The Guardian's Speaker

Volumes One - Four

Katharine E. Wibell

Phaesporia Press

This book is a work of fiction. Names, characters, places and incidents either are the product of the author's imagination or are used fictitiously. Any resemblance to actual persons, living or dead, events or locales is entirely coincidental.

The Guardian's Speaker
Volumes One - Four

The Guardian's Speaker Omnibus

Volumes One - Four

All Rights Reserved

Copyright © 2020 - 2021 Katharine E. Wibell

Paperback Edition

V1.0

ISBN-978-1-957796-05-5

No part of this book may be reproduced, transmitted, distributed in any form or by any means, mechanical or electronical, including recording, photocopying or by any information storage and retrieval system, without prior written permission by the author, except in the case of brief quotations embodied in critical reviews and certain other noncommercial uses permitted by copyright law.

Cover Design: OliviaProDesign

Visit us on the Web! KatharineWibellBooks.com

Phaesporia Press

DEDICATION

To the men and women who sailed over oceans,
Forever altering the landscape of our history
Leaving only dragon-headed silhouettes
To invade our dreams.

INTRODUCTION

Nordic Family Names

For this novella series, I am using the family naming system that was used by many of the Nordic peoples during the Viking era. As they were patriarchal societies, family (last) names are derived from the first name of the offspring's father, to which the word for *son* (*-son*) or *daughter* (*-dóttir*) is attached as a suffix. For instance, my father's name is Peter Wibell. If I were to use this naming system, my last name would be *Peterdóttir*. If I had a brother, his last name would be *Peterson*.

Groups of family members, too, take different plurals. If the family members are all sisters, they retain the *-dóttir* suffix but in its plural form; for example, *Peterdóttirs*. But if one or more male siblings are included, then the last name of the whole group requires the plural *-son* suffix: *Petersons*. The same applies if the group consists entirely of males: *Petersons*.

Singular and Plural Forms of Ancient Nordic Words

In creating this series, I have tried to remain faithful to accepted historic pictures of the Nordic way of life during the Viking era as I delve into their mythology of that time. With this in mind, I use a number of old Norse words, which have different spellings for singular and plural versions rather than simply adding an *-s* to the end of the word as modern English usually does.

Following are some rules of thumb I have learned over the course of this project:

- If a singular word ends in *-a*, the plural is often *-ur*. (Example: *völva, völvur*)
- An *-unn* or *-inn* singular ending changes in the plural to *-nar*. (Example: *Jötunn, Jötnar*)
- A word that ends in *-i* will have an *-is* ending in the plural.
- A singular word that ends with a consonant followed directly by *-r* has a plural form with the consonant plus *-ar* or *-ir*. (Example: *drengr, drengir*)

The Guardian's Speaker
Volumes One through Four

Table of Contents

Dedication i
Introduction iii

Volume One 1

    Epigraph 1

        Chapter One 3
        Chapter Two 8
        Chapter Three 13
        Chapter Four 18
        Chapter Five 23
        Chapter Six 28
        Chapter Seven 34
        Chapter Eight 39
        Chapter Nine 45
        Chapter Ten 50

Volume Two 55

    Epigraph 55

        Chapter One 57
        Chapter Two 62
        Chapter Three 67
        Chapter Four 72
        Chapter Five 78
        Chapter Six 83
        Chapter Seven 89
        Chapter Eight 95
        Chapter Nine 100
        Chapter Ten 105
        Chapter Eleven 110

Volume Three ... 117
    Epigraph ... 117
        Chapter One ... 119
        Chapter Two ... 124
        Chapter Three ... 130
        Chapter Four ... 135
        Chapter Five ... 141
        Chapter Six ... 147
        Chapter Seven ... 153
        Chapter Eight ... 158
        Chapter Nine ... 163
        Chapter Ten ... 169
Volume Four ... 177
    Epigraph ... 177
        Chapter One ... 179
        Chapter Two ... 185
        Chapter Three ... 190
        Chapter Four ... 197
        Chapter Five ... 203
        Chapter Six ... 209
        Chapter Seven ... 215
        Chapter Eight ... 221
        Chapter Nine ... 227
        Chapter Ten ... 233
    There Is Always More to Come… ... 239
    Note From The Author ... 239
    About the Author ... 240
    Appendices ... 243
        Appendix I ... 243
        Appendix II ... 245
        Appendix III ... 252

The Guardian's Speaker

Volume One

Epigraph

Hard is it on earth, with mighty whoredom;
Axe-time, sword-time, shields are sundered,
Wind-time, wolf-time, ere the world falls;
Nor ever shall men each other spare.

Völuspá - The Prophecy of the Seeress

CHAPTER ONE

I have always seen them. Some call it a gift; others, a curse. To me, it is as natural as seeing one's own shadow on the earth or reflection in the waters. Everyone has one—a guardian spirit. It is these invisible female presences that eternally watch over mankind. We call them fylgjur.

They begin life when we begin ours, connected at first breath and severed at our death rattle. They remain nameless, these invisible protectors. Though I call mine Thray....

"Lif?" Thray crawled up the stained hem of the young woman's dress, small claws tugging at the homespun cloth. Her bushy tail brushed against Lif's neck as the iridescent squirrel whispered directly in her ear. "Is it them? Have they returned?"

Lif peered at the horizon. Where the fjord met the open sea, several dark smudges were growing ever larger. They might be ships, but it was hard to tell at that distance. With the sun setting behind them, the dazzling light hindered any hope of identification.

"Possibly. My eyes are not as keen as yours."

Lif carefully made her way down to the pebbly shore and waited. She knew that if those were aquatic vessels, they would have to pass right by her as they made their way to Thorinheim, the largest trading town on the island.

The redheaded woman had never ventured farther than Thorinheim; she had never cared to. What could any other village offer her that her own could not? She had a house to live in, food to eat, warmth during brutal winters. Besides, leaving the island would mean she would have to travel by boat to reach the mainland, and that was one thing she could not do. Each time Lif set foot on one of those rocking wooden contraptions, she immediately needed to vomit. Why had man ever desired to go to sea? What compelled so many of her people to live on the water? She liked her home and her simple existence on the outskirts of town. She did not mind weaving cloth, mending shoes, milking goats. This quiet way of life was perfect for her and her sister-in-law, Driva.

"It *is* them!" Thray's softly vibrating voice announced as her whiskers tickled Lif's cheek. The shimmering rodent scurried around to the girl's other shoulder and stood on hind legs, her small, clawed hands atop Lif's red hair. "You can tell now. Right, Lif?"

Thray was correct. The three longships were close enough for Lif to watch them lower their sails. A fylgja, this one a magnificent iridescent goshawk, flew around the largest vessel's central mast.

Summer's raiding was at its end. Lif's siblings were returning, hopefully with vessels full of wealth and wares to sell at the market. Climbing back up the steep slope, Lif said, "We must inform Driva. She will want to greet Ottar."

"She is good to your brother."

Thray stated the obvious, for never was there a more devoted spouse than Driva. She was the ideal wife: dutiful, hardworking, and prudent. Lif often wished she could have a life like her sister-in-law's, but that was a daydream; such frivolities were best left to children.

"Ottar's returned!" Lif shouted through the open doorway of their home. "Their ships are sailing into port right now!"

A tall cat fylgja languidly on top of the nearby woodpile, licked her paw, and yawned. Thray darted down Lif's back and approached the larger creature. Their noses momentarily touched in greeting, although Thray's twitched continuously, a nervous habit. Lif smiled as the cat licked the top of the squirrel's head, which caused the rodent's fur to take on the green hue of new growth in spring. The feline, in turn, flicked her tail several times as her own color changed from a similar green to pale blue to green again.

"He is home, then." Driva acknowledged from within the smoke-filled house, where she was cooking. The tantalizing aroma of roasting animal flesh permeated the air.

"Yes," Lif assented as the other woman stepped out into the evening air, wiping sweat from her brow.

Driva was not considered beautiful. Of average height, her features were plain, even a bit severe. She was older, too. Ottar was her second husband, her first one long dead from a drunken skirmish in town. Two small boys, Budvar and Gratti, sprinted around her skirts, followed by their fylgjur in the form of pups.

Driva wiped her hands on her apron dress. "Ottar will want food. Can you greet him for me?"

"Can we go, Mamma? Please?" asked Budvar, the older rascal. His large blue eyes sparkled just like his father's when he knew that he was going to get what he wanted.

Driva looked at the younger woman, who smiled and nodded. Lif liked her nephews, even though they were a handful and hard to keep up with.

"Do not leave your aunt's sight," Driva cautioned them, but the boys were either too far down the path to hear or did not want to acknowledge their mother's warning.

Líf had to hurry to keep up. Thorinheim was two miles down the road. By the time they reached the town's outskirts, she could see that the longboats were already moored and being unloaded. Large crates would be carried straight to Jarl Harek's household. He would receive a third in tribute before the rest was distributed to those who had spent the past months acquiring the foreign riches. Newly enslaved captives, bound by ropes, were prodded into a tall, fenced enclosure to await the next day's sale.

"Hold up," Líf implored, but the two boys had ducked around some townsfolk and disappeared among the crowd. Gratti, the youngest, charged into an elderly fox, passing right through the fylgja. The fox's snarl of discontent was inaudible to the boy.

Líf frowned as she muttered, "They will be fine."

"They deserve a good smacking," tittered Thray from her living perch.

The thought of Ottar enforcing any sort of law among his children was amusing. Líf's laughter drew suspicious looks. Once again, she resolved not to interact with Thray while they were around others. Although most people knew about her gift, it made many of them uncomfortable.

Líf slouched low, hoping to disappear in the crowd as her nephews had so easily done. Unfortunately, her presence was more tangible to fylgjur. Although it was best to pretend that all such creatures were invisible to her, it was difficult. When she accidentally stepped on a marten fylgja's tail and heard it shriek, she tried not to recoil. At least Thray understood her. The squirrel hunkered down and for a long while remained silent.

Where were the boys? Líf began to search in earnest. Though no one would intentionally harm the children, weapons were being unloaded, stacked, and left unguarded; exhausted seafarers, their emotions strained, would brook no interference; and barrels of mead were being uncorked to replenish empty drinking horns. Somewhere, a puppy yipped.

Why was she so small? Líf wondered yet again. Why was she shorter than almost everyone else? Her head barely reached the average man's shoulder. Standing on her toes, she could just make out her nephews running down the dock to hug their father. Their fylgjur wriggled so excitedly that one almost slipped off the wooden planks. Ottar's older wolfhound fylgja bent down to nuzzle the pups' heads.

"See, they are safe," Líf whispered reassuringly to herself.

Thray looked up. "You were the one worried, not I."

Still, Líf could feel the little creature's heart slow its rapid beating.

Moving closer, Líf took a seat on an empty barrel, one that had once held pickled herring, by the smell of it. She watched as husbands were reunited with wives, children with fathers, brothers with brothers. There would be a great celebration tonight.

Everywhere, iridescent beasts crawled, slithered, and flew about. Voices of all sorts were talking at once. The cacophony made Líf's head hurt, and she rubbed her temples.

With a shrill cry from above, the goshawk descended and alighted on a branch of a nearby cypress. Thray leaped off Líf, vaulted into the tree, and disappeared behind a veil of deep-green needles, only to reemerge a moment later next to the proud-looking raptor.

"I knew I would find you here."

Líf spun around as the epitome of fierce, untamed beauty strode toward her. Tall, blond, with piercing sky-gray eyes, the woman trimmed in furs and wearing men's garb crossed her arms in front of her breasts and continued, "Don't act so shy. You will never get a man that way."

"Look who is giving me advice," Líf sniffed indignantly. "You who have sworn off men. Or have you changed your mind?"

In the cypress, the goshawk peered down with wicked intensity as the woman blatantly displayed a well-used war axe nocked in her belt. Its once-shattered handle had been smoothed to form its current grip. The hilt of a *seax*, the small dagger often used by her people, was tucked into her left boot.

"My husband is dead. I am still in mourning. Or have you forgotten?"

"You, mourning? Ha!" Líf was surprised at the unconcealed strength that stole into her voice. "I doubt you shed a tear last year. I don't think you liked him very much."

"He wasn't much from the beginning." The tall woman's face cracked in a wry smile. "Hello, sister."

"Welcome home, Hervor."

The pair embraced. Hervor almost lifted Líf off the ground. Once released, the smaller woman teetered as air reentered her lungs.

Hervor actually smiled—a rare and glorious sight. Looking much like their brother, Hervor was the oldest of the three siblings. She was strong in both physique and will. Her fighting spirit had won her recognition as a shieldmaiden, one of the female warriors of the community. Though most women retired from the field of battle when they married, Hervor had never agreed to that. She had continued to raid with Ottar and her husband and had kept on doing so even after the latter's death.

Thray jokingly claimed it was a good thing Hervor's husband had not returned last fall, for it was confusing since both men of the house shared the same name. Líf chastised the little rodent. Still, her sister had never appeared to mourn. Was it really true that in Hervor's eyes her husband had never been good enough?

Nonetheless, it was surprising that Hervor had not remarried. She had always attracted strong men and was naturally at ease with the opposite sex.

This was not a gift Líf shared. In fact, her brother was the only man around whom Líf was comfortable.

Both Líf's siblings teased her about finding a husband. Although they never meant to be cruel, the unspoken truth hung thick in the air, along with the smell of fish and unwashed bodies from the town's markets. Líf would never be asked. She was regarded as almost inhuman, for she was the only person who could see and talk with the fylgjur.

This suited Líf just fine. Why would she need a man? She had her family and she had Thray. She would never be alone as long as she lived.

"I want to show you something," Hervor said matter-of-factly.

"What?"

"You wouldn't have to ask if you just followed me." Hervor headed off, into the heart of Thorinheim. The goshawk took wing behind her.

"Come on," Líf said as she waited for Thray to jump to her from the tree. Running to catch up to her sister, she dodged bustling people and their ever-shadowing fylgjur.

"Where are we going?" Thray asked impatiently.

"I don't know," Líf replied.

"Ask her."

"I did. Or were you not paying attention?"

Thray nipped the corner of Líf's ear, causing her to yell out. A woman tugged her daughter hastily away, and Líf's cheeks grew hot.

Up ahead, Hervor had hoisted herself atop one of the fence's thick wooden rails. She waved at Líf. "Climb up. Come on."

Sighing, Líf clambered up next to her far more athletic sister. Below them, men and women moved about, fylgjur in tow, like a herd of cattle. Emaciated and tired, they hung their heads, not one daring to say a word. Each was tied to a massive rope in one continuous line. The ends of the rope were secured to metal fixtures embedded in a heavy fence post.

"What?" Líf questioned once more. "I see you brought back a large number. They all appear sickly to me."

Her sister gave her a sidelong glance. The goshawk ruffled its feathers as it perched upon Hervor's shoulder. Pulling out her dagger, the shieldmaiden pointed at the meandering mass. "Look, there. Do you see?"

Skimming the heads of those wretched people, Líf's eyes suddenly noticed the one Hervor meant. How could she not? Standing in the center of the crowd was the most terrifying-looking individual Líf had ever seen.

He was tall, like all their kind. Strong, too. This man must have been a fighter, perhaps a warrior. But he was not like the others. He was not like anyone. His skin and eyes were all wrong. He was completely black. Behind him stood a large bear fylgja, inflamed with an angry red. Worse, the man was staring heatedly at her. And only her.

Chapter Two

Thray trembled and shrank down in a bundle of iridescent fur.
Líf restrained herself from stroking the terrified fylgja, yet she, too, had an intense desire to cower under this horrid man's gaze.

"You should not be afraid of him," chided Hervor. "Remember, you are out here—free. He is bound, simply chattel."

Swallowing several times to moisten her dry mouth, Líf responded in a barely audible voice. "His fylgja is a bear. You know what that means."

"That man? That *slave*?" Hervor inquired heatedly as she jabbed the dagger in the direction of the black-fleshed figure.

"He has royal blood in him."

"Impossible," Hervor retorted. She jumped down into the pit of captives.

At first, all the prisoners backed away from the strikingly tall and beautiful woman splitting their ranks. Then one found the courage to lift his head. That was all it took. One small act of bravery stoked the embers of the raging fire to come.

"Watch out!" Líf warned as several men, still bound together by ropes at their wrists, lunged at the shieldmaiden.

Hervor never flinched. She was in her element. Grabbing the first by the connecting rope, she pulled the man toward her. She slammed her elbow into his jaw, then shoved him back into the crowd. Without hesitation, she confronted the second threat and kicked him in the sternum. That man fell backward. The slaves tethered to either side of him were wrenched to the ground. The life of the last man to attempt to strike his oppressor was ended by the sharp, pointed edge of the shieldmaiden's small blade.

The lithe blond surveyed the enclosure with searing eyes. Above her, the crimson goshawk screamed. No one dared approach; many pushed and shoved to get away. The captives tied to the dead man cautiously tugged the ropes to slide the body toward them but halted under Hervor's gaze.

Reassured, the shieldmaiden looked up at her sister and gestured to the one figure who refused to move aside. "This man, this *creature,* has a bear?" she asked once more, as if expecting her sister to correct a mistake.

Líf nodded slightly. She was still aghast at Hervor's blatant disregard of her own safety.

Hervor strode up to the man whose fierceness matched hers. He did not move or display any signs of fear or respect toward the woman who controlled his fate. The slaves flanking him tried to hide behind the man with the strange black flesh, clearly wishing he would stop angering the woman brandishing her weapons.

"I don't see how," Hervor sneered. "He might have Døkkálfar in his veins, but nothing more."

The insult made Líf feel queasy. Had her sister gone too far? Comparing anyone to those dark and twisted creatures that resided beyond Midgard would normally be considered an unforgivable slight. But a man such as this had never been seen before in Thorinheim. A man with skin of coal—that should be impossible. But here he was.

There was a flash of movement.

A gasp of surprise.

In a burst of brute strength and agility, the black slave seized Hervor's seax with one hand and her throat with the other. Twisting the shieldmaiden's wrist at a horribly unnatural angle, he pointed the blade right under her chin. If she tried to move, the knife would cut her flesh.

The man locked eyes with Líf. Behind him, his fylgja snarled at the circling raptor. Hervor attempted to disarm the man, but the muscles in his forearm tightened, as did his grip. A red bead of blood splashed onto the woman's chest.

"All you have done is seal your fate," Hervor spat out in a voice struggling for air.

The man ignored her. Instead, he spoke directly to Líf. "Buy me."

"What?" Líf's hands trembled as she realized that her sister was completely helpless.

"If I am to be sold as a slave, buy me."

"I..." Líf looked desperately at her sister. Hervor's face was turning blue, but she held her defiant glare.

"I can't."

"Free people own property. Even women. Add me to yours."

He was right. Unlike barbaric societies, Líf's ancestors had always allowed women to own wealth and even land. They could keep their possessions separate from their husbands' or fathers'. Líf's possessions were few. She had never gone raiding, and her parents, long dead, had left everything to her elder siblings.

Still, she had been gifted some items from Ottar's summer expeditions.

Was it enough? A slave as strong as this man would bring a high price; there were few others among this human chattel as healthy as he. Moreover, Hervor's life hung in the balance.

"I will," she said, then forced herself to speak louder. "I will buy you."

The man released the shieldmaiden.

Hervor spun around and pressed her dagger to his cheek. A long line of red emerged against the black skin. "You will regret this."

"No!" Líf implored, though she did not know why. Hervor had every right to strip the man's *hugr* from his body and send it to Hel. That slave had threatened her sister. Still, she had made a promise to the brute. "Please, Hervor. Leave him be."

Hervor took several deep breaths before she spat in the man's face. She could not see the large bear that loomed over her, a trail of luminescent slaver dangling from his scarlet lips. Calmly, she turned away and climbed up alongside Líf.

"We are not buying him," she snapped.

"I have some coins, some jewelry," Líf countered. "I can."

The blond touched the cut on her neck before rubbing the residue of blood between her thumb and forefinger. A wry smile crossed her face. "I *do* like his spirit." She leaped off the wall and strode toward the men recording the spoils of the summer raids.

Líf regarded the black-fleshed slave. He nodded back, as if to confirm their agreement. Hurriedly, she climbed down and followed her fylgja toward the safety of her two siblings.

It was not until the next afternoon, by which time all the men in town had sobered up, that the distribution of treasure began. The entire village came out to observe what was given and who received it; others prepared to bid and barter for what they desired. No one in Thorinheim worked today. This was a celebration, one in which all the gods would be honored in gratitude for their protection and goodwill.

Bathed and dressed in their finest attire, men and women displayed their wealth by the rings on their arms and around their necks. The rings were status symbols, proof of who held more honor and authority.

Driva looked marvelous. Her colorfully embroidered gown was trimmed in the expensive foreign material called *silk*. She was one of three women in Thorinheim who owned that strange, light material brought over the mountainous mainland from the East. Ottar had always treated her like a queen; today she clearly looked like one. Her hair was plaited and ornamented with copper beads. She wore four silver rings on her arms, and a thick gold ring hung about her neck.

Hervor was also magnificently attired. For these ceremonies, she had chosen to wear a long dress, although one not nearly as ornate as Driva's.

However, the luxurious trimmings proved she was no mere peasant. The softest white fur of Arctic fox was complimented by black mink. Her dagger was sheathed in a decorative scabbard made from some sort of speckled cat, although Líf had never seen such an animal. Hervor's hair was braided and beaded like Driva's, but she carried her short axe and round shield upon her back.

Both boys stumbled out of the house, shoving and each taunting the other for appearing too womanly, for not a spot of soil was on their clothes. They looked like miniatures of their father, wearing wooden swords belted just like Ottar's very real one.

"I think you look very pretty," Thray said as she groomed her metallic whiskers. Her mood was calm and complacent, and her fur was a rainbow of oily sheens.

Líf wished she could believe the little creature. No matter how precisely she braided her red locks or how pristine she kept her clothes, she never felt that she looked as good as the rest of her family. Worse, wearing all those heavy copper rings made her feel slow and uncoordinated. She readjusted the crescent-shaped neck ring so that Thor's hammer, Mjölnir, was centered. This was her finest piece of jewelry and the first gift Ottar had bestowed upon her when she turned of age.

"Everyone ready?" Ottar asked. After a quick head count, he led the family into town.

Thorinheim seemed to have swollen with an influx of people. Even the farmers from the very outskirts of the territory had arrived to watch and partake in the exchanging of goods. Ottar steered his family directly into the grand mead hall. This was not only the largest longhouse in the city but also the proud residence of Jarl Harek. At the back of the main room, the *jarl* sat next to his wife upon the high seat, an outward symbol that honored both his power and status.

Now well into middle age, Harek had engaged in many battles and survived countless summers raiding in the West and South. He quietly observed the notable households arrive and take their seats around the perimeter of the room. His boar fylgja, covered in silvery bristles and sporting two long tusks, reclined at his feet.

Princess Thoren was close in age to her husband, and her face always displayed a subtle scowl. Her sparrow hawk perched in the exposed roofbeams. Thoren had never spoken to Líf or shown any interest in meeting her. Why would she? Líf was only the crazy sister of Harek's best warriors.

A pile of golden objects, coins, and rare cloth was displayed in the center of the room. Even Líf was awed by the dress shirt of deep purple—a color their people could never figure out how to replicate. The shirt was probably worth more than the gem-encrusted goblet next to it. Then again, what did Líf know about the value of such things?

Harekson, the jarl's eldest child, rose from where he was seated, approached the mound of wealth, and began removing objects. Most of them would be melted down and reformed into the cumbersome rings; others would be kept as tokens or used for their designated purposes. The purple shirt was among his selections.

With a nod from the jarl, Harekson took his seat. The remainder of the plunder would be distributed among those mighty warriors who had obtained these precious objects. As the official leader of the raiding party, Ottar was first. He chose several pieces, far fewer than he deserved, then took his seat.

Hervor was next. No one objected when she took a large portion. Since as a woman she could never receive her rightful title, these spoils were her compensation. Although it was never openly acknowledged, everyone knew that it was she, not her brother, who made the crucial decisions during their foreign excursions. In truth, Ottar's grand longship, *Wavecutter*, should have been hers. Unfortunately, there were certain things a woman could not purchase. A ship of any size fit into that category.

And so it continued, until every surviving man had claimed his fair share. Then the second round began. This was the purchasing of goods, in particular those of living flesh. The first five slaves were brought in, led by collars and rope. Starting with the strongest, each would be bid for by those who needed extra hands in their households or fields. The rest would be sold in other villages on the island or shipped to the mainland.

It was no surprise that the black slave was first. Líf fumbled with the clasp of her neck ring; it was all she had with which to purchase the man. Hervor glanced at her, rolled her eyes, and began to slide an arm ring over her wrist.

"Number one." Harekson spoke loudly. "This man is clearly young and strong. Look at his musculature and the fire in his eyes…"

While Harekson rambled on about the supposed attributes of the slave, Líf overheard young Budvar ask his father, "What's wrong with his skin? Is he sick?" Like herself, the boy had never seen a person, man or woman, who had skin of any color but their own. Líf listened attentively.

Ottar replied in a hushed tone so as not to disturb the current oration. "He is not ill. He comes from a foreign land, one that has many others like him, where there are almost no men of light flesh. You see—"

Ottar stopped as Harekson called out, "Who would buy this man?"

Líf had begun to raise her neck ring into the air when Hervor grabbed her arm and held it down with assertive pressure. She nodded toward the jarl. Harek had raised two fingers. The gesture was slight, for his palm still rested on his knee, but the action was enough. If the jarl wanted the slave, no man could counter him.

Realizing what had occurred, the black slave stared directly at the young woman. Líf caught her breath as a sense of terror erupted inside her.

CHAPTER THREE

"Number two!" Harekson shouted as the black slave was pulled outside by his neck ring. He would be picketed near this longhouse until Jarl Harek decided what to do with his new possession.

Líf shook as the man passed by her, close enough that she could have touched him if she dared. His bear fylgja trundled behind him, its red color not as brilliant as before.

"Is that finished now?" Thray questioned. Her small nose was tucked against Líf's ear.

Líf gazed at the neck ring in her hand and traced the outline of Mjölnir, the hammer of Thor. This symbol was a reminder that the god of thunder and war was also the protector of common people. The talisman would protect her against evil. But who would protect that slave?

The second captive was purchased by the jarl's second son; the third, by a distant farmer. By the end of day, only half the slaves remained. Ottar had not bought any. He said that the pair he owned were quite enough for the household of six. At seven and nine years of age, his boys were old enough to help with chores, and Líf and Hervor readily assisted Driva.

Outside, the sound of hammers drummed in the evening air. Effigies of the gods were being erected for the honorary celebration of the successful homecoming. Tonight, small fires would be lit near the base of each crude figure, illuminating the food, trinkets, and other offerings collected in preparation for morning's light.

Most of the wives, along with the single women and children, began to return home for the evening. The men hauled the long tables, moved outside for the afternoon, back into the longhouse. Benches were repositioned as the second evening of food and drink was about to begin.

Hervor would remain with Ottar; she was one of the few women to drink with the other warriors and the jarl. Princess Thoren would take her place at her husband's side for the initial toasts before politely excusing herself and the remaining female spouses.

Líf did not want to leave the hall for fear of spotting the slave she had failed. But she was not her sister, and the thought of lingering in the company of all these imbibing men was worse than being observed by the dark eyes of the strange foreigner.

Mustering her courage, Líf left the mead hall. She was the last to do so. Outside, the air had chilled, and the semicircle of effigies cast eerie shadows upon the ground around the entryway. Thray's claws dug deep into Líf's neck. Never visible to the common eye, these marks would surely have bled if the fylgja had been a living squirrel.

"Let's go home," Thray said timidly.

As Líf turned the corner, she saw two of the jarl's new possessions tied to separate posts. Nearest was the dark-skinned man. His bear, for the first time, sat complacently next to his reclining human.

What should she do? Líf wondered. There was no reason for her to ever talk to that man again. He was not her problem. Yet she had failed to fulfill her promise.

Tiptoeing up to the slave, she peered at him to see if he was asleep. The second captive was snoring steadily, but this man was silent. She looked at his face. His eyes were closed, and he did not stir.

Hoping not to disturb him, she whispered, "I'm sorry."

"Wait." The man suddenly reached out and grabbed hold of Líf's wrist, not to hurt her but to halt her retreat.

His action shocked her. Should she order the man to let her go? Should she strike out or scream for help? She caught him looking at her long and hard. In the gloom of nightfall, the whites of his eyes spoke for him, and Líf found herself asking, "Why did you want me to buy you?"

"Hamingjur."

Líf blinked. Hamingjur were one of the four parts that made up a person. *Hamr* was the physical appearance; the *hugr* was thought, personality, and the only component to survive in the afterlife; of course, the fylgjur; and then the hamingjur. A *hamingja* was your luck, your good or bad fortune. It was passed down through the family, like eye and hair color, although no one could physically notice hamingjur. They were just there.

"What about them?"

"I can see them. This is why I came here, to the North."

This man was a liar! Líf stepped back, but the man's grip did not slacken. "No, you were captured by my siblings and brought here."

"That is incorrect."

Thray curled tighter around Líf's neck. "He's crazy. Let's go back."

Líf chewed her lip. "I want to know more. If you can see them, what do they look like?"

The black man inclined his head and released his grip. "I haven't the right words. Think of them as a second self. A figure always behind the person, illuminating the human in an aura of light. They are all female, that we know, though I have never seen a face nor any specific features.

"A person can have a strong hamingja, which often corresponds to good health and prosperity. But sometimes a hamingja gets sick, begins to wither and dim until its light goes out."

Lif's mouth went dry. "What happens to the person then?"

The man looked over at the who was slave sleeping nearby. "His hamingja is no more. I do not know what his future holds, though I am certain it is nothing good."

Lif knew that the final ceremony in the morning would involve live offerings and usually included the ritual human sacrifice of one or more slaves. There was a good chance that the slumbering captive would be selected for that honor. He was too weak and sickly for much else.

"Why *did* you come here?"

"Where I am from, there is a plague affecting hamingjur. They are dwindling away. I left to discover the cause. I have been traveling for years. My journey has taken me farther and farther north until your people discovered me. Your ships can travel far beyond places to which I can walk or swim. I let them take me."

"You think the cause for the dying hamingjur is in Thorinheim?"

Thray shifted uncomfortably on Lif's shoulders.

The man shook his head. "No. Your village is no better. I believe the answer lies beyond Midgard."

"What do you mean, we are 'no better'? Have you noticed something wrong here? Is my hamingja ill? What of Ottar's and Hervor's?"

"Your siblings' hamingjur are as well as most. At least for now."

"And mine?"

"Yours is the reason I wanted *you* to buy me. I have never seen a hamingja as brilliant as the one that clings to you. I think yours will last long after all others fail."

Thray sat up. "What are you thinking, Lif?"

Lif realized the little squirrel believed this man. She also realized that she was going to do something utterly illegal. With racing heart, she told him, "Stay here. I will be right back."

Spinning around, she headed toward the entry of the mead hall. All the while, Thray tittered in her ear, "Stay here? Really? Where else would a chained slave go?"

As usual, Thray was right. What Lif had said was stupid and poorly thought out. Where could a chained slave go? No, not chained. He was bound. Tied up with thick cords, he would never be able to free himself without the correct tools.

The townsmen had stacked their weapons just inside the entryway as a sign of trust and to minimize drink-inspired manslaughter. Jovial voices boomed from within. Good-natured laughter and raucous singing filled the air with a sense of reckless foolhardiness.

Everyone was relaxed and enjoying themselves. Everyone but Líf. Her heart pounded so loudly that she was afraid those inside the longhouse would turn to stare angrily at the sweat-peppered woman.

"This is wrong, Líf," Thray squealed as she realized her human's intent. "So very wrong."

Crouched low and stretching her arm around the doorframe, Líf ignored her fylgja. There were a number of swords and seaxes leaning against the wall. If she could just wrap her fingers around one—

There was a loud banging on a table. Líf froze as a grizzled man lurched to his feet, drinking horn in hand. Did he see her? If she was found out, she would be punished. They might even beat her. Well, a beating was the best option now.

The drunken fellow swayed slightly as the others watched. "Welph...I sssuggest another song for Odin an' his mighty hammer."

"Thor, you fool," said a neighboring fellow who was far less inebriated.

"That's wa' I said." The man swayed again. "To Thor an' his axe." He took a large breath and began to bellow. "Oh! Thor..."

His friend pulled him down to the bench as the entire room took up the boisterous chant. Líf released her pent-up breath. Still watching the celebrating men, she felt her fingers slip over metal. She needed only to stretch a bit farther...

The blade tilted sideways and slid down the length of her palm. Without thinking, Líf closed her hand around the weapon and, with as much care as she could, pulled the sword into the dark with her. Her hand dripped a trail of blood out the door.

Trying to ignore the pain, she hurried to the waiting slave, knelt on the damp ground, and began to saw through the thick rope. The captive remained silent as the first cord popped. Líf's body was shaking, which made cutting the ropes that much harder.

"Take a breath," he said soothingly. "You're doing fine. You were not followed. No one else is around."

Following his advice, she continued at a slower but steadier pace. She was terrified. Hoping to distract herself, she began talking. "My name's Líf. Líf Lothbrandóttir. What's yours?"

"Líf?" the man said in a way that caused her to look up. A slight smile crept onto his face. "Call me Brasir."

With a second pop, the cords around the man's waist and arms fell limply onto the ground.

"Was' going on?"

A voice from the direction of the once-sleeping slave sent daggers into Lif's heart. Wide-eyed with fear, she turned to look as the captive with the mouse fylgja sat up. "Get me next! Free me!"

What was she to do? She could not spend all night cutting these captives free. One was bad enough. She would get caught. She would be found out. She would be punished.

"I can't," Lif's voice shook. "I'm sorry. I'm so sorry."

"If you don't free me, I will tell them what happened here," the man threatened in a menacing voice. "Cut my bonds, or I swear I'll make you wish you had."

Chapter Four

L if couldn't breathe.

There was no escape; she would be found out. If she ran, this other slave would alert the men in the hall. He would identify her. The punishment for freeing a slave not one's own was severe.

Líf had dropped the sword at the sound of the man's voice. Scanning the ground, she tried to see where it had fallen. On hands and knees, she fumbled through the underbrush, mud clinging to her fingernails. Her gown was already ruined.

"No, no, no!" Líf cried in alarm. Beside her, Thray, too, searched for the lost weapon.

There was a gurgling gasp.

The bound slave's head was pulled back at an awkward angle. Red liquid spurted from a line across his throat. Brasir stood behind him, dripping sword in hand.

Líf froze.

A man had been killed in front of her. A slave had died because she'd set another free.

Brasir dropped the weapon and lifted Líf to her feet. He bent down until his face was at eye level with hers. "We must *go*."

Líf tried to focus on Brasir's features. He did not appear violent, though clearly he was unafraid to execute violent acts. She nodded in consent. As the dark-skinned man led her away from the longhouses and out of Thorinheim, they passed the post with the dead captive. All she could think was that the poor man's luck truly *had* run out.

Once in the neighboring woods, Líf came to her senses. "No, this way," she said, turning in the direction of her household.

Without a question, Brasir followed Líf so closely that she imagined it would appear to anyone wandering the forest that a large shadow was walking behind the small woman. The thought did not amuse her.

When they arrived at the house, Líf brought her finger to her lips. She peeked inside the door. There was no sound, no ray of light. The others must have gone to bed. Driva was always first up in the morning, preparing the meal before any of the others stirred. Líf crept inside and retrieved a small candle and flint.

Brasir waited for her, eyes alert for any movement other than the wind in the trees. She gestured for him to follow once again. They made their way to a small shack in back of the house and entered.

Once the candle was lit, Líf looked around. There wasn't much. The place was only used for storage and slaughtering pigs in the fall. There were several hooks near the ceiling for the swine, and a few odd tools for the garden. There wasn't even any straw to make a bed.

"This is all I have," Líf said apologetically.

"Thank you." Brasir pointed at her. "Your hand. Let me see it."

In all the excitement and the rush of adrenaline, Líf had forgotten about her wound. Slowly, she opened her palm. Her hand and arm up to the elbow were covered in blood. The sight almost made her faint.

Brasir gently took her hand in his. With a scrap of cloth that he tore from his tattered shirt, he wiped off the outer layer of dirt that had stuck to the tacky liquid. Líf winced when he neared the split flesh.

He released her hand. "The cut is long but not deep. You should clean it before you sleep. You were brave out there."

"No. I wasn't."

He smiled at her. "Don't fret. Remember, your hamingja is strong."

"I've never been called strong before." Líf was not sure she ever wanted to be associated with the word *strong* again.

Leaving the candle with Brasir, she headed in to clean up. Her gown was stained with splatters of blood and large blotches of mud. She stripped off the damaged garment and kicked it into the corner of her sleeping nook. Once in her sleeping shift, she began to untangle the knots in her hair and pick out the clumps of soil. Then she slipped outside to the barrel where rainwater was collected to minimize trips to the river. It was a relief to wash her face and hands.

She was almost ready to crawl into her bed when she heard Hervor approaching. She recognized her sister's hot, determined tread.

"Good. You're still up," Hervor said loudly. From the smell of her breath, she had been drinking but not to any great extent. "You won't believe what has happened."

Líf was glad it was dark, for she could feel her eyes growing wide. Trying to sound calm, she asked, "What's happened?"

"That slave you wanted has disappeared, and another has been slain. The men in town are forming a search party. What good it will do, I don't know; most of them are barely able to stand as it is. Then again, Ottar is with them, so maybe there is hope."

"The slave is missing?" Líf tried to sound genuinely shocked. She knew she was a horrible liar. Her sister would see right through her.

"She knows. She knows. She knows," repeated Thray, scurrying back and forth on the ground.

"Good thing we did not waste our wealth on him. Odin above! This has been a strange night." Hervor turned to leave.

Líf went weak in the knees and had to grab the lip of the barrel to stay upright. Then her worst fears were realized. Hervor suddenly pulled out her axe and ordered, "Líf, stay back! There is someone in our shed."

The dull glow of the candle's light could be seen flickering through cracks in the wood.

"Hervor, no!" Líf gasped. She ran past her marching sister and blocked the shed's door.

"What have you been drinking?" Hervor demanded as she pried her sister away. "You could get hurt. Get back."

Líf stumbled and fell to the ground. As she tried to stand, she reached up and grabbed the axe's short handle. Hervor had kept the damaged weapon, for the iron was still good and she had discovered it was ideal for throwing. The shieldmaiden stared at her sister in disbelief. Then the door swung inward.

Brasir looked right at the struggling pair of women.

Hervor's outraged voice broke the prolonged silence. "By Thor's hammer! Líf, what have you done?"

All three of them crammed into the small shed. Líf fully expected Hervor to be furious. She stood rigidly in front of her sister and listened to her tirade of profanities.

"What were you thinking? Odin above! You weren't, of course, or we wouldn't be in this position. Do you know what you have done? Balder's luck! He must be returned immediately."

"No."

"I *will* take him back, one way or another."

"Hervor, he sees hamingjur. He's like me in that way."

"That's ludicrous. Hamingjur are invisible. You can't just see them. That's crazy. Insane."

"Am I insane? People think that of me."

This caught Hervor off guard. She stood there, forming words and stopping before any sound came out. Flinging the door open, she strode off into the darkness, twigs snapping under her boots. Minutes later, she returned. Scowling at the pair and shaking her head, Hervor grunted, "Ragnarök cannot come soon enough."

Then she sighed. "What are you going to do with him? Jarl Harek will have a real search party come morning. Pray that this slave is killed on the spot. You won't want to be around otherwise."

"We have to hide him," Líf urged.

Hervor pointed to Brasir. "That is a fugitive. That is stolen property. *That* can get us killed—or worse, sentenced to full outlawry. He *has* to go back. At once!"

"Brasir says that the hamingjur are dying. He means to find out why. Without our hamingjur...can you imagine?"

There was another long look between the sisters before Hervor grumbled, "I can't believe I am saying this, but if...if I believed this insanity...and we helped the slave—"

"Brasir," Líf corrected.

Her sister was not amused. Through gritted teeth, she continued, "...helped *Brasir* get away, what's next? He will still be caught and killed. You can clearly see he is easy to identify. He is the property of the jarl."

"But what if he weren't?" Líf asked tentatively. "What if he became a bóndi, a freeman?"

"Only the owner can free a slave, Líf." Hervor referred to the age-old law. "Jarl Harek knows the sl—Brasir," she corrected herself, "fled. I cannot fathom Harek agreeing to free this runaway. Skin him, maybe. Free him, never."

"But what if I told him about the hamingjur?" Líf knew the answer before Hervor's dry laugh confirmed it.

"Don't even try."

Brasir stood quietly next to the sisters. He did not once interrupt. The man was very respectful. Líf did not want to see him killed.

"What about our king?"

"Our king? You dare propose going over our jarl's head to protect this man? No, Líf. That you cannot do."

"But he has the authority."

"You cannot bring stories of dying hamingjur and expect the king to grant your wish. I'm sorry, Líf, but that will not happen."

"Are you telling me that I shouldn't try? That there is no chance to save Brasir's life?" Líf was angry. Maybe her sister believed her, maybe she didn't. Either way, it did not matter. Hervor wasn't even going to try to help. "What about the next Thing?"

"Women cannot attend the Thing." Hervor's voice was steely. This law had never been looked upon favorably by the shieldmaiden.

"No, but Ottar can. He can represent us. He is respected. He would have the best chance..."

Hervor's bleak stare caused Líf's hopes to wither like the sick hamingjur.

In one last attempt, she argued, "Then I will talk to the king myself. I will make him believe me. And if he doesn't, our family's name won't be dragged through the dirt, since I am already the crazy sister."

When Hervor responded, she sounded almost sympathetic. "And how will you travel to him? We are on an island, surrounded by water. You have never been in a boat for more than a few minutes before turning green as new growth."

"I…well…" Líf was out of ideas.

At her side, Brasir said, "I will leave."

"What? You can't!" Líf was taken aback. "They will kill you when they find you."

"No, they won't," Brasir stated assuredly. "You are not the only one with a strong hamingja."

Hervor backed the man. "Let him leave, Líf. If he is discovered here, our entire family will be punished. This way, you can say you tried your best, and we will not be blamed. Think of Gratti. Think of Budvar. You don't want harm to come to them."

"The shieldmaiden is right," Brasir agreed gravely. "I will be placing you at too much risk."

Looking sorrowfully at the dark-skinned man, Líf asked, "How will I know you are safe?"

He placed a hand on her shoulder and gave it a squeeze. "You are a good person, Líf Lothbrandóttir." Brasir slipped past the sisters and followed his large fylgja into the night.

As Líf watched him go, a part of her wished that she, too, could so easily disappear in the dark.

Chapter Five

It was early, far too early for Lif's liking, when someone entered the Lothbranson household. Driva, the only one awake at that hour, greeted the unexpected guest. Bedding rustled and footsteps padded as others began to stir. In the sleeping nook across from Lif, the two boys mumbled, still half asleep. They would soon be snoring once more. Lucky them.

Lif slipped a dress over her thin shift and quickly brushed her hair before stepping into the main area. Skeggi, one of Ottar's oldest friends, was already making himself at home as he tore into the grainy wheat loaf, dipping the heel into soft egg yolks. He would never insult the house's matriarch by denying her the privilege of serving him.

Rolling her eyes, Lif sat on a low stool off to one side. Thray climbed up to her lap, stretched, and yawned.

"Good to see you, Lingy!" Skeggi boomed. "You are looking quite cheery, as always."

Lif gritted her teeth at the sound of her given nickname. When they were children, Skeggi had associated the color of Lif's hair with her favorite berry, the lingonberry. Even though they were grown now, he had never stopped using that horrid name.

Ottar, seated next to his friend, gave Lif a sympathetic look. Hervor, on the other hand, barked out, "What brings you here, Skeggi?"

Bits of yolk dangled from the man's beard as he smiled at the shieldmaiden. He had always been one of Hervor's admirers, though he had never had a chance. Even Hervor's goshawk glared at Skeggi's plump seagull with clear distaste.

"We are called for a hunt. The jarl's request."

"A hunt? At this hour? You are either too early or too late," smirked Lif. She had never cared to hunt, but she knew something of what the sport entailed. Or did she?

Hervor cast her sister a look of warning.

"Oh," Thray murmured uncomfortably. "*That* sort of hunt."

Skeggi was unperturbed. "Harek wants his missing slave. Since he's not been able to travel of late, I think the notion of a good chase thrills the ol' bastard. This might be a fun one, Ottar. The slave might not be alone. Someone had to free 'im. It seems whoever lifted Then's sword at dinner cut 'imself doing so. The stupid fool should be easily identified."

Líf glanced at her hand. She had not wrapped her wound, and the nasty split section of flesh could be seen easily by anyone who cared to notice. Driva was passing out breakfast to those in the room and approached the young woman. Awkwardly, Líf tucked her injured arm behind her back and grabbed the plate with her other hand.

Driva raised an eyebrow but said nothing. Leaving the adults to eat, she went to coax her lazy boys from their bed.

"Who is coming?" Ottar asked between bites.

"More than last night, though we are a sorry lot."

"How is *your* head this morning?" Hervor questioned with an exaggerated pout. "Remember, we will be *beating* around bushes, *splitting* thickets, *pounding* through puddles."

Skeggi took a swig from his cup. "Water is a great healer," he retorted, then grinned. "Could you be a dear and fill up my glass?"

It was too early in the morning to draw out Hervor's mean side. Líf sprang to her feet, unfortunately dislocating Thray in the process. "I'll get it."

As she took the cup from Skeggi, he grabbed her wrist. "Lingy, what'd ya do to yourself?"

Líf noticed a drop of blood rolling down the side of her arm. Her wound must have reopened. Had she gone pale? Trying to cover her tracks, she playfully said, "You know I am bad with knives. You would never want to see me on the field of battle—I'd likely impale myself on my own axe."

Skeggi laughed and let her go so he could wipe the tears that bubbled up in his eyes. "Yes. That is the truth."

Líf flashed a smile before running off to fetch the water. Outside, she took several gulps of the crisp fall air.

Thray scrambled up to perch on Líf's shoulder and warned, "He almost caught us!"

"Us?" Líf stated still in a panic. "What of Brasir? You know Skeggi is an excellent tracker."

"You know how skilled your siblings are as well. *Both* of them."

Líf looked at the squirrel. Her fur swirled all sorts of sheens in the morning sunlight. "Do you think Hervor would…?"

"All you can do is ask."

Once the others strapped on their weapons, Líf found a moment to pull Hervor aside. The shieldmaiden gave her sister a warning look. "Don't even."

"Please."

As the men walked by, Ottar called, "We'll be waiting by the path."

Hervor watched them leave before she hissed, "The man is foolish to think he can evade us. I won't risk my reputation by throwing others off his track. Let his hamingja protect him if he believes in it so much. I must go."

Líf stood in the entryway of the house until they disappeared. Her body was flooded with a mix of emotions. *Run, Brasir. Hide. I hope you know you are being hunted.*

"What are you daydreaming about?" Driva questioned. "You're almost as bad as the boys. Come inside, girl, there is much you can do to help me today."

That night, the hunting party returned. They had had no success. "It is so strange," Ottar acknowledged. "It is as if he left no tracks. Not one trace."

Hervor leaned over and whispered to Líf, "It was not I. All I did was ensure no signs pointed here, but that man must have already done that for us."

"Will you look for him again?" Líf asked hopefully.

"Yes, until he is captured."

But Brasir never was. Weeks passed, forcing Jarl Harek to assume the slave had left his territory and was seeking refuge in another's. The jarl sent word to the nearby clans and offered a reward for the return of the man-of-black-flesh, but there had been no response. Truly, Brasir had vanished.

Winter arrived and, with it, the celebration of Winter Nights. Everyone in Thorinheim would gather for several days to bring in the new year with feasting and small offerings to the gods. As the veil between the land of the living and the land of the dead was thinnest at this time, much caution was taken when speaking about the deceased, and much remembrance was shared of those who had been lost. This was also a propitious time for people to petition the divine for future prosperity.

"Are the fulltrúar ready?" Driva once again asked her children.

"Yes, Mamma," Budvar replied as he stepped away from the home altar. Several dishes of food were placed around the wooden relic that represented Thor, the family's patron god. Next to Thor was a second figurine, this one female. Freya, Driva's patroness, was honored as well, though not to the same extent as Thor.

"Hurry, children, or else we will miss the opening ceremony."

The boys rushed out the door to retrieve the picketed swine. Ottar had allowed his children, under his supervision, to choose the best of their livestock to take into Thorinheim. The large hog, whose eyes were almost completely engulfed by its dark wrinkles, trundled slowly after the boys. The little rascals who never seemed to slow down themselves had to work hard to adjust their pace to the animal's.

Líf shrugged at Driva as she shut and latched the door behind them. It was already very cold. Líf was grateful for her thick cloak and pulled the hood low over her face. Thray was tucked into the inner pocket, which unfortunately muffled her small voice.

"Just until we get into the jarl's hall," she promised her tiny fylgja.

It was still early in the day, and the sun had not begun to gleam off the mounds of snow that coated everything in a light grey color. With large snowshoes affixed to their boots, the family trekked into Thorinheim just as morning's light illuminated the town.

Ottar and the boys took the hog to the same corral that had held the human slaves. Now, it was filled with animals of all sorts, as men dressed in holy garb inspected this year's selection of potential offerings. Their divine choice determined which beasts would be humbly offered to the gods.

Hervor led the women up the large hill upon which the altar had been raised. Most of the town had assembled, along with Jarl Harek and his family.

"Who's that?" Líf questioned as she nodded at an unfamiliar face.

A woman around Driva's age, wrapped in a cloak of blue, was talking pleasantly to Princess Thoren. Strange markings were on her forehead and cheeks, runes tattooed on her pale flesh. Few people knew how to read or write runes; those who could, never did so without clear intent. For runes were infused with *seid*, magic. Whatever one wrote in runes became reality—curses, cures, blessings. On the stranger's shoulder perched a sky-blue owl fylgja.

Hervor had noticed the other woman as well, for she quickly replied in a hushed voice, "I do not know, but I can guess. Look at the crystal on top of her staff. She must be a *völva*."

Líf shivered, or maybe it was Thray. Líf had been a child the last time a völva had traveled to Thorinheim. This woman had to be a guest of the jarl, come for the new year celebration and the advent of the winter season.

"Welcome, all, to Winter Nights." Jarl Harek's voice reached even the farthest people in the crowd. "This year, we are blessed with the presence of a truly honored guest, Völva Gunhild. She will conduct tonight's celebration." He nodded to the woman, who moved to the altar. The local priests acknowledged her authority with a deep bow as she passed, but even they looked apprehensive and nervous.

Gunhild leaned her long staff against the stone slab. The crystal sparkled as she slid off her hood and exposed her rather dark hair. Her owl blinked lazily as if bored with these happenings.

"I am honored to be here in this good town of Thorinheim," Gunhild said, though she did not smile. She waited calmly as two small, furry cows, Ottar's black hog, and the most valuable of all animals, a stallion from the mainland, were led up the hill. Men assisted in tying up the legs of the beasts and then hoisted the first cow onto the top of the stone slab.

Ottar's boys bounced around excitedly. Their father rested his hands on their shoulders to steady them.

"I hate this part," Thray whispered. She had popped her head out through the cloak only to tuck it back inside the safety of the heavy layers.

Gunhild pulled out a blade. Her mouth formed words, but they were inaudible to those around her. In a flash of light and metal, the cow's heavy breathing ended in a wash of blood. Gunhild waited patiently as the male attendants quickly placed a ring of bowls around the base of the altar to collect the ruby drippings.

The ceremony was repeated three more times. Gratti sniffled a sob as he watched the life leave the black hog. The horse was too large for the slab and was slaughtered where it stood. The carcasses were removed and carried to the waiting spits in the town's center. Come evening, the roasted meat would be ready to be eaten.

Using her dagger, Gunhild spread the remaining pools of blood over the entire top of the altar. The blade skimmed the surface, pushing the last bits of residue into the waiting bowls. In the glow of midmorning, the stone slab radiated a magnificent red.

Next, the völva picked up one of the bowls, taking care not to spill the contents. With her hand, she scooped up the thickening liquid and sprinkled it over the sanctified grounds before turning to the attendees and splattering them with droplets of cooling blood.

When the red beads splattered Líf's face, she forced herself not to wipe them off. They were to remain on her for the rest of the day, a sign of the gods' blessings.

Following Gunhild's lead, the priests picked up the other bowls and moved through the crowd, offering the steaming drink to every villager. Ottar reminded his children, "You must swallow the *hlaut*. Do not spit it out, or you will anger the gods."

Gratti crinkled his nose and complained. "I hate the taste of blood."

Gunhild approached the Lothbranson family. She bent down to tilt the full bowl to Gratti's lips. "Blessed be the followers of the gods."

"Humble are we, the wicked," the child replied. He had remembered the correct words; this would please his parents. Unfortunately, the boy made a face just as he swallowed. Driva smacked the back of his head to punish the child's foolishness.

The völva moved to Budvar, then the other family members in turn, until she reached Líf.

Perched on Gunhild's shoulder, the sky-blue-hued owl blinked, first one eye and then the other. The bird slowly turned her head around to the far side, only to expose the flaming red features of a second, entirely different face. Now rippling crimson, the fylgja glared at Líf and screamed.

CHAPTER SIX

The völva showed no sign of having heard the owl's earsplitting sound. Instead, she lifted the bowl of blood to Líf's lips.

"It is not a curse," Gunhild said.

Not knowing how to respond, Líf repeated the automatic reply, "Humble are we, the wicked."

She swallowed the largest mouthful of the hot coppery liquid she could and watched as the völva moved on, the two-faced owl with its ruddy sheen still staring back at her.

"She knows," came a muffled voice.

Líf glanced down at the vibrating lump on her chest. Trying to talk without moving her lips, she asked, "Knows?"

"About us. About you, your gift. She knows."

"Someone must have told her. It is not a secret that I am different."

"If you say so," Thray chirped, climbing down to Líf's waist.

"Come on." Ottar herded his boys downhill. "Follow the others."

A group of children were gathering at the bottom of the slope. Gratti asked, "Can we play, Pappa?"

"Yes," Ottar consented. "But you must come in when the sun sets, do you hear me?"

"At sunset! Yes. Yes," both boys cheered as they ran off, swinging their wooden swords like wild men.

"You shouldn't always give in to them. They need to learn patience and solemnity," warned Hervor.

Driva looked fondly at her husband and added, "Your sister is wise."

"They will have many years for that." Ottar smiled at his wife as he defended himself. "But there will not be many more winters for them to enjoy this time."

Statues of the gods had been erected around the base of the hill. Though rather plain in detail, each bore an emblem or object that made it identifiable. Twice as tall as a man, these wooden presences appeared to wait reverently. At each statue, the völva, the jarl, and the fellow priests said a prayer, then smeared the hlaut, the consecrated blood, on the wooden feet and splattered it on the entire figure. Lines of red appeared all the way up to the rigid faces.

The townspeople followed the priests and stopped at each wooden form to say a prayer or ask for blessings. It took several hours to circumambulate the hill and perform the rites for each deity. Upon completion of the circuit, the priests and the völva licked their bowls clean. As they stood watch, the second rite began. This was the time for any person who desired to pay respects to his or her individual fulltrúi. Patron gods required extra honor.

Líf and her siblings made their way to Thor, who was by far the most popular god. Driva wandered off to find Freya. Not knowing whether it would do any good, Líf placed her hand on the statue's foot and prayed, "If it be in your will and the will of the Norns, please protect Brasir if he still be alive." Then she stepped back to allow others room to approach.

By now it was early afternoon, and the sky had begun to darken. The air was frigid; breath puffed about people's faces like miniature clouds of smoke. Having honored their gods, the half-chilled citizens returned to town and their final destination for the evening.

In the mead hall, the men and women filled the benches. Budvar and Gratti, along with several other children, slipped in and found seats wherever they could. The völva was given the position of honor next to the jarl and his family. Stomachs growled, for no one had eaten all day. This had clearly made some of the men irritable, and they struggled to remain calm. What made things worse was that the aroma of crisping meat suffused the entire hall. Finally, the doors opened wide as slaves and several bóndi carried in the perfectly cooked feast.

Jarl Harek stood up and gave one final blessing before the dinner commenced. Every family, in order of rank from the highest to lowest, ate of the pork, beef, and horseflesh. A score of poultry rounded out the meal.

Beer and mead were passed around to everyone, even the children. Driva warned, "Do not drink so fast, or your night will end before it starts."

The boys giggled, and fizzing liquid squirted out of their noses.

"Two more days of this, and I'll be ready for water again," Líf sighed as she sipped her mead. At least it was sweet.

"You can make it," Hervor grinned, shoving her sister's shoulder. "Just don't assume you can keep up my pace."

"Mmmm," Líf narrowed her eyes. "At least I know I will last longer than Skeggi."

Both women stared at their brother's friend. He was already on his second drinking horn. Or was it his third? Hervor laughed wickedly, "Skál, sister! To outlasting Skeggi!"

"Skål!"

They slammed their horns together, sloshing the sweet-smelling mead upon one another. Their laughter mingled with all the others.

Líf did not know when she had fallen asleep. She had a splitting headache and prying her eyes open was extremely difficult. Glancing around, she noted that at least half the town had passed out in the hall.

Thray raised her small head, cheek fur squished flat. She hiccupped. "Everything is moving. Stop moving."

Fylgjur did not need to eat or drink, yet they were connected with their person and knew what hunger felt like as well as drunkenness.

Líf picked up the rodent and stumbled to the door. Outside, raucous bellows and grunts only increased the pounding of her head. She shielded her eyes from the sun to get a better look and grimaced.

Men, many of whom took part in the raiding parties, were already in the midst of their sporting events. Stripped down to their pants, the current pair of wrestlers were tossing one another into the slushy puddles of dampening snow. Clumps of white slush stuck to their chest hair while steam streamed off their backs.

"I need peace and quiet," complained Thray.

"So do I," acknowledged Líf. She slowly dragged herself out of Thorinheim. On the way, she spotted Skeggi sprawled on the ground in one of the swine sties.

"Uck," Líf gagged. And her siblings wondered why she never wanted to get married!

She made her way to a spot near a grove of trees. Her face itched where the blood had dried. She knew that she must stink. Sinking down onto a stump, she wrapped her arms around her face. Thray nuzzled into a position under Líf's chin.

"Drink too much?" a friendly voice chimed in.

Sitting up, Líf saw a young man around her age grinning at her. He had red hair only a shade lighter than hers. Freckles plastered his face but not in an unattractive way.

"Uh…" Líf didn't know how to respond. She felt herself blush. Worse, when she tried to tuck back a swatch of hair, her fingers became entangled in the long strands.

"Cat got your tongue?" the youth teased, seemingly amused by her floundering. He had a nice smile.

"Eric—" A second youth approached but halted when he spotted Líf. Waving his red-haired friend to his side, the youth hissed, "Come here."

"What?" the redhead grumbled as he obeyed the summons. The second lad whispered something into Eric's ear and nodded at Líf. Eric's face became drawn. Without saying another word, the pair headed back into town. The redhead glanced back over his shoulder more than once.

Líf should not have been upset, for this sort of thing happened to her all the time. She was a freak, shunned by many, especially when her siblings were not around. At least these young men had not chosen to verbally taunt her. She was not in the mood for an auditory beating.

Líf kept to herself through the morning but returned to the mead hall and the sound of raucous song around noon. Her headache had all but diminished, although this noise would certainly not help. Ottar saw her first. His face was flushed with drink. Behind him swayed Skeggi. The man's nose was bleeding.

"Here, Líf!" Ottar's shout was far too loud. He handed her a half-full cup of ale. "You missed it! This sorry chap," he said, slapping Skeggi on the back, "made a pass at Hervor in front of everyone. Guess what she did?"

Líf sniffed the warm beer. It smelled sour. Crinkling her nose, she said, "Hit him."

"'Ow'd you guess?" Skeggi asked in full surprise. His words sounded distorted, probably due to his broken nose.

"Just a hunch," Líf retorted, wishing she were not so sober.

"Maybe she's prophetic?" Skeggi slurred, leaning against Ottar's shoulder. "She could be a—" He glanced around as if looking for someone in particular. "A völva." Then, pointing to his own chest, he added, "I like völva. Vulvas? I like women."

Líf turned away from Skeggi's oafish smile.

Ottar warned, "Be careful, Skeggi, or this time you might lose an eye."

"Lingy loves me," he mused, just as several of his friends walked by belting out some song of the sea and lured the drunken fellow away.

"He means well," Ottar apologized.

Handing back the cup of beer, Líf smiled. "So, Hervor broke Skeggi's nose again? When will he learn?"

They watched the men trip over themselves and tumble to the ground. Ottar sighed. "Sometimes I don't know if Skeggi is capable of learning."

Líf laughed along with the shrill snickers of Thray. At Ottar's feet, his wolfhound fylgja scratched behind her ear and groaned with contentment.

"Ottar the Untouchable, I've been looking for you."

Harekson approached. He used Ottar's moniker as a sign of respect. Líf's brother had been given it years ago, when he'd become the only man to leave the field of a particular battle without a scratch. Harekson had also been drinking, though from the way he walked and spoke, it was hard to tell. He positioned himself in front of Ottar, rudely cutting Líf off without even a glance of acknowledgment.

At least her brother had the good sense not to befriend Harekson and his comrades. These young men, all from higher-ranking houses, expected to receive their fathers' governing titles. Although they went on raiding missions, their need for honor and notoriety was never as strong as Ottar's or even Skeggi's, for that matter.

"I have just come from talking with my father." Harekson spoke formally. The one thing he never took for granted was his duty as future jarl. "Your success during the raiding season has not gone unnoticed. He wishes to make you a *godi* come summer."

"I am honored that Jarl Harek believes I am worthy," Ottar acknowledged humbly.

"A godi!" Líf exclaimed. Though Ottar should not express his feelings, she could. A woman was not held to the same standard as a man. "Really?"

"Yes." Harekson turned and gave her a belittling look. His eyes narrowed; clearly, he was appalled that a woman had interrupted him. Turning his back to her once again, he finished his conversation with Ottar.

"Word just arrived that Godi Thren has died. You know his sons as well as I do. They do not deserve their father's honor. This is why my father wishes to pass the title to you. It will be announced at the Thing. You will have to delay your raids for a few months this year, since you will be expected to attend the assembly. Do you think you can manage?"

Líf was not sure the question was meant as an insult, but it sounded like one. Ottar inclined his head respectfully. "I am here to serve the jarl's will and the will of the gods."

Harekson nodded curtly before leaving.

"That's exciting news!" Líf beamed.

"Or terrifying," Ottar countered. He nodded toward Hervor, who was giving a young upstart a lesson in sword fighting. Actually, it looked more like a *beating*.

"Oh. True. She will not be pleased.

Ottar swigged the rest of his ale. "For now, let's keep this to ourselves."

During the communal supper, Jarl Harek turned to the seeress and made a formal and public request.

"Völva Gunhild, would you do me the great honor of reading into my future?"

At the sound of his voice, everyone grew quiet, even those typically too drunk to do so. The practice of magic was both a blessing and a risk—future events could be altered; the balance of life could be affected. Völvur were even able to harness spirits to do their bidding, such as hindering a warrior in battle or assassinating a person. Using seid to kill was forbidden. If a völva were found to have interfered with the Norns' chosen death for an individual, her life would be forfeit. It was no surprise that murder by spirits rarely occurred. This, however, was different. To ask for a reading of one's future was a customary request from the host of a visiting völva.

Gunhild looked expectant. "As you wish, Jarl Harek."

Fur blankets and rugs were gathered and passed to the woman. Gunhild took a seat on the pile and settled herself until she was comfortably cross-legged. She wedged her *gandr*, the staff that marked her status, between her legs in a very suggestive position. Holding the long rod with both hands, she closed her eyes and began to yawn.

"What's happening, Pappa?" Budvar was curious about this strange ritual.

"She is allowing the spirits to enter though her mouth."

The völva leaned back and began to hum. Wordless sounds of the ecstatic trance caused many to shift uncomfortably. Gunhild's eyes rolled beneath her closed lids. Her lips, then her body trembled as if in the grip of sensual pleasure. She began to speak in a husky voice.

"I see this hall adorned with garlands of new growth. Standing in its center is a man. A man of a different color...."

Chapter Seven

"Brasir," Líf whispered.

She knew Hervor was looking in her direction, but she could not tear her eyes away from the völva for fear of missing any part of the prophecy.

Gunhild's words were replaced by sounds of pleasure, but the jarl coaxed her to continue. "This man that you see, is he bound? Is he meant to be a sacrifice during Sumarmál?"

The völva's breathing became rapid. A film of sweat coated her tattooed skin. "Death," she said. Her voice rose hysterically. "Death! Death! DEATH!"

In one final, gasping scream, Gunhild went limp and fell back onto the soft pile of furs. Her staff was still tucked against her body. No one was allowed to touch her. The spirits must depart from her body on their own, undisturbed. Food and drink would be offered when she arose.

The hall was silent; there was no conversation. Their skald, the poet, began a well-known ballad. Soon, the festivities continued as if the past hour had been completely forgotten.

Líf couldn't drink. She had barely eaten all day, but she felt nauseous. Gunhild must have been talking about Brasir. He was alive. But to be standing here in this hall could only mean that he would be captured and most likely lose his life.

"I feel ill, Líf," Thray whispered. The poor squirrel was a dark purply-blue color.

"Me too."

Later that night, when the babel of drunkenness had died away and was replaced by the rumble of snores, Líf slipped away to return home. Ignoring the freezing air, she broke the thin layer of ice that covered a nearby stream and jumped naked into its water. Her entire body stung from the bitter cold. It took several hours to warm back up, despite being seated next to the cookfire, wrapped in blankets and furs.

"I will talk to the völva tomorrow while everyone else is merrymaking," she affirmed.

"Whatever you say," Thray mumbled, yawning sleepily. The fylgja was exhausted as was Líf. Together, they slept well into the following morning.

"She is gone, Líf."

"What do you mean, she is gone?" Líf questioned Ottar in horror.

"She left early this morning in the same karve that transported her here. She was in a hurry."

"No. That can't be!" Líf exclaimed. She ran down to the docks. There were fishermen's skiffs, the jarl's five longships, one cumbersome knarr that toted goods to and from the mainland, but the völva's small ship was nowhere to be seen.

As Líf made her way back to Thorinheim, sorrow clung to her like Thray's sharp claws. Children were laughing. Men were showing off their feats of strength. Women were enjoying one another's company away from their households. Young girls were flirting with hopeful suitors. This was the final day of Winter Nights. She should be happy. She should be having fun with others her age. Most were married by now; many already had second babies on the way. This celebration had been her chance to befriend someone, anyone, outside the family.

Líf spotted the red-head named Eric playing *hnefatafl*. As the defender, his pawns were trying to protect a larger piece that represented the king. By the looks of it, both he and his opponent were currently in a draw.

Ottar had taught her this game of strategy years ago; it had become their tradition to play it every winter when the snows were too deep to travel. Seeing an opportunity to help Eric, she walked over, but she still felt awkward approaching the youth.

Eric looked up as he held the pawn between fingers. His marten fylgja stared at her as well. The youth's eyes grew wide. His jawline twitched. Those subtle signs were all she needed to see, and she veered away. Whatever Eric's friend had said had forever tainted Líf in his eyes. She chose to spend the rest of the day accompanying Driva as her sister-in-law visited her lifelong companions. At least the older women would politely bring her into their conversations, though it was only small talk.

This evening would be the most boisterous yet, fueled by round after round of toasts. Every time a cheer was given, each person in the mead hall would raise a glass and drink deeply. Most would be incoherent by nightfall. In the morning, they would return home and continue their lives as usual.

Such was the way of this celebration. Líf was tired of all the excessive drinking. She was tired of all the merriment. She was tired of all these people.

Stealing away after the sixth round of goblet guzzling, Líf and Thray wandered back home.

Slipping on slush, they paused at the crest of a hill and looked back at the village below. Bonfires blazed. The mead hall was aglow in the ring of light, a beacon for the ever-watchful gods. Stars had begun to speckle the sky. Soon the rippling northern lights would emerge.

Voices could be heard. Someone was climbing down a nearby wooded slope. In the deepening night, it was hard for Líf to identify the man.

"Your name is Líf, right?"

"Yes," she replied tentatively.

The figure stepped into the moonlight. "My name is Eric."

"Ah…" Líf fumbled with words. Why was she so terrible at this? Why did Hervor make it look so easy?

"Líf, he has introduced himself. Say something," Thray prodded. Her little heartbeat thrummed excitedly.

"May I walk with you?" he asked.

All she could do was nod.

Eric moved to her side. He was tall. Not only taller than Líf—taller than almost everyone else. Líf took a step toward home, then halted. A single woman was not permitted to walk alone with a man who wasn't a member of her family; they were required to have an escort. But Hervor and Ottar were getting drunk in the mead hall.

"No. You can't."

Thray cocked her head as she stared at Eric's marten.

"Have you never been alone with a man before?" Although his voice was gentle, he smelled of alcohol.

Thray stirred uncomfortably. "We must return, Líf."

"I need to go," Líf said to the young man as she backed down the trail.

"Not so fast, *freak*." This second voice came from a man who had approached from behind to grab hold of her.

"No!" she shouted as she tried to shake off the offender. "Let go!"

The man shook her violently as he worked on restraining her flailing arms and legs. Thray was flung aside.

"Thray!" Líf screamed. She could not see where the little rodent had landed, but it was somewhere down the slope.

"Hurry, Eric," grunted the brute as he squeezed Líf. He was so strong, so terribly strong. "Grab her feet. We need to take her into the woods."

Eric hesitated for a moment, but locking eyes with his companion, he began to constrain Líf's legs.

"Please. Let me go," she whimpered. "I won't say anything. Please. Please, Eric!"

There was a bit of doubt on Eric's face as he hauled her by her feet into the forest. Maybe she could use that doubt to her advantage. She tested the waters. "You know you don't want to do this. You know it. You can stop this right now if you want to."

"Oh, shut up!" sneered the other man, who held her arms and chest. "If you be good, girl, and stay nice and quiet, I promise you will enjoy this. If not...well, you wouldn't want that."

Eric was not going to help her. They were dragging her farther away from any hope of discovery. In sheer panic, Líf screamed, "Help me! Somebody, help me! Please!"

Suddenly, Eric's companion threw her to the ground. He grabbed her dress by the neckline and slammed a wide hand across her face, making her ear ring so loudly that she could not understand what the man was ordering her to do.

Líf blinked. Her lip throbbed. Moving her tongue tenderly over it, she tasted blood. The man shook her again. Líf barely made an effort to respond. Why was this happening?

This was her fault. She should not have left the hall early. She should have suffered through all the toasts and the stupid boasts. That seemed a lovely alternative now.

Thor protect me, she prayed silently.

"You got it?" sneered the unnamed man, mere inches from her face.

Líf could barely mumble a coherent sound.

"We need to keep moving," he ordered.

Eric pulled her arms, but she remained a limp mass in his grip. The second fellow followed them with keen eyes, his hand ready to strike again.

"She's heavier than she looks," griped Eric. Panting, he dropped her. His breath and sweat stank of drink.

Eric's companion gave him a shove. "Move aside." He finished hauling Líf into the sanctuary of tall, looming trees. The wooden sentinels creaked and groaned. Their canopies momentarily showed starlight.

Finally, they stopped. Without releasing her, the man bellowed, "I'll hold her. You go first."

Eric stepped up.

A larger shadow followed silently. The shifting blackness reached around Eric's head and, in a movement perfected with practice, snapped the youth's neck like a twig. The marten fylgja disappeared instantly.

The limp body crashed to the ground before the other man realized what had occurred. Brasir lurched at the second offender and shouted, "Run, Líf!"

She blinked again.

Suddenly she heard Thray's admonitions. "Get up! Hurry!"

Her fylgja had found her. Líf struggled to her feet.

She had barely righted herself before something seized her ankle. She fell forward, her head slamming against a mess of roots.

Her sight wavered. She rolled onto her back, trickles of warmth spilling into her eyes. Everything blurred. Bodies moved, fading in and out of shadow. Grunts and groans of men surrounded her. A large red bear held something small and furry in his teeth. Then the tiny animal disintegrated in a medley of color.

Darkness kept trying to claim her.

Who was calling her name?

Where was Thray?

Someone was stooping over her, lifting her. Her head was gently tucked into the crook of a neck. The skin was dark as the earth, dark as the night, dark as the blackness that swallowed her.

Chapter Eight

The first sensation she felt was fire. The pain was scalding as if a heated brand had been pressed against her flesh. The burning feeling pinpointed her forehead.

Lif's eyes fluttered open. At first, the world was blurry. Blinking away the initial tears, she recognized the roof beams of her sleeping nook. Driva leaned over her, strained features crosshatched by lines that could only have been created by intense worry. She was pressing something onto Lif's brow that intensified the pain.

"Oh, girl!" Driva breathed in relief. "The Norns have not called you yet. Shh. Shh. Stay still." She smiled dryly before asking the dazed woman, "Do you know me, child?"

Lif started to nod, but a new wave of pain made her feel as if her skull were actually splitting. Her sister-in-law placed Lif's hand on a saturated cloth. "Hold that steady. Don't let go. Your wound is still bleeding."

In the main room, heated voices rang out. Ottar sounded furious. "The whole time? The *entire* time? And not one word?"

"I'm not going to ask what you would have had me do," growled Hervor in reply. "I already know what you *think* you would have done. But that's not the case. Clearly. You weren't in my position."

"So, you are absolutely fine with risking all our lives? Your sister's? Mine? Your own nephews'?"

"Stop it, Ottar. Do you think so little of me for this single decision? Do you think I never considered the possibilities? Never worried about the outcomes?"

Their brother was spitting mad. "You couldn't have, or you would have dragged him back to the jarl as soon as you saw him."

When Driva looked over her shoulder in the direction of the argument, Lif took the opportunity to sit up. Her sister-in-law reached over to gently push her back down.

"No," Lif uttered, swatting at the unwanted help. "Let go." Just speaking sent torrents of pain through her. She felt drained. Drained of energy. Drained of blood. Her already pale skin was a new shade of white.

Shaking her head, Driva stood behind Lif to prevent the girl from falling backward as she struggled to her feet. Slowly, they made their way toward the angry voices.

Hervor faced the back of the house and so was the first to spot her injured sister. "Lif! You're awake! Go lie down!"

Ottar spun round; the fury in his eyes lessened as he observed his sister's unsteady form. Lif grabbed hold of one of the inner posts to support herself. Her other hand held the rag to her forehead; blood oozed between her fingers.

Brasir knelt between the older siblings. His hands were bound behind his back, wrists secured to ankles. He was gagged but did not struggle. The captured slave held his position with remarkable confidence and self-possession. He looked at Lif with relief.

"Don't be angry with Hervor." Lif spoke slowly and concentrated on enunciating every syllable.

"Lif," Ottar began kindly, but his eyes and his tone implored her to stay out of the conversation.

"Did he tell you he saved my life? Did you give him a chance?"

Ottar grew serious. "He is the property of the jarl. You know this. He must be returned."

"Men tried to rape me! Rape me!" Lif screamed. The sudden exertion caused the entire world to sway. Letting the rag fall to the ground, she gripped the post with both hands. She felt Driva's strong but gentle hands supporting her shoulders.

Her siblings remained quiet, but neither looked directly at her. Lif found enough energy to continue, "You weren't able to help me. If he had not been there—"

"You shouldn't have left the hall."

To Lif's surprise, it was Hervor who spoke. Lif looked aghast. "Maybe I shouldn't have. Maybe this was all my fault."

Ottar jumped in to defend his younger sister. "It isn't your fault, Lif. What those men tried to do to you..." He couldn't finish.

Tears trailed down Lif's face and mingled with the rivulets of fresh blood. "Brasir saved me. He *saved* me. We owe him. *I* owe him."

"No, you don't." Once again, it was Hervor who took on the role of antagonist. "You freed him, and he saved you. There is no debt to pay. And Ottar's right. He must be returned. He had his chance. Two men have been killed. I'm sorry."

But Hervor did not sound sorry. Lif studied her brother, who now appeared to be the more open of the two siblings. "Ottar, he sees hamingjur! Did Hervor tell you? Did he? Brasir is here to discover why they are dying.

He is here to help. We can't send him back to be harmed or killed. What if he is the only one who can stop whatever is happening?"

"Hervor shared this with me," acknowledged Ottar. "You are a thoughtful person, careful in your decisions. Always have been. But think, Líf. Where is the proof?"

"He…" Líf looked at Brasir. Beyond him, the faces of the boys peeked in at the door. They must have been sent outside while the adults assessed the situation. "He pointed out a slave whose hamingja had disappeared. That slave died a short while later."

"You mean Brasir killed him a short while later," Ottar sighed. "Is it possible that this man you freed had already intended to kill the other slave and made up the story of the hamingja to get you to trust him?"

"Brasir wouldn't have done that," Líf retorted, yet she wondered if that could be true. Could he have been lying to her the entire time? Had she been manipulated from the beginning? Brasir's eyes were fierce. He was certainly capable of murder. But there was no reason for him to rescue her. He had risked his own life in order to bring her safely back home. Risked and lost.

"If he is telling the truth—" she began, but Otter countered, "We cannot keep going back to ifs."

Líf spoke as loudly as her throbbing head would allow. "If he is telling the truth, we could all be in danger. Our family. Our friends. Our people. I ask for time to discover proof of his story. Time for him to convince you, all of you. If he is telling the truth, we let him go free. If not, we send him back to Jarl Harek."

Hervor pursed her lips. Ottar looked at his children, then at Driva. "There needs to be a set time limit. This man," he looked at the captive, "*Brasir*, has to show us unquestionable evidence that what he says is real."

"Of course," agreed Líf. "Until the spring. Until Sumarmál. Winter has just begun, and nobody will be traveling. There is little risk that he will be discovered with us during that time. When Sumarmál arrives, the ice will have melted. Ships will be able to venture out. If he is truthful, Brasir might find safe passage to the mainland."

Ottar and Hervor exchanged looks. Hervor was dubious but nodded assent. Ottar turned to Líf. "We will keep Brasir over winter. But he is *not* a free man. He must stay inside, under our watch. We can't have him disappearing again."

"Thank you!" Líf exclaimed.

Sighing, he added, "The *weregild* will need to be paid to the families of the dead. Today I must publicly attest to the killings with the charge that these men dared try to rape a fellow citizen and a sister to me. Still, I will have to pay out the blood money at the next Thing, as per our law. Let us hope all recourse will end there."

Líf knew she was indebted to her brother. "I will work extra hard to pay you back. I promise." Slowly, she turned around and stumbled to her bed. She did not feel strong enough to remain standing.

Both Hervor and Driva tended Líf's wounds. Hervor helped restrain her sister while Driva sewed up the gash in Líf's forehead. Halfway through the process, Líf passed out.

The following afternoon, Líf sat on the edge of her bed, glad that she was finally permitted to move about. The pain of her wound still screamed, but her strength had increased.

"Beauty is not a required attribute of a great woman," Ottar said as he inspected his wife's handiwork. "Plus, with your hair done right, no one will notice the scar."

Hervor must have overhead their brother, for she added, "Every man likes a few scars. Even women. They are arousing."

Líf's fingers hovered over the cut, but she did not dare touch the skin. She had refused to look at herself in the polished looking glass the household shared. She knew half her face must be covered in nasty, swollen bruises and cuts.

She slowly stood up and stretched her stiff legs. Brasir was tied to one of the posts; his bear fylgja rested by his side. Thray had been nestled in Líf's sheets but now sniffed the ursine's wide face.

Kneeling next to the dark-skinned man, Líf was finally able to say, "Thank you for what you did for me."

No longer gagged, Brasir replied, "It was only right."

By the next day, Líf was able to complete her daily work without help from the boys. She was very slow, but she could lift, carry, stir, and fold everything she was expected to. In the harsh reality in which they all lived, there was no time for bed rest. By week's end, Líf was almost back to normal. Although her head still pained her, that did not matter. Her life was a simple pattern of daily acts repeated from sunrise to sunset.

Brasir remained tied to the post. He was taken out several times a day under the watchful eye of Hervor and Ottar to do his business. He did not complain about his situation and always thanked them when offered food.

The boys found him fascinating. Their fear of someone different from themselves had disappeared by the second day. They were often found questioning Brasir, asking about everything from the color of his skin to where he was born.

Líf would have liked to listen in, but there was always something that needed mending, something that should be cooked, something that needed to be seen to.

Ottar had informed their own slaves about the captive. He warned them never to mention his presence to anyone, on pain of their lives. They were instructed to act as if Brasir were invisible.

Two weeks later, Líf was busy mending a mound of worn-out blankets. The weather outside was worsening, and everyone needed extra layers at night. Brasir, who had been quietly watching her work, said, "I can help if you wish."

"You sew?" Líf asked skeptically.

"A little."

No one was around. Driva and the boys were tending their livestock. Ottar was purchasing goods in the town. Who knew where Hervor had wandered off to this time? What harm could it cause?

Líf carried a pile of threadbare cloth and fur skin blankets over to Brasir. Taking a seat next to him, she started to hand him a needle. But his hands were still tied.

"Maybe you should ask permission?" Brasir suggested.

A strong rope tied around his torso tethered the man to the post. His legs were bound at the ankles. Even with his hands free, he couldn't run. Líf untied the ropes at his wrists. Brasir rubbed his raw skin tenderly before threading the needle.

They had been working for an hour when Driva and Hervor walked through the door.

"What in Hel's name is going on?" Hervor questioned angrily.

"Don't be mad," Líf retorted. "He is only helping. It was my decision. And not that it matters to you, but he told me to ask."

Hervor looked furious. But Driva, having picked up a blanket, asked, "He did this?"

"Yes."

"Well, I'll say one thing, he has the most perfect stitching."

The shieldmaiden glared at the blanket then back at Brasir. "Don't get used to this."

That was the only time Hervor threatened to curtail Brasir's assistance with Líf's chores. Every day, Brasir would offer to help with some little task. He did everything without complaint. Not long afterward, Driva began requesting his help with her chores. The more work Brasir took on, the longer the lead rope he was given. Soon, he had the full run of the house.

One day, Ottar needed help. "Hervor?" he shouted. "Where are you? I have a wagon full of firewood waiting to be unloaded."

"She's out hunting snow hare," Gratti replied as he clambered over Brasir's back.

Líf offered, "I can help."

"A storm's coming, and I'm in a hurry." Ottar was obviously irritated. "Of course, I sent the slaves to check the traps today."

Clouds were darkening the sky in an ominous fashion. "Will Aunt Hervor be okay?" Gratti asked.

"She'll be fine," Ottar said without a trace of doubt. "I don't know if I can say the same for our wood. It needs to stay dry."

Brasir stood up slowly and allowed Gratti to slide gently to the ground. "Let me be of assistance."

Ottar contemplated the offer. Behind him, the wind was picking up. He walked over to Brasir and looked at him, studying his eyes, then untied him completely. "Come on, then. All of you. Let's make quick work of this."

With wind whipping about them and snow starting to fall, the family worked as quickly as they could, carrying all the wood inside the house. Brasir's large armfuls were of great help and sped up the process immensely. As he carried in one more huge load, Líf said to Ottar, "I think he is starting to grow on you."

"I think," her brother responded, "that you should not mix daydreams with reality."

Yet, as Ottar picked up another bundle, a clear smile crossed his face.

Chapter Nine

That night, Brasir was allowed to sleep untethered. With the storm beating upon their thatched roof, it would be useless for him to try to flee. Moreover, he clearly showed no intent to run. He had curled up in his mound of blankets next to the cookfire while his bear fylgja slept soundly beside him.

The days passed. Winter's snows grew with each wave of blizzards and shrank from snowmelt in between. On pleasant days, Brasir might be spotted out in the yard, allowing himself to be tackled by the boys as they played their game of raiding.

Soon, Jól was upon them, a sign that after two and a half months, midwinter was finally here. This was a seasonal celebration marking the rebirth of the sun, for by now it was dark almost all hours of the day. Several weeks of merrymaking would commence and culminate in a final celebration known as Jólablót. Like Winter Nights, the entire population was expected to come to Thorinheim for the last three days to conduct ritual offerings, ensuring that next season would bring a bountiful harvest.

A large tree trunk, stripped bare of limbs, would be blessed and then burned in the mead hall to warm everyone inside. The celebration would commence with a feast. This time, boars would be slaughtered and eaten in honor of the goddess Freya. Decorative goats made of straw were set in the hall in remembrance of Thor and his favorite animal. Odin, disguised as Jolfaðr, would arrive on Sleipnir, his eight-legged horse, and bestow gifts upon the good children.

Líf was not ready to attend a public celebration and asked to stay behind. The family had come to trust Brasir and so allowed her to stay at the house with him, but they gave her a seax blade to keep on her person at all times.

"Would you just say that I am ill," Líf suggested as Ottar kissed the top of her head. Líf cringed when she felt his lips touch her scar. It was not painful, but the idea of the grisly wound revolted her.

"Someone will come and check on you each evening," her brother assured her.

She watched as the rest of her family headed toward Thorinheim, leaving deep trenches in the snow in their wake.

The days passed quietly. Líf replicated as many of the ceremonies as she could with the little fulltrúar. Brasir observed in humble silence.

On the third day, Ottar and the others returned home early. His face was bleak. Something was wrong, very wrong.

"What's going on? What happened?"

"To bed, boys," Ottar ordered. His sons obeyed; Gratti sniffled as he walked past. Once the children were quiet, he finally explained. "Bad omens came with the final sacrifice."

"Omens?"

Ottar was thoughtful for a time. "Yes. The blood ran black."

"The animals were sick," Hervor said. "Blood doesn't look like that."

Líf turned to Driva, who admitted, "The animals could have been sick."

"All of them?" Líf needed to know.

"Yes."

"Don't you think that's odd?"

"Of course, I do," Ottar agreed. "Five animals from five different households all bled black. For some reason, the gods are not happy with us."

Brasir was seated in his designated spot. He kept quiet but was clearly listening to the conversation.

Líf suddenly thought about drinking tainted liquid. "Did you…?"

"Of course we didn't." Ottar shook his head. "All of Thorinheim is in an uproar. Some drank the hlaut, but I think that was foolish. We left so that the godis and the jarl could discuss these matters further."

Thray chirped up, "Could it be the hamingjur? A sign that they are ill?"

Líf caught Brasir's eye for a moment. Cradling the little squirrel, she whispered, "I don't know."

That night, she dreamed of the fulltrúar. As she approached the little idols, liquid began to ooze from their carved eyes and mouths—blood as black as coal. She woke up coated with sweat.

The sun shone brightly in a clear and icy-blue sky. Driva had stoked the fire into a crackling blaze that chased away the winter chill. As he often did, Brasir stood outside watching the children play. He was not only fond of the boys but also immensely patient with their rough antics.

Líf approached him. "Morning, Brasir."

At first, the man didn't appear to hear her. He stared intently as Gratti clawed his way out of a snowdrift. Slowly he turned and blinked.

"Líf," he said in acknowledgment. He looked back at the boys.

"Is something wrong?" Líf asked, worry knotting in her throat.

Driva was walking by and paused long enough to hear Brasir say, "It might be nothing."

Several days later, Gratti came down with a fever. "Everything hurts," the boy whined, shivering. "I'm cold, Mamma."

Driva watched over him like a mother hawk. Her feline fylgja curled up on the boy's chest along with Gratti's pup. Gratti coughed several times.

"Here, sweet boy." She pressed a cloth full of fresh snow over Gratti's flushed face.

"Mamma, I don't feel good." He continued to whimper.

Brasir kept Budvar company. Unable to play with his favorite companion, the older boy also appeared gloomy. This continued for the rest of the week. Gratti showed no sign of getting better.

Clearly, Ottar was worried. And Driva, who never allowed herself to show fear when her boys were present, was even more worried than her husband. When the shieldmaiden left to fetch a healer, Brasir was forced to hide in the shed.

Upon her return, Hervor brought ill tidings. "The healers are overwhelmed. This sickness is everywhere, and it is spreading. Several children have already died." She kept her voice low to prevent the boys from overhearing.

Driva's breathing was ragged. She left to tend to her youngest child.

"Lif," Hervor added, "Tell Brasir to come in. Help is not coming."

Lif ran into the yard and wept. The idea of losing Gratti was too hard to bear. It took a while for her to calm herself and knock on the shed's door. Brasir opened it.

"You can…you can come back inside," she sniffled. "I'm afraid, Brasir. I'm afraid for Gratti. It's his hamingja, isn't it?"

Brasir looked sad. "Yes. It has been fading. I wasn't sure at first, but last night it disappeared."

"You should have said something!" Lif shouted as she struck him. He did not budge as she beat her fists on his chest. Tears poured down her cheeks. "You should have told us! But you kept it to yourself! We could have…we could have…."

She sobbed as Brasir gently ran his hand over her mess of red hair. The man did not look at her when she finally stepped back. Instead, he was staring at Ottar. How long had her brother been standing there? Had he seen Lif's angry reaction?

Ottar turned and walked to the house. Lif and Brasir followed. After Driva heard what had happened, she sat quietly next to her desperately ill child. Gratti's fever was searing. Snow had been packed around him where he lay. The central fire had been allowed to burn down in the hope that the cold air would help break the fever.

"My little boy," Driva cooed. "My sweet, sweet child. I give you my hamingja if it can save you. I give it all to you most happily. Oh, sweet boy."

She kissed the top of his sweat-soaked head.

Brasir stared at the ground. Líf couldn't stand the sorrowful crooning of the heartbroken mother. Driva's constant prayers continued well into the night—an uncomfortable atmosphere for uncomfortable dreams.

"Get up, Líf! Now!" Hervor shook her sister awake in the early hours of the morning. "We need your help."

"Gratti?" Líf asked as she tried to shake off her sleepiness.

Hervor handed Líf a pail. Bits of snow clung to its bottom. "No. The Norns did not call him. His fever broke. It's Driva. She has the fever now."

Líf was still trying to understand. "Driva?"

"Hurry!" Hervor was already moving outside. "We need more snow."

Driva moaned in her feverish fit. She must not have left the boys' bed. Instead, Gratti had been moved to his parents' bed, where Budvar now held him close. Ottar packed snow over his wife's body. Brasir helped, his face devoid of emotion.

Líf and Hervor collected more snow until all but Driva's face was buried beneath an icy white blanket. Her cat's hue was almost black.

"Driva? Driva, can you hear me?" Ottar beseeched his wife. His eyes were wild. "I don't understand how this happened so quickly. She was fine. She was just fine." Turning to the man next to him, he demanded, "What's happening to her? Tell me!"

"She gave her hamingja away," Brasir said bleakly. "She gave it to your son. She had no more protection."

"No. No, no," Ottar touched Driva's forehead. The woman's breathing was becoming shallow. "Driva? I'm going to pass some of my hamingja to you. To help you fight this."

"You can't."

Brasir's statement was not what Ottar expected. He snapped back, "She is my wife!"

"She is not your blood."

Ottar lunged at Brasir. Both men fell to the floor. Their fylgjur snarled. Shocked, the others watched the men fight each other. Each landed blows. Blood and spittle flew through the air. Then Hervor stepped in to try and halt the foolishness.

Líf glanced at Driva and watched as the sick woman's cat fylgja closed its eyes. In the next moment, the feline blew away like a handful of ash thrown into the wind. Her voice breaking, Líf cried out, "Ottar! Hervor! She's gone. Driva is gone."

"Driva, no!" Ottar untangled himself from Brasir, who watched him stumble to his dead wife's side. The boys' sobs rang out.

Driva was buried in a field where the prettiest little flowers bloomed in the spring. It took both men and Hervor to dig a deep pit in the frozen ground. When the seasons next changed, they would commission a marker for the grave.

Death was a common occurrence in the lives of Northmen. Old age was not revered. The highest honor for a man was to die in battle. For a woman, it was the legacy that her sons would create.

"Will Mamma go to Valhalla?" Gratti asked as they stood near the new mound of dirt.

"No, little one," Ottar explained. "Women are not welcomed there."

Hervor's jaw twitched, but she did not say a word.

"Where will she go, then?"

"To Hel, most likely. There she will stay, in the gray with your grandmother and her mother before that."

"Some say," Hervor added, "that a woman who has lived a life of notoriety might go to Fólkvangr."

"But of that we are not certain," countered Ottar grimly.

Hervor was first to leave the graveside. The rest stayed for a time and watched as snowflakes coated the upturned soil.

As the boys began to walk back to the house, Ottar spoke to Brasir. "Your answers lie outside Midgard? Well, then, we need to ready a ship."

CHAPTER TEN

The weeks passed as they prepared for their treasonous act. Ottar never paused to question his newfound beliefs; his first priority was to assemble a crew for his ship, which was moored in the inlet near his home. Of course, Skeggi was the first man to step up. Anything to do with Ottar and Hervor was fine by him. Besides, he had never been fond of Harekson and was happy to give that little prick the middle finger.

Together Skeggi, Ottar, and Hervor assembled a tried-and-true group of seafarers who were loyal to a fault. All had served under the Lothbransons at one time or another. They respected the siblings to a degree most others could never hope to attain.

Spring was around the corner, though it was still bitterly cold. Goods were acquired slowly, so as not to cause alarm. They hoped to leave as soon as they were able and return before they were missed.

"Do you really want to risk this?" Líf asked her brother one day as they watched the men inspect last year's sail. "What of your future title as godi? If Harek realizes you have left, you will never receive that honor."

"What is a title when one's own children are in peril? I doubted Brasir once. I asked for a sign. The gods gave me all the proof I would ever need."

"But does it have to be you? Budvar and Gratti have just lost their mother. Surely, there are others who could lead this mission."

"Hervor cannot be seen to captain the ship, as she is a woman. At least, not officially. And since *Wavecutter* is mine, I must be on her, or the others could be accused of theft. It is my duty to go. Yours is to remain here with my boys. Pray that we return before Sumarmál. It shouldn't take long, just to the mainland and back."

"Pappa!" Budvar shouted as he ran down the slope. "Harekson the Wolf is approaching with several others." The boy used Harekson's official moniker. "He is heading to the house."

"Where is Brasir?"

"At home with Gratti."

"Find him and tell him to hide; make sure your brother doesn't give him away. Líf, come with me. Let's see what Harekson the *Wolf* wants."

Wolf! How odd, thought Líf. Harekson's fylgja was a boar, like his father's. Though in regard to his fierce temperament, maybe the title was fitting.

They intercepted the future jarl before he arrived at the house. His mother had accompanied him, as had several other people.

"So, you have been keeping secrets from me," Harekson stated. His boar fylgja grunted angrily. "I don't like being kept in the dark."

Ottar was quiet and waited for the accusation.

Thray dug her nails into Líf's back hard enough to make her jump. Harekson gave her a sidelong glance before he continued. "Did you really think you could keep me from finding out about your upcoming journey? I thought I told you not to leave before the Thing."

Turning to Princess Thoren, he asked, "Are you sure this is the man you want to elevate? He does not listen very well."

"I heard you," Ottar acknowledged. "But I feel this short trip needs to be made. Some time ago, it was brought to my attention that an illness has been spreading among the people."

"Yes, that was a terrible time for us all—"

Princess Thoren interrupted. "We were sorry to hear about the loss of your wife. She was a very kind woman and a good mother."

"She was that and much more," Ottar admitted. "But that is not the sickness I was referring to. There is an illness affecting hamingjur. Draining them until they are nothing."

Líf gasped at how forthcoming Ottar was with his information.

Her brother continued, "I am traveling to the mainland to find the truth of it, if it be the will of the gods."

"Hamingjur dying?" Harekson laughed, his dark beard catching some of the breeze. "I didn't peg you as superstitious."

"I remember a man speaking of such things." Princess Thoren always spoke in a monotone.

"Brasir?" Thray asked, but Líf did not dare respond to her fylgja.

Harekson scoffed again. "Age does wonders for one's mind."

Thoren ignored her son. "We are here to express our sympathies—"

Her son cut in. "And to say this: I will not alert my father of your little venture *if* we come to an agreement."

"Agreement?"

Harekson looked in the direction of *Wavecutter*; its silhouette could be seen through the trees. "Yes. It is high time that I marry. Your sister is eligible."

"Wait, I–" Líf began in a clear panic. Her brother must save her from this horrid match!

"Not that one." Harekson refused to acknowledge Líf. "The other one."

"Ottar, you can't," Líf implored on Hervor's behalf. But he could. He was the head of the household. It was his right to marry both of his sisters off to whomever would most benefit the family.

Glancing at the house, Ottar saw the two boys waiting on the stoop. Somewhere inside was the man who could ruin those children's futures, risk their young lives. He stretched out his hand. "It's a deal."

In turn, Harekson clasped Ottar's forearm. "We will announce this match after your acceptance as godi. You should be proud, *brother*."

That last word sent shivers down Líf's spine. When the visitors had left, she turned on Ottar. "Hervor is going to kill you. How could you? Marrying her off without her knowledge!"

"I hope it does not come to that. I have time to come up with a plan. For now, I have kept my family safe—and that criminal we are hiding, alive. I did what I had to do."

"You may be right, but Hervor will be *furious*."

"She will. And I will be the one to tell her."

Ottar was lucky to be alive after Hervor's fits of rage. Unfortunately, the same could not be said for the shed after she had hurled her axe through the wall again and again. She barely missed Ottar's head, though she claimed that had been deliberate.

Only days away from setting sail, another crisis emerged.

"They took him!" Skeggi bellowed. "They found him helping your slaves in the field. There must have been a terrible struggle, for both of your slaves are dead."

"Who took him?" Hervor's question sounded like she was accusing Skeggi of mismanaging their cargo.

"Some of Harekson's companions. They are headed to Thorinheim."

"And you didn't stop them?" Hervor was beside herself. She had had very little patience since her brother's arrangement. The shieldmaiden reached for her axe.

"Wait!" Ottar commanded.

"Are you going to let them take Brasir after all this?" Hervor gestured to include the house, though her meaning was understood.

"If we interfere, they will know we are involved."

"What, then?"

Líf was holding Thray. Too tightly, for the little squirrel bit her hand in warning. Loosening her grip, Líf listened, hoping there was a way out of this mess. The boys, who had been playing hnefatafl on the floor, looked at their father with worried expressions.

"Odin's missing eye!" Ottar swore. "Líf, get the boys into the boat. Pack only the most precious things. Skeggi, alert the men that we are leaving immediately. If they are not all present, we will have to be shorthanded."

"Let me come with you," Líf begged. If Jarl Harek had Brasir, she wanted to help free him.

Ottar was in no mood to argue. "For once, Líf, listen to me. Do as I say!"

Everyone scattered. Thray would not stop talking. The rodent's incessant chatter was only making things worse and adding to Líf's worry.

With the boys' help, she collected the family's most valuable items and heirlooms: the fulltrúar, all the arm and neck rings, the fragments of ingots for trade, Driva's lovely gowns, several changes of clothes, and a set of drinking horns, believing they would need the last item soon. The boys gathered the hnefatafl pieces and their wooden swords so they would not be bored. After passing their wares and belongings up to the men in the boat, she helped the children board.

"Well, Lingy, are you ready?" Skeggi handed her a short axe whose handle had shattered over the winter and was in want of repair.

"Ready?"

"Well, I don't know about you, but I intend to be with Ottar. The boys will be fine. Guthorm Blood Cheeks will watch them."

Together they ran all the way to Thorinheim, slowing only when they approached the mead hall. Boughs, green with new growth, were spread about as if Sumarmál had arrived early. The only other reason to decorate the hall in this manner would be if Princess Thoren were pregnant again.

"Shit," Skeggi swore as he saw Brasir struck in the head with the butt end of a two-handed axe. One side of the captive's face was already swollen.

A small rock bounced off Skeggi's head, causing them both to jump. Hervor and Ottar, crouched near a neighboring building, waved to them.

"What in Hel's half-rotten heart are you two doing here?" Hervor was not grateful for their unexpected assistance.

Skeggi puckered his lips as if to kiss her. That move almost lost him an ear. Ottar filled them in. "Harek found out that Brasir was working in our fields. We will not be able to trick him any longer."

"Then what are we doing out here?" Líf asked as she awkwardly lifted her short axe. "They are killing him!"

"Give me that before you hurt someone." Hervor snatched the weapon away. "We have to wait. It is impossible to attack the hall and succeed. Our best chance is to wait for them to chain Brasir outside."

"He'll be dead by then," Líf pointed out. Her siblings were the fiercest fighters in the entire area. Why were they acting so timidly now?

"Hervor's right," Ottar said, and pointed. "Look. Quiet, all of you."

A group of men dragged the unconscious form of Brasir to his original post and began to tie his bindings, far more securely this time. He was still breathing, but for how long? Jarl Harek and his sons watched the entire procedure, then tested the ropes, before returning to the hall.

One man was left on watch. Hervor rolled her head back and grunted. "Tord, the luckless fool."

In one swift action, she hurtled Líf's small axe into the back of the man's skull. Brains and red fluid spilled onto the ground. All four rushed forward, Líf the only one without a weapon. The others quickly cut the bindings and lifted Brasir onto Skeggi's back. Since Skeggi was the stoutest person in the group, he had the best chance of hauling Brasir away from this mess.

"Wait."

Everyone looked up. Harek's youngest son stood before them. Hervor clenched her jaw, readying herself for what must be done.

Sigird was a boy of only thirteen, who had sailed on his first raiding party last summer. The teenager kept his eyes on Hervor's axe. "There is a cart over here. It will be faster."

Skeggi, Ottar, Hervor, and Líf all looked at one another.

"Hurry," Sigird implored. "Someone else could have heard you."

Ottar and Skeggi lugged Brasir's body to the cart. Taking the place of the draft horse, they pulled. Hervor eyed Sigird warily as she and Líf pushed the cart from behind.

At Thray's suggestion, Líf asked the boy, "Why are you helping us?"

"My mother wishes me to go with you."

"With us?"

"Yes. I am a third son. No property will come to me. No title. I must earn honor and status through my own endeavors. That will not happen here. But to go on a journey with real purpose, that could change my future. Let me come with you."

Ottar considered the youth carefully. "You can come. But only if you help us push."

Together, they transported Brasir to the longship. The crew had made her ready and were waiting for their captain's command. Shoving off, they rowed toward the main fjord that led to the open waters. Hervor stood at the prow and shouted commands.

As the shoreline receded, Líf tried to glimpse the only home she had ever known. Flames leaped into the air, while billowing black smoke obscured its location. There was no going back. No returning. Only forward. Always forward.

The Guardian's Speaker

Volume Two

Epigraph

Hearing I ask from the holy races,
From Heimdall's sons, both high and low;
Thou wilt, Valfather, that well I relate
Old tales I remember of men long ago.

Völuspá - The Prophecy of the Seeress

Chapter One

Unapologetic. Detached. Heartless.
Fire is all these things. It eats through cherished items with an unstoppable hunger and tears apart the lives of any caught in its searing grasp. It does so without intent and without mercy. It was this most powerful force of nature that now thrust out its long fingers to claw at the sky.

Líf watched in horror and awe as generations of memories were consumed in the column of flames. She had lit the fire herself—not the actual spark, but a metaphorical one. It was through her actions that her family's home and all their material belongings would be forever lost. Lost under the blazing embers, buried under a thick coating of ash. Lost to the rightful owners, for those who hunted them down would claim the property as their own. Lost to the progeny who would never know from whence they came.

"It's my fault, Thray," Líf confessed as trepidation curdled like sour milk in her stomach. "Mine and mine alone."

"But by saving *his* life, you might end up saving all others."

Although Thray's words were sympathetic, her voice was mournful. She meant well, but nothing she might say could provide any consolation. Líf watched the island she had called home slowly recede as the longship *Wavecutter* headed out of their home fjord and into the ice-choked sea. The feeling of foreboding grew stronger.

Perched upon Líf's shoulder, her fylgja shifted uncomfortably. As Líf's guardian spirit, Thray was linked to Líf, her feelings and her well-being. Although every person had one of these female presences watching over them, fylgjur were as different as the people they protected.

Thray was a squirrel whose fur usually shimmered with iridescent color. Just now, the little rodent's hue was a deep green that continued to darken.

"I don't feel well," Thray moaned.

At the same time, a wave of nausea rolled over Líf like the waves that rolled under her brother's ship. She turned around barely in time to vomit into the water. Just as she thought the worst was over, her insides knotted up and she began to dry-heave. This continued until the length of her throat felt as if it had been scorched by the fire that destroyed her home.

Líf hated boats. She hated being on the water. She even hated the unknown man who had come up with the clever idea that people should travel on the ever-rocking sea. She had never been able to withstand the movement of waves underfoot. Why had she thought this vessel would be her salvation? Or was she being punished? Were the gods angry with her?

"I will not die," Líf assured herself as the world tilted beneath her. "I will not die."

"You talking to your fylgja?"

Líf's brother, Ottar, walked over to her as easily as if he had been born on water. This ship and its voyages were ingrained in every fiber of him, from his blond hair to the sparkle in his blue eyes. To him, this wooden contraption was more than a temporary home on the water; it was part of the family, a member that Líf would not miss when it died. Then again, the boat was their only chance of survival.

"No," Líf admitted. Her ability to see her fylgja as well as everyone else's was unheard of. This unnatural skill singled her out, but not in a good way. She was shunned, feared, and mocked by the people. "I just—"

Líf could not finish her sentence. She leaned over the wooden siding and heaved again, onto a large drift of ice. The fjord was unusually full of the frozen floating debris for this time of year, which made the passage even more difficult.

Ottar helped her sit down and rubbed her back. "It's all right. You have been focusing on survival. Now that you are out of danger, your body has begun to realize that you are sailing."

He spoke soothingly, as if she were one of his young boys. They, however, like their father, appeared at ease on the longship. Fighting another wave of nausea, Líf envied them and their tolerance of this wretched movement.

Ottar's fylgja had the form of a large wolfhound. Her iridescent nose nudged Thray, who had curled into a ball on Líf's lap.

"Take it easy," Ottar advised. His breath puffed pleasantly about his face in the chill of the air. "Hopefully, the next few days will not be so trying."

"Did he say *days*?" Thray whined. She sat up in dismay but flopped down almost immediately, her body so limp that it slowly slid off Líf's homespun dress. "I won't last days."

Líf would have rolled her eyes had she not feared it would make her more seasick. There were more than fifty people on the wooden vessel, and she was the only one unable to function.

Well, that was not exactly true. Near the stern of the boat, Brasir was still unconscious. Turning her head in his direction, she stared at the man who had altered the course of her life. His face was misshapen under the swelling bruises and the dried, crusting blood. After the brutal beating he had received, he was lucky to be alive.

Brasir had not grown up in the seaside town of Thorinheim or in the surrounding area. An outsider, he was strikingly different. His flesh was the color of charcoal, and his eyes were almost as dark. He and his bear fylgja had traveled from lands far to the south on a quest, one that might save not only the lives of his people but the lives of theirs as well. Líf's siblings had captured him for the slave trade. These same siblings now risked everything to free this man, a man who had been sold to Jarl Harek, a nobleman and the ruler of Thorinheim.

"How is he?" Líf would have pointed to Brasir, but the boat listed sideways, causing her stomach to knot.

Ottar continued to stand. His body adjusted so easily to the ship's rollicking motion that he never lost his balance. "There is a good chance he will survive."

"Then there is a small chance he won't." Líf heard her voice tremble. Or was that just another symptom of her current predicament? "What happens to us if...? We have lost everything."

"That's where you are mistaken." Ottar looked at his boys, the ship and its crew. "Brasir claims his hamingja is strong. Believe him."

Still staring at the unconscious man, Líf felt strangely uncomfortable. She wished she could see Brasir's hamingja, but no one was able to see one's own luck—or anyone else's. No one. Yet, according to Brasir, that was no longer the case.

Just as Líf could see fylgjur, Brasir claimed to see hamingjur. Líf had had to take him at his word. It was a strange realization. Then again, her family had done the same with her their entire lives: believed her. Accepted her. Trusted her.

There had to be some purpose to this; there must be. Of all the people in all the nine worlds of Yggdrasil, she had crossed paths with the one individual who was as unique as she. What was the reason? Everyone was compelled to follow their predetermined fate. Was this their destiny? What was the Norns' plan for them?

Líf stroked Thray's shimmering fur. The little creature had curled up into a tight ball on the deck. Several of the men nearby cast suspicious looks at the young woman. She knew they did not understand her.

Brasir had been traveling north when he was captured. Though he never mentioned his exact destination, he had admitted that he was trying to leave Midgard, the world of men. This was insanity. Men were not to leave their world. Monstrosities and creatures that haunted nightmares lurked in the outer reaches of the universe. One rarely heard that a person had left the comfort of

Midgard; rarer still was to hear that one had lived long enough to return.

These facts had not deterred Brasir. His purpose was far too great. He was trying to save the hamingjar, everyone's hamingjur—the personal luck that is passed down through family lines. Without luck, a person can be easily killed in battle, succumb to an illness, or die in any number of freak accidents.

Lìf knew that people are comprised of four parts: the hamr, their physical body; the hugr, their mind and soul; the fylgja, their personal guardian spirit; and their luck, their hamingja. A person cannot survive—at least, not for long—without all the parts of the self.

For some unknown reason, hamingjur were dying, fading away into nothingness. Along with them, their people grew weak and died, just like Driva, Ottar's wife. Lìf's siblings were determined to free Brasir so he could continue his search for the source of this strange, invisible plague. Although their plan had gone terribly awry, perhaps he could still complete his mission, if only *he* could survive.

Unable to see hamingjur, Lìf had no way to gauge the strength or weakness of Brasir's hamingja. Instead, she stared at his bear fylgja. Brasir's guardian spirit was a medley of different colors. The ursine's eyes appeared dazed, probably due to her human's current state.

Please wake up soon, Lìf implored silently.

Orders were shouted from the prow of the longship. The crew members followed them without hesitation. Budvar and Gratti, Ottar's young boys, "assisted" the rowers with their work. Perched on sea chests, they mimicked the experienced sailors, who began to turn the vessel in a new direction, one that would take them around the far side of the island before heading toward the mainland. If the men were irritated by the children, they did not dare complain about it in Ottar's presence.

"You said you'd raided once before. Then act like it!" Hervor, Lìf's oldest sibling, shouted from her post. Everyone listened when she spoke. All knew too well the result of angering the shieldmaiden. Although female, she was one of the best warriors on the boat, maybe even the best.

The poor teenager receiving the verbal beating eyed with uncertainty Hervor's dagger and her unusual, short-handled war axe. The haft of the axe had broken two years ago, but preferring the shorter grip, the shieldmaiden had smoothed down the rough knob rather than repair it.

The boy swallowed and nodded before weaving around the rowers to untangle the ropes near the mast. His yearling buck fylgja stumbled after him, never quite able to secure solid footing.

Ottar snickered before explaining. "Young Sigird will quickly learn to pull his weight if he is to remain aboard *Wavecutter*. Hervor never allows excess weight to slow down *her* ship."

Lìf was grateful that Hervor was her sister, for otherwise the shieldmaiden might have already tossed her overboard. Still, she felt sorry for the youth as he fumbled with all those cords. Sigird had taken a huge risk when he disregarded the authority of his father, Jarl Harek, to help those who had abducted his parent's slave. Hervor should show the frightened thirteen-year-old some respect. However, upon observing the stern gaze in her sister's clear gray eyes, Líf knew she did not have the courage to tell Hervor such things even if they rang true.

The shieldmaiden was in her element. Barking orders to the men under her command, she would have been a great leader for their jarl's fleet if she had been born male. Unfortunately, that was not her destiny. The ship, the captain's title, the public recognition and honor of successful expeditions had all gone to Ottar. There were certain things a woman could not do. Well, not in the homeland; however, at sea this woman held unquestioned command.

Hervor caught Ottar's eye. She would never demean her brother in front of the men, though it was clear she was not pleased by his lollygagging while everyone else was working hard to keep the ship moving through the strong winds. Ottar flashed her a smile.

Líf shrank down on her bench and waited for Hervor's anger to be unleashed. It was, but not at Ottar. Instead, she began hounding the other men for even the smallest flaws.

"Guthorm, this is no time to sleep! Skeggi, are you going to let those two children row better than you? No? Then pull your damn oar!"

Líf felt Ottar's hands on her shoulders. "Don't lie down. You will make things worse." He helped prop her up in a more vertical position. "I'd best get moving before Hervor skins all these men alive on my account."

Thray clawed her way back onto Líf's lap. Her fur was still an ugly shade of green, although flickers of blue appeared here and there. All the while, wind tugged at Líf's unkempt red hair. Looking up, she spotted Hervor's goshawk clinging to the top of the mast. The poor bird's head was tucked under a wing as she tried to withstand the growing gales.

Suddenly, the raptor screamed.

Líf sat up and turned to stare in the same direction as Hervor and her bird. Behind them were longships. Five of them. And they were heading directly toward Wavecutter.

"Row faster, boys!" Hervor shouted. "We are being pursued."

Chapter Two

"Pull!" Hervor shouted as the men's oars cut into the water. "Pull!"

Ottar lurched into an open seat across from Líf. A shiver of energy rippled through her as she heard her sister shout, "Battle formations! You know what to do!"

The impromptu benches amidships, made up of storage containers and sea chests, could seat more men than the benches in the narrower prow and stern. The warriors quickly positioned themselves so that each side of the vessel became a mirror image of the other—an open seat on the starboard side was matched by an identical open space on the port side.

"It's for balance," Líf told Thray, although she assumed the fylgja knew this as well.

"Sorry, Lingy." Skeggi, Ottar's oafish friend, seated himself behind her and readied an oar. "Looks like we're fated to entertain one another," he teased.

For once, Líf did not grind her teeth at the sound of the horrid nickname. True, her hair was a shocking shade of red, but that did not give anyone the right to compare her to every bird, leaf, or berry sporting the same color, even her favorite lingonberries.

"You're lookin' a bit green," Skeggi noted. Was he actually smiling under his thick beard?

"Pull!" Hervor bellowed.

Unrattled, Skeggi continued to speak calmly. "It's not a color that suits your complexion."

Líf was too terrified to care about his insensitive humor. Turning toward him, she asked, "Is there something I can do? To help, I mean?"

Her sister's voice continued to ring out over her hurried conversation. "Faster, men! Or did I bring only sickly runts with me?"

Líf could see Skeggi's face screw up as his muscles strained to pull the oar. The drag must have been immense.

In the rush to escape Thorinheim, they had had to cast off without a full crew. Out of the fifty-two people on board, five were not part of *Wavecutter's* true crew.

"How many men are we down?" Líf asked between the crew's synchronized strokes. She had to wait several minutes before Skeggi was able to respond.

"Thirteen. Twelve, if young Sigird pulls his weight."

"Eleven." Líf gestured toward the wooden oar near her. "After you instruct me." She waited for Skeggi to chastise her, mock her skinny arms and lack of experience.

Instead, he chortled but then told her, "Ya can't be much help today, but watch the men. Ya tighten your stomach and use yer feet to press into the floor while pulling with yer arms. We'll make a mariner out of you yet."

Wavecutter was a drakkar, a long, narrow, flexible longship designed for the specific purpose of raiding and plundering. Her beautiful carvings differentiated her from the less decorated skeids. At both ends, brilliantly painted reptilian heads sneered menacingly. Although the actual purpose was to scare away the creatures of the deep, striking fear in the hearts of men was an added benefit. With her wide sail snapping in the wind like a vast wing and the row of colorful shields hanging over her sides like a layer of overlapping scales, she truly looked like a dragon preparing to render the flesh from the bones of its prey.

The vessel was fast, made for speed, and the swiftest boat in the fleet. She was aptly named, as well, for the clinker design allowed her overlapping wooden planks to flex over the waves, preventing breakage. Eighty-five feet in length, *Wavecutter* easily held sixty men and had room for as many as seventy-six. Now undermanned, the question was, would she be fast enough to evade her pursuers?

Thray dug her sharp nails into Líf's shoulder as she stared behind them. "Líf? Líf, they are gaining on us!"

Líf glanced at the approaching boats and recognized the four skeids and single drakkar. They belonged to Jarl Harek, which confirmed her fear that he had ordered his men to recapture Brasir and punish those who had freed him. They had followed Ottar's longship down the fjord and into the open sea. Now, with their quarry in sight, the jarl's ships gave chase as *Wavecutter* raced toward the mainland.

From somewhere behind Skeggi's thick shoulders, young Sigird shouted, "Those are my father's ships! Harekson has to be on *Squallsubduer*, the drakkar. He will try to sink *Wavecutter*."

"With his brother on it?" another man asked.

"He has no fondness for me," Sigird stated sullenly.

Skeggi boomed out, "Harekson has always wanted to compare cocks with Lothbranson. He has always refused to accept that he is *lacking*."

"Enough," Ottar said. "Harekson's vessels are lighter than ours, for they did not have time to load them with supplies; we are carrying a heavy cargo. Most likely, he has full crews while we do not. At present, *Wavecutter* is slow and overburdened. Those ships have a great chance of cutting us off from our destination."

Líf watched as the pursuing ships gained ground and sailed parallel to them. "How could he know where we are heading?" she asked.

"He doesn't," Hervor replied. "The jarl's ships are swift enough to prevent *Wavecutter* from reaching shore. Look, there! The skeids are moving ahead of us to force our return."

"Not to destroy our ship?" Líf asked Skeggi. She looked back at Sigird.

Skeggi leaned toward her and said in a low voice, "Harekson has always desired his own ship. He has been eyeing *Wavecutter* ever since her maiden voyage. He would rather take her whole than send her to the depths of the sea as a gift for Rán."

On the water, *Squallsubduer* kept pace with *Wavecutter* as the skeids shifted position and created a barrier. The crew awaited Hervor's orders.

The shieldmaiden's eyes gleamed. "Let's take them out to sea," she shouted. "Turn the ship around!"

"You heard her, men," Ottar bellowed. "About face!"

As several crew tended to the sails, the remaining men drove their oars into the water. *Wavecutter* displayed that incomparable ability of longships and slewed to a halt. The sail snapped loudly, and the rigging groaned in preparation for a most impressive changeover. The sail and all its accoutrements were swiftly rotated around the central mast. Crew members reversed their positions on the benches as Hervor strode to the opposite end of the ship. Another sailor released the steering oar, lugged it to the other end of the drakkar, and locked it in place. Suddenly, what had once been the stern was now the prow, and the magnificent vessel began to move in the opposite direction.

At the shieldmaiden's command, all able-bodied men heaved their oars. "Row!" The ship headed into deeper waters.

"Hard a port!" Hervor ordered. "Let's make it clear we're not going home!"

Líf felt the raw power of the drakkar as it began to spin away from the island to face the open sea. Salty spray spurted up from the ship's sides, coating everyone in a wet film.

"A storm's coming." Thray confirmed what Líf was thinking. Although the sky was cloudy, there was no sign of rain on the waters, at least not yet. But the wind had steadily picked up.

"Why go out to sea?" Líf asked the nervous rodent. "If their ships are faster, wouldn't they just cut us off again?"

"I don't know. Trust your sister. That's all we can do."

Behind them, the five vessels had also reversed their positions. They were closing in, but not nearly as fast as Líf originally feared. Several skeids were unsuccessful with the changeover maneuver. They had to be turned around manually and their sails and rigging untangled. All appeared to be wary of approaching. Maybe *Wavecutter* could stay ahead of them. But what would happen at night? At some point, the men would need sleep. Were Harekson and the other ships holding back to conserve their energy? Were they planning to attack once Hervor's crew had exhausted themselves?

In a sudden burst of wind, *Wavecutter's* sail billowed out unexpectedly, and the ship lurched violently.

"Get it down!" Hervor shouted. "Take it all down!"

Líf hurried over to the mast. She might not know how to sail a ship, but she was an expert at folding a sail for storage. Small and agile, she was the first to assist those already struggling to lower the wind-strained cloth.

Everything happened quickly. The men on the benches pulled their oars as hard as they could. Others tugged at the ropes and rigging. Líf was holding the edge of the sail when the wind shifted again, causing the heavy fabric to billow in the opposite direction and smack her in the face.

There was no time to right herself. Stepping back, she tripped over a crate near their water barrel and fell. Strong hands clutched her before she hit the rough planking. Looking up, she saw Brasir staring down at her with one eye, the other hidden under a swollen lid.

"You're awake," Líf started to say, but the wind took the sail in a new direction, causing it to crackle loudly.

Once certain of the woman's footing, Brasir released her and began lowering the sail with the others. He clearly knew what he was doing.

"Are you leaving the mast up?" he asked Hervor.

Without even a look of surprise at the upright fellow, she replied, "For now. Find a seat and get to work."

Brasir took the empty spot in front of Skeggi. Uncertain what to do, Líf carefully walked toward the prow and her observant sister. The five longships continued to pursue them like hounds after a fox.

Another shower of sea mist fell upon them as *Wavecutter* navigated the churning waters. The waves were growing larger. The ship rocked more than Líf expected, and she almost fell a second time. This time Hervor assisted her.

"Find a seat and lie low," Hervor advised. She was on high alert, her eyes constantly darting from their pursuers to her crew and the worsening weather.

"It feels like a storm," Líf acknowledged. Thray growled in her ear.

Hervor agreed. "I am planning on it. Look ahead of us, slightly to port. What do you see?"

"Water, sky, clouds," Líf answered hesitantly. The entire seascape was shrouded in a gloomy gray. Then she spotted a subtle change in color, something several shades darker than the rest of the horizon. Was it a column? Or perhaps a wall?

"There!" she exclaimed. "You are right." Líf's heart thrummed almost as fast as Thray's. "Is that our destination? Is that where we are heading?"

Longships are perfect for deep sea travel. They can handle massive waves and strong winds. Still, to plow head first into an enormous storm was a risk that most sane captains would avoid at all costs.

Hervor cracked a smile. "Those bastards might be able to outrun us, but they have to find us first. Go to the boys and keep them as calm as you can. Whatever happens next, don't panic."

"I'm panicking," Thray uttered. "I'm already panicking."

Líf trembled as she wobbled over to her crouching nephews. Their earlier enthusiasm had been wiped away. Though silent as the dead, their wide eyes could not hide their fear. Gratti blinked away tears, although his older brother, Budvar, refused to cry. Thray muttered something to the boys' fylgjur, who were whimpering. The shimmering blue-black pups cowered beside the bench.

The ship jumped a large wave, and everyone was soaked. Small pools of water sloshed over the wooden floorboards. A rumble of thunder cut through the crashing waves.

"Row, men!" Hervor had not once stopped overseeing the ship. "Let's drive *Wavecutter* into the heart of it!"

Ottar, who was working alongside his crew, cried out, "Rán will not get her offering today. Valhalla awaits us!"

The other men shouted in kind, "To Valhalla!"

Rain began to fall slowly at first, then turned into a wall of icy particulates. Visibility dropped by half. The roar of wind and waves sounded like gigantic monsters bellowing war cries. Thunder resounded through the darkening skies. Suddenly, a spear of raw white light blasted the waters in front of the ship.

Chapter Three

They had barely entered the storm before they narrowly avoided the first strike of nature's wrath. The explosive boom that followed caused many of the men to flinch.

"Don't stop!" Hervor's voice was barely heard in the clamor. "We must push farther in!"

When a second bolt of lightning lit the sky on their right, the boys leaned into Líf's arms. She tried to shelter them, but what could she actually do? All three of them were soaking wet and shivering. There had been no time to set up a makeshift tent from a sail, nor would there have been room, for the men were still rowing haphazardly into the squall, and the mast was upright. If the ship were struck by lightning, it would go down in smoldering flames.

Líf felt helpless. She could neither steer the boat nor defend it if the other vessels caught up with them. All she could do was maintain a false sense of calm so her nephews would not do something foolish out of fear.

"That's what I thought. Harekson never had balls to begin with. He's retreating like the scared cur he is," Hervor exclaimed with a wicked sneer.

Líf glanced back. The other drakkar had turned back toward the island. Though that might have brought Hervor some cheer, there were still four skeids to contend with. Though not pretty, they were meant for battle.

"Is...is Thor angry with us?" Gratti stammered as jagged lightening pierced the clouds.

"Thor?" Líf looked about warily. "I don't think so."

"Then why is he trying to hurt us?"

"I'm not sure that is his intent," Líf assured him. Seeing the terror in the boy's blue eyes, she added, "Though he is a god, he probably doesn't realize we are out here. The clouds could be hiding us from his sight."

It was a lie. Not a good lie, but it was all she had.

Gratti clutched an amulet he wore on a little chain around his neck. It depicted Mjölnir, the God of Thunder's fearsome hammer. Ottar had given it to him several summers ago when the boy feared his father would be killed during the summer raids. "We should let him know we are here. Do you think we could sing to him?"

The storm was worsening. Unable to come up with a better idea to distract the boys, Líf replied, "I think we should."

Her nephews considered several ballads. Choosing the "Song of Thunder," they began, their voices both shaky and sweet. Líf began to sing, and their strange prayer drifted over the wind-tossed sea. Ottar's strong voice joined in and was followed by those of the crew. The untrained sound of their combined voices combating the raging storm was inspiring.

Hervor did not sing. Instead, she kept watch over the turbulent water. A strange mist had blurred sea and sky. As soon as their vessel was enveloped in the gray murk, the shieldmaiden gave the command to be silent. They no longer rowed but let *Wavecutter* drift as she might over the undulating waters.

The glow of lightning allowed brief glimpses of the other longships' silhouettes. Most were still rowing in the belief that *Wavecutter* was still up ahead. In the momentary flashes, Líf spotted one of the pursuing skeids just several hundred yards from their location. Though the mist seemed to protect them from being seen, she prayed to the gods to let the other vessels lose their way in the gloom.

"Go away. Get lost," Thray muttered. Her beady eyes peered out from the soaked skirts of Líf's dress.

The storm lasted for many hours before at last leaving them adrift for another day in the unnatural fog. The crew remained silent as they bailed water out of the boat, for they could not chance being discovered unprepared. Both children understood the need for silence, saying barely more than a few whispered words. Everyone rested as best they could. Men alleviated their boredom with impromptu dicing tournaments like býta or bragðr, while hnefatafl, the strategic game of war, kept the boys entertained. In the chill air, ice formed over the puddles in the darkest hours. Although this was an improvement over the stinging cold of sloshing water, as long as they were trapped in the moist grayness no one could get dry or warm.

In a sulk, Thray watched Líf eat a piece of pickled herring. The oily fish was not as tasty as salmon, but it was the choice protein on extended voyages, for it could last weeks in the briny containers. Yet how long would the crew drift about? Out at sea, the unpleasant chill lingered.

"I wish I could see something," Líf whispered to her fylgja. "I'd like to spot anything other than mist."

"Maybe I can help," offered the little squirrel. She shook her coat, and her fur changed from a pale white to a deeper blue. Then, leaping from bench to bench, Thray scampered up the mast and disappeared in the gray haze.

When the small creature returned, she shook her head in dismay. "It's all the same. I'll try again later."

Yet there was no need. That night, the sky cleared; by morning, the shroud of fog had dissipated.

"Guthorm," Hervor ordered, "hand me the sun crystals."

A leather pouch was passed to the shieldmaiden; she rummaged through it and pulled out a polished, domed stone. Raising it to her eye, she peered through. Grimacing, she made a motion with her fingers, and a swatch of leather was handed to her. Líf observed in amazement as Hervor deftly arranged two of the domed crystals at either end of the leather before rolling them up tightly and tying it off with string.

Once again, Hervor raised the device to her eyes. Her lips silently mouthed words. After returning the stones and leather to the pouch, she shared what she had seen. "I have spotted three of the skeids. The fourth appears to be missing. Pray that the gods are in our favor."

A fellow crewman murmured, "Pray that Rán is satiated."

Scanning the horizon in the direction of the enemy's ships, Hervor asked, "Our location?"

Líf suspected that her sister already knew it but was following protocol out of respect.

"We should be two days south of Snæland." Guthorm was studying the constellations above. "If we continue on this route, Garðar's Ile is shy of a week before us."

"Rig the sail. We must head toward Frigg's Vessel." The shieldmaiden pointed to a constellation slightly southward. "If the skeids wish to pursue us, let's not give them a chance to restock their supplies."

Líf was confused. That direction would take them farther away from any landmass. The only things out there were inhospitable seas and the denizens of the deep. Why didn't Hervor race toward land? Wouldn't it be better to flee on foot or make a stand on solid ground? Why remain upon this floating vessel longer than they must? And *why* was she the only one not at ease upon the waters?

Thray must have felt Líf's uncertainty. "I know what your sister is doing," she murmured. "Those ships are fast; we could never dock before they attacked. Hervor is trying to starve them out. She thinks they are not stocked with supplies, since they had no time to prepare. We have food for days—weeks, even. If they follow us, it will not be for long. They will not risk starvation."

"How did you come up with that?" Líf whispered, quite impressed.

The squirrel, a medley of colors, sniffed. "You are not the only one I talk to." She scampered up the mast to circle the ever-watchful goshawk.

Living on a ship was nightmarish. At least that was Líf's opinion. Amid the bouts of seasickness, the stench of unwashed men, and the lack of privacy and space, there was also the horrible biological issue of doing one's business. The crew members and even the boys did not think much upon the matter. They would lean over the side of the ship to relieve themselves or use one of the treacherous-smelling slop pails. Hervor, never batting an eye, would do the same. She would peel down her pants, claiming she could piss as well as any man. Hervor was never one to be embarrassed around those of the opposite sex. She even chose to wear the garb of men when away from their homeland.

The first time Líf had to relieve herself, she was mortified. These were her siblings' companions, who would watch her with teasing and possibly lustful eyes. She tried to postpone the inevitable, but when the moment came, Ottar moved to assist. Using a blanket as a sort of impromptu wall, he tried to lessen her sense of shame. It was a nice gesture, but it did little. When the deed was done, her face stayed as red as her hair for several hours.

Why didn't Hervor force the ship to race to land? Wouldn't it be better to flee on foot? What about making a stand on solid ground? Why would anyone stay upon this floating vessel longer than they must? And once again, *why* was she the only one not at ease upon the waters?

"I told you," Thray explained the next day. "As fast as the other ships are, we could never dock before they attacked. Hervor is right in trying to starve them out.

"What about me? Will I last?"

"Quit complaining," tittered Thray before taking on a greeny hue. "Turn around, you're about to be sick."

By the following day, the one positive fact was that the fourth longship was nowhere to be seen. Maybe it had sunk in the storm. Maybe it had sailed in the wrong direction and was lost. There were plenty of maybes, but what did that matter? *Wavecutter* was in clear sight of the three surviving skeids.

As Líf hung limply over the gunwale, her stomach on fire, she recognized the colors on the other ships' attached shields. Some were nobles' households; others were warriors who could rival her siblings' crew. There were so many that Líf refused to count them, knowing it would only make her feel worse.

Pickled herring did not taste as good coming back up as it had going down. Wiping her mouth on her sleeve, she watched as fish began to pick at her clumpy gifts. More than ever, Líf loathed whomever had invented the boat.

Refusing to move, she picked out her siblings' voices over the chatter of the crew. With the sail doing most of the work, there was no need for them to row, and they gossiped idly like the elderly women in Thorinheim.

"Less than that," Ottar stated dubiously.

"You might be right," Hervor admitted with a sigh. "Have you thought about a plan for your children? Líf will be of no help."

There was a long pause before Ottar answered her. "Protect them as long as we can."

Another lengthy pause.

Hervor stated grimly, "The men know our chances if it comes down to it. I had hoped we had more time."

"So did we all."

Líf stayed in her position. Surprisingly, it was more comfortable than it appeared. She continued to watch the skeids close the gap between themselves and *Wavecutter*. With the slight rocking of the waves and the early spring sun above, she drifted off to sleep.

Her dreams were filled with images of home, impressions of the faces of those she used to know, echoes of long-gone laughter and song. Suddenly, Thray's sharp voice cried out, "Líf, wake up! You must see this!"

During her nap, the other longships had almost reached them. The sight of their crews moving about caused Líf to lurch to her feet.

"Watch it!" a man growled as she stepped on a boot.

Swiveling around, she almost rammed into Guthorm Blood Cheeks. He looked at her with a bit of sympathy. His rosacea-blotched face had scared her when she was young, but now she was indifferent to the man and his stoat fylgja. "'Ave you ever seen it happen before?" he asked. "Watch. Behind you."

Out on the waters, the skeids were positioning themselves extremely close to one another, so much so that when one rocked too far sideways, the sound of groaning wood from the neighboring ship's planking was heard.

"What are they doing?" Líf asked in astonishment. A good captain would not risk his ship crashing into another. These crews were far too skilled for that, even in stormy seas.

"Keep watching." Guthorm spoke right behind her. She could smell his breath and sweat.

The middle ship was taking down its sail and undoing the rigging, while the other two moved into positions parallel to it before throwing ropes and ties to the central vessel. All three ships lashed themselves together. The outer two extended their ocean-facing oars, while their individual sails billowed as one massive sail.

Líf's voice trembled as she asked again, "What *are* they doing?"

"They're creating a platform."

"Why?"

"They are preparing to attack."

Chapter Four

"Oars out!" Hervor cried.

The crew was already scrambling to their seats. Working in small teams, they pulled out the blocks that sealed the oar holes when not in use. Next, the oars were set into position. Ottar took control of the steering oar at *Wavecutter*'s stern. On Hervor's command, he altered their course away from the enemy.

Responding to Hervor's tactics, the combined skeids used a *beitass*, or stretching pole, to extend their sails to their maximum breadth. Both parties understood that if they met, an all-out battle would commence.

"Faster, men!" the shieldmaiden bellowed. "Let's make her fly!"

Lif trembled with fear and excitement. She watched as the composite skeid easily jumped over a large wave. The horrible noise made by the rubbing and bending of wooden planks sounded like the scream of some unthinkable sea monster.

Ottar gave Hervor a nod, and she ordered, "Secure the shroud, Guthorm! Sigird, make yourself useful."

Without being asked, Brasir assisted the men as they tightened the support ropes that kept the mast in place. Just as they finished, Ottar adjusted the steering oar. Suddenly, the entire longship picked up an enormous amount of speed. With sail strained to the maximum and the crew rowing as hard as they could, *Wavecutter* sprinted through the sea's churning waters.

Behind them, the combination vessel seemed to snarl as it, too, caught the wind and lunged after the drakkar. Yet, now comprising three ships lashed together, the massive device was far slower than its individual parts would have been. This gave *Wavecutter* the advantage.

"They were too excited, just like a lad his first time," guffawed Skeggi. "Blew their load too early. Look at 'em floundering."

Skeggi was seated on a crate in front of Lif. His portly seagull fylgja laughed from the air. Líf started to relax, but the look on Hervor's stern features warned her that this race was far from over.

The chase continued for some time as the combined skeids fell farther and farther behind before fading in and out of sight. Only then did Hervor order the crew to haul in the oars. *Wavecutter*'s pace slowed, and the crew took advantage of the much-needed reprieve.

"Are they gone?" Líf asked no one in particular, although Thray assumed the question was directed to her.

"Let me see," tittered the fylgja, who then leaped over to the mast and scurried up the post. At the top, Hervor's goshawk alighted next to the curious rodent. They must have exchanged some sort of words, for the goshawk took wing and flew in the direction of their distant enemy.

The sight of Thray clambering down the wooden mast reminded Líf of stories about Yggdrasil, the world tree. She glanced at her nephews. Their faces were pale and strained.

"I couldn't see them, Líf," Thray announced matter-of-factly.

"Did you tell her to search?" Líf nodded toward the sky where the goshawk was soaring.

Thray blinked at her. The rodent's shimmering eyes kept their secrets. Fylgjur were guarded when it came to interactions with their own kind.

With the immediate danger averted, Líf stumbled over to her nephews. Sitting down, she pulled Gratti onto her lap. "Did I ever tell you the story of Ratatoskr?" She looked at Thray, who was grooming her bushy tail. The boys had indeed heard this story many times, but it was all she could think of to get their minds off the continual terror of the past few days.

Budvar, at nine, was just old enough that hearing these children's stories would normally have insulted him. Only recently, he'd thought them far too childish for a young man of his age. Yet he scooted closer to Líf and did not balk when Gratti nodded.

"Well, then, you both might help me with it," smiled Líf. "Ratatoskr is a squirrel who lives on Yggdrasil. He does not care to travel to the nine worlds that are tucked among the tree's roots or branches. He does not care about the people or the gods who live in those worlds nor about what happens to them. They bore him. As a result, Ratatoskr has always yearned for amusement."

The boys were listening intently. Their fylgjur pups snuggled up to their ankles, though their humans would never feel their glistening fur or hear their yips of excitement. Fylgjur were intangible to mortals. Well, to all mortals except for Líf.

She continued, "Ratatoskr does have two companions. They are the only two creatures in the entire universe that he would willingly interact with. Can you name them?"

"Níðhöggr, the dragon," Gratti said as he pointed to one of the carved faces on the interchangeable prows. "He eats the roots at the base of Yggdrasil."

"And?" Líf prodded.

"At the top, there is an eagle..." Gratti began, then hesitated.

"An eagle? You sure?" asked Líf.

"The..." the little boy scrunched up his face, trying to remember. Two years younger than his brother, Gratti was still learning the ancient stories.

It was Budvar that answered, "A hawk, Veðrfölnir."

Gratti looked disappointed with himself, but Líf reassured him. "That is a confusing answer, since Veðrfölnir often perches atop the head of a gigantic eagle in Yggdrasil's canopy. It is unknown whether Veðrfölnir and Níðhöggr have always despised one another or if that is the result of Ratatoskr's doing."

Thray must have surmised the inspiration for this particular story. She sniffed at Líf indignantly before running back up the mast to await the return of her goshawk friend.

Líf pretended not to notice as she continued, "What is known is that the squirrel takes great pleasure in scurrying up and down the trunk of Yggdrasil. Sometimes he passes along gossip between the hawk and the dragon; other times he spreads insults." Turning to Gratti, she whispered, "You hook-beaked birdbrain." Then she caught Budvar's eye. "You ice-breath corpse eater."

The boys started to laugh and began to invent insults that Ratatoskr might have used for the creatures that resided in the world tree. Glancing up, Líf saw Brasir watching them. Was that a smile? It was hard to tell with his face so mangled.

Regardless, Líf and the boys continued their fun until she felt a sharp bite from her squirrel. "Ow!" she hissed at Thray. "What in the names of the gods possessed you to do that?"

"I had to get your attention. The skeids are back, but your sister is not doing anything about them."

Thray was right, as usual. Still connected by their rope tethers, the ships were racing toward *Wavecutter*. Hervor stood watch. Maybe this was patience. Maybe this was madness.

"What is she waiting for?" Thray asked before Líf could. The young woman shrugged, almost dislodging the vibrant orange rodent.

There was another murmured conversation between her siblings that Líf yearned to overhear. Ottar waved his boys over. As he bent low to have a few words with the children, Hervor strode to the other end of the ship and shouted her command. "Pull out your weapons, men! It's time to bloody our swords!"

"Or axes." Skeggi grinned as the storage compartment was opened so their armory could be distributed. Those who served as archers aligned themselves on the side approached by the enemy. Hervor lifted her axe in the air. She cried out, and the crew began to bellow and scream in wild rage.

"We're fighting!" Líf cried out in alarm. "Why aren't we running? We are clearly faster." Instead of asking her sister, she made her way to Ottar and his children. He handed both of them small seaxes and gave Budvar a shield to hold over their heads.

"I don't understand," Líf said in dismay as she observed her brother inspecting his sword.

"We could continue this dance on the water, but there is no honor in running from a fight."

"What about living?"

"One can only enter Valhalla if one dies on the field of battle showing absolutely no fear."

"Only men enter Valhalla," corrected Líf, "and I am beyond simple fear. This is madness."

"This is strategy," Hervor's voice interjected. "Those lardheads have been breaking a sweat struggling to keep up with us. Look around. My crew has been given time to rest as well as to prepare. When those others arrive, they will be tired and scrambling to gather their weapons. Look," she said, pointing. "You can see that a great number of their shields are still lashed to the sides of those ships. They may outnumber us, but I promise it won't stay that way for long."

"They're almost in range," reported a short, stout man known as Ulf.

The shieldmaiden turned back toward the enemy. "Ready?"

Archers nocked their bows and pulled them back. Behind them, a row of men holding circular shields waited.

"Hold! Hold!" Hervor shouted. Ottar passed Líf a shield. Though it could not have weighed more than ten pounds, it felt far heavier. Perhaps that was due to her lack of muscle. As she grasped the shield by its umbo, or recessed central knob, she wondered how long she could maintain her hold. Her hand was small and sweating.

Her sister shouted, "Shoot!"

Like a flock of sparrows, the lethal projectiles flew through the air. In a large arc, they drove into the wooden siding of the skeids, plummeted under the watery surface, or burrowed their shafts deep into living flesh.

Alarmed voices were heard as the combined skeids began to turn in an attempt to pull alongside the drakkar.

"Once more!" Hervor commanded. "Fire!"

This time, the second wave hit more of the intended targets. Immediately, a row of shield bearers moved to the front to create a wall of wood, as return fire began to pepper *Wavecutter*. Thray squealed as an arrow shattered near Líf's feet.

Through gaps where shields didn't quite overlap, *Wavecutter*'s archers released two more rounds. Líf crouched low near her nephews. She could hear cries of pain and the splintering of wood as more arrows crashed into the ship's floor. One man on the port side of *Wavecutter* was impaled. Spitting out blood, he keeled over the side before anyone could help him.

A loud crack rang out, paired with a jarring sensation. The tip of an arrow had forced its way through Líf's shield only inches from her eyes. Someone screamed as Líf fell back against the side of the ship. The person would not stop crying.

Thray spat out, "Quiet, Líf! More are coming. Worse is coming!"

It was Líf who was screaming. Clamping her jaw shut, she tucked herself into the smallest ball she could and closed her eyes. Men rushed about, orders were given, wood cracked; and then the smell of smoke caused her to sneeze.

"Protect the sail! Roll it down! Don't let her burn!"

"Fire?" Líf was up in a flash. More arrows bit into flesh and ship. This time, their tips were alight with tufts of orange. The skeids were trying to burn the drakkar! Stamping on the small whips of flame, Líf realized that others were less concerned about the flooring and more about protecting their now lowered sail. If the flax and woven horsehair caught fire, then sail, mast, and rigging could all combust in a matter of minutes.

More and more archers were dropping their bows to use other weapons. Why were they giving up on a long-range defense? To make matters worse, large quarrels were hooking into *Wavecutter*'s panels. These short, heavy arrows were connected to ropes.

"The ropes!" Thray pointed out as she observed the chaos around them. "Líf, look at the ropes!"

Suddenly those tethers snapped taut, and *Wavecutter* was jerked sideways. Líf realized what was happening. "They are pulling us in! They are going to try to board us! We need to sever the ties!"

Dropping her shield, Líf pulled a hand axe from a dead crewman's grip. Rushing to the far side of the boat, she squeezed next to Guthorm, whose shield was part of the wall defense.

"I need to cut the cords!" she cried. He glanced down at her with a raised eyebrow. Raising the shield, he allowed her just enough room to lean over the ledge and slam the axe down on the rope. Half of the cords popped. She did it again. This time, the rope was severed and fell limply away.

A large shadow appeared above her; there was a crackling pop as Guthorm caught the arrow in his shield, preventing it from slicing into her head. Unfortunately, at such close range, the wood could not entirely prevent calamity—the tip was now embedded in the man's arm. Blood dripped onto Líf as she hacked at a second cord. Other crewmen followed her example.

More quarrels carrying ropes rained down from the sky. One projectile dug into the shield of a man standing near Líf. When the cord tightened, the poor mariner was hauled over the side and plummeted into the sea.

"Up!" Guthorm grunted. He grabbed Líf's braided hair and jerked her violently to her feet. Just in time, too, as *Wavecutter* rocked into the skeids.

She would have been crushed like the crewman in the water.

The next wave separated the ships, which prevented anyone from leaping between vessels. But the gap was closing fast.

As the waves rose higher and higher, the ships continued to slam against one another, cords tangled, people slid through invisible fylgjur and stumbled to the floor. Water sloshed over the side; no foothold could be found, and Líf felt herself tumble. The next wave rolled her right into the mast.

The impact was jarring. Looking around, Líf could not see her fylgja anywhere. "Thray? Thray, where are you?"

She tried to stand, but the drakkar bucked and kicked, making standing impossible. The sea roiled as violently as it had in the massive storm, but the sky remained blue, and the wind was no more than a mild breeze. As she clung to the mast for security, a crate of food slid by, bowling over several men.

"Líf! Líf!" cried the squirrel's sharp voice from above. "I'm here!"

Thray gripped the mast near its top. She, too, was having trouble maneuvering. "In the water, Líf!" the fylgja warned. "Look in the sea!"

When the next wave passed, Líf stumbled to the side of the ship away from the battle—or what would have been a battle had any of the combatants been able to stand and fight. Careful not to fall overboard, she peered into the salty abyss.

A massive school of fish was swimming in strange, flowing movements. Sun glinted off their silvery forms as they progressed in a synchronized fashion. They were rising, slowly making their way toward the turbulent surface of the water.

Líf had observed schools of fish many times in the streams and fjords at home, but never like this, never at sea. There were hundreds, thousands, maybe millions, and they all kept their positions, never bumping or encroaching on their neighbors. They....

They were not fish. They did not have fins or tails. There were no mouths searching for food. These were the diamond-shaped scales of some great creature moving underneath the vessels. Líf caught the glimmer of the same scales in the distance. Following their movement, she ran to the opposite side of the boat. Ignoring the men and other objects that teased her peripheral vision, she scrutinized the waters. The creature was there. Its massing form could envelope all four longships as if they were nothing.

Then the monster broke the surface.

Chapter Five

"Hervor!" Líf cried out, but not in time. A column of water shot up and rose several hundred feet into the air. The liquid explosion halted the chaos on all of the vessels. Everyone turned to watch. Everyone but Líf.

Her focus had shifted to the rising mass far off in the opposite direction. The glimmering of scales flickered maddeningly as the creature continued to contort its position. She stumbled over to her sister.

"Hervor!" Líf called out again. "Behind you! Look behind you!"

The shieldmaiden's eyes opened wide. "Jörmungandr," she hissed before desperately trying to warn her men. "Hold tight!"

"The world serpent?" Líf asked in disbelief as the water around the longships began to bubble and boil, even though the temperature remained frigid. Another undulating mass of scaly hide rose next to *Wavecutter*. The resulting ripples grew to the size of giant waves and caused a series of powerful impacts. The first wave crashed over the side of the ship and toppled scores of men as the vessel worked hard to stay above the breakers.

Ropes groaned and snapped. The turbulent sea separated the ship from the skeids. Once free, a series of waves slammed into the drakkar. *Wavecutter* reeled sideways. Cargo, weapons, and men were tossed about. Líf was crushed behind Guthorm and another brawny fellow.

Hervor's voice cut through the clamor. "Quick. Over here. We need to counterbalance her! Hurry!"

The men struggled to run up the steepening incline, leaving Líf helpless against the force of gravity. A heavy crate of wares was sliding right toward her. She tried to jump away, but the listing ship caused her to lose her footing, and she tumbled over the side.

Líf's back smacked the water. Her thick layers of clothing weighed her down like an anchor, and she began to sink. Through the stinging, salty murk, she saw *Wavecutter*'s mast dipping dangerously low over the sea. If the ship overturned, there would be no hope of making it to the surface. She would be crushed beneath it and dragged down to the depths.

As the drakkar attempted to right itself, Líf struggled to shrug off her outer layers. The water was icy cold, but she would rather freeze than drown.

Fighting to pull the heavy cloak over her head, she felt a disturbance in the water. Something had fallen overboard, but she couldn't see what it was. Then something touched her.

Líf started to scream but stopped; she would lose too much air. Kicking frantically, she struck something, then nothing. Suddenly, her entangled cloak was jerked over her head.

Brasir was beside her. The heavy fabric disappeared into the depths as he grabbed her hand and began to kick toward the surface. Below them, the water shimmered as a section of scales began to rise. There was nothing they could do to escape.

The pair were lifted rapidly through the water and into the air. Higher and higher they rose until the creature underneath them had created a massive arch so tall that Líf could observe the ships far below.

The trio of skeids continued to collide with one another. Bits of wood cracked off; one mast shattered and took out the central mast as well. The falling sail enveloped a number men before dragging them down to the bottom of the sea, into Rán's rapacious embrace. However, *Wavecutter* was not in her line of sight, so Líf could not determine how badly the drakkar had been damaged.

She dug her fingers between thick overlapping scales as her body began to slide down the massive form.

Now she screamed.

"Líf, are you there?" Brasir shouted. He was clinging to the serpent's opposite side.

"Brasir! How do we get down?" Her fingers were growing numb and turning blue, and she felt her grip loosening.

"Hold your breath, Líf!"

"Why?"

The gargantuan serpent had begun to slip back into the water. Líf clung to a section at the peak of the creature's arched body. The sudden drop as the serpent's back plummeted to the rippling surface caused her to slip. She watched helplessly as Brasir was flung into the sea. Then it was her turn.

Líf was not a great swimmer, but she knew she had to get away from the sea serpent's body, or there would be a good chance that she would be crushed by it or sucked under the churning surface.

Brasir swam toward *Wavecutter*. Líf followed in his wake, berating herself for not having learned to swim in rough waters. Why was the ship so far away, she wondered. Why were they not getting closer?

The answer was obvious. The ship was retreating, leaving behind her the horrors unleashed by the angered monster. If *Wavecutter* did not stop, there would be no chance for Líf and Brasír to climb aboard. They would drown, freeze—or worse, be eaten.

With a serpent this size, how large would its maw be? Líf imagined the colossal head, with its mess of fangs longer than the tallest mast, looming up to swallow the skeids whole. Would that monster even notice a morsel as small as Líf? How horrifying to think she could be conscious and feel herself sliding down the waterlogged gullet of that reptile.

"Keep moving, Líf!" Brasír shouted through chattering teeth. He had turned to see how far back she had fallen.

Tired and sore, Líf struggled to keep up with the dark-skinned man. "They're leaving us," she uttered between mouthfuls of water. She was both exasperated and disheartened.

"No. They are waiting," he countered.

How could that be true? she thought. *Wavecutter* was still far away, and the swirling currents were tugging her everywhere but toward the longship.

After a wave shoved her underwater, Líf reemerged. Her limbs were sluggish and heavy. Her body heat was dissipating. "I can't..." she moaned.

Brasír halted. Líf thought she heard a growl as he swam back to retrieve her. His large hands prevented her from sinking, but she was obviously slowing him down and causing the man to tire rapidly.

Once again, Líf realized she was proving a burden. Maybe it would be better if she did sink to the bottom of the sea to become fish food. Her current situation would only confirm everyone's fears. She was not only useless but also a danger to others.

The tears that trickled down her face were lost in the salty splatter of the sea. Her eyesight blurred, but she could not pause her desperate swimming to clear her vision. All she could hear was her own heaving breath, the crash of waves, and the harsh cries from injured ships and men.

It seemed like ages before *Wavecutter* rocked in front of them. Ropes and arms reached over to haul up the waterlogged pair. Once on solid planking, Líf struggled to slow her breathing, which was rapid and harsh.

Hands hurriedly stripped off her clothes. Storage panels in the hull were opened, and a few blankets that were still slightly dry were quickly wrapped about her. Enveloped in a tentative warmth, she stared up at the clear blue sky, not focusing on the people circling her until Thray's almost-black eyes blocked her sight.

"You're safe now, Líf," the squirrel purred as her fur slowly brightened. "You scared me. But you're safe now."

Beyond the little rodent, the iridescent bear rose to her feet. Wrapped in thick furs, Brasír stood next to the ursine. Soon, two other small forms collided with Líf's prostrate body. Her nephews threw themselves on her, hugging her tightly. Intangible to them, Thray passed through the children and ruffled her fur once she was safely atop Líf's head.

"I'm okay," Líf reassured them meekly. She still did not believe she had made it back.

"We thought Jörmungandr had eaten you," Gratti whimpered into Líf's sopping hair.

Most of the crew was lined up on one side of *Wavecutter*, Ottar and Hervor among them. Budvar blurted, "Jörmungandr is going to drag the other ships down with him! He is angry."

Thray questioned, "Is it really the world serpent? Why would he be so far from his home?"

Slowly standing up, Líf wished she knew the answer. As she stepped next to her siblings, she stopped, horror-struck at what the crew was watching. The trio of skeids had all but fallen apart. The one with the most damage was sinking fast, but the connecting ropes were pulling the others down with it.

Even from this distance, they could hear the desperate shouts of the crew. Men jumped off their dying crafts to swim toward open waters. The enormous serpent's long form occasionally surfaced but did not seem to deliberately attack the doomed vessels.

"We should help them." Líf's teeth chattered with the cold, and she felt as if her insides had turned to ice. She looked on in dismay. Those people were from Thorinheim. They were men around whom she had grown up. In attempting to capture Wavecutter and the runaway slave, they had only followed the orders of their jarl; they had only obeyed the law. Why should they die for having done what they believed was right?

Ottar must have been thinking the same thing. He looked at Hervor. The shieldmaiden scowled at the ever-expanding wreckage of the ships. "We cannot risk *Wavecutter*. She has sustained enough damage as it is."

Líf felt nauseous as she listened to her sister's words. Still, the fierce blond woman's eyes softened. "However, if that foul creature goes away, I will permit the ship to search for any survivors that Rán has not claimed. But first, we must move farther away."

Before Líf could ask why, she observed Hervor staring into the water. Following the shieldmaiden's line of sight, Líf noticed the faint glimmer of scales far below. If the sea snake actually was this long, could it truly be the world serpent?

Once the ship was settled in its new position, Líf rested under a blanket along with her nephews. She slept for a few hours until Gratti crawled over to her and spoke into her ear, "Did you see its face when you were in the water?"

His blue eyes sparkled with curiosity rather than fear. It was amazing how young children could sometimes recover faster than adults.

"No," Líf said. She did not want to imagine what foul features that beast would have.

"What about a tail? Did you see his tail?"

"No. Why are you asking these questions?"

Gratti blinked in disbelief. "Because of what *you* told us. The story of *The End*. The serpent's purpose."

Líf's confusion showed on her face, so Budvar chimed in, "The day that Jörmungandr releases his tail from his mouth will be the day Ragnarök begins."

"Ragnarök?" Ragnarök was the end of times, when gods, monsters, and men would be wiped from existence. She knew the story of Jörmungandr well. It was told to terrify children so they would not leave their beds at night. But many believed it to be a prediction, not only of the future but also of the termination of life. Líf had never considered the tale to be real. At least, not until now. It was only a story—wasn't it? And there was still much more time before it occurred. There had to be.

Líf tried to think whether she had seen any beginning or end to the mammoth snake. If the monster was Jörmungandr, he would be far from his territory. He was meant to encircle Midgard until Ragnarök. What if…?

No. She had not seen an end to the creature. Still, Líf needed reassurance. Making her way to Ottar, who was also resting on the floor, she asked, "What do you think that serpent is?"

Her brother's look confirmed her fears. She repeated Gratti's question. Ottar turned to peer at the floating wreckage before suddenly announcing, "Jörmungandr is gone!"

Chapter Six

The sea was calm, almost perfectly flat. Only a few small waves and no wind at all ruffled the water. Without the shadow of clouds upon its surface, the entire expanse was as smooth as a looking glass.

Yet Líf knew what sort of foul monstrosities lurked beneath the water. Where had Jörmungandr gone? Had he left to find new prey? Was he searching for landfall? Or had he, perhaps, returned to the deep until the end of time?

Scattered across the silky sea, bits of rubbish and wood fragments were all that remained of the skeids that had been torn apart before sinking to the ocean floor. Several panels of overlapping planks floated in the placid sea, along with the top half of a buoyant barrel and a scrap of cloth entangled with an oar. Slowly a gentle current carried the debris past *Wavecutter*'s grim-faced crew. Their serene view was shattered by the frantic cries of men struggling to stay afloat among the wreckage.

"What should we do about them?" Guthorm Blood Cheeks asked Hervor. In the bright sunlight, his rosacea flush was even more vibrant.

"Their lives are in the hands of the gods," said the tall blond woman. "Let us hope they can last long enough. Those who are meant to enter into Rán's water-filled hall will do so. No one can escape one's fate."

Once again, both Líf's siblings shared the same line of thought. But as the number of voices lessened, Líf felt her nausea build. Thray shivered upon her shoulder, mirroring her human's emotions.

"Do you hear that, Líf?" the small squirrel crooned. Fylgjur senses were far keener than those of humans.

Líf listened intently. At first, all was relatively quiet. Then there was a slight thumping against the side of the ship. It was probably more debris from the skeids that had reached *Wavecutter*.

She leaned over the drakkar's side and craned her neck. The source of the noise did indeed originate from the skeids, but it was not some piece of a doomed vessel. A corpse, floating face up, rocked gently in the water, bumping against the wood planking. The discolored flesh and milky eyes stared sightlessly at Líf.

"That was Oggi the Younger." Sigird had walked over to see what she was looking at. At thirteen, he was a man in all respects—but just barely. He was pale, almost as pale as Líf's normal hue. His jaw was clenched with an inner determination, although his eyes told a different story. He had been affected just as much as she by recent events.

"Stop acting like an ergi," grunted Ulf the Short to the teenager, "or people will believe you are one. Help shove the corpse away from the oars. We're going to see who's still kickin'."

Líf did not dare offer Sigird assistance. Ulf had used an epithet so offensive that, under normal circumstances, would have provoked a deadly fight. Every man in their society—as well as shieldmaidens like Hervor—strove for drengskapr, the supreme ideal. A man manifesting drengskapr was called a drengr. Such a man should have boundless courage as well as a high-minded nature and should be among the most manly of warriors. To be masculine in features and character was essential; to show no fear in the face of certain death was esteemed above all. How else would one earn the right to enter Valhalla at one's death?

An ergi was the opposite of a drengr. Some men, like cowards and cheats, deserved the association. Yet the unfortunates who received that title were often mocked and harassed, even sometimes killed, for simple weakness of mind or body. If a man were found doing woman's work or suspected of showing affinity for his own sex, he would bear that label forever. Líf remembered when one man deemed an ergi was found beaten to death. His corpse had been dressed posthumously in his wife's clothing, the runes for ergi carved into his back with a knife.

She glanced at Brasir. Over the winter, he had helped her with her chores. Did that mean he was an ergi? He certainly did not look like one. Then again, Brasir, too, was quite different from the average man. Maybe the fact that he was gifted exempted him from such a dishonorable title.

Perhaps Ulf was trying to ignite some sort of fire in the boy or harden him for battle, but Líf felt the insult had gone too far. Of course, she could not say so; a woman's attempt to defend a man's masculinity or bravery would have the opposite effect. Sigird buried his emotions as he pushed the dead man away from the longship. As *Wavecutter* slowly made her way to the center of the wreckage, he was called to repeat the act several more times.

Ottar stood with his boys. Pointing out bits of debris or bloating bodies, he talked them through this horrible situation and explained the harsh reality of life outside their seaside town. For the first time in a long while, Líf wished she were young enough to take refuge from such a tragedy in her brother's arms. Having reached womanhood years ago, however, she was expected to stomach this gruesome sight. Moreover, at twenty she should have been comforting her own little ones—that is, if she had ever found a man willing to wed a "crazy woman."

Thorinheim was not perfect, especially with respect to Líf and her strange ability, but it was her childhood home. It had been her shelter and the foundation of everything she had known and experienced. Nonetheless, she had never desired to participate in the bloodshed her siblings engaged in during their summer raids.

Now, the longship was surrounded by the bobbing remains of men who had teased her, called her names, and harassed her mercilessly for years on end. Líf took no pleasure in the stiffening, bloating corpses, which had already begun to attract hungry aquatic life. Instead, she felt immensely sad.

"Is anyone alive out there?" Skeggi called. His portly seagull screamed in the sky as she flew over the sprawling waste.

Along with several other shimmering fylgjur, Hervor's bird circled the debris. Below them, crewmen scoured the wreckage for any sign of movement. Líf knew they hoped to spy a waving arm or desperate face. She was the only one who searched for something different.

When a man died, so did his fylgja. The animal would vanish in a wisp of sparkling granules that were carried away on the wind. If a person were alive among all these dead, she should be able to spot their guardian spirit swimming or floating nearby. Yet all she saw were limp corpses partially submerged in the salty waters.

Some had died during battle; their bodies were spiked with arrows or rent with gaping wounds. Others had drowned when their vessels sank or when they no longer had the strength to stay afloat during these last few hours. More had perished from the frigid waters, unable to stay warm until help finally arrived.

"Is anyone alive?" Skeggi boomed out once more. "Anyone?"

As Sigrid worked hard to shove away the dead bodies and other wreckage that hindered the longship's movement, Líf spotted a body sprawled out on a wooden platform. Alongside the still form, a metallic blue fox shivered uncontrollably.

"Over there!" Líf shouted as she made her way toward the prow and Sigrid. The boy had just pushed the platform away when she shouted, "That man is alive! Pull him back!"

With Ulf's help, they used an oar to pull the wooden raft alongside *Wavecutter*. Other crew members hoisted the unconscious man aboard and checked his breathing and temperature. Líf leaned over, caught hold of the listless fox by its scruff, and dropped it into the longship. She was grateful that her gift allowed her to interact with all fylgjur, not just her own.

Líf ignored the strange looks from the sailors, but a sharp bite on her neck caused her to tear up while she muffled a cry. Thray was angry at her for touching another person's fylgja. The squirrel was red with rage.

"You know they can't be separated for long," Líf snapped as she touched her sore neck. The wound did not bleed, though it felt as though it should have. It may have been invisible to others, but the throbbing pain was as real to her as Thray was.

The fylgja continued to glare at her before seeking solitude atop the mast. Líf did not care to argue with the squirrel, nor did she check on the man, who was now being wrapped in heavy blankets. Instead, she turned back to the sea and searched for more survivors.

Another eight were saved from Rán that day. All suffered from severe hypothermia, and two died within the hour. The man with the fox fylgja was the first to recover enough to speak.

"For those who don't know me, I am Einar Threnson. I work for the family of Jarl Harek." He looked at Sigird, who had recognized the redheaded man. "We were ordered to bring back this ship and the jarl's slave with it."

Líf heard Brasir's bear snarl menacingly, though the black-skinned man remained icily calm.

Clutching his blanket with blue-tinged fingers, Einar made the mistake of looking right at Ottar as he asked, "What will you do with me?"

Hervor stood rigidly next to her brother. Her jaw twitched with irritation. When she answered, Einar realized his error.

"You do know you are at *our* mercy?"

Einar refused to answer her. Nodding, he locked eyes with the shieldmaiden—a risky action that might prove fatal. She could have him thrown overboard, nailed to the mast, or gutted at her feet. Silently, he chose to accept his fate without fear.

"The Norns have not ended your life, nor will I," Hervor told him. "You and the rest of the survivors will be set free once we reach land." Líf suspected Einar's bravery had saved his life.

"Aw, Hervor," Skeggi joshed as the shieldmaiden walked by. "I knew you had a heart."

Holding her breath, Líf watched her sister turn slowly to face the foolhardy oaf. The shieldmaiden rarely used verbal retorts; actions were much more effective. Líf half expected Skeggi's nose to be broken again. Yet there was no sudden movement on Hervor's part.

But Skeggi's face suddenly lost its joyful glow. Slowly, the man eased backward, exposing the dagger perfectly positioned at the level of his scrotum. Líf coughed out a laugh, for she knew that even this close call would not dissuade Skeggi's constant pursuit of her sister.

"He'll never learn," she said aloud, then realized that Thray was still perched atop the mast. Fylgjur could hold grudges longer than Líf cared to try, so what was the point? Besides, she had done the only logical thing. Líf sighed. She would never intentionally upset Thray, but the idea of being separated from one's fylgja made her shiver.

Walking past the captives, she noticed that they constantly gave Brasir dark looks. Why wouldn't they? Wasn't he the source of their current predicament? Líf understood the hatred that radiated from their crimson fylgjur; still, their pain and suffering were nothing compared to what would come if Brasir were to fail in his quest.

She wandered over to the dark-skinned man. His face was still severely disfigured, possibly by some of the same fellows who had been saved from the frigid waters. Yet he did not outwardly show discomfort from the wounds inflicted upon him.

"Does it hurt?" Líf asked, for she did not know what else to say.

"It's just pain." He looked at her with his one unswollen eye. Under his gaze, Líf suddenly became self-conscious and pulled some of her hair low to cover the long scar on her forehead. Brasir had saved her on the night she had received the scar, just as he had saved her in the waters. Would she ever be able to return these favors? What use was she on this journey, when she was the one who kept causing problems?

"Let's turn this ship around!" Hervor cried out, interrupting Líf's depressing thoughts.

Just as before, the men did an about-face; the sail was raised; and the prow became the stern as the older Lothbranson siblings took their positions at opposite ends of the vessel. With barely a pop-up shower to slow their progress, the longship fairly flew toward the mainland, ready to relieve itself of its precious, though dangerous, cargo.

Over the next few days, the captives were treated with respect and were allotted the same amount of food and care as Wavecutter's crew. The only difference was that they were restricted to one end of the ship, while Brasir, along with Ottar's boys, remained on the other. Líf stayed near her nephews and the foreign man, which resulted in more scowls and foul remarks from the skeids' survivors.

What did she care? She was used to men disliking her because of her ability. Harassing her because she associated with the strange man was not very different. Still, when she helped distribute the rations, the jeers and crude gestures increased—delivered quickly and timed just right so that neither Ottar nor Hervor noticed.

One man with atypically dark hair snagged Líf's wrist as she handed out dried meat. "Why don't you share some of your love? Or are you only attracted to darkies?"

Einar, who was standing nearby, overheard the rude remark. Jerking the man's hand away, he growled, "Leave 'er alone." Catching Líf's eye, he apologized, "Sorry. He forgets he is not still in the homeland."

Rape was only permitted on foreign soil if the woman was of foreign blood. Líf gave a quick nod of thanks before clambering back to the refuge of her nephews.

Such was her life until the evening Ottar announced, "Jarlbörg is in sight."

Hearing the capital's name, Einar jumped up, causing Ottar's men to unsheathe their weapons. Even Einar's own companions shot him dirty looks. Undeterred, he implored Hervor, "Halt the ship. Do not go there."

Skeggi, who was near Líf, uttered in a low voice, "Maybe the sea destroyed some of his...." He tapped the top of his head. "Ya know?"

"I am not a malicious man," the captive began. His fylgja bristled at his feet.

"Shut your trap an' sit down," snarled the man who had offended Líf the day before.

But Einar's worried look bothered Ottar. "What is it?"

"I would have killed any of you in battle, but I do not wish those who spared my life to be massacred." The derisive looks from the men around him shifted to wariness and skepticism. Einar continued, "When Harekson left us, he sailed straight to Jarlbörg. Thor's hammer! He's the king's grandson—pray for swift deaths."

CHAPTER SEVEN

"So, the weasel didn't flee home." Hervor stared at Einar for a long moment. "He thinks he is so smart, doesn't he?" Without looking at her brother, she ordered, "Steer *Wavecutter* to Gerðr's Fjord. Mast down. Let's pull in nice and slow."

"If only she asked that of me," Skeggi quipped.

Líf shoved an elbow into his brawny side. "Do you want her to carve out your heart right here and now?" Before he could answer, she continued, "And don't joke that she already has your heart."

"It's not my heart I want her to have but my—" Skeggi reached for the bulge in his pants just as Hervor strode by. "My back has indeed been acting up."

Ottar's friend was teetering on the brink of disaster. Shaking her head, Líf began, "I swear, Skeggi, one day—"

"Lingy, it's not like you to swear. Quite unbecoming." He grinned, exposing the missing tooth Hervor had knocked out shortly after they'd both hit puberty.

Líf bit her tongue so not to get sucked into one of Skeggi's unending word games. That man made her head ache. She returned to her designated spot and watched her nephews play-wrestle with Brasir. Remaining seated, the man allowed the boys to shove him backward as they roughhoused from sheer boredom.

They had been on the water for over a week, and Líf was impressed with Gratti and Budvar's good behavior in such tight quarters. If they had been at home, the boys would have been able to wind down only after running for miles through the woodlands and over the fields. Climbing, jumping, and pestering Líf was a daily affair; yet on *Wavecutter*, they were much calmer and more manageable. Still, it was clear they were getting restless and yearned to leap off the boat and run free on solid ground.

Líf shared some of their feelings. More than she needed to expend energy, though, she yearned for a day without vomiting up her stomach's contents. Landfall should have been a dream come true. Now, it was less a dream and more a nightmare.

"Move aside. Make way!" Ulf bellowed as he and a score of other men began the slow and dangerous process of lowering the mast. The heavy beam could easily throw off the balance of men and ship or shatter bones if dropped. Líf pressed up against her brother as she watched the crew expertly maneuver the mast to the floorboards.

Once the long beam was down, the drakkar's profile would be transformed. On land, an observer at the right angle and distance might even overlook the oncoming vessel until it was too late. The low, sleek design allowed the longship to slip over the water so unobtrusively that it could be mistaken for part of the waves. That would have been easier had *Wavecutter* been one of the less decorated skeids, and not a brightly adorned warship. However, there was no need to draw unnecessary attention to her as she entered the fjord.

The men were quiet. Though not gagged, the captives were carefully watched to make sure they would not call out for help. The crew paddled up the fjord. Birds twittered in the sky above. From time to time, a fish leaped near the shoreline.

Ottar steered the ship toward a pebbly beach. Dropping anchor, he and Hervor exchanged words before selecting several men to scout the town. Jarlbörg was located in the next fjord, and they needed to find out if Harekson was indeed in the city. Unfortunately, both Hervor and Ottar would be easily identified, so Guthorm Blood Cheeks took command of this venture. He and half a dozen others leaped overboard, waded toward shore, and disappeared over the rocky slope.

"You will be released," Ottar assured the captives, "but not until we know we are safe."

Low grumblings were hushed by the threat of thirsting blades. And so the rest of *Wavecutter*'s crew waited. Even though Sigrid had bloodied himself the summer before, Líf thought the boy seemed too young. As he sat on his bench and stared at his hands, his yearling-sized buck's shimmering eyes darted about warily.

Skeggi unleashed his twisted sense of humor. "Cheer up, lad. You may have a family reunion sooner that you think."

Sigrid was serious. "My brother will kill me. In his eyes, I have betrayed him as well as our father."

"Let's hope your grandfather sees it differently."

The boy's eyes widened in recollection, and he called out, "Hervor! Ottar the Untouchable!" His voice was louder than expected, and he shrank down cautiously. Nobody wanted the ship and crew found out.

When the siblings approached the teenager, Sigird explained, "My mother sent me with this." He rolled up a sleeve to expose a very ornate arm ring. "A gift from my grandfather to her, and now a message for him. If I give this to my grandfather, he will believe what I say."

"Which is?" Ottar inquired quietly.

"That the slave, Brasir, must be freed so he can pursue his quest."

"It appears," said Hervor, "that we owe much to Princess Thoren. Now we have to get you in front of King Thorkell before your prick of a brother finds us out."

It was several hours before the scouting party returned with news. Guthorm talked as he shook off the water he had just waded through. "*Squallsubduer* is anchored in the harbor. Once we spotted his ship, we searched the city for signs of Harekson."

"And?" Ottar inquired while Hervor remained silent.

"We found some of his men in King Thorkell's mead hall. Let's just say they were very loose lipped. Harekson is in Jarlbörg, but not for long. He intends to propose that the entire Lothbranson family be sentenced to full outlawry at the Althing, in front of all the jarls, the godis, and the king."

"The Althing is this year?" Líf referred to the largest council of elders and rulers. Held once every nine years, a representative from each jarl's household and the most important godis from all four quarters of the kingdom would meet with the king to establish new laws and deal with major grievances. It was always held before the independent quadrants convened their annual Things, similar but far smaller assemblies.

If a person was sentenced to full outlawry, he or she would be cast out of the kingdom forever. Considered outside both the law and society, an outlaw forfeited all rights to property or wealth and could be slain by anyone without repercussions. To die in full outlawry was a disgrace and would almost certainly prevent one from entering Valhalla. This was one of the worst possible punishments, surpassed only by the fearsome ritual of the Blood Eagle.

Líf was confused. "It's far too early, even if it's the right year. Sumarmál has not even occurred. That's over a month away." She realized the pensive expressions of her siblings indicated the discrepancy was also recognized by them. The timing of blóts and religious ceremonies, as well as governmental assemblies, were determined by the lunar calendar and did not change.

Hervor looked worried. Her brow furrowed as she asked her brother, "Did you know of this?"

"If a call for an early Althing was made, it must have occurred while we were preparing to leave or after we left." Ottar pursed his lips.

"What are we going to do?" Líf asked.

"I will go to the Althing," Ottar said. He turned to Hervor. "I'll take five men. We will purchase horses in Jarlbörg and ride to Haugr. I must try to settle this. You stay with the ship and the crew. You must take care of my boys until we return."

He selected Guthorm, Ulf, and Skeggi, his most trusted men. For obvious reasons, Sigrid would accompany them. Brasir would also come, for he could not be granted the rights of a bóndi, a free man, unless he appeared in person.

Hervor's expression was sour. Once again, she was prevented from attending simply because she was a woman.

"I want to come with you, Pappa," Budvar stated with all the authority a nine-year-old could muster. "I will soon be a man and I...I should come along."

Ottar smiled at his young boy. "I see that. Well, while I am gone, you are the man of the family. You will need to watch over your brother and your aunts. Isn't that right, Hervor?"

For the first time in a long while, Hervor did not grimace at such a remark. She inclined her head ever so slightly, then walked off to inspect the damage from the sea battle.

Ottar continued, "Remember to keep everyone safe and a watchful eye on your captives at all times."

Budvar, looking so like his father, stood up straight and glared at the hostages. "I will, Pappa."

Two of the men spent the remainder of the day bartering for the half-dozen horses. As evening approached, they made hurried farewells before heading inland, hoping that their bizarre mission would succeed.

Budvar took his newly ordained position seriously. With an almost comically severe face, he strode up and down the length of the ship until long past sunset. The men repairing *Wavecutter* had stopped work with the waning light. The captives were tied together with spare rope to prevent them from leaping overboard while the drakkar was at anchor. At this late hour, most everyone was settled in for the night.

Líf nestled next to Gratti, who was softly snoring in the crook of her arm. She called out to his brother, "Budvar, it's past time for bed."

The summons drew some snickers from the captives huddled in the stern. Budvar looked mortified before retorting, "I'm the man of the household now."

Physically tired and emotionally exhausted, Líf could not allow that statement to stand. "Get over here. Now!" she barked. The venom in her typically kind and understanding voice was unusual. Sulking, her nephew walked quickly to her side and sat down in one dejected motion. Come morning, Líf thought, he could be angry at her all he wanted.

The stars still glittered brightly in the sky when Líf awoke to the whispers of voices. Budvar was up and moving toward the hostages, who watched him with mocking expressions. He had a little seax in his hand.

Where had he found that? Líf slowly eased Gratti off of her while

Budvar hissed at the men, "You take that back!"

"Budvar—" Líf's soft voice distracted the boy. As he looked over his shoulder, there was a flash of movement. He tumbled backward, the knife fell from his hand, and the dark-bearded man who had harassed Líf grabbed the child in his arms.

"Budvar!" Líf's anguished cry alerted the crew.

"What in Hel's name is going on?" Hervor asked. Now wide awake, she saw her nephew's dangerous predicament.

"It's past time for me to be leavin'," grunted the large fellow holding Budvar. "Untie me, boy."

In an act of spite that would have normally earned praise from Hervor, Budvar kicked the man's shin. In response, the captive pressed the tip of the little knife against the child's temple. The boy froze, his eyes widening.

"Any more movement, and the boy'll earn his first and only scar." The brute scanned hands hovering above weapons. "Now, untie me!"

Gratti whimpered behind Líf's skirts as he watched his brother turn pale. Budvar fumbled with the knots around the man's wrists before crying in dismay, "I can't!"

"But I can!" Líf shouted out before the man could harm her nephew. "Let me. Please."

"What are you doing?" chirped Thray in a worried tone as she clambered up Líf's skirts.

The man considered her offer, then nodded. "Hurry up."

Hervor watched motionlessly as her sister slowly walked past her. Líf desperately tried to remain calm. What would happen if her fingers shook too much to unbind the man?

Taking a long breath, she worked on the intricate knot around his wrists. Who had come up with such a confounding thing? It certainly was good at staying together. Worse was the horrible angle she had to work from, as the captive's bound hands kept a tight grip on Budvar and the knife. A bead of sweat rolled down the bumpy ridge of the scar on her forehead before landing on the fraying tether.

"What's taking so long?" the man grumbled as he continued to hold the seax next to Budvar's face.

"I've almost got it," Líf lied, hoping that one of the gods would take pity on her plight. It was Thray who pointed to a loop and whispered, "Tug that one."

The cords unraveled, and Líf cautiously stepped back. But the man did not release Budvar.

"Now the others."

Líf glanced at her sister, who gave her a stiff nod. The shieldmaiden was clearly forcing herself to refrain from striking the brute down. With her nephew's life at stake, the risk was simply too great.

She moved over to Einar and worked on releasing him. Was that pity glimmering in his gray eyes? Shouldn't he be thrilled to escape with his comrades? Once free, Einar rubbed the marks on his wrists.

Líf moved once again. As she turned away from the others, she heard a grunt and a huge splash. Spinning around, she realized that the man holding Budvar was no longer on the ship. Neither were her nephew or Einar.

"They're in the water," affirmed the small, anxious squirrel.

A flurry of activity followed. As the rest of the captives were restrained, Hervor and several others leaped from *Wavecutter* into the sea. Líf hurried to the side of the ship. Below, Einar held his hands up, acknowledging his recapture. Budvar floundered into Líf's outstretched arms. Hervor had reached the rocky beach; axe in hand, she rushed after the escaped man.

"I'm sorry," Budvar sniffled as he tried to hold back tears. "I'm sorry."

"I know," Líf soothed as she worked to dry off the sopping wet child. His brother stood nearby, his face also scrunching up from crying.

When Hervor returned, she looked less a woman and more a raging Valkyrie ready to reap the dead and dying. Her pale-blond hair flew wildly about her face. "He's gone," she seethed. "If he reaches Harekson and tells him about Ottar, our entire plan is for naught."

Chapter Eight

o you think that's where he went?" Thray asked as she folded down her normally fluffy tail fur. The result made her look more like a rat than a squirrel.

"Thor's hammer!" Hervor swore. She glowered toward the ridge where she had lost the fleeing captive.

The whirling thoughts in Líf's head frightened her. If Harekson were informed of her brother's plans, he would do everything in his power to end not only Brasir's life but Ottar's as well.

Hervor turned her attention to Einar. Her axe was ready to mete out punishment. "If you desired death, you are about to receive it."

Einar tried to stand up but was shoved to his knees by several of the crew. He defended his actions. "I tried to prevent escape. If I hadn't acted, all the others would have been released. You would have had no chance to recapture us all." As he spoke, the captives behind him looked as if they, too, wished Hervor to strip the hugr from his body. "I had hoped Hogni would be…"

Einar's line of thought shifted. He nodded toward the tethered men. "We are good people who only want justice. You saved us, Lothbrandóttir; you showed mercy. You did not have to, yet you did. Though we all desire freedom, Hogni should never have threatened the child. There is no honor in that."

"Why would you not help your comrades escape?" Hervor was skeptical of Einar's professed good intentions.

"You saved us. You saved me. We all know you, either personally or by reputation. You keep your word. You promised not to harm us and to let us go after your venture is complete. I believe you. I have never borne ill will for you or your family. I only wanted the slave returned to our jarl. But if Hogni informs Harekson, your family will receive punishment, one that many of you do not deserve." He looked at the boys tucked up against Líf's skirts.

Hervor adjusted her grip on the axe before returning it to its loop on her belt. "I will not take your life, but I cannot speak for your companions."

The other captives cast dark looks at Einar who, in turn, lowered his head in acknowledgment. If he lived through the night, it would be a miracle. No one on the longship would make a move to save the man if he were attacked, not even Líf. One must always take responsibility for one's actions if one hoped to receive blessings from the gods.

When Líf's thoughts turned back to the missing captive and Harekson's wrath, Thray knew what she was thinking. "Don't be ridiculous," the squirrel chittered. "That would never end well."

Nevertheless, Líf looked at her sister. "Let me go after Ottar."

Hervor was not the only one to belt out a harsh laugh. Undeterred, Líf continued, "I'm serious. That man, Hogni, will try to find Harekson. But he is on foot and has nothing to trade for a horse. He can only travel so fast. If we buy a steed, I can ride after our brother and warn him."

Her sister looked thoughtful. "You are using your head. That's good, but someone else must go. It is far too dangerous for you."

"She's right, Líf," agreed the squirrel fylgja. "Let her send another."

"What about the boat?"

Budvar's voice shook. "That man was saying things. Bad things. He said he would tell all of Jarlbörg where we were hiding. He said we were all doomed."

The shieldmaiden approached Einar, who was still kneeling. "Is this true?"

"The boy is correct. If you stay here much longer, you risk being discovered and captured."

"Loki's bindings!" she snarled. Looking over the rest of her crew, she grimaced. "We are already too short."

"What does she mean?" Thray whispered as she curled around the back of Líf's neck.

"I think *Wavecutter* does not have enough crew to sail her as it is," Líf explained. "Between those who died and those who are away, she is extremely shorthanded."

Shaking off the boys, Líf approached her sister. "Hervor, let me go after Ottar. If you do not have enough men now, you cannot risk sending someone who can be of help to you. You must stay with the ship and take her offshore. I can do this. If I can get a horse, I can find our brother."

"And if you are captured? Women are not allowed near the Althing."

"Remember, I'm just 'that crazy Lothbrandóttir.' How could I be suspected of intending to do harm?"

Hervor studied the ridge. Her jaw twitched in agitation. "There is nothing to be done tonight. The stables will be closed. No one will sell a horse at this hour." She removed one of her arm bands and gave it to her little sister. "*Wavecutter* must leave this fjord before first light. Pack some food and go ashore. Find a place to settle in. In the morning, get a steed and ride swiftly. Hogni will have had a huge head start."

Lif nodded. There was no need to say more. She collected some provisions while the rest of the crew prepared *Wavecutter* to set sail, and then she waded toward shore.

"I'll be all right," she said, partially to reassure herself.

"Of course you will," her sister agreed. "You are the daughter of Lothbran the Cunning."

As Lif watched *Wavecutter* sail away, she shivered. Or was that Thray.

As Lif approached Jarlbörg, her red locks were still entangled with bits of twigs and leaves from where she had curled up to sleep. Tired and a bit sore, she wandered around the foreign town until she found the stables.

It was still very early, and nobody appeared to be around. She knocked on the warped wooden door. "Hello? Hello. I need to purchase a horse."

Heavy footsteps resounded just before the door creaked inward. "What? Are the stars even in bed yet?"

An elderly man with big, sloping shoulders towered over her and eyed her with suspicion. And why not? Her forehead broke out in a sweat, and she was unable to lock eyes with the man.

The only items Lif had ever purchased were a few fabric swatches and some produce that their farm's rocky fields could not grow. She had never bought anything as valuable as livestock and never been in a position whose dire nature imposed time limits. She needed a mount, and quickly.

"A horse, you said?"

"Yes," Lif piped out.

A large, lumbering dog fylgja loped around with a heavy gait similar to that of the man's.

"And what would a nice little lady like yourself need a horse for?"

Unable to speak the truth, Lif quickly spat out a lie. "To tend to the fields. My husband is away at the Althing, and the only horse left at our household went lame yesterday. I need a strong one to help plow the fields in time to sow our seeds."

"Why not send a slave to do this errand? Shouldn't you be more concerned about managing your farm?"

"Do you think I would trust slaves? They would probably buy some half-dead mare and pocket the rest of the gold."

The man looked insulted, "There are no half-dead mares in my stable. Gold, you say? Follow me. I'll show you our best draft horses."

A mount built for speed would have been ideal. However, Lif came away with a shaggy, sturdy horse perfect for pulling a plow and other farm equipment. Swiftness was not in its genes. Next to it, she felt small and fragile. The creature looked as if it could not care less about moving any faster than at a plodding walk. Using Hervor's arm band as payment, Líf was able to barter for a worn-out saddle and a bridle as well. The stable owner was pleased with his new wealth.

Líf had to be assisted to mount the tall beast, which was quite mortifying in itself. Then came the task of getting the animal to move. She kicked her heels into its ribs and tugged at the reins, yet the horse continued to languidly graze wherever it liked.

Refusing to acknowledge the mocking eyes of the stable master, she struggled to pull up the horse's head. Despite her efforts, all she provoked was a sharp, indignant snort.

"Come on, you darn thing. Don't you know we have to gallop away?"

The horse did not react to her sense of urgency but instead meandered over to a scrubby bush near a fisherman's hovel.

The town was starting to awaken. In the distance, men were approaching. She heard one voice say, "Things'll be set right. Just you wait."

A second one bellowed, "That's one of them! Stop her!"

"Líf, that's us!" squealed Thray. They both turned to see Hogni and two other men running toward them.

"Move, horse," Líf begged. "Move!"

The bleating of a goat behind a nearby picket fence startled the steed, who finally took notice of the petite woman's commands. The great beast lurched into something resembling a gallop. Massive hooves kicked up snowy clouds into the air behind him.

"Hold on, Thray," Líf warned, struggling to steer her mount down the main road that led inland and, she hoped, in the direction of Haugr and the Althing. Behind her, the shouts of the angry men faded.

Don't give him a horse, Líf thought in a panic. She knew Thray was scared too, from the way she dug her claws into Líf's flesh. Those sharp, shimmering nails could bore through all but the thickest material.

Although Jarlbörg had been left behind some time ago and there was no sign of pursuit, Líf refrained from rejoicing. She was ahead of Hogni for the moment, but that could change at any time. A faster horse and a party bearing weapons could alter everything. Moreover, her dratted steed had slowed down again to a simple trot.

"This whole idea is unsound," complained Thray. "Listen to me."

Líf gave the fylgja a sideways glance. True, Thray was her personal guardian, but she was not always right. If Líf had listened to the opinionated squirrel, Brasir would still be enslaved by Jarl Harek, and the future of the hamingjur would be at risk. Still, she knew never to bring up such things to a fylgjur; they were strangely proud creatures.

For a while, the pair continued down the dusty road, heartbeats still far more rapid than usual. Líf's neck developed a crick from continually looking behind them in fear of Hogni and his mates. Thray was luckier; she could perch backward on the young woman's shoulder or on top of her head. Much to Líf's relief, the little creature offered to be the sole lookout.

Where was Hogni now? What had the man said to get others to help him? The truth, probably. He was a crew member on a ship owned by his jarl's son. They had been sent to capture or kill the people who had stolen the jarl's slave and to return the stolen property. During the ensuing battle, his ship had been destroyed and he himself captured and bound. Everyone who heard Hogni's tale would believe the Lothbransons were in the wrong, for they had stolen from their jarl. But that was only half the story.

"Líf?" Thray shifted her position atop the woman's red hair.

"What?" asked Líf as she tried to rouse a burst of energy in the sluggish draft horse.

"I think there is a fylgja flying behind us."

"What?" Líf asked again. She craned her neck about, but saw only a colony of swifts flitting in the air. "I don't see anything."

The squirrel slid down onto Líf's shoulder and paused before jumping onto her lap. "We should go faster. This is not good."

"Why don't you tell that to this wretched animal?" Líf snarled as she kicked the horse.

The beast took a few peppy steps, then paused to chew on a tuft of grass.

"You have to do something, Líf." The fylgja growled in a feral way. She scurried up the horse's neck and whispered in its ear before sinking her metallic teeth into its neck.

There was no bite mark, for fylgjur shouldn't be able to interact with the physical world. Still, the horse whickered and broke into a gallop.

"How did…?" Líf began, but the rodent had curled up in her cloak to escape the tug of the wind.

"You can't get caught!" Thray exclaimed.

They were racing down the open roadway, hopefully putting a good distance between themselves and their pursuers. Líf clung to the horse and prayed she would not fall off.

The gods must be favoring her. She was going to make it to the Althing. She would be able to warn Ottar. Everything would work out.

Then she saw it—a simple choice that could eliminate any hope of success. Just ahead, the road forked in three directions. Líf had no idea which one to take.

Chapter Nine

"Whoa." Líf slowed the horse until it halted.

Thray poked her head out from under the flaps of cloth. Her iridescent eyes were dazzling. "Which way?"

"I don't know."

"How are we going to get to Haugr?"

Líf wanted to scream. "I've never been away from Thorinheim. How should I know?"

The Althing was to be held inland, but the mainland was vast. How naive had she been to believe the road led only to Haugr? Of course the road would split toward other towns and villages; this was the center of their kingdom, not a small island.

"What are we going to do?" The fylgja's questions only fueled Líf's growing stress.

"Three roads. Three options. One right, the others wrong." Líf spoke aloud, hoping it would help solve her problem. But was the answer really going to reveal itself to her like visions to a völva?

"Need help?"

The dry, crackling voice startled Líf, almost causing her to tumble off the horse. A small, ancient-looking man walked slowly toward her across a fallow field. His wide-brimmed hat prevented the rising sun from blinding him, and his wispy beard had become entangled in the brooch pinned to his right shoulder.

Líf considered him for a moment. He clearly had no idea who she was, nor could he be a thief, for he needed his staff to stand erect. Perhaps the old man genuinely wanted to assist a wayward traveler.

She would have asked Thray her opinion, but the squirrel had once again buried herself in Líf's cloak. Besides, if the man noticed her talking to the fylgja, he might become suspicious.

"I have an important message to deliver to someone at the Althing. I need to know which road to take."

"I see," the man wheezed. The wheeze turned into a coughing fit, and it took him a moment to collect himself. In addition to being frail and small, his brimmed hat tilted downward. Perched atop her horse, Líf could not see his face to make sure he was all right.

Just as she was about to ask, the elder spoke. "You are searching for Haugr, then. Take the left path to the next fork, then veer right. That should take you to your destination in two days' time."

"Thank you," Líf said. "Is there anything I can give you in gratitude?"

She had been taught the proper etiquette and thus to respect gift giving. One must always honor those who offered help.

The man laughed so hard that his entire frame shook, and followed that with a second bout of hacking coughs. "Off with you, child," he said, waving her away.

Somehow, Líf was able to kick the horse into a trot. She shouted back once more, "Thank you again, and may the gods bless you!"

It was a good half hour later when she realized Thray had not stirred from her position. "Are you coming back out, or are you asleep in there?"

"Is he gone?"

"The old man? Of course," Líf replied, her curiosity piqued by Thray's strange reaction. "What's wrong with you?"

A moment later, the tip of the squirrel's nose appeared as she sniffed the air. "He was not *right*."

"His directions?"

"No, no. *He* was wrong."

"How so?"

"Did you not notice? He...he did not have a fylgja."

Thray's comment startled Líf. "That's impossible," she said as she tried to recall the man's guardian spirit. But she had no memory of it.

Thray's observation had to be incorrect. A person could not survive without a fylgja, and vice versa. His must have stayed out of sight like Thray had. Nevertheless, a long shiver ran down Líf's spine.

The next two days did not diminish her discomfort. Both Líf and Thray remained constantly alert for their pursuers. And they *were* being pursued; periodically, the little squirrel spied a winged fylgja. As Líf was never able to catch a glimpse of the creature, she could not tell how far back it was, and possibly Hogni as well.

The fear of capture motivated Líf to ride until well past dark and rise before first light. She could not risk being found. But the long hours found her growing ever more exhausted and reliant on her guardian's continued encouragement to keep going.

"We should move off the road," Thray's sharp voice urged.

The rodent's words pulled Líf from her daydreams. They were traveling up rocky slopes. Ahead lay a strange outcropping of jagged stone whose shape was reminiscent of a long-dead giant's sharp teeth.

"Haugr. We're here."

Sliding off the horse, Líf led the steed behind some boulders to tether it before following Thray around the perimeter of the outcrop. The sounds of voices and men at camp rose from below—a cacophony of hammers pounding stakes, whickering horses, booming bouts of laughter, and crackling cooking fires.

Keeping low to the ground, Líf peeked over the strange, jagged rock to see the setting up of the Althing. It was as if a village had erected itself overnight. Búðir had been almost completed for every godi and jarl and even the royal family. These tented structures or booths would serve as homes for each of the representatives over the coming weeks while the Althing was in session. When not assembled for debate, the men would gather in their búðir not only to create alliances and strengthen old friendships but also to witness and sanction nids.

A nid was a formal and severe insult that was given either verbally or by means of a rune stick. Words held power, which was magnified when the nid's runes were carved into the wood. To bestow an unwarranted nid was as heinous an act as the rape or murder of a free person and punishable by full outlawry.

Líf shivered. How foolish men were to try and manipulate seid, magic. Haugr's hill was already infused with seid; the location was sacred and revered. Numerous raised rune stones the size of men were scattered about, each revealing tales of a specific god or goddess. Líf was not quite literate, but she recognized some of the beautifully intricate images adorning the somewhat rectangular objects. Long after the Althing was over, the tented roofs torn down and the wooden booths rotted, these stone structures would remain.

The only other objects to stand the test of time were the seats for the Speaker of the Althing and the king. Both seats had been carved into the tallest rocky outcrop (appropriately named Lögberg, the Law Rock), from which the two judges could oversee everything taking place in the session. Unlike the king, the Speaker or Lögsögumaður was chosen from among the godis at the beginning of the Althing to serve as the judge representing the common freemen—a counterbalance to the king.

Líf saw that this selection was occurring now. The holy grounds had been blessed with sacred fire, and now several godis stood at the center of the assembly. Each argued why he should be chosen, emphasizing his knowledge of political diplomacy and the law.

Watching them made Líf a bit sad. Ottar would have made an amazing godi. He had a way of solving issues rationally. He was never quick to judge nor as hot-tempered as Hervor. Levelheaded and just, he might one day have earned the esteemed privilege of being chosen Lögsögumaður. But that was not to be. Each region had a fixed number of godis; titles were either passed down through bloodlines or awarded to worthy men. When Ottar chose to free Brasir, he had relinquished any possibility of receiving that honor. Worse, he and the rest of his family risked banishment from the kingdom.

Líf slunk away and began scouting the perimeter. If she had made it to Haugr, surely so had Ottar's party. Where were they hiding? She didn't have to wonder long, for suddenly Thray sprang away, leaving Líf in the one area where women were never permitted. Unable to call after the little creature for fear of being overheard, she quietly made her way back to her horse. She spotted the beast languidly chewing some pale green shoots while two strange men circled him.

"Who you think he belongs to?" one asked the other. In the unseasonable cold, their breath wafted like miniature clouds as they spoke.

"Bring him to our búðar for now. Someone'll come and claim him."

"Loki's luck!" Líf swore as she watched her horse being led away. Now she had no escape plan. If spotted, she could only run, and she knew she was not fast enough.

Thray scurried up to Líf. A large, glimmering wolfhound fylgja followed her. The wolfhound sniffed the air and cocked his shaggy head. A moment later, Ottar waved to her from the cover of some boulders.

"Hurry up, Líf," Thray tittered. "You have been wanting to speak with him. What are you waiting for?"

Knowing that her brother could not see fylgjur, she asked, "How did you find me?"

"I had this gut feeling," Ottar said.

Líf glanced at the dog as it stretched and yawned.

"Why are you here, Líf? What happened to Hervor?"

"She's fine, but she had to leave the fjord with *Wavecutter*. One of the captives escaped, a man named Hogni. He is coming to find Harekson to tell him of your plans. You had to be warned."

"So *you* came?" Ottar sounded impressed, but somehow Líf felt insulted.

"I may be a woman, but I can ride a horse and deliver a message."

"Bravery is a Lothbranson trait," Ottar forced a smile, then looked towards Haugr. "I must alert the others. Come."

Her brother's camp was a prudent distance from the Althing. Every precaution had been taken. Once Líf's warning was relayed, the expressions of surprise and disapproval on the other men's faces dissolved.

Sigird's face was as steely as his tone. "I must see my grandfather tonight. No more waiting. We need to find a way into that village so I can enter his booth. The great decrees begin tomorrow. We still have a chance to explain to my grandfather and defend your actions before Harekson's proposed decree is instigated."

"His búðir is surrounded by the others. All the jarls will have men on watch, none more so than King Thorkell," added Guthorm.

"True, yet few outside Harekson's party would recognize us," countered Skeggi. "And during the Althing, no blood may be shed on the sacred grounds of Haugr. What if we walk in without weapons as if we belonged there? Who could tell? Aren't there always new faces at these meetings?"

Sigird nodded. "He is right. My grandfather might not even recognize me. He hasn't seen me in years. If we could just enter his—"

The teen was cut off by Ulf. "Walk in without weapons? Are you askin' to be slaughtered?"

No warrior wanted to be caught unprepared. However, Skeggi argued Sigird's case. "It would look as if we belonged. You know the policy."

"Ha! That's why I'll never be asked to be a representative."

"Sure. *That's* why…."

As the men began to bicker, Ottar raised his voice. "Enough! Ulf, you and Guthorm stay here with Líf and our weapons. Skeggi, Sigird, and I will slip into the Althing."

"What about Brasir?" Sigird asked. "He must be present, but he will draw attention to us."

The youth was right. How could they walk the black-fleshed man through the camps and not be noticed? Brasir's freedom and life were in the balance, but his very presence could ruin his only chance.

Chapter Ten

From the snarls and low growls of the fylgjur, Líf knew they were as frustrated as their people. Fused with the very essence of their humans, the shimmering creatures clearly indicated the men's emotional states.

"He might hide better in the night," Sigird suggested hopefully, when no other idea was offered.

Other than the minor twitch of his jaw, Brasir did not appear angry with this narrow-minded notion of his dark-skinned pigmentation. The boy was young and trying to be helpful, and Brasir was the only black person he'd ever seen.

"The night would draw more suspicion," countered Ottar. "We would appear to be up to something, skulking about the camps after most have retired for the evening."

Brasir strode over to Ottar. "I am a foreigner. There is no denying that fact. So treat me as one." He stuck out his wrists. "Tie me up. Surely giving gifts of living flesh is not uncommon during these treaties."

"Brasir!" Líf uttered his name in dismay. She did not want to see this man once again restrained and led as property among his enemies.

Her brother inclined his head in a sign of respect. Skeggi worked on the bonds while the rest discussed what would happen next. Then they put their precarious plan in motion.

Líf watched Ottar head toward Haugr. Atop Líf's flaming red hair, Thray stood on her hind legs to gain a better view. Even when distance had shrunk the men to the size of ants, the little squirrel was still able to describe the party until they disappeared among the búðir without incident.

"That's that," Thray noted as she slid down to Líf's shoulder. "They are out of my sight."

"They'll be fine," Líf forced herself to affirm.

Nevertheless, Ulf gave her a questioning look. The man had never been comfortable around Líf when she spoke to her invisible creature. Muttering something under his breath, he moved closer to Guthorm, who reclined against a rock, his eyelids sinking lower as his breath deepened.

Líf sat alone, which was perfectly fine with her. Thray was always nearby, and that knowledge fended off the dull pain of solitude. Her siblings' companions did not have to like her, just respect her presence enough to not harass her. Thray would never leave her. She—

Where was Thray? Líf could not spot her fylgja anywhere. The little creature appeared to have wandered off, but that was not like her. When a fylgja was separated from her human, both parties were afflicted with nausea, which increased in intensity until each returned to the other's side. The few exceptions involved individuals who had developed icy, independent personalities. Hervor was close to becoming one of those, but Líf and Thray were inseparable. Where had the squirrel run off to?

"Thray?" Líf called out quietly as she crept around the rocky terrain. "Thray, where are you?"

That's when she heard something. No, not heard; sensed. A sensation of sound that was not quite verbal. There was a glimmer on the ground up ahead. Thray stood at attention, her small body strained by taut muscles. Her entire form was a polished black. Never before had Líf seen the fylgja display so dark a hue.

The rodent did not acknowledge Líf's presence but continued to stare several paces ahead, where a second animal stood stiff and unbending. An owl in a motley of dark blues had locked its unblinking eyes with Thray's.

This was not normal, even for fylgjur interaction. Líf ran to the little squirrel and scooped her into her arms. The rodent became limp as soon as Líf touched her. The second fylgja's trance was also broken. Staring with its large, round eyes, the owl turned its head 180 degrees to expose a second face. This face was bright scarlet, darker than Líf's own hair.

In a burst of hot hues, the owl took wing and released one loud hoot before flying off into the brilliant blue sky.

Líf pulled the squirrel close to her chest and held her in a protective embrace. The small animal's face was still vacant, like the face of someone who had just died. "Thray? Thray, speak to me!"

A moment later, the black creature gasped, her eyes focusing on Líf's worried face. "They know where we are."

"Who?"

The sound of hooves clattered on stone. Líf saw a band of riders making their way toward her. Without hesitation, she turned and ran back to the camp, shouting, "We're found out!"

Ulf and Guthorm were on their feet immediately. They did not worry about the scattered equipment or the pair of picketed horses behind them.

Their weapons were drawn when the riders encircled their position.

Seven, eight, nine. Líf tried to count the riders but stopped when she spied Harekson mounted on a dappled charger. *Wavecutter*'s crewmen were outnumbered, with no chance of escape; still, they were ready to fight.

"They brought themselves a bitch as well," sneered one of the riders, who reached down to grab Líf's locks. Ulf swung his blade and would have severed the man's wrist had the man not retracted his hand.

"We need them alive," Harekson stated, displeased.

Behind him, Hogni's face peered at Líf. So, she thought, the weasel had made it to Haugr.

Harekson continued, "The Althing has begun. Take care. Try not to spill too much blood."

"But we are outside Haugr's grounds," another man pointed out.

"That's why I said not *too much.*"

Líf shot Guthorm an imploring look, hoping they would not try anything unwarranted. With a clatter of discarded iron and steel, Guthorm and Ulf reluctantly gave up their weapons. Once those items were confiscated, one of Harekson's men assisted Líf onto his commander's horse. She knew not to struggle and allowed this grim person to take control.

They would not rape her so near the Althing. Nevertheless, a single backhanded slap by Harekson could damage her face. Líf chose not to look back as she heard the grunts and groans of Ottar's men as they were beaten by Harekson's. There were some things she never wanted to see.

As Líf rode to Haugr in silence, she wondered what had happened to her brother's party. They must have been discovered. How else had Harekson known where to find her? If she were braver, she might have asked him outright; fearing the answer, she kept her tongue in check. In turn, Harekson offered no details of what was to come.

Thray remained quiet in Líf's folded arms. The little fylgja seemed to want to hide from Harekson's snorting boar.

Once in the makeshift town, Líf was taken straight to the Law Rock. Perched upon one of the two carved-out chairs was the man who had to be the Speaker for this Althing. The Lögsögumaður was a rotund, middle-aged fellow. His smile would have been pleasant but for the disfiguring scar where he had lost a bit of his cheek.

The friends around him backed away when they recognized Harekson riding with a woman. Whispers and curious stares followed the pair until Harekson halted at the edge of the circle of men. Handing his weapons to several observers, he helped Líf to the ground. Holding her wrist so tightly that she whimpered, he led Líf before the Speaker.

"I am Erikk Harekson the Wolf," he stated, giving his full birthname and given moniker. "Son of Jarl Harek of Thorinheim. First grandson to King Thorkell. I come before you with important matters that cannot be delayed, even for a night. I ask only that you hear my case. The judgment of it I leave in your worthy hands."

Had Harekson always been so eloquent? Líf wanted to defend herself, but the time was not right. There was a protocol, and she must follow it if she hoped to get a chance to speak.

The Lögsögumaður appeared both shocked and appalled. "This will be permitted. Speak, son of Harek the Jarl."

Harekson inclined his head respectfully. Maintaining his grip on Líf, he spoke loudly so that all around them could hear. "Just shy of two weeks ago, a slave rightfully owned by my father was stolen for a second time. Originally claimed by Jarl Harek, this slave had disappeared over the winter and was thought to have fled afar. Yet he was discovered on Ottar Lothbranson's farm, working alongside his slaves. Within a day of our reclaiming of him, the slave was stolen by the Lothbranson family and smuggled away on their drakkar. A friend of mine, Tord Njalson, was slain during this abduction.

"As Lothbranson and his crew are renowned for their seafaring skill and successful raids, my father thought it wise to send our four skeids after them to force them to return. In the meantime, I was sent to represent my family at the Althing."

"He lies!" bristled Thray. "He wanted to capture us himself but finally realized he couldn't. He was scared and fled. And the ships! They were ordered to sink us!"

Líf was glad that Harekson could not hear what her little fylgja was saying. Although the creature's anger matched her own, if Thray's remarks became known, more ill would result.

Harekson continued, "Hogni, one of my men stationed on a skeid, arrived here earlier today. He reported that all four ships have been destroyed, and that the few captives taken aboard Lothbranson's drakkar are being held hostage. Hogni escaped and came to warn me that Ottar the Untouchable and several of his companions are here at Haugr for purposes I hope are never achieved. They are violent men who show no inclination to obey the common laws of our society. The blood of many of our own people is on their hands."

"And what of the woman?" questioned the plump Speaker. "They are forbidden on these grounds."

A wisp of a smile twitched on Harekson's face. "After Hogni warned me of Ottar's presence, I had my own cohort keep an eye on the surrounding area. We discovered their camp and captured two of Lothbranson's men and this woman, his younger sister, whom he dared bring with him to these hallowed grounds."

Líf knew the men were staring at her with disgust. For once, this had nothing to do with her unusual ability.

"And what of this Ottar Lothbranson?"

"For all I know," Harekson admitted through gritted teeth, "he is here, inside Haugr, as we speak—possibly to seek allies in his maddened reasoning. I have brought this to you, our Lögsögumaður, to judge at your discretion. As my father's representative, I implore you to send the entire Lothbranson family into full outlawry, where they can either flee or risk punishment by dishonorable deaths. I also ask that our slave be returned to us. He is easily recognized, for his flesh is as dark as charred coal."

Before anyone else could further besmirch her family's name, Líf shouted, "I demand my say! I have a right to explain our role in the events that have transpired!"

The slap was so heavy and hard that Líf was flung sideways. Sharp pain pulsed from the five-fingered imprint, and she spat out blood. In a mix of horror and fear, Líf covered her dripping lip and tender cheek with her hands. She turned toward the Speaker, her plea silent.

Harekson rubbed his palm and snarled, "Women have no rights at the Althing. To even dare to presume such is unlawful."

The vile man bent down to pull Líf to her feet. As he did so, she hissed, "Your grandfather will back my brother and yours, you'll see."

"Too bad he does not have final authority here," Harekson sneered as he violently righted Líf.

Her eyes widened as she remembered that a verdict rendered by the Speaker must be honored, even by the king. Every ninth year, when the Althing convened, the people held more power than royalty did.

Where was King Thorkell? If he were just and unprejudiced, wouldn't he convince the Speaker to be the same? Surely her brother had had enough time to present their case to him. And with Princess Thoren's arm ring as proof, the king would back their cause.

Where was Ottar? Líf looked around in desperation, recognizing no faces other than those of Harekson and his crew. She wanted to cry out and speak the truth. She wanted to stall the proceedings until the king arrived.

Harekson must have sensed her rebellious desire and snapped, "Any word from you, and your life will be forfeit."

He peered up at the Speaker. "What say you, Lögsögumaður?"

Without a moment's hesitation, the man in the seat of power proclaimed, "The entirety of the Lothbranson household will forevermore be punished with the state of full outlawry!"

Chapter Eleven

Líf dropped to her knees in dismay. Soil and grime smeared the dull blue of her apron; the chill of the earth seeped through her clothing and skin and slipped into her hugr.

The Speaker was not finished. "They will be given two weeks from tomorrow's morn to settle all debts and vacate this great kingdom. Thenceforth, the magnanimous gods and all men will turn their backs on the Lothbranson family until the age of Ragnarök has begun."

Harekson, still holding Líf's wrist tightly, bowed with appropriate courtesy. Nodding to his men, he gifted the Lögsögumaður with many riches in return for his good service and sound judgment.

Líf was led away from the Law Rock to Thorinheim's búðir. As she approached the large structure that would normally protect their jarl from the elements throughout his stay, Harekson scanned the men milling about the smaller tents surrounding the wooden booth. Neither Guthorm nor Ulf was spotted. What had happened to them? Would Harekson risk being outlawed by ordering the murder of men just outside the perimeter of the Althing? Had their bodies been left to feed the wolves and crows that eternally hungered for the flesh of men? Líf shivered.

"You condemned a family into which you desired to marry," Líf suddenly hissed.

"What I desired," Harekson bellowed, "was a permanent alliance with those of high esteem and rank, not those of ill repute who thieve and murder."

Harekson's tented búðir was modest in comparison to his father's longhouse yet far more luxurious than Líf expected. The tented ceiling was high enough for men to stand under it. Wooden chairs, and even a simple framed bed covered in lush furs from all around Midgard, had been transported for the duration of the Althing. The thick, fluffy, animal-hide rug with black smudges on white was striking, for no creature such as that had ever been found near Thorinheim. It was clear from the careful preparation that the summons to the Althing, though out of season, had been planned ahead of time. Had her family been too preoccupied preparing for their own departure to hear word of this unusual occurrence?

Once at the center of the tent, Harekson released her, and she collapsed onto the blanketed floor. "You will stay here until your brother claims you. If he cares for you so much, he will return what is mine." He hesitated by the entrance flap that covered the open doorway. "Until then, I will send you food and drink. You are not an outlaw yet."

The foul man left Líf alone, but she knew she would not be allowed to leave. She did not have to wait for Thray's confirmation to be sure that guards were positioned outside the búðir. She was a captive, just like Brasir had been. Her freeman status had been revoked.

She waited patiently for whatever was to occur. Outside, the voices of men's fierce banter mixed with the aroma of cooking meat. They were discussing her and what would become of her if Ottar did not show up.

As far as she was concerned, for a woman of her age there were worse punishments than full outlawry. Líf tucked her knees to her chest while Thray scurried around the room with a fiery agitation.

New voices arose, louder and certainly more determined. A hand appeared at the opening, gripped the flap, yet paused as the conversation outside continued.

Thray froze in mid step. Her swirling eyes were fixed on the beringed fingers of the person about to enter.

Finally, a tall man appeared. Although elderly, his presence was commanding. "Come, girl," he said without stepping over the threshold. "Walk me to my búðir."

As Líf rose to her feet, Thray scurried up her back and jumped to her perch. The pair obediently approached the tall man. His hair, once surprisingly dark but now bleached by the years, was worn in heavily beaded braids. His thin lips were pursed, but his eyes were still fierce and keen. He gripped Líf's extended arm, not for balance but as acceptance of his gracious offer.

Stepping outside, Líf observed the king's guard delivering gifts to Harekson's men for their diligent service. They eyed Líf with a curious suspicion even as they counted the heavy ingots in their arms. Harekson was not among them.

"My grandson told me you were here." King Thorkell spoke with a voice that resonated with a strength uncommon for one his age. A bear fylgja trod nearby. Patches of iridescent fur had sloughed off over the years, exposing glimmering skin. Large, drooping lips revealed metallic teeth.

Líf concentrated on preventing her wary eyes from darting about in search of her jarl's heir. She felt terror creep up her spine even as the godlike man led her around the recently raised buildings of the temporary town.

Up ahead rose another massive, tented booth, so large that it put Harekson's to shame. King Thorkell neither smiled nor spoke as he strode to his current place of residence. His warriors and attendees numbered well into the double digits, an impressive spectacle for any Thing. But this was the Althing. This was the blessed time when their kingdom's law was solidified. This is where Líf's future had been forever altered.

Several pale-skinned slaves opened the tent flaps as the king entered. Líf followed stiffly behind. Many men were seated inside. Among them, at last, were faces she recognized.

Ottar looked at her, his features contorted in a mix of pain and relief. He must have heard about the decree. The sight of her brother's conflicted state caused Líf's stomach to knot up. It had not been her fault, not entirely; yet she still felt wretched. She wanted to call out to her older sibling, hoping for his protective assurance, but she swallowed the words. This was their king's búðir. And they were simply servants who relied on his good will.

Brasir sat nearby along with Skeggi and young Sigird. They had come here to see their king, suffering many hardships during their travels—but all for naught. Líf could not bear to look any one of them in the eye. She cast her own eyes down to the floor.

King Thorkell removed his arm from Líf's. "See to your brother, girl." His every statement was regarded as a command. The wizened ruler took a seat across the room as Líf slunk to Ottar's side.

Never having been in the presence of a king, she remained silent. Instead, Ottar had the audacity to speak next. "What can be done?"

"Very little," admitted King Thorkell solemnly. "I cannot change what the Lögsögumaður has decreed. Not as it currently stands. You and all your kin will be labeled outlaw and must leave the kingdom. The slave, Brasir, is still the property of my son-in-law, Harek."

Líf glanced at the black-fleshed man. Brasir remained focused on Thorkell as the ruler continued to speak. "I will not make a move against my daughter's husband. Not unless"—and here Thorkell looked at the familiar arm ring he had just received—"viable proof is provided that this invisible illness afflicting the hamingjur is real."

"What do you recommend?" Ottar asked earnestly. His voice was strangely clear, despite the emotional strain.

"You must flee with the slave. Leave the confines of Midgard. Do whatever it takes to bring me proof. Then, and only then, will I free the slave and support further expeditions to discover a solution.

"In the meantime," Thorkell continued, smiling kindly, "I can accept your children as wards in my house. I will raise them in protective safety until you succeed, assuming that you do. Your children will live in my household and will thus be protected from the Lögsögumaður's decree. You will not have to fear for their survival as you travel through the worlds beyond our own. Out of respect for my daughter, that much I will do."

Ottar appeared humbled and relieved.

"What of your safety, Grandfather?" Sigird's voice was tentative.

The king's face was stern as he growled out, "I am descended from Odin and rule these lands. I cannot be punished, not even by those who *overextend* their power every ninth year." A smoldering blaze flared deep within Thorkell's pale eyes.

He spoke directly to Ottar. "Head to Jarlbörg tomorrow. I will gift you supplies and sufficient wealth to hire more men for your crew. Hand over your children to my wife. She will know the truth of this act by these." The king reached his knobby fingers into one of his coffers and slowly removed a necklace of such beauty that Líf gasped. Each polished, circular gemstone sparkled in the light; together, they displayed a remarkable array of colors.

Thorkell continued, "My wife wears its twin. The craftsmanship is rare and seldom seen, found only in the sea swallowed by land. She will know and understand. But that is all I can do without upsetting the way of things. I cannot go with you, for there are dismal happenings afflicting my kingdom. This Althing was called for those very reasons. I must remain here while you make preparations in my fair city. When ready, seek the völva. She will send you on the correct path toward your destiny."

"Where is she?" Ottar inquired.

"The völva lives on the cusp of civilization. You must meet her at Spákona, the place of unbridled sight."

"So the tales are true," muttered Skeggi glumly.

The oafish man's remarks were overheard, and the king responded. "All tales have their origin, one that is fused with fact." He paused before issuing a final warning. "Be wary of those whom you trust, Ottar, son of Lothbran, and be swift to make ready. Others will come for you."

After precious wealth was distributed among them for their journey to the sea, they were dismissed. Outside the king's tent, a set of rested horses stood ready. With them were the horribly battered forms of Guthorm and Ulf. The latter had massive swelling around his jawline, likely from shattered teeth. The taller man was stooped over a wash barrel rinsing clumps of blood from his tinted hair. At least they were alive. Harekson had some sense of mercy after all.

The ride back to Jarlbörg was almost as harrowing as the race toward Haugr. They were only given two weeks' head start, a week shy of what was normal, and time would flicker past in the blink of an eye. Preparing a damaged ship for sail would consume much of it, so every day spent returning to *Wavecutter* was one day fewer in which to prepare their exodus.

"Hervor will have remained offshore," mumbled Ulf in a distorted blend of words and pained sounds as they neared their destination. "She would not stay in sight of Jarlbörg if the drakkar were at risk. How...?" He broke off, no longer able to force out words, as he moaned and caressed his inflamed face.

Guthorm came to his aid. "How will we discover her whereabouts in time for us do what must be done? The grace period will be up sooner than any of us would like."

Ottar, who was riding in front, said, "I know Hervor's mind better than any other. I will find her."

"In time, I hope," Ulf managed to mutter under his breath.

When Jarlbörg came into Líf's sight, so did a familiar winged presence. "It's *her*!" Thray chattered. Her nose twitched rapidly as she stared at the glimmering goshawk. The raptor circled overhead several times, as if searching for choice prey, before slipping away toward the horizon.

Wavecutter was audaciously sailing into the port. The sight of a foreign drakkar had drawn the attention of more than the travel-weary party. A fair-sized crowd of onlookers was appraising the vibrantly painted warship that moored right next to *Squallsubduer*.

Before the crew had fully tied down the ship, Hervor leaped onto the pier and strode toward her brother. As she passed by, the locals backed warily away from the fierce shieldmaiden.

Ottar smiled at his older sister while Skeggi asked, "How did you know we were coming back?"

Hervor, as always, was bluntly honest. "I sensed it a few hours ago, deep in my gut."

Both Líf and Thray scanned the overcast sky and caught sight of the gray goshawk's soaring silhouette. If humanity only understood how closely their fylgjur interacted with them, how connected they were, much of what seemed inexplicable would become clear. At least Líf understood. She scratched the top of the squirrel's tiny head.

Líf kept out of the way as the hurried preparations began. She said her tear-filled goodbyes to Gratti and Budvar. Though the younger boy was reluctant to see his father leave, his older brother appeared to have changed since the frightening confrontation on the ship. Budvar obeyed his parent's commands without question. Like his father, he did not cry when they parted. Gratti followed his brother's lead and snuffled far less than he might have done otherwise.

As men ran about loading supplies and repairing the pockmarked ship, Líf chose to watch people. She ignored the determined crew, of whom she would surely tire once back on *Wavecutter*'s ever-shifting deck. Instead, she observed the local folk—mothers, farmers, fishermen, and even slaves.

Most were indistinguishable from the people in her home village of Thorinheim. They moved, talked, and acted similarly, and she could easily imagine how the pattern of their lives would repeat, day after day, year after year. Yet two people stood out; even Thray took an interest.

Seated on empty barrels, the pair talked in low voices as they observed the Lothbranson longship. One slouched low as if to hide his natural height. His face had a feral look that was matched by the expression on his fylgja's muzzle. The she-wolf's lip twitched agitatedly every time her person spoke. Her fur maintained its oily shimmer but would flare up in warm hues when she turned her lethal interest toward a particular crewman.

The second man was of smaller stature. His hair was as dark as his eyes, which were remarkably different, for they appeared thin, stretched, almost annular. Hooded, the eyes brimmed with life. He wore foreign clothes: a caftan trimmed with silk that covered extremely baggy pants. His fylgja, the size of a large housecat, was also foreign to these parts. Her face retained markings of a different color from the rest of her form. Those spots created what appeared to be eyebrows and matched the color of her cheek patches.

"Do you know what she is?" Líf asked.

The squirrel replied in a hushed tone, "You know we share the same limits to our knowledge."

"Can't you ask her?"

"Can't you ask *him*?" retorted Thray sarcastically.

As if it had overheard, the strange fylgja turned and began to trundle toward them. Thray bristled in Líf's arms. Watching the squirrel, the other creature stopped and sat down in a nonthreatening position.

"Put me down, Líf," Thray whispered. "Back away and be quiet. I will commune with her."

Líf did as she was told, and in a matter of moments, the tiny creature came scurrying back. "Have them come with us."

"Come with us?"

"Your brother is looking for more crewmen, is he not?"

"You're keeping something from me. That's not like you. What is it?"

Thray's eyes sparkled more than any other part of her body, yet she refused to say more.

The two men had turned towards Líf and were watching her apparently one-sided conversation. She shivered just before she felt the sharp pain from Thray's insistent nip. Trusting her fylgja, Líf spotted Ottar, still recruiting sailors for *Wavecutter*.

Einar was entreating him, "I promise I will pull my weight."

"I do respect you and what you did for my son," Ottar admitted. "I am sure we will have use for you. Now, that leaves at least one more."

"You should hire them," Líf pointed to the men still seated on the wooden barrels.

Ottar looked curiously at the pair. "How do you know they are for hire?"

"I—" Líf hesitated and dug one of her boots into the ground. "Have you asked them yet?"

"I think it is very clear what I have been doing here for the past few days."

Ottar had a point. Still, Líf persisted. "One has a wolf fylgja. That means he is a natural-born warrior. We might need one if we leave Midgard."

"A wolf?" That was of interest to Ottar. "One skilled in battle would be beneficial, yet that is no guarantee of his character."

"I know," agreed Líf. "But I am telling you to hire them."

Ottar stared at her. "For a moment," he said, "I thought I was listening to Hervor. Very well. I will talk with them."

Two days later, *Wavecutter* took to the waters once again, this time with a full crew. Among them were the mysterious men Thray had backed and the enemy-turned-ally, Einar. Líf watched the mainland recede as she gripped the longship's side tightly. Her nausea had returned to take control. Once again, she was sailing away from the comfort of the familiar toward a far less certain fate.

The Guardian's Speaker

Volume Three

Epigraph

Thence come the maidens mighty in wisdom,
Three from the dwelling down 'neath the tree;
Urth is one named, Verthandi the next,--
On the wood they scored,-- and Skuld the third.
Laws they made there, and life allotted
To the sons of men, and set their fates.

Völuspá - The Prophecy of the Seeress

CHAPTER ONE

It takes great courage to face one's nemesis, but Líf was not born with courage. She had always viewed the sea as her greatest foe. The fluid surface and ever-changing motion that beckoned her people had stirred in her only relentless nausea.

She had therefore never desired to sail across the vast waters; but the Norns had other intentions. Although Líf preferred to imagine these female beings as three cruel shepherdesses who steered humanity and all living things onto whatever paths they saw fit, she admitted that was a naive fantasy. In truth, the Norns scored one's fate into Yggdrasil's roots, solidifying one's future. They knew the length of one's life and where it would end. Even the gods bowed to their will.

Wherever her path might take her, Líf had begun to realize that her greatest nemesis was not the sea with its rolling waves, but something far more foul: the men who had outlawed her family from their kingdom and the protection of civilization—men like Harekson, who had accused her and her siblings of wrongdoing while failing to realize that something far more important was at stake than the theft of property from his father, Jarl Harek.

True, Líf's family had stolen their jarl's slave—a man by the name of Brasir—not because they wanted the slave but because they believed in the man's gift. Brasir claimed that he could see hamingjur, the female presences that accompany each person and are manifestations of personal luck. They are one of the four parts of self that comprise a human. The others are hamr, the physical body; hugr, the soul and source of all thought; and Líf's favorite, fylgjur, the guardian spirits. Hamingjur are so powerful that they can protect against evil or cause one's downfall.

Brasir had warned Líf that a plague was destroying hamingjur. If someone's hamingja died, shortly afterward the person did too. If this were allowed to continue, all humanity would cease to exist. Brasir had been on a quest to discover the cause when he had been taken captive during last summer's raiding season. Belief in Brasir and his mission to save hamingjur had set Líf and her family on their current path. Their faith in him was great, for Brasir was the only person who had ever claimed to be able to see hamingjur. To everyone else, they were invisible.

No wonder people had not believed the enslaved man. Why would they? Clearly, Brasir was lying, spinning a wild tale so he would be freed to continue his "quest." That was what Líf's siblings had originally thought. That is what Líf would have thought, too, had she not been born with a similar gift.

Líf could see fylgjur. Like hamingjur, they were female, but fylgjur took the form of animals. The specific type of animal was dependent upon the personality of the individual person. Líf's fylgja was a squirrel whom she called Thray—who was currently nestled into a ball in the center of the young woman's lap.

Glistening in oily sheens, Thray's fur took on various hues that represented the squirrel's own emotions and thus, somehow, Líf's. Just as the small rodent's body glinted a dark green, Líf sprang to the side of the longship and threw up her meager lunch.

"She's the reason," a voice behind a nearby crate grunted. The speaker was one of the two men that Thray had urged Líf to persuade her brother, Ottar, to hire for their journey north toward the frigid wasteland.

The man, whose average height and strange, oval eyes indicated foreign blood, was perched watchfully next to his far more dangerous-looking comrade, whose scowl held a feral quality. Their fylgjur sat next to them. The speaker's strange, almost felid creature had separate patches of color over its eyes and cheeks, as well as rings around its tail. The rest of its body displayed iridescent fur, which indicated that at present the animal was calm and content. The other fylgja was a large wolf whose hues constantly flickered in hot shades. Líf feared that creature and her human. That same pairing had convinced Ottar to take the two men on as hired hands.

To have a wolf as one's fylgja meant that you were a great warrior. Wherever the longship *Wavecutter* was headed, they would need every fighter they could get. Líf trusted Thray's judgment. And Ottar trusted Líf's.

Líf was closer to Ottar than to their older sister, Hervor, who at present was commanding the crew with a sharp tirade of orders. Although Líf was the youngest, neither of her siblings had ever outwardly questioned her ability to see and communicate with fylgjur.

For this she was grateful. Of course, not everyone on the ship had the same blind faith. Líf was used to others' constant doubt and distrust and tried to ignore their skeptical eyes. But these two newcomers made her skin crawl, and she shrank under their gaze.

Although she had stopped dry-heaving, she was too drained to move away from the side of the ship. Just standing might make her need to retch again, and over the past few weeks of travel, Thray had grown increasingly unsympathetic to Líf's constant sickness.

In fact, for the first time in Líf's life, her little fylgja preferred the company of others. Instead of constantly perching upon Líf's slender shoulders, the squirrel would scamper to the top of the mast, where she and Hervor's goshawk appeared to engage in conversations. On other occasions, she would commune with the other fylgjur crowded throughout the ship, especially the strange beast with the ringed tail.

At first, Líf had pestered Thray to find out what sort of creature the new fylgja was, but the squirrel only blinked at her and emitted a low growl of discontent. It was not Líf's place to interact with other people's fylgjur or even to acknowledge another's guardian spirit. This she understood and normally accepted, but now her own fylgja no longer appeared to want to be near her.

What had she done, other than constantly feel ill during this dreadful journey? Líf tried to apologize to Thray for making the squirrel nauseous. The pair were so intimately bound that they shared emotions and even physical sensations. Surely, Thray understood that Líf was trying to fight the endless seasickness.

Still, the squirrel had sharply remarked, "Try harder," before she scurried away.

Maybe it was good for them to spend some time apart. They were both confined to the rocking vessel, so it was impossible to be separated for long. There just wasn't space to be alone or a place to hide from all those dubious eyes.

A shiver ran down Líf's spine. Or was it a tremor? She was exhausted from her body's constant upheaval and upheaving. On the other hand, it was far too frigid for their short spring. She forced herself to look at the water. Slabs of ice bobbed about on the surface when they should have long since melted. It was common for chunks of ice to break off from the great glaciers that dominated the northern lands when the weather began to warm. But strangely, this year the cold was increasing.

Everything around them screamed silently of ice and snow, from the freezing spray that stung Líf's face each time the longship tackled a large wave, to the raw air that hit her lungs like a backhanded slap with every inhale and sent puffs of white steam around her face with each exhale. Their entire environment boasted of oncoming winter, and with it, the threat that their ship would be trapped in the massing ice.

How could that be? Everything had changed. Nothing was as it should be—especially for Líf, who was neither familiar with nor adept at voyaging by sea. Her single decision to free a slave had ruined her life. Would it save everyone else's?

Líf quietly watched her siblings running their ship. At the prow, her proud and clearly respected sister effortlessly commanded the vessel. With each order, Hervor's voice boomed out in a puff of pale air. Tall—as were most of their people—and blond with keen grey eyes, nothing occurred on *Wavecutter* that Hervor did not notice.

With her modified throwing axe nocked in the loop on her belt and the hilt of her seax dagger peeping out from the top of a fur-trimmed boot, Hervor appeared to be a living embodiment of the famous shieldmaidens from age-old tales.

Lif wished she were more like her sister. A female warrior would serve a clear purpose in their upcoming trials. Lif, with her petite stature and flaming red hair, was the absolute opposite of her oldest sibling in every way, including personality.

Ottar stood at the stern, where he was in charge of the steering oar. He mirrored his older sister in height and physical attributes, including his blond hair. Yet his blue eyes remained calm and compassionate, while Hervor's were often judgmental and remorseless. After their father died, Ottar, as the only son, he had become the head of the family. Technically, all family decisions were made by him, including hiring a crew, engaging in raids, and accumulating wealth. A man was entitled to a number of legal rights, privileges, and advantages to which a woman was not. Yet here, in the middle of the vast waters, far from the mainland and its male-dominated laws, Hervor held her power with an absolute and unchallengeable authority.

"Tie it tighter!" Hervor ordered harshly. "We cannot afford the rigging to loosen during the next bout of storms."

"More storms?" Lif moaned in dismay as a youth hurried to comply with the shieldmaiden's demands.

Thirteen-year-old Sigird was the only person younger than Lif on the longship. Despite his age, she thought the lanky, dark-haired boy was far braver than she was. As the youngest living son of Jarl Harek, he knew he would never receive anything of worth from his father, for the first-born son would inherit the family wealth and the title of jarl of their trading town of Thorinheim. Sigird would have to make a name for himself. But in choosing to aid the Lothbransons, he had turned his back upon his father and brothers, including Harekson, the eldest. And it was Harekson who, if he found Sigird, would kill him for this betrayal.

Lif looked kindly on the shy and gawky youth and knew that her siblings did so as well. Had it not been for Sigird and the message he had brought from his mother, Princess Thoren, *Wavecutter* would not have been ready in time for them to flee following the family's outlawry. Once sentenced, they had only two weeks to leave port. After that time, their entire family could be hunted down and slain on the mainland without ever being avenged. Outlaws were not allowed to be housed or cared for by anyone within the kingdom. If an honorable man died while an outlaw, he would be barred from Valhalla. Of everyone she had known, it was Ottar who deserved to be welcomed into Odin's hall to feast and prepare for the end of times. Hervor would have been, as well, had she been born a male. Such was the life of an outlaw; the only worse punishment was the rite of the Blood Eagle.

This was all Harekson's fault. He had used a legal loophole to prevent his grandfather, King Thorkell, from giving Brasir his freedom. Once Brasir was declared free, there could be no retribution for having stolen him. A bóndi, a freeman, could go where he liked. He served only the king and the jarl who oversaw the territory in which he settled. Brasir could have completed his journey without risking anyone's life, including his own.

Instead, Harekson had taken the opportunity to inflict the horrible punishment of full outlawry upon the Lothbransons and besmirch their unblemished names. Brasir's life was still threatened, as were the lives of all of Líf's family. Although King Thorkell had made Ottar's sons his wards under his protection, even he could not undo what had been decreed at the Althing. The Lothbransons could never return home unless they proved that Brasir's story was true. This was the reason Líf's family would accompany Brasir on his quest. This was the motivation for all of them to ensure that the mission was successful.

Líf continued to observe her brother. Of the three siblings, he was the one who stood to lose the most, for if they failed, he would never see his sons again. That would be unacceptable for any father, especially Ottar. He would do whatever it took to succeed.

Alas, if only everyone aboard felt the same way. *Wavecutter*'s crew was a mix of those who knew and trusted the Lothbransons and those who were paid to be there. There had been no time to assemble their full crew before leaving Thorinheim, and some sailors had died during the battles at sea. Forced to flee the mainland, Ottar had had to hire strangers to man the oars for their odyssey. Mercenaries were not reliable; once their pay ceased, so would their loyalty. How long would these men continue a journey they cared little about? How much would they risk in the face of adversity? If it came down to it, would they sacrifice their lives for Brasir's success?

As the longship headed into the unknown, these questions weighed heavily on Líf, especially those surrounding the two hired hands, who continued to watch the young woman with veiled expressions.

Behind her, Líf heard the foreign man's voice once again. "Yes. She *is* the reason."

CHAPTER TWO

The wind picked up, causing the sail to snap and whipping sea spray over the thigh-high wooden siding. Damp and cold, Líf shivered. Had she ever been more miserable? In truth, she had; but at the moment, all her thoughts were focused upon this abysmal trip and the relentless, bitterly cold waters.

"Take this, Lingy." The massive form of Skeggi, Ottar's oafish friend, stooped over her. In his meaty hand was a blanket that was surprisingly dry. As much as Líf despised that nickname, she was grateful for the offering.

Skeggi wasn't really bad, though he was a constant irritant from her childhood. Although Líf preferred his absence, it was actually Hervor who was forced to deal with the majority of his antics. Everyone but Skeggi knew not to push the shieldmaiden's temper, but he could not stop himself. As a result, most of his collection of scars came from Hervor's wrath, not from the summer raids.

"You can sit here if you like," Líf said, then realized what she had done. Usually she avoided the ruddy-haired man, but somehow, having him nearby alleviated a little of the discomfort caused by the stares of the pair behind her.

At least, if those mercenaries said something derogatory about her within earshot of Skeggi, he would defend her without a moment's pause. Crewmen rarely killed one another at sea, but it was not unheard of. And Skeggi, with his dense musculature and sturdy build, clearly outweighed both men. If only his personality matched his looks, maybe Hervor would respect the besotted fellow.

Skeggi crouched next to her and asked in a low voice, "Having trouble?" Of course, he might have been referring to Líf's seasickness, but she preferred to think he could sense the undercurrent of suspicion and fear the strangers emitted.

A portly seagull fylgja perched on Skeggi's shoulder and fluffed up her feathers against the coming storm. When the sailor wiped off the brine that had collected on his neck, his hand passed right through the fylgja as if she were nothing.

Although fylgjur could contact their people if they so chose, people were unable to interact with their guardians. This was the case for every person but Líf. Somehow, her gift made all fylgjur tangible to her. This also made living on the cramped ship close to impossible.

"I...um—" Líf glanced over at the men, who were still watching her. What if they heard her? Skeggi would not always be around.

"Skeggi, quit loitering and do something of use!" Hervor's voice broke in from the prow. "All hands at the ready! Here comes the storm."

No sooner had the shieldmaiden shouted her orders than thunder pealed in the distance. The sky darkened, the waves beat against the side of the ship, and the gale clawed at cloaks and rigging.

Líf clung to the blanket, pulling it tightly down over her head. Soon, snow began to fall, lightly at first and then with relentless force. Hooding her face, Líf's view of the world around her vanished. She heard the grunts and groans of men as they struggled to keep the longship on the safest course. She felt *Wavecutter* bucking over the waves and fought to keep her own balance.

Suddenly, something slipped under her protective cloth. Thray's sharp claws pulled her little form onto Líf's lap. As the tiny rodent curled up against her, Líf understood that all was right between them if only for the moment. They stayed that way well into the night until at last the storm abated.

"Land! Land on the horizon!"

The shouts of Ulf the Short woke Líf and the rest of the exhausted crew. Líf quickly pulled off her blanket, causing her mess of red hair to temporarily block her sight before she could tame the knotted locks. Far in the distance, there was a smudge of haze that might be land.

Hervor had already pulled out her sun stones and was peering at the sky through the murky crystals. "The direction is true. That should be Argr's Fjord up ahead. We will camp on solid ground tonight."

The crew cheered; Líf was not the only one eager to stand upon soil and sand. Shortly after noon, their wishes came true. Hervor had steered *Wavecutter* well into the fjord until the waters narrowed and ice thickened upon the surface. Once the longship was anchored, the men waded to shore. Many jumped into the frigid waters without a moment's hesitation.

Líf, already terribly cold from the storm the night before, stood nervously next to the railing. Although she could swim well enough and the water was not too deep, the thought of plunging into that cold liquid was more than disconcerting.

A tall form emerged from the shore and the line of fires sputtering into existence. The only man with skin of black flesh had doubled back and waded into the frigid water, followed by a massive bear fylgja. He waved to her and said, "Jump. I will catch you."

For an unmarried woman to leap into the arms of an unrelated male was unquestionably improper. Yet this was no ordinary man. This was Brasir, the slave she had freed and the reason for their journey to this uninhabited wasteland. Over the winter, when he had lived with her family in secret, Líf and her siblings had developed a special bond with him. There was a trust and a connection that was stronger than most.

After taking a breath and checking that Thray had a strong grip, Líf leaped into Brasir's arms. The man kept most of her body out of the water before depositing her on the shore. Then, without another word, he headed off to help unload cargo near their burgeoning camp. Though several crewmen cast distasteful looks at Líf, no one said anything. She moved over to a fire tended by Guthorm Blood Cheeks. He might not be warm toward her, but neither was he cruel.

Guthorm's head wound had healed, leaving a nasty scar. The sight of it prompted Líf to hide her own scar by covering that part of her forehead with her hair. Guthorm cast her a long look, then nodded to a set of blankets drying on the ground. She took a seat and waited while those around her completed their tasks.

After they had had a chance to dry off, a number of men, including Guthorm, left to hunt wild game. His arm was still bandaged from an arrow wound, but that did not deter him. Their people were accustomed to harsh conditions. There was little hope of finding anything at that time of day, but it allowed the crew a chance to move about freely on solid ground.

Others stayed near camp to make plans for the next leg of their travels. Their destination, Spákona, was three days upriver. There they would consult Völva Gunhild, the seeress, about where to seek their answers.

The pair of mysterious mercenaries had been gone for some time when Thray's sharp voice alerted Líf of their return. "They're back!"

The men carried large bundles of wood and then dropped some off at each campfire, the last one being Líf's. While the man with the wolf fylgja stoked the flames, the other cocked his head and looked at her blatantly, as did his strange fylgja.

His audacity made Líf's skin crawl. It was almost as if the man had a hunger, but not for flesh. In Thorinheim, she could have avoided such a person. But that was impossible here. Whatever problem these men had, it would not be solved by fleeing them. She and they were on the same journey, tethered to one another by the borders of the ship.

"Do you have a problem with me?" Líf snapped with unusual ferocity.

A smile broke across the shorter fellow's face. "Is it right what they say about you? Can you really talk to fylgjur?"

Though it was true, Líf had never spoken of it in public, especially not to a stranger. She was not about to start now.

When she failed to respond, he continued calmly, "I met another woman once who shared the same gift. A völva from my birth town."

Another? Were there others? Líf had always wondered if anyone else shared her…gift. "And where is that?"

The man laughed softly. "No, you cannot meet her, for she is long dead. But I remember she told me mine was a lesser panda. Is it true? I have never seen such a thing, but I was told that she is beautiful."

Líf had not heard of that creature. She glanced down at the strange, felid-like fylgja who was grooming her left paw. "She is."

The man moved closer to Líf and squatted, his hooded eyes shining with curiosity. "Can you describe her?"

"She looks a little like a cat or a fox, one small enough that you could pick her up in your arms. There are distinctive markings above her eyes and on her cheeks, and rings about her tail. Like all fylgjur, she shimmers in iridescent colors. She—" Líf paused. "I'm sorry. I'm bad at this. I have never described one before."

"Thank you," the man said as he stood up. "My name is Roden, and this is Úlfor." He gestured to his roguish companion. "He doesn't speak much, so I do the talking for both of us. This works quite well, for I like to talk, and he, to listen."

"I've never met a true mercenary before," admitted Líf. She wondered if she should keep talking with these unfamiliar men. Yet they were no longer constrained by civilized society, so why should she consider herself to be? Choosing curiosity over propriety, she inquired, "Why do you do it?"

"My father was Rus," explained Roden. He dragged over an empty barrel that had held pickled herring. It had been tossed overboard to be cleaned on the chance they could restock during their travels, but it would now serve as a temporary seat. Roden seemed quite amenable to conversing with another person.

"A Rus?" Líf echoed. She knew that a number of her own ancestors had ventured east and mixed their blood with the rougher natives. Their descendants were known as Rus.

"Yes." Roden smiled while Úlfor stood silently behind him. "My mother was his slave. She was traded from the land that is as far east as one can go. Her entire life was spent in service to him, and I am the result. I, too, was a slave for half my life, until my father freed me upon his deathbed. It was the only gift he ever gave me and the most valuable one that I could have ever received. I serve no master but myself, and I will never serve another again. That is my vow."

"Is there honor in such a life?" Líf genuinely wanted to know.

"Is there honor in being an outlaw?"

The counter question startled Líf so much that she stood up and went to find her siblings. The men watched her go, making no effort to stop her. Líf decided that she really did not like them or their kind.

Hervor was not present, for she was leading one of the hunting parties. Ottar was nowhere to be seen, though he was certainly somewhere near the camp, as it was his duty to be. She would have to find him later.

"They did not mean it as an insult," noted Thray, who was at that moment the more levelheaded of the two.

"Then why say it?"

"You insulted them."

"I did *what?*" Líf snapped, annoyed. She trudged into the surrounding forest. The snowfall was only a few inches deep, yet her hem dragged in the frozen particles. She intended to go only far enough from the chatter of men to relieve herself in private for the first time in weeks. In those few moments, she briefly felt joy.

Above her, a flock of crows cawed as they soared northward. Thray watched them warily, for such birds were barometers of death. Clearly unnerved, the shimmering squirrel peered around in fear.

"What's wrong with you?" Líf asked, a tremor in her voice.

Thray did not reply but continued to swivel her head about.

Whenever Líf's fylgja became frazzled, so did she. Once again, she asked, "Thray?"

Suddenly the squirrel leaped off her shoulder and bounded over the snow, only to stop and sniff at a discolored patch. Líf followed slowly and bent down to look at what had caused the fylgja's fur to darken. Crimson splattered a strip of snow. Blood.

Jumping back, Líf looked around. A number of tracks led away from camp. Had a hunting party shot an animal? Were they tracking the poor thing to finish it off?

"Only boots, Líf," stated Thray as if knowing Líf's thoughts.

The rodent was correct; there were no paw prints or hoof marks.

"We should return to camp," Thray warned.

"What if something is wrong?" Líf asked. "Someone could be hurt."

"We are not fighters, Líf," countered the squirrel. "Send someone else."

Even though she knew her fylgja was right, Líf ignored the little creature's pleas and followed the footprints into the forest. The red splatters increased, clear markers of the direction of the injured fellow.

Soon, voices could be heard up ahead. Although Líf was unable to recognize the speakers, she was not overly concerned, for there were many of the crew with whom she was still unfamiliar, many to whom she had not said a word during this entire journey.

Approaching cautiously, she hid behind a cluster of pine trees. A dozen or more men were grouped around a corpse. Líf recognized only two: the dead man on the ground and the one with a sword to his throat.

A burly fellow seemed to be in charge. "I still haven't heard anything of worth. Send him after his friend."

"No, no," begged the captive. "What do you want? I will tell you, but I need to know what you want."

The leader of the band guffawed. "Isn't it obvious? Why is there a warship moored in the fjord? Why travel to the north? There is nothing here. No village to plunder. No city to impregnate. Tell me why. And then tell me how I can benefit from this knowledge."

"It's something to do with hamingjur. I don't fully understand. I signed on for the pay."

The coward admitted what he knew without hesitation. Líf was aghast but became even more so after hearing what he said next. "We are led by the Lothbranson family. They have been outlawed, and this has something to do with changing that verdict."

"Outlaws?" The leader lifted his head, and Líf thought she saw a trace of a smile. As he turned and walked away from the captive, those holding the spineless fellow slit his throat and left his corpse next to its neighbor.

Without a backward glance, the brute shouted an order. "I want their heads! All of them!"

Chapter Three

Lif backed away from the vandals. Just when she was sure she had moved out of sight, someone grabbed her from behind. The sudden action caused her to fall forward, and the man fell on top of her.

Flashes of the vile night in the forest outside Thorinheim flooded her mind. She pictured the faces of the men who had tried to rape her and remembered crying out as she struggled to crawl away.

Her offender grabbed her dress and was pulling her back to him. Clawing at the snow in front of her, Lif's hand touched something hard. In a fit of pure, fear-driven instinct, she spun round and slammed the stone into the man's face. There was a sickening crunch. Immediately she was released.

Without pausing, Lif lurched to her feet and took off toward the camp, calling for help as she ran. Before she reached the camp's perimeter, a number of the crew approached, but she sped past them.

Breathing heavily, tears pouring from her eyes, she was barely able to answer her brother's questions. "There were about twelve of them. They killed two of our men. One told them we were outlaws. They know about us. They are coming for our heads."

"I want those men found before they find us," Ottar ordered. "We can't risk them contacting others." He assisted Lif to one of the central fires. "Skeggi, find Hervor's party. Warn her."

"Of course," Skeggi uttered, then grabbed his two-handed broadaxe and disappeared into the woods.

Lif trembled as she sank onto a blanket spread on the ground. Looking down, she realized that she was bleeding; her right hand was coated in red. She cried out.

Ottar carefully wiped away the crusting residue only to expose an old scar. "It's not your blood," he reassured her.

"What?" Lif blinked. There was so much blood. It had to be hers.

Ottar took a long, slow breath. "It's not your blood, Líf."

"That man...." Líf continued to tremble. "The rock crushed his head." Suddenly she inhaled sharply. "I...I killed someone! Ottar, I killed someone. What if he was one of ours? I never looked. I just assumed. I *killed* someone." She shook with waves of uncontrollable fear, the memory of assault, the sickening crunch of a shattering skull. Over and over, again and again. Overwhelmed by emotions, Líf was unaware of Ottar's attempt to soothe her.

Thray finally got her attention. "Be sharp now, Líf. We have captives."

There were shouts and yells as a man was brutally dragged into camp, protesting wildly. Líf recognized the vandals' leader. The man glared madly about. His serpent fylgja hissed and snapped at the other guardian spirits.

"Is he the only one?" Ottar asked sternly.

Guthorm and Úlfor were restraining the brute. Guthorm spoke. "Many of them were killed in the fight. Those who resisted died. One or two may have fled. We have several men searching for them. We found the corpse of the one your sister killed."

The captive spotted Líf and snarled, "My hugr is to be stripped away because of a scrawny cunt!"

Ottar took a step closer to the fellow. "I would watch what you say about my sister. You were the one who threatened us."

"As is my right," countered the captive. "Do you know how much the heads of outlaws bring these days? The pay is good and *just*."

Ottar's jaw twitched. Hearing those words affirmed the reality of their predicament. There was nothing wrong with hunting down outlaws for pay. For many men, it was their livelihood.

"Well," began the male Lothbranson, "I am sorry our paths had to cross as they did."

"I'm not," hissed Hervor. Her party had just returned. Her left shoulder bled from a wound, and her face was splattered with red. She turned to Ottar. "We dropped the last one a mile upriver." Crimson droplets slipped off the edge of her axe as she cast the captive a look of disgust. Still speaking to her brother, she added, "I will let you have this one."

Ottar shook his head. "There is no reason—"

The captive sputtered out blood, and the tip of a spear protruded from his chest. Úlfor grabbed the man's head and pulled it back, exposing the blank eyes. He looked at Roden and nodded. The dead man's serpent was now merely sparks of dissipating color.

"What in Höðr's darkened mind have you done?" gasped Ulf. The short man looked back and forth between the Lothbransons and the mercenaries. "There was no order given."

Roden stepped between Hervor and Úlfor as his companion began to hack off the dead man's head with his seax. "Úlfor claimed the man's life so that he, and *only* he, would have the right to the bounty." He gestured toward the body. "The man he killed went by the name of Vik the Merciless. We crossed paths with him several years ago. At that time, his own lesser outlawry had been increased to nine years."

If only her group were subject to lesser outlawry, Líf thought, as she listened to this exchange. Lesser outlawry carried a sentence of only three years, though additional three-year increments could be added if the person failed to follow the restrictions placed upon him or continued to do wrong.

Roden had not stopped talking. "It appeared that Vik could not stay out of trouble. According to the common laws, Vik's head is proof of Úlfor's right to receive the bounty."

Hervor's features darkened in the evening gloom. "So be it," she said.

Squat Ulf looked at the siblings. "What should we do with the dead?"

"I care nothing about those vagabonds," Hervor asserted. "As for our men, bury the one, but let the bones of the man who gave us away be picked clean by the wolves. That ergi deserved what came to him."

Úlfor held Vik's severed head in his hands. Upon hearing the shieldmaiden's verdict, the mercenary's face grew grimmer than any of those around him. Ergi was a serious insult, used for the most disgraceful of men—those who stole, who displayed cowardice, who were weak, or who showed an affinity for their own sex. Ergi was the opposite of what their people strove to be. Such a label was an invisible brand the man must bear for the rest of his life.

Hervor continued, "We *cannot* permit betrayal." She pulled her brother to the side and spoke quietly. Had Líf not been seated nearby, she would not have overheard. "If there was one traitor, there may be more."

The oldest Lothbrandóttir flicked her axe, shaking off some of the blood. Ottar clenched his jaw. "We cannot kill our own men."

"*Are* they our men?" Hervor cast her gaze over a number of hired hands. "Look how easily one turned. We do not have their trust."

"You cannot force trust, Hervor. Only fear and hatred."

Hervor gently rotated her injured shoulder as if testing its mobility. "What then, brother?"

"We must *earn* their trust. Give them something to believe in. Respect grows. It is not birthed from nothing."

After giving the crew one last look, the shieldmaiden stated, "As I said, I will not suffer betrayal."

Ottar agreed. "Nor should you, but do not act without reason. Thus far, these men are innocent."

"Wise words, little brother," Hervor huffed before heading to their ship.

Líf could not sleep that night. Once more, her nightmares whipped her mind into a turmoil. Hervor had ordered her most trusted men to keep watch. Skeggi took the first shift. Although he might irk the shieldmaiden, she knew he would not fail her commands.

Unable to rest, Líf found the large man and kept him company. Together, they watched Úlfor walk off with the still-dripping sack that contained his prize and return later without it.

"What do you suppose he did with it?" Líf asked as Thray groomed her bushy tail. "I thought it was valuable."

The squirrel paused to consider the question, but it was Skeggi's voice that answered. "I am certain he buried it in order to collect it upon our return. There's no reason to tote festering flesh around. Maybe it will rot enough that the smell will die down before we head back to open waters."

"Is that really what you do?" Líf scrunched up her face in disgust.

"It's not what *I* do, Lingy," chortled Skeggi, using his personal nickname for her. "I prefer wealth from gold and silver. Now, *that* is tangible and instant. No waiting around."

"And no stench," added Thray, knowing Skeggi could not hear her. She eyed the bearded man and sniffed. "Well, not that extreme sort of stench."

Líf cracked a smile as the volume of snores grew around them. Thray scurried to the woman's other shoulder. "Look up! It's so vibrant tonight."

The squirrel lifted her small head toward the glistening, rippling ribbons of light that spanned the sky. Like fylgjur fur, the colors of the aurora borealis changed constantly, although tonight greens dominated. As if mirroring them, both squirrel and seagull took on a similar sheen.

Líf watched her fylgja in awe. Though she had observed this display before, it was always breathtaking. It would not be much longer before such a sight would be lost to the summer's endless daylight. Under the shimmering display in the night sky, the other fylgjur—even in sleep—mimicked what swirled above them, rendering the shoreline aglow with creatures of all kinds.

At some point, Hervor approached. The shieldmaiden never ordered her men to do anything that she was not willing to do herself. "It is my turn, Skeggi. Get some rest."

Skeggi's eyes had already begun to droop, but when he saw her, he perked up. "I can take another shift if you desire company."

Hervor shook her head and sat down. "Get some sleep."

Without another word, he wandered away to his night sack. Hervor looked at Líf. "You should, as well."

"I can't," she admitted.

They stayed silent for a time. Finally, as she scanned the still camp Hervor declared, "What you did today was very brave."

"It wasn't, actually," countered Líf. "That was just fear."

"I'm not talking about the dead man," countered Hervor as she stretched her legs before her. Like the rest of the crew, she wore trousers under a tunic, not a gown. "I'm talking about taking a risk and spying on that party. If you had not done so, tonight might have had a different outcome. You saved lives. I thank you."

Hervor had never before thanked Líf for anything remotely as important as that act. It was the first time. Oddly, there was no pleasure in it. Líf had always imagined what it would be like to walk in Hervor's tall boots. Now that she had had a taste of what others called bravery, she hated it. Madness was more like it. What else would compel a person to refuse their fylgja's counsel? Though Líf might be the only person to actually hear her fylgja's voice, others could sense their guardian spirits in different ways. Premonitions, intuition, hunches—all might be the whispers of a fylgja. Self-preservation was a powerful instinct. On the other hand, a guilty conscience could be a guardian spirit's rebuke.

Líf observed her sister. "What do you think the völva will tell us when we see her again?"

"How could I possibly know?" Hervor's response was not meant to be derogatory, only honest.

Líf scratched the top of Thray's head. "I remember Brasir saying he believed the answers lay outside of Midgard." The idea was terrifying. Men must stay in their own world! What lurked beyond its borders? Creatures and beings straight out of the dark legends of their past. According to the tales, encounters with such entities often proved fatal. "What if we must leave our world? How could we survive another?"

Hervor took a deep breath. "I am not sure…" She was oddly hesitant. "I have heard whispers suggesting men have tried. Regardless, we will fight for the right to continue."

There was a tinge of sadness in the shieldmaiden's tone. In the darkness, it was hard to tell for certain, but Líf thought her sister cast her a mournful glance. Was Hervor worried for her youngest sibling? And why shouldn't she be? Líf could not fight. There was a high probability that if this party were attacked, Líf would be the first to fall.

What use was she to any of them? She could prove a distraction or a hindrance. What if others got hurt because of her presence?

Thray whined, "I will do my best, Líf. I promise."

Líf did not reply. The snow had begun to fall once more, and she watched the snowflakes slowly passing through the glowing animals and dimming their lights ominously.

Chapter Four

"I do not like this plan, Líf," Thray chirped as she dug her needle-sharp claws into Líf's homespun dress. "We were attacked yesterday. Did your brother forget?"

Although Líf felt she should listen to her fylgja and question Ottar's recent proclamation, out of respect she waited until the rest of the crew had dispersed. It would look bad for a woman to oppose a man in public.

"Is it safe to stay here any longer? We have already been found out once. What if we are again?"

As Líf voiced her fears, Ottar looked at her sympathetically and his wolfhound tucked her ears back in a show of agitation. "We are almost out of provisions," he explained. "The weather slowed us more than we anticipated. I've sent a number of men out to hunt this morning. The others will set snares and cast nets, though with all the ice on the water, I doubt many fish will be caught. We need to eat."

Before she could chime in, her brother continued, "As for being discovered, I doubt we will be. We killed Vik's party. Without a village nearby, there is little chance that other wanderers will encounter us, much less decide to attack. More likely, anyone crossing our path would prefer to trade instead."

"But a week?" Líf asked. "Is that necessary? We are only three days away from Spákona. If we ration ourselves, we could head straight to Völva Gunhild."

Ottar rubbed his forehead and countered, "The men need time on land, and a party as large as ours must not arrive at the house of a völva empty-handed. Gifts must be exchanged. You know this as well as I do. We are close, Líf, but that should not make us foolish. If we want Völva Gunhild to receive us, we must approach the situation carefully and show her the utmost respect."

Líf looked toward *Wavecutter* and the men who were breaking the ice that continually formed around the boat. "I hate this." She did not need to explain. She knew that Ottar understood her deep desire to return home, even though they both knew that would never happen.

"This spring might be a cold one," Ottar noted, "but summer will come again. We must be patient."

Thray bristled on Líf's shoulder and muttered, "What if this is not spring? What if winter has chosen to stay forever?"

Líf stepped away from her brother before retorting, "Nothing lasts forever. Not even death. Remember, when the worlds crumble, all will cease to be." The words were anything but comforting. Neither was the following week of "rest and recuperation."

When it was finally time to vacate the camp, the red-headed man known as Einar offered to help Líf to board the longship. Though his smile was genuine, she hesitated to grasp his outstretched hand, for Einar had been among the crew sent from Thorinheim to recapture Brasir. He had fought against the Lothbransons before being captured by them. Though he displayed respect for her family for his merciful treatment and had even prevented their capture, she did not completely trust him.

Einar seemed to recognize Líf's wariness, for he stepped away and allowed Guthorm to hoist Líf's shivering body out of the fjord's frigid water. Only after *Wavecutter* was on her way did Einar cast Líf a look of dismay. His fox fylgja slumped as she sat between his legs.

"I wasn't cruel," Líf protested sulkily. But she suddenly felt that she had acted badly.

Thray curled her tail around Líf's neck. "I never said you were."

A number of the men must have heard her speaking to her fylgja, for they shied away from her. Líf felt her cheeks grow hot. She quickly found a seat near the stern, behind the men and their uncomfortable glances.

Over the following days, Líf almost felt as though she were back in the town of her birth, for none of the crew spoke to her. She was treated with indifference, even revulsion. Brasir made no effort to converse, either, yet this did not bother her, for he, too, had to deal with the crew's lack of trust, though somehow he was making far more headway with them than she was. More than once, Líf had observed him chatting with whomever was seated near him as they rowed.

Only her siblings were kind to her, yet they were kept busy steering the ship through the fjord. Left alone, Líf leaned over the side and listlessly watched Sigird and Einar use poles to break up and push away large chunks of ice. Thankfully, the frozen layer had not thickened. Though present, the wind was not enough to be of much service, so the sail had been furled. The crew struggled to row through the hard chunks that bobbed on the surface of the fjord as they eased the drakkar, their beautiful longship, farther inland.

Midmorning on their fourth day, Thray ran up to Líf in a flash of glimmering excitement. "We're here, Líf! We made it!"

No sooner had she spoken than the sharp cry of the goshawk was followed by Hervor's strident voice. "Spákona lies just ahead!"

Looking up, Líf spotted a single longhouse perched on a solitary hill. Some two hundred fifty feet long, its thatched roof was coated in a layer of moss and trimmed with snow. Solid walls were almost hidden under the low roofline, from which hung a row of icicles that nearly reached the ground. Smoke wafted from the open front door, escaped through the gaps built into the roof for light, and wriggled through holes where the thatching needed to be repaired. Clearly, the building was not regularly tended.

Yet why would it be? A völva traveled most if not all of the time, visiting villages and towns where she would use her gifts to cast blessings or foretell the future. She rarely lived among others. It was strange that such a solitary lifestyle would result in a longhouse as large as this.

A subtle yet distinct sigh of relief passed through the crew. Though not one person had voiced doubt, they all must have wondered whether the völva actually lived in a place so far removed from civilization.

Clambering onto shore, the men unloaded what they could. Ottar wanted his ship hauled onto land, for he feared that *Wavecutter* could become trapped in the ice-coated water during their stay.

Meanwhile, Líf wandered farther up the trampled path. The walkway seemed to have been cleared of snow that very morning. From her vantage point, she heard the bleating of goats from a small outbuilding where the animals were picketed. The scent of something rich filled the air—possibly slow-roasting meat and herbs.

"Spákona, the place of unbridled sight," Líf whispered, for though it was not visually impressive, the very essence of reverence surrounded it.

"She's watching us," was Thray's reply, though Líf could not spot the woman they had traveled so far to meet.

It took several hours for everyone to get situated. At last, after the drakkar had beached and crates full of offerings were made ready, Ottar led the party up the slope to the open door of the longhouse. There they waited while he crossed the threshold.

Líf remained next to Brasir, near the front of the procession. As sister to Ottar, she would have the privilege of being one of the first greeted if the völva decided to welcome them. In front of Líf stood Úlfor and Roden, for they carried an extravagantly carved chest containing the most prestigious gifts. Standing right outside the door was Hervor. It was clear that the shieldmaiden was impatient, yet she understood that only Ottar had the right to implore the völva's good will.

Soon a form emerged from the warm glow of the interior. A woman older than the Lothbrandottírs stared out at the weary travelers with a face wiped clean of emotion. She wore the same blue cloak she had worn the first time Líf had seen her. In her hand she held her gandr, the staff with a crystal affixed to its top.

With her vibrant dark hair, Gunhild might have been considered attractive had it not been for the runes tattooed on her forehead and cheeks. Líf understood a little of their meaning, which was rare, for most of her people were illiterate—which was probably for the best. To write runes was to toy with seid, magic. Everyone understood that whatever was denoted by the angular lettering would come true whether good or evil.

Gunhild's fylgja, an owl hued a pale blue, perched on her shoulder. The bird's eyes were partially closed, its body calm.

Without pausing, the völva walked slowly past the first of the waiting visitors, speaking all the while. "A woman of the shield, a brother of the wolf, a faultless guide, and a child with sight so true." Gunhild stopped before Brasir and locked eyes with the tall man. "Ah…the man with the skin of a different color. Though I knew you would come, I had hoped that you would not appear so soon."

To Líf's astonishment, Brasir suddenly dared to speak. "I have been waiting for a long time to talk to someone with your gifts."

Gunhild nodded. "And I have worked hard to avoid this meeting, yet we must all follow our designated paths."

The owl on her shoulder turned its head around to expose its flaming-red second face. Emitting a singular, piercing hoot, the now crimson bird flew silently into the longhouse.

"Come." The völva spoke loudly so that the entire crew could hear. "You are all welcome in my home. Food has been prepared, and there is plenty of drink."

That cheered up even the glummest of the crew. Smiling, the men lugged their gifts into the smoke-filled building, whereupon Ottar presented their hostess with chests filled with ingots of silver and gold, bronze arm rings, mounds of new furs, and large sections of choice cuts of meat. Already four goats were turning on spits, their skin crackling over the long central fire.

Gunhild commanded several men to haul out of a back room a few barrels full of ten-year-aged mead. The golden liquid was so rich and spicy that it went down everyone's throats far more quickly than it should have. Soon, a number of the crew displayed glazed eyes and jovial demeanor.

Líf did not partake as much as the others. Her distrust of drunken acts kept her wary, as did Thray's unsettled state. The squirrel clambered up and down Líf's back in a sort of nervous fit, her nose twitching rapidly.

"What's wrong?" Líf asked as she found an empty bench. Come nightfall, it would be her bed.

"Sumarmál should be approaching soon."

Líf thought a moment. That blót was the religious celebration that marked the beginning of summer, the raiding season, and the time to sow seeds. It occurred during the fourth lunar cycle after Jól, the winter season of gift giving. "I guess you are right. I hadn't thought about it with all this blasted cold."

"We had no spring." Thray paused long enough to peer up into the rafters, where several avian fylgjur perched. "It is always short, but this time it never even occurred."

"You know that most people do not believe in such seasons. For them, there is only winter and summer."

Thray was still dubious. "Still, summer should be approaching."

"But it still feels like winter," added Líf reflecting the little squirrel's worry. "Why does that disturb you so? We have been experiencing this for a while. What concerns you now?"

"Look! Look!" Thray's loud scream startled Líf, who sloshed some of her mead onto her gown. "Where are the garlands? The trimmings? Surely a völva would not dare ignore the coming celebration. She *knows* something."

Líf scanned the ash-tinted planking above her. Thray was right. Not one bit of greenery adorned the room. "Maybe it is too cold here to find that sort of new growth."

The squirrel growled. "Then why not travel south? Being what she is, she is obligated to perform her rituals. Unless…unless there is no need to welcome the summer."

"That's just foolishness," Líf countered quickly. Her voice was raised and slightly high-pitched. "Summer always follows winter."

Thray's teeth chattered in agitation. "You're smarter than that, Líf." The fylgja leaped from the woman's shoulder and scurried past the men waiting for the roasting meat.

Brasir stood next to the central fire. He had not talked with the völva since their exchange outside several hours ago. The seeress would decide on the time to discuss important matters.

It was well after nightfall when Gunhild emerged from a back room. Líf had never seen a longhouse compartmentalized that way and thought it a strange concept; but, then, the seeress was no ordinary person. The völva slowly scanned her observers as if judging their level of inebriation.

Brasir had refused drink. He stood up as soon as the seeress appeared. Gunhild locked her eyes upon him. "In nine days, I will give you your answer," she proclaimed before returning to her private rooms.

"Nine days?" Thray tittered as she climbed down the soft wattle-and-daub wall and leaped onto Líf's hair. "That number is sacred. Do you think that is the only reason she chose that time?"

"I don't wish to presume anything when it comes to a völva. It does not matter anyway. If she says we must wait, that is what we must do."

Most of the men were not opposed to an extended stay if they could spend it eating and drinking. Líf might have been so inclined, but one look at Brasir reminded her that each passing day could mean tragedy in her kingdom as well as his. Ottar, too, was impatient. Though he was used to being away from his children for months at a time, this was different. Unless tangible proof were found to support Brasir's theory, Ottar could never return to his boys.

Could the völva's verdict be considered proof? Líf doubted it. As the time slowly passed, she remained quiet and observant.

Finally, at no particular hour on the afternoon of the ninth day, Gunhild rose from her seat at the back of the main hall. As soon as she did so, everyone quieted no matter how inebriated they were.

"You have been patient guests, and I thank you. Now is the time for me to give an answer, though you might not wish to hear what must be said." She looked upon the expectant faces once more, then stated, "Your journey will lead you north."

One drunken bloke spoke up. "There's nothing north of here!"

A thin smile seemed to crack the seeress's face. "Oh, but there *is*."

CHAPTER FIVE

That statement shut the drunkard up immediately. Líf could feel Thray's heartbeat quicken as the squirrel pressed her warm body against Líf's neck. The völva looked about once more, as if asserting that there would be no further interruptions.

"A ceremony is unnecessary," she began, which made Líf recall the first time she had seen Gunhild prophesy. "I have known what I am about to say for quite some time." The seeress gestured to Brasir. "Come with me."

Brasir obeyed without hesitation.

Gunhild pointed directly at Líf. "You as well."

Several murmurs erupted, along with surprised looks shared between the older Lothbranson siblings. Yet neither questioned the seeress's wishes.

Líf hesitated. Why was she needed? What was going to be told to her that her siblings could not hear? There must be some mistake.

"Should we go?" Thray inquired. Her entire body was rigid.

Swallowing to moisten her dry mouth, Líf slowly followed Brasir and Gunhild into the back rooms. They passed through a small storage space filled with mead barrels, now mostly empty, and into the farthest area, which was the völva's sleeping chamber.

A magnificent bed was covered with pelts of mink, snow hare, and fox. Surely the bed had been a gift from a jarl, or perhaps even a king. A trio of backless chairs was positioned near the perimeter, along with a low table covered with rune staves and half-melted candles. The floor of compacted dirt was layered with woven rugs and more furs. A large loom was set at an angle near the base of the bed.

"Bring over the chairs," Gunhild instructed as she gestured to the space next to her loom. Brasir grabbed two chairs while Líf picked up the third. When they were as comfortable as they could be in this strange situation, the seeress asked Brasir a question in such a way that it appeared she had forgotten Líf's presence. "Your name?"

"I am called Brasir." Behind the man, his large bear's head loomed over his shoulder, even though the animal was still on all fours.

"That is not your name," Gunhild snapped in an irritated fashion. Did she think he was lying to her? Her grim stare bored into him.

Brasir's jaw twitched. "My father—"

"Your mother named you," Gunhild stated. "Not he." Before the man could respond, the völva turned to Líf. "What is your name?"

"Ah..." she answered hesitantly. "Líf."

"Speak up, child," Gunhild said, her own voice softening.

"Líf. Líf Lothbrandóttir."

The owl fylgja gave a hoot from somewhere above as the seeress looked at the pair in front of her. "Certain people are bound together by fate, a purpose set by that intangible essence that controls even the gods." She gestured to the half-woven image on the loom. The canopy of a tree could be discerned, with various birds and a stag in the uppermost branches. "Like these threads, you are designed to be part of each other, meant to form a tapestry of special beauty. But if pulled apart"—Gunhild reached for the loose end of a yarn. She tugged it, and the image began to unravel—"everything you are meant to become will be undone. You both share gifts. You are both meant for more. Remember this."

Not knowing what to say, Líf remained quiet, as did Brasir. She looked to the man who had changed her life. He, in turn, cast his gaze upon her. Gunhild held her own council for a time, then smiled wearily at Brasir. "I know your questions. You need not ask. I do not have your answers."

Brasir's features grew sullen. This did not deter the seeress. "But I know where you can find them. You must leave Midgard and find your way to the well of Mímisbrunnr. It lies inside Jotunheim, though its exact location I do not know. Within the waters of that well, your answers await. Yet your path will not be so straight."

Gunhild reached over and picked up her staff. Her long fingers ran over the crystal attached to its top. "The greater the knowledge to be obtained, the greater the offering that must be made. Travel first through Jotunheim and Svartálfheim to find your way to Álfheimr. There, the Ljósálfar, the race of the light, will assist you with the offering you will need and the direction you must then take."

"How do we leave Midgard? Where do we find the entry to Jotunheim?" Brasir's questions were practical and blunt. "Can you at least counsel us?"

The seeress's eyes rolled back in her head. She began to hum; then words formed and her voice pealed out: "Follow the star that does not move. Go northwest for the length of three days' travel on horseback. There you will come to Sormr, the Serpent's Strait. You must sail across as you continue to follow the star. Do not stop. Do not show fear, and Jörmungandr will remain complacent."

Jörmungandr! Líf shivered. Memories overwhelmed her—of the world serpent roiling the ocean waters as it rose from the depths to lay waste to ships and crew, and of her own narrow escape. If they had to pass over its back, could they do so without disturbing the gargantuan beast?

Gunhild continued, "On the far side of the river is a wall so tall no man or jötunn can scale it. The only passage is a crevice so narrow and low that a longship can just slip through if the mast is down. You will not be able to row in that underbelly, so you must enter at great speed. Be cautious. A slight miscalculation, and your vessel will break apart against the wall or become wedged in the tunnel of stone. If you succeed, you will have entered Jötunheim. May the gods look favorably upon your quest."

The völva looked at Líf from the corner of her eye. "Leave us."

As Líf got to her feet, Thray muttered, "First she wanted us here, but now she doesn't."

The young woman left the seeress's private quarters. The two who remained did not speak as she left their presence. More secrets. More mystery. More questions. When Líf entered the main hall, those waiting looked at her in expectation. She walked past everyone without stopping.

Skeggi stood next to the door. "What is it, Lingy?" he inquired.

She passed him by, unable to make herself reply. Instead, she walked out into the snowdrifts and stared at the panorama. White coated the few evergreen trees that peppered the landscape. Everything else was blanketed by the frozen particles. Under the sun, the entire wilderness sparkled in brilliant, almost blinding, light.

Thin, burning lines stung her face as tears rolled down her cheeks, the cold solidifying their trails before they could trickle off her chin. Sinking to her knees, she sobbed. Hervor and Ottar rushed to her side, yet there was nothing they could do to make her stop.

Líf stared at the open space. This was Midgard. This was her home. How could she hope to survive anywhere else? If she left this place, would she ever see it again? Men were not supposed to leave their world. They were not meant to survive if they did.

The tears had stopped forming. Her face ached from the cold. Líf, still seated on the hardened earth, took several long breaths as she tried to clear her mind of the worst of her fears. Without looking at her siblings directly, she finally addressed them. "Teach me to fight."

Ottar squatted down; his face was contorted with worry. Behind him, Hervor scowled. "What happened, Líf? What were you told?"

Forcing herself to meet her brother's eyes, Líf replied, "I need to learn how to defend myself."

"Why?" Ottar asked, as Hervor inquired, "Where are we headed?"

Behind them, Brasir emerged from the doorway. "I can tell you where my journey will lead. I will not ask you to follow."

"You know I am going with you," Ottar declared as Líf rose to her feet.

Líf realized that Brasir was about to share what Gunhild had said. To hear again that she must leave her world was more than she could bear at that moment. As she pushed past Brasir to get to her sleeping bench, the man made a move, then paused, as if he had wanted to tell her something but thought better of it.

For the rest of the afternoon, she remained curled up on the bench with a blanket wrapped around her as she tried to block out the disjointed chatter about worlds beyond their own.

Surprisingly, few protested their forthcoming attempt. Was that because the majority did not believe there was a way to exit Midgard? Or was it because those faithful to the Lothbransons would follow them all over Yggdrasil if need be? Their universe might be vast, but so was the spirit that drove Líf's people toward adventure.

The few who openly balked were among the newly hired hands. That changed when the völva made another pronouncement, "Each of you who is truly willing to take up this quest will receive the greatest riches in the end. I promise you this."

"She sees the future," one said in hushed tones.

"I'm ready to be a wealthy man," affirmed another.

The talk soon turned to the logistics of travel. What food and other provisions would need to be gathered, and how soon could they attempt this venture? Hearing all this talk made Líf sick. She seemed dazed as Thray nuzzled her face.

Hervor urged Líf to eat some supper, yet the thought of food brought a sour taste to the young woman's mouth. Sometime later, Ottar tried, too, but with the same result. Only after most others had turned in for the night did Brasir approach the bench.

"If our fates were our own, I would ask you to stay."

Líf sat up, making room for the man to sit next to her. She studied him for a moment longer before asking, "Völva Gunhild suggested that our fates were bound together, didn't she?"

"Yes," agreed the man. His bear fylgja bent down to touch noses with Thray, and the pair's colors shimmered pale blues and greens in the firelight.

"I'm scared."

"I know," Brasir admitted. "So am I."

Although this man was powerfully built, he showed more outward emotion than Líf's people would have deemed acceptable. Strangely, she found this reassuring.

"Why do you think she said that Brasir was not your name?"

"Because my father made an error. He misread the runes my mother wrote on my body with my afterbirth before she died."

"Is that what the völva told you after I left? Your true name?" Looking into his eyes, Líf understood. "What is it?"

He smiled slightly. "I have been Brasir my entire life. There is no need to change that now."

Though Líf felt that he had every right not to tell her, her own curiosity grew. "Come on. Get it out. It can't be that bad."

For some reason, the pleasant expression on Brasir's face changed. His voice became surprisingly serious. "Líf, I want you to understand that although I am not your family, I will do everything in my limited ability to protect you. I want you to know that. This I pledge to you."

"Why are you saying this?" Líf was suddenly startled.

Brasir stood up. Behind him, his bear did the same. "Get some sleep."

"He's keeping something from us," Líf whispered to Thray.

"I believe you're right," agreed the squirrel. "In fact, I know you are.

"I have one major issue with this plan," began Guthorm as he wiped sweat from his brow.

For several days, the crew had been felling all the trees they could find, stripping them of their branches, and then placing the tree trunks in a row on the ground, perpendicular to *Wavecutter*'s bow and in the direction of the north star. When enough trees had been readied in this manner, they would move the ship forward over the rollers. Even with the sun high above, everyone was chilled to the bone. Despite the cold, some of the men sweated from their exertions.

Ottar and Guthorm had just laid down a new log and were breathing heavily. Ottar glanced at his man and asked, "What is your issue?"

"How in the names of all the gods and their kin are we supposed to make it to Álfheimr? We have no map. No direction outside of our exit from Midgard. We cannot be expected to wander the realm of the jötunn endlessly and hope to find our way."

It was one of the longest monologues Guthorm had ever spoken. Yet every word was valid. Ottar's concern was evident. "We will have to do the best we can."

"I do not like this," harrumphed Guthorm as if he were his comrade Ulf. "How can we reach a place that no one knows how to find?"

Roden and Úlfor arrived and placed another log at the front of the line. The Rus must have heard some of the short man's trepidations, for he said, "I can find Álfheimr. I can find anything."

"How?" asked several of the crew at once.

Inclining his head, Roden peeled off his cloak and tunic. His body was lean and full of wiry muscle. There was not any fat on him. Turning, he exposed his back and the giant circular sigil tattooed upon his flesh. Like a wheel with eight spokes, at the ends of each line was a rune-like symbol.

Líf did not recognize the intricate design, though her brother clearly did. He stared in awe. "A vegvísir."

"What does it mean?" Líf asked.

Her brother explained as several other men stopped what they were doing to admire the large tattoo. "It means 'Wayfinder.' Whoever bears that marking will never lose their way in storm or clear weather, even when the way is unknown. I have never seen it inked on living flesh before today, for it is seid. Magic."

Roden had begun to put his clothes back on. "If there truly is a path, I can guide you to Álfheimr. But I will expect a fair compensation for my efforts."

"You will have it," Ottar said, stretching out his arm, which Roden clasped in a sign of their mutual agreement.

"Then have no fear. You are in the best of hands."

Once Roden and Úlfor left to haul another log, Líf asked her brother, "How do you think Hervor will react when she hears that she must listen to a mixed-blood mercenary?"

"Better than when I told her she was to marry Harekson."

Líf snickered. "We are fortunate *that* never came to pass."

Ottar watched as two rows of men hauled the drakkar onto the first number of rolling logs. "Let's just hope that our *fortune* holds out."

Chapter Six

"She's on the logs!" shouted Skeggi. He and Hervor were coordinating the efforts of the crew.

"Then let's begin," the shieldmaiden responded. Ottar moved closer to help oversee the activity. As the last few tree trunks were laid in front of the drakkar, the crew grasped ropes attached to the ship and began pulling it over the wooden rollers. The process was slow, but it allowed the drakkar to be transported overland.

Going around Gunhild's hill was the hardest feat and the goal for the rest of that day. As *Wavecutter* slid forward, the men positioned behind her would pick up the rearmost logs and haul them to the front. The labor was intense, but at least their journey was progressing once more.

They would spend their last night inside Spákona's hall, then begin in full force in the morning to transport the ship in the direction of the Serpent's Strait. The land would flatten out, which would allow them to quicken their pace. Still, a trip that took only three days on horseback would be three times as long with the drakkar rolling over the tundra.

The men had taken some time to hunt and fish, though there was not a lot of wildlife to be found, and Gunhild had also gifted them with bags of salt and smoked meats. Along with a blessing and the sacrificial offering of four of her goats in the name of Thor, the protector of the common people, the seeress wished them well on their final days in Midgard.

As the crew finally departed, the völva watched them trek northwest. Her brilliant blue fylgja flew with them for the first few days. The last time Líf caught a glimpse of the owl, Thray chittered to herself as the bird's shadow passed overhead. Then, with a sharp hoot, the raptor turned back toward Spákona.

Líf had never known anyone whose bond was such that both human and fylgja could exist without pain at such a distance. Gunhild must be an extremely powerful seeress. The thought of being separated from Thray caused Líf to shiver and hug the little rodent closer.

"Come, look at this!" Sigird, who had been scouting the smoothest terrain, shouted in excitement as he returned wearily on the third day. "You won't believe what I found!"

"Halt!" Ottar ordered. Everyone put down their ropes and wooden rollers. "Take this time to rest. Hervor, Brasir, come with me."

"I'm coming, too," Líf said as she hurried after her family.

Ottar looked as if he were about to protest, but Sigird reassured him. "It's fine. She should see as well."

The group had walked for several miles when Sigird halted, pointing ahead. "Have you ever seen so many?"

In the distance were what must have been more than a hundred thousand aurochs migrating across the vast expanse of plain. Though Líf had never seen them before, she recognized the beasts from her siblings' stories. The massive, reddish-brown bovines trudged slowly forward. Here and there in their midst were black bulls with a white eel-stripe down the back. Pale muzzles snorted clouds of air. Enormous horns projected from huge heads on strong, muscular bodies. They were far larger than any cattle Líf had ever laid eyes upon.

"I did not know that aurochs lived here." She was more than impressed by the seemingly endless herd. From one end of the horizon to the other, the beasts marched.

"They're not supposed to," Hervor quickly countered.

Sigird acknowledged this unusual behavior. "Could they be sick?"

"Not all of them," replied the female warrior, while Ottar added, "They could be confused because of the weather. Or they may have gotten lost."

Hervor looked doubtful. "Whatever the case, we will have to make camp here. There is no way we can cut through that herd without injury."

They turned back and informed the rest of their party. Once they had settled in for the day, Úlfor picked up his spear and two swords. The bounty hunter had procured one of the blades from a man he had slain several weeks earlier.

"Where do you think you're going?" Hervor asked tersely. She never liked it when her men refused to communicate with her. The mercenary continued without answering, which irritated the shieldmaiden even more. "I asked, where are you headed?"

Recognizing an impending confrontation, Roden answered for him. "He's going trophy hunting."

Hervor reared back at Roden's statement. "If he angers those beasts, they will gore him. Hunting aurochs is no activity for just one man."

"It is quite obvious that you do not know either of us well," Roden said as he readjusted his fur-lined hat. "If any man can single-handedly slay one of those animals, it is Úlfor. He is the best there is."

"I doubt that," sneered Hervor. She had never looked favorably upon men who were loyal only to coin.

"Have you not realized what he is?" Roden pressed. "He's an Úlfhéðinn. A wolf warrior. The most elite fighter there is. Do not look ill upon that fact."

Hervor seemed shocked. She stared in the direction of Úlfor's tracks. The all but mythic band of Úlfhéðnar warriors was revered far and wide. Extremely rare and more powerful than even the berserker forces, wolf warriors were known to attack massive numbers of men in battle without protective chain mail or helmets. Half-maddened by the drugs they ingested, they would charge into a fight howling like the animals from whom they obtained their unnatural strength.

Supposedly, Úlfhéðnar shared a bond with the wolves whose pelts they wore as cloaks and hoods. Known to bite and beat on their shields until they spat splinters and blood, these warriors were recognized as some of the most brutal opponents in combat. Their volatile behavior discouraged most people from offering them companionship or kinship. If Úlfor were indeed one of the Úlfhéðnar, shouldn't the rest of the crew be worried about his potential for rage and slaughter?

Hervor automatically reached for her axe. "If he wants to get himself killed, so be it." She loomed over Roden. "Just remember who is truly in charge, Wayfinder."

Líf cautiously approached the Rus after her sister stormed off. "Is he safe? Úlfor?"

"The man will not harm any of you," Roden promised. "He left that life for a reason."

"Isn't that part of who he is?" Líf questioned as she thought about Úlfor's wolf fylgja.

Roden lost his smile. "As long as he gets his pay, no harm will occur."

Líf swallowed and eased away from the man with the almond-shaped eyes. As she did, Thray chittered, "Your siblings must not run out of coin."

"We will have enough," Líf affirmed, though she knew neither she nor Thray fully believed it.

Before the sun had set, Úlfor returned. Carrying the massive head of a bull still dripping blood, he deposited his prize by a cook fire. Its dead eyes reflected the firelight while the fire's heat singed its ruddy forelocks.

The hunter sat next to his prize and began to hack off the pair of horns, each longer than his arm. He must have said something to Roden, for the Rus began to clean out the hollowed inside of the horn presented to him as they shared the cow tongue. Other men came up to congratulate Úlfor on his feat, though the man seemed to care little for the praise. His wolf raised her hackles, annoyed by the crowd around them.

From her seat at a neighboring fire, Hervor glared at the Úlfhéðinn.

Nearby, Thray groomed her paws contentedly as she commented, "It seems Skeggi might get a reprieve from the bulk of your sister's wrath."

Though Thray's comment was meant to be amusing, Líf did not like the thought of Hervor facing off against an Úlfhéðinn. Hervor might be one of the best fighters in Thorinheim, but she had never tested her mettle against a warrior such as this one.

The following day, the last straggling cows mourning their fallen companion were chased away from the dead ox. When the beast had been butchered and the meat salted, the ship's band continued the trek overland. The entire expanse of plain reeked from the plethora of steaming rounds that had been dropped in the snow. Líf hoped they would complete this leg of the journey as quickly as possible.

Surprisingly pleased with themselves, Úlfor and Roden proudly displayed the new drinking horns that hung from their belts like sword sheaths. Today, that pair was assigned to pull the ropes, while others were switched to hauling the rollers around the ship.

Líf watched everyone else hard at work. "What use are we if we cannot help in any way?" she asked sulkily as she walked ahead of the long vessel.

Thray had become stir-crazy on the young woman's shoulder. For days on end, Líf had slogged through the white drifts. Suddenly, the small squirrel leaped onto a mound of snow. On one hand, as fylgjur she was unable to leave footprints; on the other hand, the soft surface could not hinder her. She jumped and ran about quickly, enjoying the opportunity to expend some of her own energy. Elsewhere around the perimeter of the ship, other fylgjur were doing the same. Some even dared to wrestle with one another as they tried to alleviate their own boredom.

"I say, Líf—" Unable to halt, Thray skidded right into Líf's skirt. "Stop being so sullen. We are alive and well. That cannot be said of everyone in Midgard. Quit looking at the negatives."

Líf had to admit that the little squirrel might be right. Many people also struggled, yet Líf could not seem to rid herself of her personal doubt.

"I do want to learn to defend myself. I know my siblings scoffed at the idea, but I think it would be for the best."

"So you were serious!" Thray peeped out from under the skirt's hem before bounding ahead of the woman. Turning around, she stood up on her rear legs, her tail spread out behind herself for balance. "I think you are marvelous, and you should as well."

"You're my fylgja. Of course you say such things." Líf rolled her eyes before shaking off one of her wide snowshoes. The broad platforms tied to the bottoms of her boots prevented her from sinking too deep, but they were cumbersome. She preferred to ski, but considering the rate of everyone else's travel, there would be little benefit from that. The skis would remain with the other gear gifted to them by Gunhild. "Listen. I can't hunt. I can't fight. I'm not strong enough to move the rollers or pull the ship. I'm not even smart enough to strategize."

"That's not true," argued the squirrel. Thray never condoned Líf's demeaning herself.

"Fine," sighed the woman. "I've never been *educated* on those topics."

"That's better," Thray affirmed as she leaped upon the dress. Clambering up to Líf's ear, the little creature stuck her nose close and whispered, "Just because you were never taught does not mean you are incapable of learning. That is the greatest secret of our gender; we are smarter than men." Thray emitted a series of purring sounds—her laughter. Tussling with the long lengths of red hair, the squirrel added, "There are many different kinds of strengths. Never forget."

Líf thought upon Thray's words for some time before responding. "Regardless, I do want to learn to fight. I fear that is a skill I may soon need to call upon."

Thray flicked her tail and emitted a low growl. "If that is your desire, make someone teach you."

"I did ask," sighed Líf.

"Don't ask. Demand it."

Líf looked back at Hervor. Her older sister was a terrifying presence. Yet out of all of those here, she was the only one who could possibly understand Líf's wish.

Finding the right time to approach, Líf requested of the oldest Lothbrandóttir, "Teach me to use a sword."

"A sword?" Hervor said dismissively. "You are so small that it might topple your little body."

"A short axe, then." Líf stepped in front of the shieldmaiden. "A dagger. Anything. Please, Hervor. You know where we are headed. You understand what we might face. I must learn how to do something, as insignificant as it might seem to you."

Surprisingly, her sister did not laugh. The tall blond nodded. "Fine. When we make camp, I will show you something. But you must promise me that you will listen to exactly what I have to say and will not question my techniques."

"I will," Líf hurriedly replied. "I promise."

Hervor kissed the top of Líf's red hair. "Now, let me get back to these half-witted slackers." She turned to face those tugging at the ropes. "Were you all born without bones in your bodies? Use your weight! Show me some semblance of effort!"

Leaving her sister to verbally berate the crew, Líf walked ahead with a little more pep in her tread. She was excited. For the first time in who knew how long, she was looking forward to learning a new skill. Her life used to be full of simple tasks repeated day in and day out. When was the last time she'd had any sort of schooling? Could she even remember?

When the time came for Hervor to give her the first lesson, Líf trembled with excitement. What would she be taught to wield? A mighty sword, like her brother's? Or perhaps a throwing axe, like Hervor's? Maybe even a bow for long-range defense?

The shieldmaiden was tending a small fire, which she had built away from the main group to give them enough space to work on their movements. Her sparring shield was strapped to her back. It was almost identical to another shield that was rigged to the seaward side of the longship, where all the warriors kept theirs ready for battle. This particular shield was kept solely for practice. Perfectly circular and three feet in diameter, it was painted in triangular wedges of green and blue. At its center was the umbo, the hollow metal dome that allowed for the grip at the back. Several gashes and nicks already marred its wooden surface.

Standing up, Hervor appraised her sister. "Are you sure you're ready?"

"I am." Líf looked around for blade or spear. The only weapons were Hervor's own.

"Good," huffed the female warrior as she pulled off her shield and handed it unceremoniously to Líf.

The device could not have weighed more than ten pounds, yet it was designed such that only one hand could grip the iron bar behind the central dome of the umbo. This enabled the shield to be held farther away from the body, but it could also tire any trained warrior's arm after a time. How long would Líf's slender form last? What if she slipped and dropped it? How was she to wield anything else? How could she see an opponent approach? The shield covered more than half of her body. Though this would be good in an attack, she felt it might slow her reaction.

Lowering the rim so she could see over it, Líf nodded to her sister. "Okay, what's next?"

Hervor drew out her throwing axe, spinning it in the air before settling on her grip. The shieldmaiden grimaced. "I attack."

CHAPTER SEVEN

In a flurry of movement, Hervor charged. Leaping into the air, she slammed her axe into the raised shield.

The impact was so jarring that Líf fell backward, emitting a startled cry. Her spine crashed against the earth. Coughing, she tried to inhale. She felt as if she couldn't breathe.

Hervor pressed her boot against the top of the shield and pulled out her axe. "Stand up."

Gasping, Líf struggled to comply. Her mind was abuzz with all sorts of questions. "What was that?" she finally asked, as she looked over the edge of the shield and spied the clean split in its wooden façade. "Why did you do that? I had no weapon."

"What did you promise me?" Hervor retorted as she crossed her arms in front of her.

Líf was shaken, yet she responded, "No questions."

"No questions," Hervor repeated. "You have a weapon, Líf. More than one, in truth. Your body and the shield. Our shields are designed for more than just defense." Stepping behind Líf, Hervor manipulated her sister's body as she spoke. "With a shield, you can ram your enemy, shove them away. Use the lip to slam into arm, leg, or neck to break bone. With the correct skill, you can even disarm an attacker trying to stab around the edge. Knowing how to use the shield is crucial, and it is where we begin."

Striding back to her original position, Hervor finished, "For now, keep your mouth shut and your eyes and ears open."

The rest of the hour progressed as Hervor beat Líf about the snow-strewn landscape. Between Líf's constant falls and tumbles, the tall blond would make a corrective statement and occasionally reposition Líf's stance and form. Yet most of the learning came from actual movements and instinctual reactions.

By the time Hervor ended the session, Líf felt as if she had been trampled by a herd of aurochs. Her pale skin had already begun to show bruised patches, and she bled from a small cut on her cheek.

That night, it was hard for her to sleep through the pain, and walking the following day proved just as burdensome. When her sister made a sign for her to follow, Líf obeyed, though her reactions with the shield were slower than the day before. All the while, her injuries multiplied.

On the third evening, Thray whimpered in her stead. The little fylgja limped behind Líf, her own body sensing the torment that her human was suffering. "I don't know if it's worth it," she complained.

"I need to do this, Thray. I must," Líf affirmed as she gripped the shield once more. She barely had time to raise her shield in self-defense when Hervor, weaponless, rushed at her sister and slammed her shoulder into the circular wood.

Líf fell back from the blow. The shield hit the ground and twisted in her grasp. Suddenly, the woman's wrist blew up in sharp pain. She screamed aloud while Thray squealed.

Hervor tossed aside the shield and knelt beside her. Examining Líf's arm, the female warrior said, "It's just sprained. On your feet." She pulled Líf upright, her own face solemn. "Bind your wrist and return. An enemy will not care that you are injured. You will learn to work through the pain."

"No," Thray protested. "Stop, Líf. It hurts too much."

Líf made her way to the stored bandaging. Using fragments of wood as a brace, she began to wrap the loose strips of cloth around her right wrist as the little squirrel continued to try to dissuade her. "Please, Líf. Stop this. I was wrong. We are not your sister. We cannot endure this treatment."

Once her wrist was immobilized, Líf summoned her own depleted willpower. Seeing her rise, Thray growled, scrambled up and bit Líf's earlobe. Though no visible mark was made, tears welled up in Líf's eyes. Harshly she demanded, "Stop that!"

Thray's eyes grew wide. The squirrel clambered down and trailed her in the snow. Several men nearby watched her head off once again to train for combat.

That night, Líf's body hurt so much that she was unable to find relief. The following morning, she struggled to keep up with the caravan. She was exhausted, and her bruised body throbbed relentlessly. The worst pain came from her swollen wrist.

"Your sister is hard on you."

Brasir's voice caught Líf's attention as she once again mentally readied herself for a beating. "She wants to protect me."

"I am not so sure that is the best way," noted the dark-skinned man.

His statement annoyed Líf. How dare he judge her sister for making the effort to teach her these important skills? She scowled as he added, "She is emotionally tied to you."

"And you are not?" snapped Líf. "Could you do better?" She stared into the man's eyes. "My sister is a warrior. How dare you demean her?"

Turning away from him, Líf limped over to Hervor, who immediately began to instruct her.

"Today, I want you to show some effort," the shieldmaiden said. "Remember your footing. Keep yourself grounded. Crouch if need be. You must keep the center of your weight low so you cannot be bowled over so easily. Let's begin."

Unlike the two previous days, Hervor had brought out a second shield, which she gripped. The pair gave each other a nod, and then the tall women made her move. There was a crash as wood ground against wood, metal against metal. At first, Líf held her footing, but then the second impact occurred. Hervor had raised her own shield, using its edge at an angle, like the stroke of a sword. Líf's shield torqued away, and she crumpled amid new waves of pain. Dropping the round device, she clutched her wrist.

Suddenly, a large shadow covered her. Hervor had not stopped in her attack. The shieldmaiden made a move to ram her own wooden weapon against Líf's unprotected back. There was a resounding thud as Hervor was tossed onto her back.

Brasir stood beside Líf. "She has had enough," he growled at Hervor.

The shieldmaiden scrambled onto her feet. "Who are you to say when my sessions are done?"

"Your sister is in pain," snarled Brasir. "Injuring her now will not help her in a fight later."

"You said you'd seen battle before," hissed Hervor. "Then you know the enemy will be merciless. She must be aware of what to expect."

"She must learn the basics first. How will tolerating pain help if she is not given a chance to develop any skill?"

"There is no *time* for skill!" Hervor shouted. She was breathing heavily. The look in her eyes was searing.

"Stop this, both of you!" By now, Líf had risen. Her injured arm was tucked close to her breasts. "I thank you, Brasir, for your concern, but Hervor will teach me. This is what I asked for. I will see it through."

Brasir looked solemn. "Very well. Since that is *your* wish."

He retreated to the main encampment.

Hervor watched the man leave, then looked down at her shield. "That's enough for today." With that, the blond woman left Líf alone.

Líf was shocked. She would have continued. Pain or no pain, this was what she needed to endure to become better. She picked up the discarded shield and placed it next to the ship, to be stored on the vessel come morning. She was aware of the scornful expressions on several faces.

Thray's own colors shifted to oranges, yellows, and even whites. What was she feeling? Annoyance, embarrassment, relief? The squirrel's eyes glinted before she bounded off toward their family's campfire.

Ottar watched his sister approach. He had made no effort to express his own thoughts about Líf's wishes. He did not even berate Hervor for injuring their youngest sibling. Like Thray, he kept his personal opinion to himself. He merely handed Líf a strip of cooked beef before continuing on his way to patrol the camp.

Hervor was already seated on her night sack. Her face was stern as she stared into the flames. Somewhere high above, a goshawk cried out. Without turning to her sister, Hervor said, "He might be right. We should slow down."

"I'm doing my best to keep up. I can learn. I know I can."

"You need to be your best when we cross over." Hervor glanced at her sister's wrist. "Not like this."

"It's fine," Líf began. "I'm fine. We only have days before—"

Hervor clenched her fists, and Líf stopped abruptly. Suddenly, she realized that Hervor was terrified. She had rarely seen her sister look even remotely doubtful, certainly never frightened. Her sister was worried about their impending venture. In three days, maybe four, they would attempt to leave their world behind.

Hervor had never batted an eye at the thought of adventure or upcoming trials. But this voyage was different, for not everyone here had trained their entire lives for battle. Certainly not Líf—a small, mild-mannered woman who had not set foot outside of her home village until she was forced to flee. With only a few days left, there was no time to teach combat skills to a person who had never wielded anything more dangerous than a simple cook knife. Líf realized that Hervor was as frightened for Líf's life as Líf herself was.

The younger woman took a deep breath and stepped next to her older sibling. "We are going to be okay."

When the blond looked up, Líf could see the desperation in the woman's gray eyes. Pulling her sister into an embrace, the youngest Lothbrandóttir said, "We're going to get through this. *Together.*"

When Hervor returned the slight squeeze, Líf felt damp droplets land upon her neck and shoulder. The two remained that way for some time before Hervor abruptly leaned away. Her eyes were red and puffy. "Tomorrow we will do better."

Líf smiled. "So, are you going to tell him? Brasir?"

"Tell him what?" Hervor looked askance.

"That he was right."

The shieldmaiden gave a long stare at the redhead before breaking into laughter. "That will be the day that women are welcomed into Valhalla!"

At that, even Líf laughed.

The blessing of sleep was ripped from Líf the moment she rolled onto her wrist. Swallowing a moan, she tenderly hugged her arm close and stared up into the sky. Above her was the rippling luminescence of the Aurora Borealis. Bright as lantern light, it kept the darkest hours of the night at bay.

As long as her arm continued to throb, she would be unable to sleep. She stood up to go and relieve herself. At her feet, Thray stretched and yawned. The tiny creature's body glimmered like a miniature version of the lights above.

Using the squirrel as a guide, she followed Thray away from the camp and over a slight ridge where none could easily spot her. As she started back, Líf paused in mid-step. The camp was filled with illumination from all the fylgjur, which lay like a soft halo over the entire area. Shaped like the dome of the sky, held by each of the four dwarves at the cardinal points, the light appeared like a protective force over those who slumbered underneath it.

Yet something else far off in the distance caught Líf's eye. A second glowing dome could be seen, a smaller version of their own.

"Thray," Líf breathed as her chest tightened in fear, "we are being followed."

Chapter Eight

"What do you mean?" Thray questioned.

"Up here. Look!" Líf scooped the fylgja into her arms so the small animal could peer into the distance.

The squirrel inhaled sharply. "Warn your siblings. Hurry!"

"Wait," Líf hesitated long enough to note the direction and distance. Then she stumbled through the snowdrifts back to her family. She immediately shook Ottar, who gave his sister a look of surprise, while she startled Hervor enough that the shieldmaiden scrambled onto her feet.

"What—? What's the matter?" Ottar asked, realizing something was amiss. Hervor was already tucking her axe into her belt loop as she grumbled, "This had better be good."

"There is a group of people camped nearby. I'm worried that they might be tracking us."

"How do you know? It's too dark to see much of anything." Ottar hastily rubbed the sleep out of his eyes.

Líf realized that her ability gave her an advantage. "All fylgjur glow under the northern lights. Yours," she gestured to Ottar's wolfhound, then to Hervor's falcon perched atop her sleeping blanket. "Hers. And theirs." She motioned all around her. "I spotted fylgjur glow from a distance. There are other people nearby."

Hervor leaned into Ottar and said, "There shouldn't be anyone around us. It might not be a coincidence."

"You sure you saw fylgjur?" Ottar asked again.

"Yes," Líf affirmed. "They are probably two miles behind us, camped in the direction from which we came. They must have come across our tracks. It hasn't snowed in days."

"Very observant," noted Ottar. "Could you tell how many?"

"No. They are too far away. The glows blend together. But the light was strong enough to be seen, so there had to be a number of people."

"I'll go look," Hervor stated grimly.

"Fine," said Ottar, for there was no way he could stop his determined sister. "But take Guthorm and Ulf. Einar, too."

Hervor shot her brother a look, which forced Ottar to explain. "He wants to prove himself to us. Let him do so."

The shieldmaiden slipped around slumbering men to wake the others. Líf was almost as shocked as Hervor at Ottar's suggestion. "Do you think it wise to send Einar? He was one of Harekson's men. Can we trust him?"

"Trust must be earned, Líf. If he is never given the chance, how can he earn ours?"

From the shadows, another person approached. Skeggi, who was on watch, grunted as he cleared his throat. "What's all this?"

Ottar nodded toward those who were now heading away from camp. "There is a small party not far from us. Hervor is going to scout them out, see if they are friend or foe."

"When'd this happen?" Skeggi asked as he scratched his shaggy head.

Ottar gave Líf a quick smile. "You weren't the only one keeping watch."

"Balder's luck!" snarled Hervor as she rushed into camp. Her face was contorted in such disgust that in the dim lighting she looked as evil as a Døkkálfar. Behind her stood Guthorm Blood Cheeks and Ulf the Short.

"What did you see?" Ottar hastily inquired. "Where is Einar?"

Hervor growled at the name. "Spineless coward!"

By now, a number of the men had begun to stir and rise. They gathered around the shieldmaiden. "Harekson has found us," she spat out.

"How is that possible?" questioned Skeggi, disgruntled.

Ottar shook his head. "He must have sailed after us as soon as our outlawry went into effect."

"But how did he catch up so quickly?" It was Líf's turn to question.

Hervor hissed her answer. "We waited too long in the völva's presence, and he is not transporting his father's longship; that must have been beached near Spákona. They brought only three simple faerings."

"They can easily drag those small vessels after us," Guthorm added. "Maybe even carry them, with their number."

Scowling even more, the shieldmaiden added, "He will reach us before we can make it to open water."

"We should attack them now, while they are sleeping," suggested one of the crew.

"Do they know we are aware of their presence?" questioned another.

Ottar asked again, "Where is Einar?"

"I don't know," admitted Hervor. "We lost sight of him just as we skirted their camp."

She did not have to say more, for everyone's minds went to the same place: Einar must have deserted them. If he were to warn Harekson, there would be no chance of a surprise attack. Líf knew she should never have trusted him, yet he had always behaved so nicely.

"What do you want us to do?" Skeggi looked at the Lothbranson siblings for guidance.

"Wake the rest of the men," Ottar ordered. He shared a knowing glance with Hervor as he continued, "There is no point in expending our energy hauling *Wavecutter* with the enemy breathing down our backs. We will make our stand right here."

As the camp made ready, Ulf alerted those in command. "Quick now! Someone's approaching."

Einar stepped into sight. His hands were covered in blood and shaking. Hervor strode toward him and threatened, "I have half a mind to skin you right here and now."

The man looked imploringly at Ottar before turning to face the shieldmaiden. "I'm sorry. I stayed behind in case there were scouts present." He lifted his reddened limbs. "There were."

"You killed their watch?" questioned Hervor skeptically.

"No one woke up. There might be time before the next shift to... I would not wait if you want victory."

"The sun will be rising soon," noted Skeggi. "If you want to do this, now is the time."

Ottar turned toward his younger sister, "Líf, let's get you into the ship. You need to lie low until this is over, all right?"

"Yes. Yes, of course," Líf nodded, allowing herself to be assisted over the side of the drakkar. The rest of the men threw on their armor and charged off into the gloom, their fylgja still glowing at their heels.

In the distance, Líf could not make out individual men, yet she could see the guardians' lights and could tell when both parties met. Standing up on the decorative carved head of the snarling lizard at the stern of the ship, she noted how a number of the glows disappeared, as if multiple candles had been snuffed out.

Were the dead among her crew or Harekson's? How many could have been slain in their sleep before an alarm was raised? Who would return, and who would be left to be buried by the snow and ice?

The sun was beginning to rise. Along with it came the realization that soon Líf would lose the chance to keep watch. She sank to the floorboards and waited silently, hoping for any sign that all was satisfactory.

Time dragged on; each moment was more terrifying than the last. What if the enemy reached the longship? How could she defend herself? She had only the small seax that Ottar had given her once she was on board.

She crawled along the floor of the vessel to the storage crates and began to pry their lids off. They were full of essential cargo, but the armory was empty. All the men had donned chain mail shirts and strapped on weapons before heading off. Not one domed helmet remained. Not one spare sword, either, for they were too expensive for the common man to own more than one. The only useful things she found were the battered practice shields and a broken double-handed axe.

Claiming her splintering shield, she clutched it to her. In the now brilliant daylight, the device did not look as if it would hold out much longer. There had to be something else that could help her.

Thray scrambled around the prow. Her body no longer emanated the brilliance it did at night, though her iridescent fur refracted some of the sun's rays as she poked about the bundles of wares.

Líf spotted several spears wedged behind some crates. She did not recognize their make, but whoever they belonged to was not using them currently. She attempted to pull the weapons free, but they were pinned in their location, and the crate was too heavy for her to move. Switching tactics, she began to unload the contents of the storage bin. If she could lighten it enough, she could free the spears.

Thray scurried over to the long weapons. Though unable to manipulate the physical realm, she attempted to claw at the shafts.

Líf was infuriated that her fingers could feel the sanded wood of the long shafts but not remove them. Then she heard a soft sound behind her.

Thray froze as her shimmering eyes widened.

Dropping low, Líf removed several more containers of provisions; still crouched, she shoved the crate sideways, seizing a spear just as a heavy thud came from the stern of the ship. In a quick twist, she swung her body around and jabbed the spear at the man who loomed over her.

Her reflexes were too slow, for the man's hand grasped the spear just below its sharp point, then jerked the weapon out of her grip. A moment of terror was followed by the release of breath.

Úlfor gave her a quick sign to be silent as he crouched next to her and held the weapon at the ready.

"Others approach," Thray warned. The squirrel's teeth began to chatter in agitation.

Its body as tense as Úlfor's, his lean wolf fylgja snarled as she stared in the same direction he did. Her hackles gleamed a red far deeper than the blood splattered over the Úlfhéðinn.

More muffled noises were heard. A group of men came slogging through the snow. At these sounds, Úlfor gestured to Líf, then to the training shield at her side. She slowly bent and retrieved the round device, careful to not let it drag or drop.

He gripped it. Somehow, seeing the shield in the grasp of the fierce warrior made it look even flimsier. Úlfor gave her one last motion to remain silent; then everything occurred at once.

An unidentified man's hands reached over the side of the boat as he attempted to climb in. Úlfor rose to his feet and thrust the spear past Líf's line of vision. A scream was cut short as the bloody end of the weapon was pulled back. The hands released their grip; a heavy thud followed.

Instantly, an object was flung at the warrior, biting into the shield and almost splitting it in two. Úlfor ignored the axe as he jabbed his spear at some unseen figure beyond the boat.

A dark blur flew past. The arrow struck him in the back of his shoulder. With an enraged howl, Úlfor hurled his spear in the direction from which the projectile had come, then retrieved the axe from the shield. Ducking low, he dodged a second bearded axe, which fortunately missed its mark and soared over the ship. The wolf fylgja emitted a piecing howl that only Líf could hear.

On both sides, men were attempting to breach the vessel. Three tried to board *Wavecutter* at the same time. Úlfor grasped the shield and slammed its edge onto their reaching fingers, breaking a number of them in one stroke.

Shouts rang out.

Orders were given.

Another figure leaped next to the Úlfhéðinn, someone not of the Lothbranson's crew. Úlfor immediately attacked that fellow, who, like the wolf warrior, sported an axe and shield. Yet unlike Líf's protector, the other man's shield was new and flawless. The painted design on its surface indicated it had been commissioned by Jarl Harek for his personal crewmen.

Then the third man leaped onto the ship. Harekson stood between Líf and Úlfor, his sword ready to deliver its lethal blow.

Chapter Nine

There was nothing that Úlfor could do. He was too closely entangled with the other man to even attempt to defend himself against Harekson.

Líf held her breath as her eyes darted from the tip of Harekson's blade to the vile man's back. That's when she realized he had not seen her. She reached back, felt about, and seized the first object she touched—a sack of moderate size that contained something heavy, or so it seemed to Líf.

Harekson raised his weapon.

Thray caught Líf's eye and shouted, "Líf! Do it now!"

Springing to her feet, Líf swung the sack at Harekson's head. The blow should not have done serious damage, but the surprise attack, together with the impact, sent the man reeling over the side of *Wavecutter*. Ingots of silver sailed through the air and scattered. From below came the angered squeal of Harekson's boar.

Úlfor was still combating his man. If Harekson managed to climb back aboard, he would surely kill Líf without hesitation. There was no time to waste. Jumping behind one of the smaller storage crates, Líf shoved it as fast as she could to the side of the ship. Using all the strength she had, she lifted the heavy box up and over the railing and allowed it to fall below.

The crash was loud. Líf peered over the side. Harekson lay on the ground. She could not see his face, but she saw blood oozing from under the shattered wood. His boar was nowhere to be seen.

Right beside her, a man fell. His helmet tilted, and vacant eyes stared back at her. Nearby, Úlfor pulled the damaged arrow out of his own back. Blood stained the wolf's-hide cloak that covered his injury.

Trying to stand, Líf's legs felt weak, and she leaned against the siding. Bodies were strewn all around the ship. Blood soaked into the once pristine white of the snow-covered ground. Was it over? Or was this just the beginning?

"Let me help you with that," Líf told Úlfor, realizing he had snapped the arrow off, leaving the arrowhead in his flesh. His eyes, which had once appeared vicious, no longer terrified the woman. "Please, let me do this. You did save me."

He nodded at the divots that had been gouged into the side of the ship when the crate toppled over. "You saved yourself."

Nonetheless, he slowly turned around and unclasped his cloak. The heavy thing dropped to the floor, exposing the bloody hole in his tunic. But before Líf could retrieve any bandaging, Úlfor raised his hand.

Multiple men came running toward the ship. For a moment, Líf's heart felt as if it skipped a beat. Then she recognized the faces of Ottar and Roden among other crew. Once he saw the devastation around the drakkar, Ottar picked up his speed. He easily hoisted himself onto *Wavecutter* and caught Líf up in his arms.

"They escaped us," he explained apologetically. "We did not realize any had gotten away until we lost sight of Harekson."

"I killed him." The words felt like ice on her tongue, numbing her mouth and muting the warmth of her brother.

Ottar held her firmly at arm's length and inspected her. "You what?"

Líf pointed to the far side of the ship. "Over there."

Right at that moment, one of the crew shouted, "The whoremonger's still breathing!"

Ottar looked over the edge, his eyes wide with amazement, though he said not a word. From below came the booming laugh of Skeggi. "She'll be a shieldmaiden yet!"

By now, Úlfor had climbed out of the ship and was speaking to Roden. They both looked up at Líf. The Úlfhéðinn inclined his head in a sign of respect. She mirrored his motion.

Others were removing Harekson from beneath the wreckage of the crate. His face and dark hair were covered in so much blood that Líf was surprised he was still alive. His narrow nose was clearly broken, and red lined the teeth in his open mouth. He looked nothing like the steely fellow who loathed Líf and looked down upon her family.

In the distance, smoke began to billow from Harekson's camp. This fight was over, the battle finished.

Once on the ground, Líf looked about until she found the darkening bristles of the razorback, who lay listlessly on her side in the snow. The boar struggled for air, her color fighting to brighten. Standing behind the tusked beast, Líf looked at her brother. "Is everyone else...?"

Ottar appeared sorrowful. "Most were killed before they knew what had happened. Others made an attempt to fight." He looked at the corpses being piled away from the ship. Nothing more needed to be said.

Later, Hervor returned with the rest of the men. They dragged a faering behind them, but there was not one prisoner to be seen. "Without a full crew," she explained, "their longship could not sail again. They were as good as dead. It was more merciful to take that hope away than to let them suffer a slow death in this frozen wasteland."

Ottar seemed to have expected such brutal action. He did not look nearly as appalled as Líf did upon hearing their sister's words. Instead, he pointed to the four-oared ship.

Hervor explained, "It might come in handy. There was no use for all of them, so I had the others burned along with the bodies." She gave Líf a look of warning. "There is no time for burial, even for our own men."

"How many?" Ottar asked.

"Six or so. Eight in total, if those pass during the night." Hervor gestured to a pair of men being carried to their night sacks.

"We have one captive who lives."

The shieldmaiden's face grew dubious. "Who?"

Ottar led them to the far side of *Wavecutter*, where Harekson knelt. He had come to his senses. Bound and staked in such a way that he could not move, his attempts to rise were useless.

A smile cracked Hervor's face but faded into surprise at Ottar's next words. "Your sister's doing."

Nearby stood young Sigird, his skin pale. He spoke to his kin. "You never knew when to quit."

"Be happy, brother," sneered Harekson. "If I was freed, I would run you through."

Ottar gave Sigird's shoulder an encouraging squeeze, just as he would have done to his own sons. He turned to Hervor. "He's yours. Do with him what you will." Then the male Lothbranson, along with Sigird, turned away, leaving the shieldmaiden to kill their offender.

Líf was unable to move. She observed her lithe sister run her fingers over her hair, tucking back the loose ends that had escaped her war braids. Then Hervor squatted down in front of Harekson, close enough to butt heads with him if she so desired.

The captive spat blood in her face before sneering, "You lowlife *bitch*! And I considered marrying you."

What audacity he had! Líf had been there the day Harekson pressured Ottar into arranging a marriage with Hervor. There had been no choice in the matter, and it was probably the worst topic to bring up for one at the shieldmaiden's mercy.

Hervor made no move to wipe the spittle from her face, yet she appeared to want to rip Harekson's hugr from his body and send him off to whatever afterlife the gods saw fit. Her hand hovered over the head of her axe, ready to pull it out of her belt at the first inclination. At last, Hervor said, "A warrior's death is too good for you."

Standing up, she turned to face the cloud-peppered sky. Then, in a swift movement, the shieldmaiden knocked the captive unconscious with the butt of her axe. As several men walked by, she commanded, "Throw him on the ship. Tie him to the mast."

"You're letting him live?" Líf was surprised and questioned her sister's uncharacteristic behavior.

Hervor stepped up to Líf before she explained, "That man is the first grandson of King Thorkell and heir not only to the jarldom of Thorinheim but potentially to the kingdom itself. There is a good chance that the king will not return our citizenship if his heir is dead. Ottar deserves his sons. We deserve a home."

Líf was simultaneously shocked by her sister's decision and proud of it. Still, what issues would arise as they tried to keep an enemy captive alive during the journey ahead?

They both watched as men loaded Harekson's body onto the drakkar. Hervor gave a snort. "At least one of us got a shot at him." She eyed her little sister and grinned. Before anything else could be said, the tall blond shouted out, "I need a dozen men with me to scavenge what we can from the other camp!"

Líf left her sister to her own business.

"Your siblings are pleased with you," purred Thray near Líf's cheek. "So am I."

Líf scratched the top of the squirrel's head before going off to find some food to fill their bellies. There would be no traveling that day.

By the time all useful goods from Harekson's camp were brought back and stored, the sun had already begun to sink. There was also the issue of the injured. The pair with the most severe wounds had both died within an hour of each other. All the other wounded required time to be tended to. Both Hervor and Líf stitched many a cut and even branded shut some that continued to bleed readily.

Líf also worked to remove the arrowhead from Úlfor's back. She had to use metal pliers heated in fire and quickly cooled in the snow. Once the point was removed, she carefully sewed up the split flesh.

As unpleasant as the situation was, Líf was grateful she could contribute something. These men had all ensured that the mission would be able to continue. There was still a chance for success.

By Ottar's command, the venture continued. There were at least three more days of travel before they would reach Sormr. With the combined provisions, there was no risk of running low any time soon. However, the fact that snow had begun to fall again was quite worrisome. If the drifts rose too high, pulling the drakkar overland could become impossible.

Shortly after the party departed, Líf noticed Harekson's boar stumbling behind the ship, limping and glazed. If the tie between man and fylgja were not so strong, the poor beast would have collapsed from the pain it was certainly enduring. Líf felt sorry for the creature as she observed it struggling.

Yet why should she be so concerned? The beast was the fylgja of Harekson, their enemy. Then again, it was not the boar's fault that her person was so vile.

Petting Thray's back, Líf asked her little friend, "Do you think a man's personality can affect a fylgja's, outside of the animal form? Or for that matter, can a fylgja's affect a man's?"

Thray squinted back at her suspiciously. "Are you trying to blame me for something?"

"No. Of course I am not," Líf countered. She was quite surprised at the squirrel's reaction.

Her fylgja flicked her bushy tail three times. "We are bound in many ways, yes. But not in *every* way."

Líf was puzzled. Was that the answer to her question? It sounded far too vague. And it was not like Thray to take offense. They used to be so closely bound with one another. This journey, along with its trials, was causing a fissure to form between them. Líf's mood soured.

During one of their rests, she spotted Einar sipping water from a pouch in the shade of the longship. His fox was curled up at his feet. Elsewhere, men chatted and relaxed in small groups, but Einar was alone. No matter what he did, he was considered an outsider.

Had she misjudged him? Twice now, he had saved her family; yet they still looked at him with distrust. He was not here for pay, nor was he one of the trusted crew the Lothbransons had brought with them. He did not fit any category. But did he deserve the alienation and isolation? Having a fox fylgja often indicated that the person was deceitful, but that was not always the case. It could also imply that one was cunning and sly—qualities that could prove beneficial.

Walking over to him, Líf honestly said, "I want to thank you for what you did the other day. It was smart to hold back and kill those on watch."

At first, Einar's eyes were full of pity; then he blinked, and his face became collected and calm. "I can only do what I think is right and what might gain me entry into Valhalla. As I said before, your family is honorable. I value that, else I would not be here."

At their feet, the squirrel and fox touched noses. Both animals' iridescent fur rippled in new waves of color.

"Well, for what it's worth, I am grateful," Líf acknowledged before picking up Thray. Realizing what she had done, she felt her face pale and waited for Einar's reaction.

Surprisingly, he looked at her without revulsion or discomfort. For a long moment, it was clear he was considering the actions of the woman who speaks to fylgja. Finally, he said, "It's worth more than you know."

Everyone had stopped, frozen in their tracks. All eyes were turned upward, staring in the same direction. No one dared speak.

Before them rose an incomprehensibly gigantic wall. Although pale and sheer like the glaciers they knew, this was not made of frozen matter. Magnificent sections of stone had been stacked perfectly and locked into place. Not a single gap could be seen, not one imprecise calculation found. Soaring into the dome of the sky, the massive structure was encased in a film of white where snow had formed ice so polished that its unbreakable core could be discerned even at this distance.

Standing between her siblings, Líf finally found her voice. "Do you think the gods made this?

Without looking away from the wall, Ottar admitted, "That's unknown. One thing is for certain: whether god or jötunn, it was not man."

CHAPTER TEN

"It has to have been the gods trying to protect us," Líf said as she took in the unbelievable sight. "For why would jötnar barricade themselves behind it if they love slaying mankind?"

"Maybe it was the Asgardians; those deities care for us. Or maybe it was something else." Ottar finally turned to his crew, though his voice was low enough that only his sisters could hear. "Whatever its origin, we need to make our way through."

He gave a sharp whistle, and the men began to haul the ship forward. They reached Sormr's shores at midday and made camp. Hervor wanted to start fresh in the morning. The waterway was wider than expected, and she did not want to attempt to find the sole entrance to Jötunheim in the dark.

"I'm not sure I'm ready for this," Líf admitted to Brasir as they observed the elder Lothbransons, along with a number of the crew, inspecting the water. There was something unnatural about the area. With the temperature as low as it was, the river should have been covered in ice. Yet it was not. The stony shoreline was clear of frost and snow. As far as they could tell, even the opposite side of the crossing held no threat of frozen buildup. And the water itself, though irrefutably cold, continued to move rapidly.

Brasir stood by Líf. His large bear fylgja had risen on her rear legs as she, too, peered across the expanse. Crossing his muscular arms in front of his chest, Brasir said, "That is perfectly acceptable. If any person said he was prepared for the unknown, I would question his sanity."

Was Brasir trying to be funny? Or was he just being logical? Líf raised an eyebrow as she tried to figure out the dark-skinned man.

It was Brasir who spoke next. "How is your wrist?"

Líf lifted her arm. The swelling had gone down but the tenderness remained. "Improving. As is my training." She did not know exactly why she felt the need to defend her earlier decision, but she did.

"I wish you could feel safe again," said Brasir.

"There should be nothing wrong with a woman learning the arts of combat," countered Líf.

"There isn't anything *right* about learning to fight in response to the threat of death."

Líf was quiet for a moment before saying, "It may not be right, but it's the way things are."

"Unfortunately, it is," the man agreed.

"Brasir," Ottar's voice called out. "Help us with the mast."

He headed away at the summons. A number of men were lowering the mast to the floorboards of *Wavecutter*. If the völva was right, they would not be able to sail the ship through the fissure with the mast erect. It was heavy and required the utmost care to take down without cracking the wood or injuring a fellow crewman.

Harekson, who had been kept onboard during their travels, was now tethered to the sculpted prow. None of the men dared lower him to the ground lest he try to bolt or do harm to others. He was often left alone, blindfolded, until it was time to offer him food. Since his imprisonment, he had only recently eaten several meals.

Hervor suspected that he understood their need to keep him alive and was trying to rebel. His threat to starve himself might have been a larger concern to them had his own hunger not won out.

At first, Líf had thought it strange to blindfold their prisoner, for it did not matter if Harekson saw where they were headed. When she asked Ottar, he explained that this was done so he would not struggle and injure another. Unable to see, he could not come up with a creative means of freeing himself and so remained at the mercy of the Lothbransons.

Harekson's boar was near the stern of the ship. The creature looked dejected, and Líf could not blame her. There was always something pitiful about a fylgja unable to maintain contact with her human. The animal's coloring appeared dull and failed to shimmer in as wide a range of hues as those around her. The other fylgjur acted as threatening barricades, brutally attacking the boar when the pathetic beast stepped out of line. She was restricted to a small area under the constant watch of her fellow entities.

Thray must have observed Líf's line of sight, for the tiny squirrel shivered. "I don't ever want to be separated from you."

Líf raised an eyebrow. Hadn't the little creature chosen to stay away from her? Of course, when it was Thray's choosing, it was all right, but not if Líf walked away. Surprisingly, this realization did not irritate her, but it did make her more curious about fylgjur morals.

"Can she swim?" Líf found herself asking the iridescent creature. "All of you can swim to an extent."

Thray was thoughtful. "Only if her human can. Are you worried she won't be able to board?" The squirrel looked around. "Are you concerned that not all of us can access the ship?"

The camp was filled with a few avian fylgjur and many mammalian ones. Some species were small enough to climb on a shirt or a shoulder or to fly in the air. Yet there were others.

At home, fylgjur would board via the docks. Some could even climb over a ship's side. But what about the rest?

"A little," Líf admitted.

"That is quite kind of you, Líf. But please trust me, that should not be *your* concern."

Eyeing the sullen boar once more, Líf headed off to find Hervor. If they were to remain on land for the rest of the day, at least she could be practicing with a shield.

There was something eerie about waking up in the shadow of the gigantic wall. It was so tall that it held off morning's light until the hour was far later than everyone wanted.

Hervor was irritated. She'd woken up that way. Líf thought there was something about setting off later than planned that made her sister quick to react. Once the ship was moving at full speed, crossing Sormr should take only a few hours. Yet, not knowing where the exact opening lay was troublesome—as was the knowledge that they would most likely have only one chance to make it through.

By the time Líf had rolled up her night sack and blankets and gone to break her fast, she noticed that most of the fylgjur were positioned along the perimeter of *Wavecutter*'s deck, as if waiting for their people to join them. Even the boar was there, her color brighter than the day before.

"How?" Líf asked in awe.

Thray sniffed, "I merely expressed your concern before I went to sleep. That's all."

"But how?"

The squirrel's glistening eyes danced with swirls of color. That was all the answer Líf would receive.

Everyone worked in a well-trained and precise manner. Each member of the crew knew his job and completed it without waiting for a command. However, it still took them several hours to slide *Wavecutter* into the water after loading the ship.

By the time Guthorm finally barked out, "She's ready!" the sun was well into the sky.

Líf had been the first one on the vessel as the ship returned to the waters. Hervor was next, followed by Ottar, then the rest of the crew. She eyed Harekson, remembering his strong grip and the impact of his slap on her cheek when he had threatened her life at the Althing before having her family banished. She prayed that his bindings would remain tight.

"What do you want to do with him?" Skeggi asked Hervor as the crew readied the oars. The ruddy-bearded fellow picked part of his morning meal out of his teeth as he nodded to Harekson.

Their captive was still tethered to the prow of the ship, standing upright in the spot where Hervor usually presided. The shieldmaiden looked less than thrilled at having the man on the drakkar. "Move him to the center. He can sit on the mast. I think a night propped upright will wear him down a little."

Skeggi smirked. "As ya command."

Líf felt her skin crawl as the man was led past her. She slipped next to her sister. "Are you ready for this?"

Hervor looked from Líf to the impressive wall behind her, then shouted out, "Steer us true, Ottar! The rest of you—row!"

Wavecutter lurched forward as she cut through the liquid beneath her. Frigid spray splattered faces and hands. Behind them, Úlfor rowed the little faering. Both mercenaries had insisted upon bringing it. Though Ottar feared the loss of two more men, Hervor granted Úlfor permission to transport the small vessel if he felt that he could keep up. Roden had had to remain upon the drakkar; as a Wayfinder, he was too valuable to risk. Somehow Líf wondered if this was just an excuse to get rid of one of the men who challenged her sister's authority. For how could one man attempt a feat at which a ship as grand as *Wavecutter* might not succeed—and on a faering meant for four?

Sensing the longship racing across the water, Harekson threatened, "No matter where you go, you cannot escape retribution. The world may be wide, but it holds you in its grip. Others will come for you and hunt you down. Your bounty is enough that even the most beneficent farmer would consider laying down his plow to track you."

Hervor ignored the captive as best she could and continued to shout, "Row!" on beat, although the severity of her face suggested she was considering other alternatives. Ottar remained calm, focusing on the direction in which they must head.

Harekson tried to shift his position but was unable to move much. The way his wrists were tied caused the ropes to cut into his flesh. He verbally abused those around him for the better part of an hour before he finally said, "I'm sure even some of your hired help would be interested in how much your heads cost. Do you want to know? Do you dare ask?"

"Someone shut 'im up already," Ulf grunted as he pulled his oar.

Skeggi rose to do so, but Hervor shouted, "Stop!"

She strode up to the prisoner, grabbed his hair and jerked his head back, exposing his throat.

At Líf's angle, she could not tell if her sister's dagger was still tucked in her boot.

"Is that you, my *love?*" Harekson's voice dripped with poison.

Pulling his head back even farther, the shieldmaiden hissed, "You think men will come after us? You believe they would value the pay to follow us to the ends of Midgard? Maybe." She yanked away the blindfold along with a clump of dark hair. "But we will not be in Midgard much longer."

Harekson's sneer suddenly disappeared when he laid eyes upon the massive wall. Hervor returned to her post, leaving him muttering, "This cannot be. This cannot be."

The waters were so clear that it seemed as if one could look all the way down to the depths. Yet not a fish was spotted anywhere in the strait. The few birds flitting in the sky avoided the channel as well. It was as if the wildlife did not feel safe around the waters. Or was it the presence of the wall? The ship slipped into the shade of the gargantuan structure.

"You're mad! You're all actually mad!" Harekson gasped as he realized that they were veering right at the wall and not parallel to it. "Cut me loose! Do not take me with you!"

"Collect yourself, Harekson," boomed Skeggi, who had never liked the fellow to begin with. "You should be ashamed of your lack of spine."

"Odin above! Set me free!" Harekson began to struggle. Blood dripped from his wrists onto the damp floorboards.

"Now you can gag him," said Hervor, smirking.

Einar lurched up from his seat to do the shieldmaiden's bidding. As he was forcing a wad of cloth into the enraged man's mouth, his own face was struck by a flailing elbow. Stumbling back, he held his jaw while blood oozed from a split lip. "Loki's offspring! That hurt!"

Between the pair, the fox snarled while the boar squealed. Upon Líf's shoulder, Thray began to emit a low growl. "The waters. He's there."

Without questioning, Líf leaned over the edge of the ship. Deep below the drakkar were the flickers of scales the size of one's hands. Slowly easing back, Líf turned to her sister. "Jörmungandr is with us."

Hervor took a peek. Her body stiffened briefly. She shouted out to the crew, "How does one enter Valhalla?"

"Through death!" the men shouted back.

"And how must one act upon entry into that golden hall?"

"Show no fear!"

"Show no fear!" Hervor repeated as the crew and the ship picked up speed. It felt as if *Wavecutter* were soaring. Without the hindrance of waves, she crossed the channel faster than even Líf could have hoped for. They could make it out of Midgard! They would!

As the shieldmaiden smiled at those hard at work, her eyes landed upon Einar. The man's lip was swelling quickly, and he tried to wipe some of the blood onto his sleeve. He turned and hacked. The red-hued spittle landed in the water.

Líf could almost hear its impact. Or was that the thud of her heart as she watched the dark stain disappear. In the depths, the mass of scales began to rise. The world serpent was stirring.

Líf grabbed Hervor's arm. With a nod and a point, she showed her sister the frightening movement rising toward them. The shieldmaiden pulled herself up onto the prow as she searched for the opening in the wall.

"Do you see it, Ottar?" she asked. Did her voice waver for a second?

Sensing something awry, their brother replied, "No, I—Yes! Yes, I see our mark. It's coming up."

"Prepare to turn her!" Hervor commanded. "We must enter head on."

That's when the first wave hit. The water rose and fell, crashing against the side of the ship. Several of the men and the loose seating slid about. Líf almost lost her own footing, but she grabbed hold of the railing beside her.

"Where'd that come from?" one man asked.

"Did you see it?" another inquired.

Harekson's eyes widened even more as he was bounced about despite his bindings.

"Don't stop rowing!" barked Hervor. "Don't you *ever* stop rowing!"

At the stern of the vessel, Ottar quickly shoved the steering oar into the water, causing the longship to spin. In seconds, the front of the drakkar directly faced the wall and the tiny, dark smudge near the waterline. The little faering could not be spotted.

Everyone aboard the longship was doing his best to pull the oars simultaneously as a new set of waves shoved them sideways. Ottar struggled to maintain the ship's direction as Hervor yelled commands. But for the shieldmaiden's keen eyes spotting upcoming impacts, *Wavecutter* would be far from their objective.

Farther upstream, a geyser of water erupted. Frigid liquid spewed high into the sky. All at once, a section of the serpent broke surface. Its gigantic proportion was matched only by that of the wall.

"Hold on!" Hervor warned as *Wavecutter* rocked violently, barely able to right herself.

Drenched in unbearably cold water, the crew kept rowing as Ottar realigned the ship yet again.

The shieldmaiden reassuringly held onto Líf's shoulder and shouted, "Faster, men! Row faster!"

In all the tumult, success at the nearly impossible task of speeding headlong into the crevasse of the stone was becoming less and less probable. Jörmungandr slowly rose. More and more stretches of scaled body were sighted. Soon *Wavecutter* would be tossed about in its wake until the ship shattered and sank to the sea floor.

"Líf, it's coming!" cried Thray in terror. The frightened fylgja was referring not to the horrifically large sea serpent, but rather to their impending crash into the immense wall. They were off course. Ottar was doing his best to correct the trajectory, but was there time?

In the next leap over rolling waves, the longship realigned herself.

"Hold her steady!" Hervor shouted. Her voice blended with the grunts and cries of the men. Their angle was perfect. "Pull them in!"

Frantically, the men hauled the oars into the vessel and expertly stowed them along the central walk next to the mast. There would be no more chances to change direction. One final wave forced its way under them. Riding its crest, the ship rose from the water.

Líf could see that the fissure was now too low. She instinctively warned, "Everyone, get down!"

Pulling Hervor along with her, she dove to the floor just as the top of the prow collided with the roof of the opening. The serpent-headed topper sheared off and was flung overhead. A man cried out in pain. Splinters fell down upon Líf, as did fragments of stone amid the grating sound of the ship until the wave had passed them by. As the water level dropped, the longship slid through the darkened cavern.

The light was almost extinguished. Líf could barely make out the passing of stone as the ship began to slow. How thick was the wall? Was their nearly devastating crash enough to keep them from making it to the far side? What if they were stuck in this tomb of water and rock forever?

"I love you, Thray," Líf whispered to the shivering squirrel.

"I love you, Líf," the fylgja replied.

Suddenly, light broke into the gloom of Líf's thoughts. Up ahead, the opening to Jötunheim appeared to beckon their ship to enter. Carefully rising as high as she dared in their low environment, Líf and Thray caught their first glimpse of the world beyond....

The Guardian's Speaker

Volume Four

Epigraph

I remember yet the giants of yore,
Who gave me bread in the days gone by;
Nine worlds I knew, the nine in the tree
With mighty roots beneath the mold.

Völuspá - The Prophecy of the Seeress

CHAPTER ONE

Men are not meant to leave their world. They cannot survive. Only death and destruction await those who try.

Since the creation of the nine worlds, mankind has remained within the borders of Midgard, surrounded by Jörmungandr, the world serpent, and barricaded behind impregnable walls. There was not meant to be a way out. None had dared or were meant to challenge these known facts. That is, until now...

Líf quickly tried to recall everything she had heard or been taught about those ill-fated attempts to travel outside the world of man. Though it was never openly discussed, any attempt to do so was not only discouraged but also understood simply to be impossible. Yet the young woman's family and crew were about to leave Midgard and enter Jötunheim, the realm of the giants.

Crouched on the shattered prow of *Wavecutter*, their longship, Líf squinted at the oncoming light that marked the exit from the narrow stone fissure through which they were sailing. The fissure's rough ceiling, mere inches above her head, grated against the prow's splintered end, where the ornamental face of a serpent had once perched. It had been sheared off upon entry into the tunnel, when the ship had nearly collided with the inconceivably tall, thick barrier. The wall had been created before time was conceived, to prevent the jötnar from encroaching upon the newly created race of man.

Jötunheim was both wilderness and wasteland, the opposite of Midgard in every way. Civilized society resided on one side of the wall, while the horrific and monstrous giants lived in primordial brutality on the other. No wonder the gods hated the jötnar; the massive brutes made a mockery of their notions of culture and intellect. And of all the gods, Thor, the lightning bearer, hated them the most.

As the light ahead of her brightened, Líf's narrow fingers unintentionally played with her neck ring and the carving of Mjölnir, Thor's war hammer. The symbol protected those who wore it, for Thor was the god of the common people. But where were the gods now? Surely, if something was harming mankind they would be aware of it. Why had they not intervened? Why was this the only mission in all of Yggdrasil to attempt to prevent the annihilation of the human race?

A plague was killing people—a sickness taking the lives of men, women, and children. This invisible destructive force was spreading. If it were not stopped, would anyone survive? Most people were unaware of the oncoming calamity and did not know about its effects. The few who did, denied its existence, for this illness specifically affected hamingjur.

Each person, each human, was composed of four distinct parts: hamr, the physical body; hugr, the soul and mind; fylgjur, the guardian spirit; and hamingjur, one's personal luck. Without all four parts of the self, a human could not survive. When someone's hamingja was destroyed, he or she would easily fall victim to disease, a freak accident, or some other fatal occurrence. The human would not survive.

Like fylgjur, hamingjur were invisible female presences. No one had ever seen them. That is, until now. A man known as Brasir, who was traveling on this very ship, could see hamingjur—not unlike Líf, who had been born with the ability to communicate with fylgjur. How had the only two people in all of Midgard with these unexplainable gifts discovered each other? And why? There had to be a reason. But what?

"Líf, I'm scared," whimpered Thray, Líf's own fylgja, who took the form of an iridescent squirrel. The tiny creature curled around Líf's neck and shivered as the pair of them squinted to make out the first glimpse of the world beyond their own.

As Líf's guardian, the small animal was never comfortable in a situation that could cause the woman harm. Poor Thray. How would she and all the other animal spirits fare when they learned that their people had chosen to disregard what was natural, chosen to risk their lives in a world not their own?

These questions faded away in the brilliant light that swallowed them. *Wavecutter* was passing through the opening. Líf shielded her eyes as she tried to adjust her sight to what lay beyond.

As soon as the blurs gained color and form and the panorama took shape, she inhaled sharply. They had entered a basin, a large lake that hugged the stone wall blocking entry into Midgard. The basin, and hence the ship, was surrounded by barren land covered in snow far thicker than where they had come from. Here, it appeared that winter had also chosen to stay through what should have been their short spring. In the distance, sharp spears of craggy rock jutted from the ground, as if a jötunn's broken ribs had been pulled out of its back and left to form an eerily jagged mountain range.

Nothing stirred. Not one bird flew in the air; no creature walked upon the land—at least, none made of flesh and blood.

A goshawk fylgja took wing as she emerged from the shadowy underbelly of the wall. Crying out with unbridled energy, the magnificent bird glimmered high in the sky, encouraging the few other winged fylgjur to follow her boldly into the unknown.

"Is he behind us?" asked Líf's sister, the only other woman on the ship. "I cannot tell." Hervor was a shieldmaiden, one of the few female warriors in their society and someone not to cross. It was her fylgja that soared overhead. The voice of this tall, blond woman with piercing gray eyes oozed skepticism as she scanned the stern, where their brother was supposed to be positioned.

Though slightly younger, Ottar could have been Hervor's twin, except that his eyes were blue and kind while Hervor's gray ones retained the heat of challenge. Just now, Ottar was stooping over one of the newer crewmembers whom they had hired at Jarlbörg, the capital.

"Thorid's having a bit of trouble breathing," Ottar stated dryly as he lifted the prow's splintered wooden serpent head off the man's chest. Sprawled on the floorboards, the poor fellow coughed up blood.

The short, squat man called Ulf chimed in over the groans of a redheaded fellow with a fox fylgja, "Einar's leg was caught under the mast. It's only sprained, not broken, thank the gods. But a good bit of flesh has been rubbed off."

The mast had had to be lowered for passage through the fissure, for the crack in the wall was neither tall enough nor wide enough to sail through. The crew had maneuvered the longship into position using the oars, increased their speed, then pulled the oars in at the last moment. Only the perfect mix of luck and skill had enabled the vessel to squeeze through the opening.

Ulf shoved another body with the tip of his boot. "Harekson's still breathing. With the bump he took to his head, I had hoped…"

Many others glared at the unconscious body of the man responsible for Líf's family's banishment as well as the deaths of a number of crewmen. Most wished him dead. But he was a hostage, one whose life was valued, and possibly the key to revocation of the banishment decree.

Skeggi, a large burly fellow and lifelong friend of Líf's brother, replied to Hervor's earlier question. "I don't see him."

"Pity," the shieldmaiden replied flatly. She returned the seax dagger that had fallen out of her boot during the earlier commotion and readjusted the throwing axe that was tucked into an iron loop on her belt.

Líf was mortified. It was certainly true that Úlfor, the powerfully built mercenary who had chosen to row the faering, a tiny four-oared boat, could never have survived the crossing once the enormous sea serpent

Jörmungandr awakened; but Hervor did not have to be so cold about it. Líf had started to like Úlfor. He was one of their society's elite warriors, who was not only an asset to their quest but also a hero, for he had saved Líf's life during an earlier attack.

Quickly looking at Úlfor's friend, Roden, she noticed that the man's eyes kept wandering back to the black crevice that split the wall at its base. Roden was a Rus, a people related to her own who had traveled, settled, and intermarried with the barbarian tribes in the east. Known for their trading connections, the Rus roamed far and wide to bring back the rarest merchandise. Roden had been a slave but was now a bóndi, a freeman. Fiercely protective of his rights, he had joined the crew purely for the pay. Yet Líf thought there was something kind in his strange, hooded, oval eyes.

"Should we offer him our condolences?" Líf asked Thray quietly. Though everyone on the ship was well aware of her so-called gift, they were not comfortable when she demonstrated it in front of them.

The little squirrel flicked her tail in irritation. The rainbow of colors swirling about her fur shifted to darker hues of discontent. "If you must."

"I thought you liked him and his fylgja," Líf remarked as she recalled the strange little creature called a lesser panda. No such animals lived in her home kingdom.

"What I feel for them is none of your concern," snapped the squirrel as she swatted at a section of Líf's flaming red hair.

"You're just being irritable," retorted Líf. She tucked the swatch behind her ear, then pulled it back to cover the long scar on her forehead. "I know you do not like our plan."

"I would like it better if there really *was* a plan," sniffed Thray. "Passing through several worlds just to double back makes no sense. If our goal is Mímisbrunnr, the well of knowledge, then we should go straight there. That well must be nearby."

"You heard what we were told," Líf said, but she chewed her lower lip with worry. It *would* be easier to head directly to Mímisbrunnr, within whose waters lay the knowledge of how to stop the plague affecting the hamingjur. But nothing was that easy. Líf scratched the top of Thray's head affectionately. "We need a worthy offering to give to the well. Only the Ljósálfar can help us with that."

"The elfin race of the light may be wondrous," began Thray, "but to reach the Ljósálfar, we must travel through lands that are less than hospitable. And winter strengthens unabated."

"How do you know?" Líf looked at the thick mounds of snow.

"I can feel it. Can't you?"

"No."

Thray's nose twitched once more. "Humans…." She leaped from Líf's shoulder and scurried off.

"Oars out!" Hervor barked.

The able-bodied men slid the oars through the oar holes in the side of the ship. With everything occurring so fast, the stoppers had not been put into place; this allowed the crew to set up faster than was normal.

Within their kingdom, a woman would never have been allowed to take command of a drakkar, especially one as magnificent as this highly decorated, brilliantly painted warship. According to legal documents, *Wavecutter* belonged to Ottar. Yet out at sea and away from the homeland, Hervor had always been the unquestioned commander—until recently. Crew hired for this trip knew little of the shieldmaiden's past and trusted her less. Once again, their grumbling was overheard, though it was impossible to tell from whom it came.

Lif observed her sister tense up. The shieldmaiden hated to be challenged and was raring for a fight. Yet surprisingly the tall blond remained calm—at least for now.

"We must move the ship away from here and make landfall. We have injured to tend to and shelter to seek."

As if on command, snow began to fall from the gray sky. Like plumes of downy feathers, the thick clumps at first melted into furs and cloaks, until everyone's clothes had become chilled enough for the clumps to stick, powdering everybody in white.

Wavecutter sliced through the lake. Frigid water sprayed up from the prow and sides and continued to dampen the already sodden crew. Lif shivered in dismay and wrapped her meager cloak more tightly around her. She watched the men grit their teeth as they rowed steadily.

Why must it be so cold? She was used to brutal winters, but that was when she had had a home to live in, a comfortable bed to sleep in, and a fire to keep her warm. Now, all that was gone—all sacrificed for this mission, one they could not fail.

Something bumped against the outer planking and was followed by another thud. Hervor was already staring ahead when Lif realized what was happening. Unlike on the other side of the wall, the waters in Jötunheim were freezing over. The lake shore was not as close as they had thought, and soon the ship was forcing its way through thick sections of ice and snow.

Growling, Hervor strode up and down the longship, giving orders either to row through or to push aside the frozen fragments. The ship's progress slowed, becoming almost negligible.

"What happens if we can no longer move forward?" Lif asked, expecting to hear a response. She immediately realized that Thray was not in earshot. Louder, she called out, "Thray?"

The squirrel's face poked around one of the storage crates that served as a rower's seat. Blinking, the fylgja hopped into Lif's awaiting arms. "Are you worried?"

"Someone needs to be," Líf admitted, a little surprised that her fylgja was so relaxed in their current predicament.

Thray stretched and yawned. "Put me down outside the ship." The squirrel acknowledged the shock on Líf's face and quickly added, "I will not freeze unless you do, and you can swim. I will be fine."

Líf trusted Thray above all others. Leaning over the side, she carefully dropped her glimmering fylgja upon a raised chunk of ice. The little creature's claws held her securely as she leaped from fragment to fragment until she reached an unbroken expanse of white. Soon, the fylgja returned and, near the base of the drakkar, called out, "I know the way. Follow me. I will guide you through the thinnest ice."

Líf seized her sister's shoulder. Leaning close to Hervor's ear, she said, "I have a way to get us across the lake." The shieldmaiden raised an eyebrow as Líf continued, "But you're *not* going to like it."

Chapter Two

"I'm listening," Hervor said.

Líf nodded toward the ice. "Thray can guide us through the thinnest ice so we can get as close to the shore as possible. But..." Líf did not know how to broach the next part.

The shieldmaiden was quick to understand. "Only you can see fylgjur. You would have to guide us."

"It's your ship, Hervor." Líf did not argue. She respected her sister and did not want her to think otherwise.

The tall blond caught their brother's eye as she replied to Líf, "It's a Lothbranson ship. We are all Lothbransons, the three of us. You will tell Ottar where to steer *Wavecutter*. Let's just get her to shore."

After the orders were relayed, Líf took control of the ship. The realization was both exhilarating and frightening. What if she ran the drakkar into underwater rocks or got it stuck in the thickening ice? Yet, as long as Thray was confident of their path, Líf would be as well. At least there was no massive serpent slithering under the surface.

As much as she tried to ignore the chatter of the men behind her, she still overheard the gripes and slurs made by some of the crew. Now they were all directed at her.

"Why don't we just stay home with the children and let the women sail, raid, and run the government?"

A second voice snickered but was cut short so abruptly that Líf looked back. Hervor loomed over a man and pressed her dagger against his throat. She bent down as if to whisper but projected her words so all could hear.

"Any issues you have with the way I run the ship will be brought directly to me. Have problems serving under a woman? I assure you that you do not need a cock to steer a ship." Hervor slid the blade down to the man's groin in a threatening way. "Care to test that theory?"

The man shook his head, and the shieldmaiden smiled sweetly, "Do you understand, Arto?"

"Yes," he said through gritted teeth. Next to him, his goat fylgja bleated.

"Good." Hervor slapped the side of her blade against his cheek before she stepped away.

Refocusing on her own job, Líf made sure the drakkar was angled in the direction of Thray as the little fylgja leaped over the ice. The squirrel bounded ahead, then paused long enough to stand up on her rear legs and observe the following vessel before moving again.

Wavecutter groaned in discontent as she forced her way through the ice but continued to crawl forward. Finally, Líf shouted, "Stop rowing!"

Thray was scurrying back. The fylgja chirped, "That's it."

Líf searched the flat white blanket of snow that surrounded them. "Where's the shore?"

"Another hundred yards out. You can walk from here." Thray jumped up and down as if to display the integrity of the surface, yet fylgjur could not affect the physical world, so the act was pointless.

Behind them, Ottar's voice asked, "What's going on, Líf?"

Without answering, she carefully lowered herself onto the broken sections of ice bordering the ship, then swiftly leaped over to the unfractured expanse. The ice held her weight. But would it hold the rest of the crew? She was the smallest one among them other than Ulf.

"We are near enough to shore to walk there."

"Okay, then." Hervor stepped up to the prow. "Everyone overboard! Lower the planking and unload the ship. We need to make her as light as possible to haul her onto land."

As much as some of the crew clearly wanted to complain, they held their tongues as they obeyed the command. Crates and barrels were quickly removed and carried to solid ground. Bundles of weapons were piled nearby. The two injured men were carefully set down near their personal effects. For the first time, Harekson was untied from the mast and half dragged onto shore.

Líf felt the difference the moment she stepped off the ice and onto frozen earth. The ground was hard and bumpy. Brushing away the snow, she noticed that there was neither soil nor sand, just fragments of stone—and not the smooth, polished ovals that covered her home's beaches. No, these were shards, rough-edged and sharp. The farther down Líf dug, the more stone she revealed. Was all of Jötunheim rock? Were there no plants? No animals? This world must truly be a wasteland if that were the case.

Hervor was overseeing the crew as they attached thick ropes to *Wavecutter* in order to haul the ship out of the water. Ottar had left to find Roden, who was rearranging the crates. Líf knew her brother would relay his sympathies for the loss of Ulfor, his companion.

It was never easy to accept the loss of an offering claimed by Rán. In their underwater hall, the jötunn giantess and her husband ruled over all who drowned at sea. Unfortunately, even the greatest of warriors who met that fate would never gain access to Valhalla. Just like life, the afterlife was harsh and uncompassionate.

"Why are you still glum? You wanted to be here," noted Thray as the squirrel's eyes darted about warily.

Líf nodded toward Roden. "I feel sorry for him. Maybe Hervor should have forced Úlfor to sail with us. I wonder if his stubbornness had anything to do with the fact that he was Úlfhéðnar."

"I think it quite strange that a man such as that wolf warrior would want to try to enter this world by himself, but I know little of the male gender."

"As do I," sighed Líf.

"But he is not dead."

Líf looked incredulous. "How do you know? Can you sense his fylgja?"

"No," sniffed Thray. "I can see him. Look."

Emerging from the darkened hollow of the fissure was the small, four-oared vessel. Standing at its prow was a glimmering wolf. Behind the fylgja, Úlfor—drenched, shivering, and looking as wild as ever—steadily rowed in their direction.

How could he have survived all the tumult caused by Jörmungandr? The world serpent should have sunk the faering and drowned the man, or worse. Yet here he was, seemingly unharmed by the monstrous snake's movements.

"Úlfor!" Líf cried. Running toward the shoreline, she waved at him with the impulsive excitement of a child.

Soon the muscular warrior was greeted by his comrades and offered a place to sit, warm himself, and rest. The crossing in *Wavecutter* had been so extremely difficult and dangerous that Úlfor's ability to survive on his own in the small craft had been unthinkable.

Although Hervor gave Úlfor a begrudging nod of acknowledgment, she left the mercenary to his own devices. Líf wondered if the shieldmaiden envied his success.

"What Úlfor did was imprudent and irresponsible," Líf assured her sister.

"True," the shieldmaiden replied, "but no less noteworthy."

"Of course, only his own life was at risk," added Líf. "He was not in command of more than fifty men."

Hervor looked at her sister thoughtfully. "I wonder if a man who so recklessly puts his own life at risk can be trusted to come to the aid of others." Her distaste for the Úlfhéðinn was evident.

When the blond finally approached Ottar and the pair of mercenaries, Líf followed. Hervor cast Úlfor a judgmental look before asking Roden, "Since you are supposed to be our guide, where are we to go from here?"

Roden's eyes widened, and he rubbed his callused hands as if to ease away a cramp. "Are we traveling more today?"

"No. We all need time to rest after that ordeal."

"That's a relief," Roden said with an earnest smile. "I will tell you more when we head out in the morning." Before either Hervor or Ottar could protest, he warned, "We cannot bring the drakkar."

Both Lothbransons were appalled. "You expect us to just leave her? Here in Jötunheim?" There was an edge to Hervor's voice.

"What? Do you think the jötnar will have use for her? The ship is too small a plaything."

Ottar was as dubious as his older sister. "And what of the faering?"

Roden looked apologetically at Úlfor. "We must leave her here as well."

Líf expected her sister to make a snide remark about Úlfor's wasted effort, but Hervor kept quiet. She nodded to her siblings, and the three left. Hervor and Ottar headed to check on *Wavecutter* while Líf began to prepare for the evening. As she arranged the family's night sacks, she realized that Brasir's was not among them.

Líf spotted the tall man on the opposite side of the camp. With flesh the color of coal, he was easy to identify, even in the growing gloom. His large bear groomed herself near Brasir's bedding. This did not feel right. The freed captive had lived with the Lothbransons since true winter began, and had been treated as if he were a relative. His presence by their fire would be missed.

Thray sensed Líf's discontent. "Are you jealous that Brasir has made new friends?"

"No. I mean, I don't think so. I just—"

There was a commotion in the camp. A brawl had erupted, causing others to gather around. Though fights would occasionally erupt during long expeditions, this one was atypical, for instead of even sides, three men were brutalizing a fourth. That man was sprawled on the ground, where he was kicked and stoned repeatedly. Líf glimpsed both Ottar and Hervor heading toward the fray.

"What should we do?" Thray asked. Her fur bristled.

Drunken fights were not their source of entertainment. Yet this was different, and curiosity got the better of Líf. Carrying Thray, she moved closer to the now separated men.

"This isn't the first time, either," Arto told Ottar. "Several days ago, I caught him looking at Hrek. Isn't that right, Hrek?"

An attractive younger man nodded. "I said my piece before."

"It's not...what you think," gasped the victim of the uneven brawl, then wheezed. One eye was swelling horribly. The rest of him was in even worse shape. His name was Toini; he was one of the men hired at Jarlbörg, and he typically kept to himself. The injuries he had received from Arto and his companions' beating were severe. Gashes from jagged rocks covered his face, and blood pooled about the tears in his clothing. His polecat fylgja struggled to crawl onto the man's chest.

Arto sneered, "That ergi put his cock-loving hands on mine. My friends and I will not abide an ass-fucker. It ain't right. You know the law, Lothbranson. All ergis forfeit their rights based on the choices they make."

"If this is true," Ottar's face was stern, "then I will not counter the law. But consider that every able body is needed from now on. The dead cannot help us with our upcoming trials."

By now, the entire camp seemed to be clustered around the men. Líf's heart beat quickly as she looked at the injured fellow. How had an ergi traveled with them for so long undetected?

The derogatory title *ergi* was reserved for those who possessed effeminate traits or displayed unmanly behavior. Cowards and cheaters were never looked upon fondly, but the worst were those with an affinity for the same sex. The ideals of manliness had been prescribed by the gods and instilled in Líf's people from childhood. Still, she did not wish to see more death. Too much had already occurred.

Each of the other three assailants claimed to have been approached by the ergi. Nothing Toini could say or do would counter so many accusations against him. Ottar stepped back, for he was neither accuser nor accused. The law dictated that Arto and his companions would decide whether to spare Toini's life and let him remain with the people. The killing of an ergi was looked down on, but these men were far beyond the boundaries of civilized society. What rules, if any, now applied?

Líf waited for the final verdict. All that was heard in the ensuing hush were poor Toini's ragged breaths. The man had closed his eyes and lay still in the frigid slush.

Arto picked up a blood-splattered stone and handed the rock to Hrek. "One more for good measure," he said.

Hrek hurtled the sharp projectile at Toini's unprotected face.

Líf turned her head away, but it was already too late. A sickening crunch was echoed by a ferocious howl—a sound not made by the polecat. She heard blood spurting from the wound as Toini's fylgja faded from sight.

Suddenly, Hrek collapsed. His flailing arms and leaden body toppled onto Líf. The pair hit the ground, and she was momentarily blinded by a spray of red.

Crying out, she struggled to wipe away the liquid coating her face as she extricated herself from beneath Hrek's body. The man's head had been split in two; the tip of the spear emerged from his left eye socket.

There was no time to question. There was no time to act. Hrek's killer stood over Líf as he jerked his vile weapon free.

Chapter Three

Several pairs of hands assisted Líf to her feet.
"How dare you?" Arto's voice bellowed. "You had no right!"
Úlfor wiped the gray matter and blood off his spearhead. At his feet, his wolf fylgja snapped her jaws threateningly.

Roden swiftly stepped between his friend and Arto, momentarily passing right through the slavering wolf. Scowling, the Rus replied, "There was no need to do what *you* did." He raised his arms to block the fellow from striking Úlfor.

Arto snapped back, "No need—but *every* right." When he reached for his sword, Ottar intervened.

"Enough! No more killing. I said we need a living crew."

"I demand *my* revenge," Arto shouted, unafraid of either the roguish Úlfhéðinn or his own employer.

"Are you Hrek's kin?" Ottar asked.

"No."

"Then you cannot take Úlfor's life. We may not be in Midgard, but we are still men and have laws to follow."

Arto looked as if he were going to physically lash out. "So says the outlaw," he hissed before stepping back and releasing the grip on his sword.

Several men moved Hrek's body away from the camp and began the difficult process of burying him in the frozen, stony ground. Ergis' bodies, however, customarily were not buried but left for carnivores to feast upon. Toini's corpse had been abandoned by everyone but Úlfor. Even Roden had departed.

Líf watched from a distance as the wolf warrior attempted a feat that would take more than a few men hours to accomplish.

"You're going to help him, aren't you?" Thray questioned. She had not left Líf's shoulder since falling off when Hrek's corpse knocked them to the ground. The squirrel already knew the answer.

"I think so," said Líf, glad that at least her fylgja understood her. She found a pick in the pile of tools, walked over to Úlfor, and began to hack away at the jumble of rock under the snow.

The process was lengthy and grueling. Líf was impressed that Úlfor, who had forded the waters in the small boat despite a shoulder wound that had not completely healed, had the stamina for this task. What drove the man to continue to shovel away stone? He must be far more powerful than he looked, and he looked monstrous.

Though the reputation of someone who assisted an ergi often became tainted, it was clear that Úlfor would never be accused of being less than what he clearly was: a drengr, the ideal man. Fierce, unrelenting, and a natural-born fighter, he would certainly be honored wherever he went if he chose to tell the tales of his exploits. Yet the man spoke only rarely and never shared anything about himself.

Líf stopped scooping away loose stone with her now blistered hands and eyed Úlfor's temporarily discarded weapon. "That's your Úlfhéðinn spear. I've seen how good you are with it." Though crusting clumps of gore still matted her red hair, Líf had taken the time to change her blood-drenched clothes. Not wanting to mislead him, she quickly added, "Can you show me how to use one? I know I'm not a man or a shieldmaiden, but—"

"Your sister is working with you on the shield," Úlfor grunted. His voice was rough, though Líf could not tell if that was its normal tone or if it was gravelly from not having spoken recently. Either way, the conversation ended.

By now, the pit was deep enough to allow them to lower Toini's body into it. The Úlfhéðinn grabbed the corpse under its arms.

"I know," Líf acknowledged reluctantly as she picked up the legs. Why, in death, did a man's weight seem to triple?

Together, they placed Toini's body in the hole. As Líf stood looking down at the vacant expression on the man's marred features, she felt the need to say something.

"May Hel welcome you to her hall and drink with you in death."

Úlfor nodded at her words, then began to pile the stone back into the pit. Having no shovel, Líf had turned to leave when she heard the wolf warrior speak. "I will show you some of what I know...for...you understand better than most."

Puzzled by these words, she left to find Hervor and practice with the training shield before retiring for the night. Líf knew her sister was not pleased that she had helped to bury the ergi, and the shieldmaiden did not go easy on her despite her exhaustion and her throbbing hands. Although Líf left the sparring session feeling particularly battered, she did not regret her decision. Burying Toini felt right; she was not ashamed of what she had done.

During the night, the man injured by the broken prow died. Once again, their journey had to be postponed until he, too, was buried in the stony ground. Úlfor and Roden used that time to hide the faering under a snowdrift. Travel packs were made up and all transportable wares distributed among the crew. Each person received skis to help them move swiftly over the snow. Those who had brought chain-mail shirts and helmets donned them. A stretcher was constructed from driftwood and scrap cloth to haul Einar until his leg mended. Harekson was uncompassionately revived; bound like a slave, he was forced to walk between two of the larger men.

Both Ottar and Hervor looked forlornly at *Wavecutter*. The ship had been hauled farther inland and lowered carefully to rest on her side. Brilliantly painted and exquisitely adorned with detailed carvings, the drakkar was still magnificent, though considerably damaged.

"Maybe the snow will cover her and the jötnar won't find her," Líf offered. Neither of her siblings replied. They all realized that the fine craft might be destroyed before their return. If that happened, there would be little hope of surviving a return to their world. Once again, Líf tried to console them. "There has to be a reason for all this. Our paths are preordained. Why would we be sent here, if not to save our race?"

Ottar lifted Líf up and kissed the top of her head. "You see the best."

Tears welled up in Hervor's eyes, and the shieldmaiden blinked them away. "Let's be off," she said. Yet the forcefulness in her voice had faded.

Partly out of respect and partly because she had not skied in years, Líf slipped back and allowed her siblings and Roden to take the lead. Until now, her life had revolved around the household. As a child, she had loved to slide down the large slopes with the thrill of the wind in her hair, seeing the world around her blur past. But this was different. This was not childish fun. Besides, the terrain was predominantly flat.

As she used the poles to help propel herself forward, Líf's thin arms felt strained from the exertion she had forced upon them the night before. She was unable to keep pace in the long caravan, and men began to slide past her. Líf soon fell behind. At least she was not alone; for Brasir had volunteered to stay at the rear and make sure stragglers were not left behind. At first, Líf was embarrassed to find herself in that category, but she soon realized that she was content with his company. Even better, she was reassured and entertained when she discovered that Brasir, too, struggled with his skis. Although Líf began to remember the proper technique, the black-skinned man continued to flounder.

"Are you all right?" she asked, trying not to sound amused.

"I've never skied before," admitted Brasir, somewhat abashed.

"Never? And you waited until now to admit this?"

"I had hoped—" Brasir grunted in frustration as his legs almost slid out from under him.

Líf quickly reached over to help the man balance. His muscles were unusually tense. "Relax," she said. "You have time to learn while the ground is still flat."

After receiving some pointers, Brasir explained, "We do not have snow where I come from. The air is too hot."

"Too hot for snow?" Líf giggled. "Are you from Muspelheim? No snow? I cannot envision such a place. Especially now." She shivered, surveying the white-coated landscape.

Brasir's bear and Thray trekked ahead of them, the squirrel bouncing about the ursine's heavy feet. The two fylgjur both shimmered in a plethora of calming colors.

Trying to keep up with Líf's now steady pace, Brasir turned to her. "You are very empathetic."

"Why do you say that?" Líf asked. Thray glanced back at her.

"Because of what you did last night. You are kind, Líf. Not many would be as open-minded about people who are not well *understood*."

Líf hesitated before responding, then chose her words with care. "Well, *I'm* not really understood…although at times, I think you do. Why did you not offer to help?"

"It was not for me to judge," said Brasir rather bluntly.

"Judge? A man was dead. Why should there be any question that he deserved a proper burial?"

"Did he? Deserve it?"

Líf stopped and gave him a long, hard look. "I don't think I like this side of you, Brasir."

The man shrugged. "People do not have sides. We are much too complex for that."

As she tried to think of a response, Líf heard her fylgja call out, "Something's happening up ahead!"

Those at the front of the caravan had come to a stop and were waiting for the rest of the group to gather. There was much chatter among them. Scooping up Thray, Líf skied over to her siblings, where the talk seemed the most serious.

Unintentionally loudly, Skeggi boomed, "Have you ever seen anything like it before?"

Hervor glared at the large oaf. "How could we? Jötnar have not entered Midgard in a millennium or more."

"What's going on?" Líf asked.

Skeggi pointed ahead of them. "Footprints, Lingy. Giant footprints."

"Jötnar?" Líf gaped at the huge divots in the snow. Three times the size of a man's, the nearly oval markings did resemble shoes.

"They're not fresh," Ottar reassured her. He was a skilled tracker. Though these prints were not of their world, they could be observed, interpreted, and followed like any animal's. "The morning's flurries have already begun to fill the hollows. There are two of them—by their gait, not traveling at a great speed."

"Can we avoid them?" Guthorm Blood Cheeks asked. The fellow's rosacea flush was partially hidden by the thick fox-fur trim about his neck.

Roden Wayfinder shook his head. "I can only steer you on the most direct course. It is not as if I am reading a map. If you want me to continue to access the power of the vegvísir, you must follow where I lead."

Líf chewed her bottom lip. True, Roden bore tattooed upon his back the magical sigil, which ensured that its bearer would find his destination; but was there no leeway to avoid a potential calamity?

She was not the only one concerned.

Skeggi scoffed, "You're telling me a couple of jötnar were out on a midnight stroll, and we are going to follow them?"

With a sympathetic look, Roden affirmed, "You asked my help, which I will happily continue to give, but you must not question my methods. Doubt births weakness, and weakness leads to destruction."

Sigird's voice revealed how scared the thirteen-year-old was. "What if we are spotted? Jötnar eat men for breakfast."

Harekson tried to speak, but his mouth had been gagged due to his incessant complaints. Sigird warily glanced at his oldest brother. He must have caught Harekson's eye, for the boy seemed to shrink where he stood.

"So we are told," remarked Hervor. She waited for Ottar to decide what course of action they should pursue.

Reinspecting the nearest footprint, Ottar said, "They walk faster than we do. At the rate we are traveling, there is a good chance we will not spot either of the giants. We will continue forward as planned, but I want everyone to be on guard. If you spot movement in the distance, or even anything unnatural, you must inform me immediately."

Arto muttered under his breath, "Is there anything *natural* about what we are doing?"

The caravan began to move again. This time, Líf remained near the front. She wanted to look at the massive footprints before they were overrun by numerous skis. Were there other signs that jötnar lived nearby? A tool of some sort? Surely, they used them to build the mead halls and walls so often mentioned in the tales of the giants. Líf pondered such things in silence.

The day dragged on, as did the next day and the one after that. For a full three weeks, they moved ever forward, never spotting a wisp of smoke from a fire or a mountain-sized hovel of the enormous natives. Did jötnar actually live in this world? Were the "footprints" something else entirely? Had the giants finally been slaughtered by mighty Thor and the other gods?

For some reason, Líf felt disappointed. She missed her two nephews and, one day, would love to tell them she had seen the gargantuan men of this wilderness. How often had the boys sat next to her as she told them stories about Járnsaxa, the unusually beautiful jötunn who had become one of Thor's lovers and was the only jötnar upon whom the god of thunder had ever looked kindly? On the other hand, perhaps it was better if none of the native inhabitants were found, for most jötnar were evil, wicked beings, like Geirröd, one of the few opponents who had come close to killing the protector of mankind.

No one had spotted an animal or plant living in this inhospitable environment. Surviving solely on their resources had begun to cause tension among the men. If Jötunheim were as large as Midgard, how long would it take for them to travel across it? They were running out of supplies. Along with the fear of starvation was the fact that the snow had not stopped falling. At first it was light, but now storms arose, forcing the party to stop for a day or two.

The only positive event was that Einar's leg mended, and he was able to trudge along with the rest of the group. The redhead had given Líf a big smile the first time he walked on his own two feet. His fox fylgja had flickered a brilliant, cheery yellow.

One evening, Líf scooted close to her siblings, who were seated on the ground next to her. Huddled together in blankets, their body heat was all that made this particular storm remotely bearable. Boulders protected them against the worst of the wind but did nothing to keep the cold from seeping into their bones.

"Tell us a story, Líf." As Ottar spoke, his teeth chattered. The question was like one of those his sons would ask. Hopefully, the boys were faring better in Jarlbörg as wards of the king.

Líf blew her breath onto her gloved hands, to little avail. The fires had been blown out, and if the storm did not stop, the crew would begin to lose fingers and toes to Fornjót's bite. She had seen it before. Appendages of those caught in winter storms would blacken and later fall off.

"Any will do," Ottar encouraged.

Líf gently touched the spot where Thray had buried herself under the woman's tunic in an effort to escape the fierce wind. "I don't know which one to choose. This cold—it's all I can think about." Between the gales, Líf caught glimpses of the strange, elongated spires of a distant mountain range. Their tips disappeared in the clouds. "They remind me of broken ribs," was her comment.

"Maybe they are," agreed Ottar as he pressed closer to his sisters. "When Ymir, the first jötunn, died, his body became our earth. Maybe he was large enough to have formed Jötunheim as well."

Without thinking, Líf began to recite verses from the well-known poem *Grímnismál*:

"From Ymir's flesh the earth was made,
And from his blood, the sea,
Mountains from his bones, trees from his hair,
And from his skull, the sky."

The strengthening tempest enveloped them in a whirl of white and grey. Heavy snowflakes struck each other and thrashed about as if possessed by the lust for battle. The icy haze shifted and moved in the howling wind.

Líf continued:

"And from his eyelashes the cheerful gods
Made Midgard for men's sons;
And from his brain the hard-tempered clouds
Were all created…"

Staring ahead, Líf could almost envision massive bodies striding in the murk of the storm, covered in frozen armor. As she was about to recite the next verse, Ottar suddenly clamped his hand over her mouth, while Hervor hissed, "Jötnar!"

Chapter Four

Shrouded in flurries of white, two silhouettes moved steadily past. The pair's shadowy forms, much larger than a man's, were lost in the haze. Yet they were as real as any of the crew and the fylgjur crouched by their feet. After a few more moments, the presences disappeared from view.

Líf realized she had been holding her breath and gasped for air. Her deep inhalations were far louder than her normal, calm breath. How silly she had been to worry that the two jötnar would hear her over the rushing wind.

Suddenly Hervor hissed, "Shhhh!"

They waited quietly for a time. All three were afraid that any movement they made would lure the giants back to their location. Líf's heart thrummed swiftly, while Thray's beat faster still.

"They're gone," Ottar finally said. His voice was barely audible above the raging storm.

"Do you think I summoned them…somehow?" Líf had to ask.

"Don't be silly," dismissed Hervor. "That was a coincidence. We are in their territory. We were bound to run into a few at some point."

"If you're sure," mumbled Líf, though she was not. The dubious look on Ottar's face worried her. "What's wrong?" she asked him.

As her brother continued to stare at the gray murk, he explained, "Most beasts would seek shelter in a storm such as this. It's strange to see anything moving about without apparent purpose."

Suddenly, a large, snow-covered mass rushed toward them. Hervor reached for her axe while Ottar attempted to stand and draw his sword.

"Did ya see them?" Skeggi's voice was surprisingly subdued. "Jötnar! Right here in our camp!" The man looked wild, his bushy beard crusted with ice and his wide shoulders slumped under extra furs.

"We did," Ottar acknowledged right before Skeggi blurted, "They strode right past, only a few feet away. I was certain one would step on us."

"Do you think they saw you?" asked Líf.

"No," Hervor was quick to reply, "for if they had, they would have attacked. We were lucky this time." Turning to Ottar, she added, "We need to move away from here as soon as we can."

The storm did not relent for the remainder of the night. In the cool light of morning, the party reassembled. Much of the talk focused on their near escape. Several men speculated about what might have happened if they had been discovered, but Líf preferred not to harbor such grim thoughts.

No one could agree on what the jötnar looked like. Some swore they were twelve feet tall; others, thirty. A few dismissed the size difference but claimed they had three heads and five limbs. However the giants were described, they were always grotesque and inhuman.

Any traces of the local inhabitants had been swept away in the storm. Although Roden led the caravan forward, there was no way to tell if they were following the jötnar or moving away from them. This made Thray nervous. Actually, everything was making the tiny squirrel nervous.

Thray could not settle down when perched upon Líf's shoulder. The animal fidgeted with unrestrained energy as she scurried over the snow. Her little head looked about continuously, ears and nose twitching and tail flicking violently whenever she paused.

Líf would have worried about the fylgja's health even if Thray's well-being had not been linked to her own. And Líf was fine, at least for now, although she was always hungry, as the rations had been cut. However, as the days passed, hunger began to affect the men, too. Occasional spats broke out, and one morning, a mob of eight hired hands encircled the Lothbranson cookfire.

Arto, waving his sword in the air, led the assault. "What have you done to us, Ottar, son of Lothbran? They call you untouchable, but I don't believe it." The group of mercenaries had drawn their weapons and pointed them threateningly at the three siblings and their close companions. As tensions rose, more of the mercenaries joined in. Some bore bows; others, spears. "You have dragged us into this frozen desert and are letting us starve to death. For what? No answer is worth our lives. We came for pay. I can speak for the others and say that none of us agreed to this."

Rather than brandish a weapon, Ottar calmly tried to resolve the issue. "I know none of us realized the challenges that we would face. And I know that traveling in this cold wasteland with dwindling reserves is difficult, even for the mightiest of men—"

"You know nothing," snapped a man to Arto's left.

Hervor lurched forward, axe in hand. As she did, a second fellow rammed the handle of his own double-handed axe into her back, knocking her down. Several other disgruntled men pointed their blades at her neck. The shieldmaiden reluctantly relinquished her weapon.

Ignoring the fallen woman, Arto sneered at Ottar. "We will not die here simply for your sake, *Untouchable*."

By now, the crew members were set against each other, the group divided nearly in half. Even some from Thorinheim had sided with Arto in this matter. Úlfor, Roden, and a few others waited on the outskirts to see who came out on top. Mercenaries followed the money, not the cause.

The leader of the mutiny declared, "We are leaving, Lothbranson, and we are taking your ship."

Ottar stepped forward, but before he could speak, a fist punched his face. He coughed and spat red.

"And doing what?"

The question came from none other than Roden. "You can't sail a drakkar with less than half a full crew, not if you want to succeed in *that* crossing. And how will you find your way back to the longship? You will surely get lost in the storms."

The rumble of disgruntled voices was heard. Arto faced his followers. "He is right. We will be lost." Then he turned to the Rus. "But not if we have a map."

Several men strode toward Roden who, along with Úlfor, was preparing to fight. Although the two companions were surrounded, they did not appear terribly concerned.

With a smile, Arto barked out, "Escort them back with us!"

As the men began to follow Arto's commands, Skeggi laughed so loudly that everyone paused. "I'm going with you. Why, you may wonder. Because I'd like to see ya try and steer a ship. I watched how ya fumbled about not sure which rope hoists the sail and which secures the mast. You're gonna run her ashore, and I want to see that happen."

"Can you not steer?" a man standing behind Arto questioned.

Arto glared at Skeggi. He looked as if he wanted to drive his sword through the barrel-chested man.

"He may not be able to, but I can." All eyes turned to Harekson. Someone had untied the prisoner, for he stood outside the mass of readied weaponry, rubbing his bloody wrists. "Even with half a crew."

Líf's heart sank. Harekson, though not as skillful as her siblings, was a fine commander. He had always wanted to call *Wavecutter* his own. Now he would have the chance.

With a grim look, Harekson addressed Ottar and ignored Hervor, for in his eyes a woman had no worth. "You are undone, Lothbranson. You should have taken my offer when you had the chance."

Hervor cast Ottar a questioning glance as Harekson continued, "Sigird, little brother, it would have been better if you had been stillborn."

Clenching his jaw, the teenager glared at his kin, yet he could not defend his honor with several blades facing him.

As Roden's captors began to escort the Rus back the way they had come, he shouted, "I don't know much about you, Harekson, other than the fact that you are their king's grandson. Nor do I actually care. But what I do know, beyond the shadow of a doubt, is that you and your men will not make it home. With *or* without me."

Harekson lifted his hand, signaling everyone to halt. He moved closer to the foreign mercenary. "Why is that?"

"Because you will run out of food first. You don't want to starve? Then you must *not* return the way we came."

Lif could almost feel the chill of Harekson's look.

Thorinheim's heir growled, "Then what do you suggest?"

"There are other ways—" Roden began but stopped short. His eyes widened in horror.

One by one, the others turned in the direction the Rus was facing. Four jötnar had appeared at the top of a snow-covered slope. The mammoth beings were around nine or ten feet tall, and their unusually round eyes were focused on the angry, disorderly camp.

Although they appeared much like any man, each sported something abhorrent. The tallest had what looked like part of an additional face on one side of his head. With a full third eye, second nose, and drooping mouth, this false face appeared to hold no life in it, though fearful to look upon.

To his right stood a jötunn with a second set of arms under the first. These extra limbs were thin and scrawny, clearly overshadowed by the powerful musculature of the dominant pair.

The third had an extra eye centered on his forehead, although it looked cloudy and dull. When he blinked, all three eyelids closed simultaneously. The final creature dragged a leg that did not appear to have a knee. They each held a cudgel in their disproportionately large hands.

In a voice that sounded as if it rumbled up from the pit of the earth, the first one grunted, "Humans."

The smallest jötunn, the one with the bad leg, began to laugh hysterically. The sound was eerie and surprisingly high-pitched. Then, as suddenly as it had begun, the laughter stopped.

"Run!"

The word was shouted by a number of men. The entire crew bolted away from the massive brutes. Many men abandoned their supplies, while others grabbed travel packs in mid sprint. Lif had to leave hers behind. There was not even time to grab her drinking pouch before she fled with her family.

No one looked back at the conferring jötnar. The crew had barely clambered over the nearest stony slope when the thunderous footsteps of the charging giants were heard amid their excited bellows.

Men began to run pell-mell in different directions. The lucky few who wore skis quickly raced away. Several archers took aim at the enemy, but their arrows bounced off the giants' skin as if it were made of stone. The jötnar charged after the largest groups.

As Líf forced herself to sprint along with her siblings, something large crashed nearby. The cluster of crewmen around them prevented her from seeing what was happening. A second explosion of snow burst to the right.

Why was she so short? Her lack of stature not only hindered her sight but also forced her to work harder to keep up with the longer-legged men. A third impact was followed by screams.

"Duck!" squealed Thray as something large soared overhead. The object exploded into a snowdrift, sending mounds of white into the sky.

Líf was yanked to one side. Hervor held her by the wrist and pulled her behind the rock that had barely missed them. It was almost half the size of a fish barrel. Had it landed on them, they would have been crushed. Jötnar must be tremendously strong to be able to hurtle such heavy objects so easily.

Another boulder rolled past, splitting the men's ranks even further. Now, most groups had five or fewer men; at ten, Líf's was the largest. With a nod from her sister, she ran alongside. But where was Ottar? She scanned the area but could not spot him. What she did see made her blood curdle.

The four-limbed jötunn was brutally beating a crewman to pulp with his spiked cudgel. With all the blood and mangled body parts, it was impossible to tell who it was. The other three giants continued to follow Líf's group.

Why hers? Why not anyone else's? Einar must have seen the terror in her eyes. His face paled as he spoke. "My leg can't handle much more. I have to slow down. I...I will lead them away."

"Are you crazy?" Líf asked. By the look on his fox fylgja's face, this offer was not a welcome one. "They will kill you."

"Better me than any of you," he said bravely, though his voice cracked as he spoke.

Without slowing down, Hervor nodded her head and honored him by saying, "Valhalla awaits you."

Einar split away. He slowed down as he cut in front of the jötnar's path and headed west.

Líf felt a catch in her side. Tears streamed down her face; the trails of hot ribbons froze on her cheeks. She knew she could not continue at this speed much longer. With more than one misstep, she clambered to the top of a ridge.

Glancing behind her, she saw Einar dive under a swing of the largest Jötunn's weapon and scramble out of range. The glimmer of a silvery fox shadowed him. Yet the Jötunn did not deviate from his original course. He, along with his kin, continued to pursue Líf's party. Even the one with the gimpy leg followed like a dog after a hare.

"I don't understand," Sigird exclaimed in exasperation. "Why are they still after us?"

Hervor grimaced. Her face was flushed from exertion. "I see now," she muttered before ordering, "You three head to the left. You two, go right. Sigird, Líf, keep running."

"What's your plan?" the boy asked.

"I'll let you know if it works," huffed Hervor.

Behind them, the jötnar hesitated briefly as they glared at the dispersing figures. This was the break Líf needed. She and the others began to increase the distance between themselves and the monstrous creatures.

With a growl, the two-faced leader of the giants charged. Out of all the potential targets, they chose to follow both Lothbrandóttirs.

"Hurry, Líf," implored Thray. "Keep going!"

The snow grew deeper. Despite all her effort, Líf's pace began to slow. Sliding down the last slope, she landed in a drift as high as her waist. The terrain had flattened out, yet it would be next to useless to try trudging through the frozen precipitation. In the wide-open expanse, there was nothing to shelter them, nowhere to hide. Dark formations in the distance looked like stony hills, but they were too far away.

In far fewer strides than it had taken Líf, the jötnar mounted the ridge. The largest laid his eyes upon her, for she was now the straggler. Almost as one, they jumped down to the snowy plain.

Thray scrambled in front of Líf. Able to run upon the snow, the little fylgja frantically raced around the redheaded woman but was unable to proffer any tangible help beyond constant encouragement and warnings.

"Líf, behind you!" cried Sigird as he threw his axe over her.

Had the axe it hit its mark? She couldn't tell. She tripped in a buried dip in the ground and fell into the snow. Turning around in a panic, she tried to scramble backward but floundered in the drift.

Then the massive shadow of the largest jötnar covered her.

Chapter Five

The dual-faced behemoth stopped so abruptly that two of his followers struggled to halt at his flanks. He snarled in frustration, and loathing simmered deep within his eyes. The brute's chest rose and fell dramatically, as did those of his companions. They looked at him, and he looked directly at Líf.

The young woman felt as if she were frozen stiff amid the heaping snow. Though out of range of the cudgel's swing, she could be overtaken in several short strides. There was no chance of outrunning the jötnar. Would her sacrifice allow the others to flee? Was this the reason the Norns had fated her to make this journey? Her life would be given so that Brasir could succeed in finding the hamingjur's cure.

"Líf?" Thray whimpered somewhere behind her as the fourth Jötunn slid down the slope, almost bowling over the four-armed figure.

Without taking his eyes from her, the lead giant signaled the others to hold back. The smallest and most recent arrival gaped at the clear and easy target before them. The largest looked beyond Líf at the fleeing crewmen, while the giant with the third eye hissed, "They retreat to their shelter."

"Kill them now!" trilled the gimp. He took a step forward, causing Líf to shrink down, but the four-armed behemoth pulled him back.

"Let them be," advised Three-Eyes. "Their lives never last long...and they will end sooner out here."

With a pitiful groan, the small Jötunn questioned, "Why?"

As their leader stared at Líf in disgust, the three-eyed monster counseled his kin, "The humans will hide in their gifted lands." As if speaking directly to Líf, he said, "If ever they leave, we will kill the little invaders. Skin them for bedding. Tan them for boots."

For the first time, Líf took note of the crude clothing the jötnar wore. Furry pelts draped them like heavy cloaks. Loosely stitched trousers covered their legs. Soft, knee-high boots protected their toes from Fornjót's bite. The one with the true third eye sported a rudimentary ring of twisted metal around one large bicep. Though clearly barbarous, they were far less bestial than Líf had feared.

But why let her live? Was this some cruel trick? A barn cat would sometimes tease its prey for the pleasure of it. Was that what these giants were doing? Letting her think she had a chance for survival before stripping her hugr away?

The four giants stood still, as if waiting to see what Líf would do. Trembling, she rose to her feet and turned her back to the massive beings. She began to slog in the opposite direction, where the shocked face of Hervor stared back at her.

Several men were with the oldest Lothbrandóttir. Whether they had prevented the shieldmaiden from charging into a doomed situation or she had realized they were powerless to change the inevitable, they watched in astonishment as Líf was allowed to stumble away.

A roar burst forth, one so loud and vile that Líf actually felt the sound slam into her body. Blinking back more tears, she trudged toward her waiting sister. Lacking the strength to look back, she asked, "Are they gone?"

"No," Hervor replied. "They watch."

Still fearful, the small party trekked toward the grey blur in the distance. Perhaps those hills would hide them from the ever-glaring eyes of their massive enemies.

"What do you think they meant when they said this was 'our shelter'?" Sigird questioned. The thirteen-year-old was apprehensive for good reason. "Where are these 'gifted lands'? We are in the middle of Jötunheim."

No one responded. Above them, Líf heard the cry of the iridescent goshawk. As it circled in the air, suddenly something occurred to her. "Thray, do jötnar have fylgjur?"

"It appears not," replied the squirrel in her soft rumble as she shimmied up the hem of the apron that covered Líf's underdress.

"I wonder how that works? How can a person survive without a guardian nearby?"

"I wouldn't call them *people*," noted Thray as her small claws raked the brooch on the shoulder she was aiming for. "And maybe they have some of a different sort, a kind that neither you nor I can see."

That thought was unsettling.

Finally having ascended to the top of Líf's red hair, the small, shimmering fylgja asked, "Are those trees?"

Líf squinted at the growing blur. "I can't tell."

Thray's keener senses, which allowed fylgjur to perceive oncoming danger sooner than their people did, saw what to Líf was still a blur. "Yes. They are trees, ugly as they may be."

Soon, others concurred with Thray's observation. Since Líf was the only one who had heard the squirrel, she was not surprised when the scrawny branches and thin green needles were discerned. The copse was comprised primarily of spruce and a few bare-limbed rowans that clustered in defiance of the surrounding land. Ironically, there was never a more welcoming sight than the sinister appearance of gnarled trees twisted by strong winds and the weight of snow-laden limbs. Trees meant shelter and wood for fires.

As they approached the outer greenery, Hervor observed, "Even these are not natural." Noting her little sister's questioning glance, she explained, "They are far too tall. The rowans are the size of aged oaks. And look how high the spruces tower over those."

"Maybe something in the water makes everything grow so big," Sigird suggested, just as a shadowy form emerged from the tangle of trees.

"If that be the case, I better stop drinkin'. Don't want to be too big for the womenfolk." Skeggi winked at Hervor, who returned his look with an exasperated groan. Totally oblivious to the shieldmaiden's distaste, the oafish fellow boomed, "'Bout time you all arrived. We been—"

"Who is here? How many made it?" Hervor was in no mood for banter. She strode into the brush to take a look for herself.

"What?" Skeggi asked Líf.

She smiled. "I'm glad you made it."

"Me too, Lingy. Me too." The barrel-chested man gave Sigird a playful slap on the back as he led them to the copse. "Where's Ottar?"

Líf froze. "He's not here?"

Skeggi's normally bright features darkened. He shook his head.

"That's all right. He'll come," Líf tried to sound assured. "We just need to let him know where we are. Signal him somehow, that's all."

"We can light fires…" Skeggi began, but his words faded away.

As they walked around the abnormally thick trunks, Líf realized that a number of the crew had also taken refuge here. About half of the original party either squatted on the ground or leaned against the huge trees. Hervor had found Ulf and was discussing something with the stout fellow when a pair of men on skis slipped into the circle. One was Guthorm Blood Cheeks.

"Hervor." He nodded in respect and then shouted, "Follow me! Everyone!" Though tired and winded, the men rose and trailed Guthorm through the grove.

On the far side, the land flattened into a wide plain. Positioned a respectable distance away was what appeared to be an abandoned longhouse. The structure was as large as Jarl Harek's mead hall in Thorinheim. Although the wooden planks were covered in thick green moss and the thatching had caved in, the frame still stood.

"Jötnar?" asked Sigird, who was not as easily intimidated as Líf.

"No," huffed Skeggi. "It's too small for those brutes."

"Who built it?"

"Where did it come from?"

Questions erupted from the men. Having scouted the area, Guthorm explained, "There is no living soul around."

"Abandoned?" questioned Hervor.

Guthorm grunted. "Doubtful. There are burial mounds in the back. I spotted a pair of rune stones." He did not have to say that he was illiterate, for most people were. Only a few had studied the marks and could wield the magic of the written word. "There is still furniture inside, though most has been corrupted by rot. There was one set of bones on the floor. Looks like whoever built the hall died long ago."

Like a she-wolf protecting her pups, Hervor clearly wanted to keep the men close. "We will stay here tonight. Build a fire outside the doorway to signal to any others nearby. Darkness comes early, and the glow will be a beacon to those who are lost."

"One more thing," Guthorm added. "There are horses here. Wild, from what I can tell. Maybe descended from those who came before."

This was excellent news; even Hervor smiled. "We must thank the gods. Guthorm, select some men and round up a couple of steeds. We must offer a good sacrifice tonight. And then we will feast."

There was a cheer.

Líf did not join in the exuberance. Moving closer to her sister, she whispered, "Are you not afraid that the jötnar will return?"

"Their comings and goings are out of our hands," Hervor admitted. "Yet we can be warmed, fed, and rested if they choose to attack."

Líf hesitated before asking, "Did it work? Your plan? I still don't understand what you tried to do by splitting us up back there.

Hervor studied her sister carefully. "I noticed that the jötnar did not act like typical predators, singling out the weakest prey to kill. When hunting for food, you take what you can get. If that was the case, they would have picked off a few men and stopped. They didn't do that—not even to Einar as he fled."

Líf listened intently as Hervor continued, "The jötnar did just the opposite. They went after the largest groups. I assumed they wanted to corral us in order to inflict the most damage. That meant they were not merely a hunting party. However they view us, their desire to kill was either pure hatred or a need to defend and protect themselves. I split us up, hoping that they would also split up in order to chase us down. So, no, my plan did not exactly work."

Líf wished she had the shieldmaiden's keen sense. "But why let us go?"

"I have no explanation for what they did, yet I feel it has something to do with this place." Hervor pointed to the dilapidated longhouse. "If the jötnar avoid this area, this is where we need to stay. At least for now."

Brasir stepped through the open doorway into the waning daylight. He held a bundle in his arms, but when he spotted the Lothbrandóttirs he gently put down his burden and went to greet them. He extended his arm, and Hervor clasped it as any man would.

"It pleases me that you are here," said the shieldmaiden, "but next time, if ever the men are forced to split up again, you are to remain near us. This will all be for naught if you are lost."

The black-fleshed man understood Hervor's temperament and took no offense. "I assure you, I will be by your side till the end. Our fates are bound."

"So it seems," Hervor agreed. They studied each other for a long moment before she let go of his arm. A sense of playfulness flickered between them, though it was not evident in their words or actions.

"Is...?" Brasir looked past her, jaw tensed. "I will help search tonight."

Suddenly, Líf choked up. Ottar was alive. He could not have been killed by a jötunn; he was fated for better things. He had to be.

Leaving the pair, Líf slipped past Brasir's discarded bundle, which had fallen open to reveal a pale femur, and entered the murky longhouse. The thatching had almost completely deteriorated, and large sections of the roof had fallen in. The largest roof beams were still connected to the peak like bony fingers positioned on a corpse. A mixture of dust and snowflakes hung heavy in the air, lazily drifting through the remaining sunbeams.

Could she blame her tears on the aerial contaminants? An adult woman was not supposed to cry in public unless a death had occurred. And for all Líf knew, her brother was alive and searching for them.

Thray nuzzled her ear. The tiny creature's colors had dimmed and become sallow. As Líf began to explore, the fylgja said, "These were men. Look!"

Líf spotted a rusting sword that appeared similar to those the warriors wore. Yet by its side was a dagger forged from a white metal she had never seen before. Had she not touched its perfectly smooth edge, she might have thought it was bone. When she picked it up to view the ornately rendered features of the hideous beast engraved on the pommel, the leather on the handle crumbled in her hand. The lethal side of the blade was slightly curved, with jagged teeth like a wolf's. The weapon was loathsome. She dropped it, then kicked it out of sight.

Ducking under a sloping section of mildewed thatch, she entered the back rooms. A wooden bed listed at an odd angle. It was decorated with delicate and elongated carved images of deer running through a forest filled with leaves. Although the bed seemed large to Líf, it was too small for the jötnar to comfortably sleep in. Could this have been built by humans? If so, who were they, and why had they traveled so far from their home world?

A shrill scream outside caused Líf to wince. The sound of a dying horse always made her feel sorrow, which was further intensified by the feeling brewing in her belly. Yet she knew that the cries would bring joy to many others, for they would be well fed come nightfall.

The sounds of shuffling bodies in the main room reached her ears, and soon a warm glow fended off the gloom. Líf retraced her steps and joined the men who gathered around the flames massing in a long, raised pit at the center of the hall. A few of the crew removed the sagging thatching to prevent it from catching fire.

Brasir was searching for something on the ground. Realizing what he was trying to find, Líf pointed toward the dark corner. "Over there."

The man retrieved the discarded sword and dagger, then nodded to her before exiting the longhouse.

Líf tended the fire as the men slowly settled in for the evening. Slabs of horseflesh were roasting over the flames. Hervor's face was smeared with red. She must have officiated at the sacrifice and thanked the gods.

"I would have offered you some of the hlaut," the shieldmaiden began, holding a shallow stone bowl containing the blessed blood, "but it cooled too quickly. I was lucky to sprinkle it around the longhouse before it froze." She flipped the bowl upside down, and a section of blackened ice slipped out, only to sizzle and stink up the flames.

"Where'd that come from?" Líf nodded at the bowl.

"Ulf discovered it, along with a butcher's block and some other items too damaged by the elements to save. There must have been a small village here. Several other households were found, though they are even more dilapidated than this structure. All are empty. Although heavy furniture remains, it appears that the owners left some time ago."

"Who were they?" Líf asked, hoping her sister had an answer.

Hervor shrugged. "Whoever they were, I am grateful that they left this place for us."

By now, all the men had clustered inside the main hall and were staring ravenously at the roasting meat. At least now they were focused on the meat and not on Líf. They were a mix of the original crew and the hired hands, and not all of them were fond of taking orders from a woman.

Líf felt compelled to ask, "Are *we* safe here?"

"For now," admitted Hervor.

Was there a hint of trepidation in the female warrior's voice? The thought startled Líf—but no more so than the sudden clamor outside.

The man on watched alerted those inside. "Others approach."

Weapons were sought and grasped. Hervor, one of the few still carrying a shield, ran to the front to create a wall of defense. It was too dark outside to see who or what lurked beyond the firelight. There was a bestial sound, almost a moan.

Harekson emerged from the gloom, along with Úlfor and Roden. They carried a limp body. Dropping her shield, Hervor ran toward them crying, "No! Ottar, no!"

CHAPTER SIX

L if caught her breath and her legs instantly weakened. She struggled to remain upright as she stared wide-eyed at the inanimate body of her brother.

Someone pushed her aside. Several men, along with Brasir, ran to help. Who knew how far Úlfor and Roden had carried Ottar?

Was he alive? As he was carefully brought indoors, she tried to spot any sign of his chest rising or his eyes rolling beneath his closed lids. Líf began to follow the others but stopped abruptly. "Thray," she asked, "do you see Ottar's fylgja?"

"No," whimpered Thray. "She's not here—but neither are the others."

That was true. Harekson, Roden, and Úlfor had walked past her without their guardians beside them. Their fylgjur were alive and could not be far away. Turning to the man on watch, Líf demanded, "From which direction did they come?"

The man pointed in the darkness, and Líf immediately trudged off.

"Where are you going?"

Rather than answer, she remained alert, searching for any unnatural glow in the distance. Above their heads, the sky rippled with the aurora borealis. Its ever-changing hues were mirrored by Thray's shimmering fur.

"There!" chirped the squirrel as she leaped off the woman's shoulder and ran toward the light.

Chasing after the rodent, Líf came upon the small group of fylgjur glimmering like the sky above them. All, that is, except Ottar's; his wolfhound's light was dull and wan. Úlfor's large wolf pulled the shaggy hound by its scruff, while Harekson's boar nudged the listless dog's rump. Roden's lesser panda tugged or shoved the canine whenever she could get her paws against the dog.

Ottar's fylgja still existed, which meant that he, too, was alive—but for how long? As Líf bent down to help the unconscious wolfhound, she felt a sharp bite from Thray, who was scurrying around her ankles. The squirrel bristled and emitted a low growl. Líf knew she was never to interact with another person's guardian, but these were not normal circumstances. How could Thray be so enraged? Yet the small rodent chattered her teeth and flicked her tail as she stood between the young woman and Ottar's fylgjur.

Líf had to content herself with walking alongside the animals as they struggled to return the canine to her human. As they got closer, other lights began to appear around the outskirts of the tree line.

"More of the crew have found us," Thray assured Líf, who glanced indifferently at the glows.

Arto and a good fifteen men caught up with Líf as she stepped within sight of the watchman. They all looked grave as they entered the dilapidated longhouse. As the night progressed, another couple of men returned, but Líf did not care. Her focus was on her brother and the fylgja at his side.

"One of the jötnar's throwing stones caught him," Roden explained. "There was nothing we could do. No way around it. We thought they had left, but then the four-limbed fiend attacked."

Hervor knelt next to her brother and held his pale hand in hers. There were long moments when Ottar did not take a breath. His ribs were shattered, and one of his lungs may have collapsed. His chain-mail shirt was no defense against crushing stone.

"He's dying, isn't he?" Líf saw that the wolfhound's fur was blackening.

"I'm sorry," responded the Rus in earnest. "He was a good man."

"He's not dead yet." Hareksons's voice conveyed a strange kindness that Líf knew stemmed from respect.

Yet she did not want kindness. She was far too angry. Ottar's life did not deserve to end this way. Was this sacrifice enough for him to be chosen for Valhalla? If not, what was worth this loss? What did it even mean to have gods watching over them, if they did not actually care?

She grabbed her neck ring, the one engraved with the image of Mjölnir, Thor's hammer. Ottar had given it to her, for the amulet was supposed to protect the wearer. Yet what protection had she ever received? Violently jerking it from around her throat, she threw it into the fire and stormed into the back room, away from the rest of the crew. The food would be ready soon, but she was not hungry. Too furious to cry, she curled up in the back corner. Somehow, amid her grim thoughts, she fell asleep.

"Líf, Líf!" Thray's chirps awoke the young woman far earlier than she would have preferred.

Blinking and stumbling to her feet, she croaked out, "Ottar?"

"No, Líf," the squirrel thrummed. "You must come outside."

Having fallen asleep in all her clothes, Líf was soon weaving around snoring men as well as her own siblings. Hervor's eyes were closed, and her head rested upon Ottar's shoulder. The pair truly looked like twins, even though they were not.

Once out of sight of the morning's watchman, Líf finally asked, "What's this about, Thray?"

The squirrel looked around, perturbed. Suddenly there was a high-pitched bark. By the edge of the copse was a fox fylgja whose fur glistened in whites and pale blues. The creature was hunched and shivering.

"Einar," Líf breathed out in a puff of air.

"See!" Thray leaped excitedly into the air. "They need help!"

Líf hurried back inside in search of assistance. But how could she dare awaken her sister, who had probably tended to Ottar all night? She did not trust most of the men, and the others might look at her as if she were crazy. Then there was Skeggi, snoring loudly in the back. It would take a bucket of frigid water to rouse him.

Bending over the only one who would help, Líf gently touched Brasir's shoulder. The man opened his dark eyes, immediately alert. Before he could ask a question, Líf whispered, "Follow me. And bring a weapon."

As they plodded into the copse of spruce, Líf explained, "I saw Einar's fylgja. I think he is in trouble."

The pale fox appeared ahead of them; twitching her tail, she guided the pair away from the grove. They had walked almost a mile when the fox barked. Einar lay under an outcropping of stone. His skin was drained of color, his eyes were half open, and he trembled mightily.

"Gods above!" Brasir exclaimed. He peeled off his outer cloak and wrapped it around the redheaded man. "You're all but frozen. That must have been a frightful night."

Einar's teeth chattered so much that it was hard for him to get any words out. "I t-t-tried to lead them a-a-away."

"I know," Líf murmured, as she too removed her cloak and threw it over Einar's back. "You were very brave."

"We need to get you to our fires," Brasir said as he helped the smaller man to his feet. Einar had worn no gloves, and his fingers were an ugly shade of purple. He struggled to make his legs move. He would lose some fingers and toes, but if they hurried, he would live.

Together, they half carried, half dragged Einar to their camp. As soon as he stepped inside the longhouse, Líf halted by the doorway. There were plenty of men to help him from here on, and she was not ready to find out whether her own brother still drew breath.

The morning was crisp and clear, with the taste of frost on the tongue.

A few wispy clouds meandered overhead, though larger, more solid sovereigns of the sky massed in the distance near the mountains. Wandering about the dilapidated village, Líf approached the pair of rune stones that marked the burial mounds. About six feet in height, the sturdy slabs were engraved with elegant, interwoven imagery akin to that on the bed frame, but these did not depict deer. The first showed a man in wolf furs fighting jötnar with a spear; the second showed a king healing a bedridden fellow.

Líf was not literate, but she still recognized some of the runes that wrapped around the edge of the rock that framed the images, and guessed at a few more.

"What's it say?" asked Thray. Strangely enough, fylgjur struggled to comprehend runes. The idea that such symbols could represent sounds or words was almost unfathomable to them.

Líf tried to understand the angular lettering as she inspected the stone that bore the king. "It says…um…Guðmundr, son of… some name…I think it says Úlfhéðinn. Maybe it means he was the son of a wolf warrior?" Líf skipped several words until she spotted a few she knew. "…Ruling justly over…more words I don't know… a warrior's paradise?"

Turning to the other monolith, she again struggled. "Dedicated to the memory of Úlfhéðinn, mighty father…something, something, something," Líf sighed. "This is useless. They are just markers of the dead."

Shaking her head, she had started to return to break her fast—for her stomach now reminded her that she had missed last night's meal—when she noticed a small heap of upturned soil, almost like a miniature grave. This had to be the spot where the dead man's bones were laid to rest. Had Brasir taken the time to honor the departed? Why would Brasir care that much for a person he had never met?

As if waiting for her, Einar stood in front of the longhouse. Líf could not understand why the men had let him go out into the cold only minutes after he had arrived in such a wretched state. He grinned widely and waved at her in what Líf perceived as a highly careless manner.

"What are you doing? You need to warm yourself!"

"I'm fine," he said, still waving at her in amusement.

"Stop that! Why are you not wearing gloves?" Líf snatched his hand. Though he felt warm to the touch, surely his body needed more care.

"I'm fine now," he insisted as Líf inspected his fingers. They were pink and full of life.

"How?"

Einar chuckled. "I don't know."

"Líf!" She turned at the sound of her brother's voice behind her. Ottar rushed outside to snatch up his little sister in his arms.

Unable to comprehend what she was seeing, Líf shrugged out of his grip and stood back. Ottar sported a full smile. He moved as if he hadn't a scratch on him. But what of his ribs? After all, his body had been crushed by the heavy throwing stone.

"Your...your...?" Líf started to question him as she attempted to pull up his tunic.

"Gone. All gone," Ottar proclaimed. "Every cut, broken bone, scrape, or scar has vanished. It's the same for all the others."

Líf stared at her brother in disbelief. Abruptly, she touched the scar on her own forehead. The skin felt smooth and unblemished.

Hervor approached, looking younger than she had in a long while. She handed Líf her neck ring. There was only minor tarnishing on it. "I had it pulled out," she said.

Ottar beamed. "The gods are pleased with us."

The fingers of Líf's free hand trembled as she continued to brush her forehead. "I've never heard of the gods doing this." She stared at the longhouse. "What *is* this place?"

"Paradise?" suggested Ottar.

"Guðmundr's paradise," uttered Líf absentmindedly, for none of this could be real.

"Where did you hear that name?" Ottar asked with a laugh.

"It is written on the rune stones. They talk of a king called Guðmundr and his father, an Úlfhéðinn."

"Not an Úlfhéðinn," Úlfor's voice cut into their conversation like the sharp edge of Hervor's axe. "*The* Úlfhéðinn." He and Roden had joined the small group.

"That can't be," countered Roden, quite shocked.

"The Úlfhéðinn are named after an ancient king," Úlfor explained, "one who was fabled for slaying jötnar. He was known to all as Guðmundr Úlfhéðinn and was said to have traveled into Jötunheim, where he discovered the Glæsisvellir."

Ottar frowned in concentration, then murmured, "The glittering plains. A land of youth and eternal health. At its seat of power is Údáinsakr, the warriors' paradise, where no man can die of wounds or age."

"Yes," Roden agreed. "A kingdom within Jötunheim, ruled by men."

Einar's brow furrowed. "I thought Guðmundr was a jötunn, as was his son Höfund."

"Some have said so," noted Roden. A well-traveled mercenary, he had heard many interpretations of the myth. "Jötunn or man, in the tales he was always kind to humans. We may have stumbled upon his home, or at least the place whence the stories were derived."

"Why would those who came here choose to leave paradise?" Einar questioned again.

"Well, someone had to have left," Roden said thoughtfully, "for how else could those stories have come to our ears?"

"Show me the stones," said Ottar.

Her siblings and the cluster of men followed Líf as she led them to the ancient carvings.

Hervor ran her fingers over the image of the original Úlfhéðinn. "So, the stories are true. That means we are not the first people to enter Jötunheim." She turned her attention to the four sizable burial mounds. "How many do you think lived here in the time before our fathers?"

"It would be impossible to tell how many are buried in each," Ottar replied. His blue eyes sparkled with wonder.

Yet not all were swept up in these larger mysteries. Surprisingly skeptical, Einar wanted to know, "How could one die in a land that prevents it?"

Ottar shrugged. "Maybe these were killed outside of Glæsisvellir. We all saw how jötnar react to the presence of humans."

"Then what of the dead man in the hall?" Guthorm had joined the group. He looked cynical. "There were bones in the mead hall when we arrived."

Líf considered the problem. "What if he too died outside the boundaries? Maybe his companions brought him here in the hope of saving him, but it was too late?"

"Then why did they not bury him?" again Guthorm's question held merit. "Why leave him to rot? And why, if there is such a place where immortality is granted to those living within, did they abandon it? Where did they go? Why did they leave? Why not stay forever until the beginning of Ragnarök? This place holds magic, but its source might not be as benevolent as it appears."

CHAPTER SEVEN

The older Lothbransons shared a look.

Speaking to her brother, for in her mind only he held authority equivalent to her own, Hervor suggested, "I think we should stay here, gather food, take stock of our resources. There are ample trees from which to construct new skis, and a large herd of horses that the men could train. With mounts, we could not only travel swiftly but also haul more supplies for the journey ahead. One of our men has even found a frozen spring due east of us. Who knows when we will have another chance to restock and recuperate?"

"Wise words, sister," agreed Ottar. He tenderly touched his ribcage as if a phantom pain had begun to ache. "As much as I would wish this venture over, we must not be hasty, especially when it appears that we have been given an incredible gift. If we are to stay here for any length of time, our first objective should be to repair the roof of the longhouse. Why not be comfortable as we prepare?"

"Excellent," Hervor affirmed. The small group began to disperse to spread the news and organize the crew. Guthorm hung back to walk alongside Ottar and express his concern. "This is not a world for men. If those who were given this gift, as you call it, have all vanished, how long do you think we can risk remaining in these parts?"

Ottar's features held little fear. "Long enough, good friend. By the way," he said as he tugged the ends of Guthorm's beard, "your grays have left you." As the pair headed back, Ottar smiled as Guthorm attempted to inspect his facial hair with new interest.

Now, only Úlfor remained at the runestones with Líf. His wolf fylgja sniffed at the base of the large markers and whined. There was a subtle change in the man's demeanor such that he appeared to worship the carved image of the Úlfhéðinn, although he never touched the stones.

Something about the area held Líf in place, as if the earth called to her to press closer. There were many tales about the dead rising to haunt the living and spread plagues and famine. Most revolved around men who had died tragically through deceit and murder. Others focused on those who had not been properly buried. Only after their bones were given the respect they deserved did the spirit relinquish its hold on the land. Líf shivered as she saw how the frost had already coated the newest grave.

Úlfor pulled his seax from its sheath. The small dagger glinted in the sunlight, brighter than even the fylgjur. The glimmer drew Líf's attention away from the burial mounds. The wolf warrior turned the knife upon himself.

"What are you doing?" Líf gasped as the mercenary slit his wrists.

Allowing the blood to splash over the top of the monolith, he explained, "An offering is needed."

The red liquid spilled down, filling the carved pathways and outlining the entire image in vibrant color. Úlfor knelt in front of the rune stone, and the streams of red soaked deep into the snow around him.

Afraid for both the man and his actions, Líf rushed to find the Rus, who had begun to fell trees. "Roden, hurry! Úlfor has harmed himself. He intends to offer himself as a sacrifice."

Dropping his axe, the foreign man ran swiftly back to the stones. Úlfor sat motionless, his head on his chest and his arms limp at his sides. A pool of crimson bloomed around his upturned wrists.

"What have you done?" Roden cried. He sprinted over and seized hold of one of the dripping red hands. Breathing heavily, the Rus stood, then flung the warrior's arm down. "And I thought you were mad before!" Spinning on his heels, Roden strode furiously away.

Úlfor's wolf fylgja, bright and luminous as the full moon, loped from around the nearest mound. The man looked at Líf unapologetically. "It is my right to give honor when due," he told her. Carefully washing his wrists in a patch of unblemished snow, he added, "Why does it concern you, a woman, what a man does out of respect for a greater power?"

Líf felt her cheeks flush. "Can I not worry about my friends?"

Úlfor paused in shaking off the icy particulates that exposed his now perfectly healed flesh. "We are not friends, Lothbrandóttir. I was hired for your cause. Do not mistake our relationship."

Repelled by the Úlfhéðinn, Líf returned to the longhouse and the sounds of animated voices. They were so loud that she could not help but overhear the speakers as she gnawed on a piece of cooled horseflesh.

"How dare you?" Hervor snarled from a back room. "Who do you think you are?"

"I would ask you the same thing, *woman*," Harekson retorted. "You dare to defy your superior! You cross the line."

"You are not—" The shieldmaiden was cut short by Ottar's voice.

"Harekson, what would you have us do?"

"First, bind the bitch so she can learn her place."

There was a scuffle, a clang of weapons, and a thud. Líf rose to her feet, but someone gently forced her down. Brasir sat next to her and shook his head. The men in the hall had fallen as silent as corpses in the ground. The talk in the back room continued.

"You can't take away my men," sneered Hervor. She was spitting angry.

Harekson, sounding almost as enraged, countered, "You cannot command men. Your loins prevent it and probably other things as well. Wombs wield no power."

"Erikk! Enough," Ottar interjected, using Harekson's given name. Líf knew they had grown up together, but using a first name was a sign of familiarity and closeness, and neither man was close to the other. Yet for some reason, Harekson ignored the slight.

The heir to Thorinheim spoke slowly and calmly. "You know I am right, Lothbranson. Three more men are dead. How many are you willing to sacrifice on this fool's errand? The only sickness that is spreading is in your minds. The only deaths are the result of the choices you are making."

As the voices quieted, the crowd grew. When Líf stood up this time, Brasir did not move to stop her. Was he not as curious as the rest of the crew? she wondered. She maneuvered herself as close as she dared to the back room and pressed her ear to the wall.

"If you want my ship when this is over," Ottar said, "you can have her."

"No!" gasped Hervor.

The male Lothbranson was not finished. "But you must ensure that my boys are pardoned, and Líf as well."

After a long, drawn-out pause, Harekson responded, "You know I cannot promise that. It is not within my power."

There was another long pause. This time, it was Ottar who spoke first. "Then leave, Harekson, and take all who wish to follow you. If you are able to reach *Wavecutter*, try to sail her back to Midgard. I will not stop you and neither will Hervor."

There was a low growl; nevertheless, the shieldmaiden did not speak.

"But," Ottar continued, "you cannot take Roden with you. He is bóndi, a freeman. You cannot compel him to follow you. If you do, you will force my hand. I do not want to fight you, Erikk; I never have. I respect you too much. But I will stand for what is right, even if you do not see it that way."

Líf's heart thrummed so loudly she was afraid she wouldn't hear what was said next. Finally, Harekson agreed.

"Have it your way, son of Lothbran. I will permit your endeavor to continue its course, but I smell mutiny in the air. And know that when it happens, I will be waiting."

Someone was approaching. The crew scurried away, acting as if the entire conversation had never occurred. Líf was not as quick as the others. When Harekson strode out, he almost collided with her. He flung a look of distaste at the young woman and left the building.

Both Hervor and Ottar appeared. Hervor's words dripped venom. "I wish you'd let me restrain him. No good will come of it as long as he is free."

"But he *is* free," countered Ottar. "We are all free and alive. And to keep it that way, we must focus our attention on our objective and not let outside worry cloud our thoughts."

"I think that is a narrow-minded approach," the shieldmaiden retorted.

Ottar sighed wearily. "Only time will tell. For now, we are unchallenged, and much work must be done."

The next three weeks passed more quickly than expected. They discovered that Glæsisvellir was a plain in more than just name, for the snow had hidden rich soil and tender grasses. Observing the wild steeds digging up shoots, the men realized that the ground was no longer stony.

Twenty horses were corralled and broken. The shaggy, stocky beasts were far hardier than any Líf had seen before. Without saddles, they were hard to ride, yet they could pull crude sleds and haul bundles of supplies.

Skis were constructed in vast numbers. Everyone received a set, and spares were packed along with smoked horseflesh and grouse that had been discovered seeking refuge in the grove of trees. A small store of salt had been found in one of the ruined households, as well as several sets of fishing gear, although no fish could be harvested in the frozen spring.

Hervor oversaw the construction of new shields. They had plenty of wood, but viable metal was scarce; moreover, the process took time. Only a few shields could be made, and there would be no spare for Líf to use.

With her siblings so busy, Líf had almost given up hope of learning to defend herself. Then one day, Úlfor approached her, holding a staff with a crudely whittled end.

He handed it to her. "You want to learn to use a spear. Here."

Líf held the wooden shaft that was as tall as she was. "I'm confused," she admitted coldly. "I'm no shieldmaiden. I'm just a *simple woman*." She threw the handmade spear at his feet.

Úlfor walked away without retrieving his gift.

"Why did you do that?" Thray questioned. "We both know you want to learn to wield weapons, as unsafe as it is."

Líf chewed her tongue in frustration but did not respond.

Thray poked the woman's cheek with her soft nose. "So what if he insulted you? Prove him wrong."

Looking at the spear, Líf wondered if Thray could be right. She *did* want to learn. The idea that one day she might not be such a burden to others, that she might even be an asset, was empowering. Seated on her shoulder, her fylgja sniffed, "You're as muleheaded as your sister."

As quickly as she could, Líf snatched up the wooden spear and chased after the Úlfhéðinn. "Úlfor, wait! I'm sorry." The man turned and watched her approach, while Líf implored, "I do want to learn. Please, teach me."

The warrior rubbed his eyes as if they were tired. "You're too emotional."

"I know," confessed Líf.

"Think with your head. That is essential."

"I'll try."

"Then come." Úlfor led her away from the center of camp. "Time to sully your gown."

Just as she had been after her bouts with Hervor, Líf was sore and tired after the session—but she felt more fulfilled than she had in a while. On her way to wash up, she passed several of Arto's comrades muttering amongst themselves. They were uninterested in the crazy Lothbrandóttir and paid her no mind as she turned the corner.

From past experience, Líf was careful not to encourage lustful behavior. She knew that without the bounty of available women, men might be moved to take advantage of the few they could, so she remained cautious around those whom she didn't trust. Líf kept her head down as she slipped past but stayed alert to sights and sounds. As she splashed water from a catch basin onto her face and neck, she heard one of the crewmen groan, "He could have made it. It wasn't right, what we did."

Another one countered, "How could we have known? He was hurt and slowing us down. Arto made the sensible choice. Now we must live with it."

"It's been weighing on me these past weeks."

"We'll have no more of that sort of talk. It's over and done with."

After the men dispersed, Líf whispered, "I think they killed someone."

Thray growled, "I think you're right, Líf."

"We should tell my siblings."

"Did you see their faces?"

Líf paused. "Not really."

"*I* don't know who they were. I doubt you do. How can you accuse anyone when you do not know who the culprits are?"

"Arto is one of them. We heard that much."

Thray's whiskers flared as she talked. "Your siblings are fully aware of Arto's treachery. With tensions this high, we are lucky the crew has not rebelled. It's only the loose agreement between Harekson and Ottar that holds us together for now."

Acknowledging the fylgja's concern, Líf said, "You don't want me to say anything in case the actions cause unwelcome reactions."

"You are right. I don't," agreed Thray. "Not now. Not about this, but we should be on our guard."

"When have I not been of late?"

"Tomorrow we continue our journey into jötnar territory," said Thray as she peered into the white-hued distance. "They could be watching Glæsisvellir, waiting for just that moment." Nodding toward the crew who were loading supplies upon crude sleds, she added, "These men must fully support your siblings' commands. A fractured unit would be disastrous."

"I know, but a man was killed."

"So? So what?" barked the squirrel. "Do you even know his name? Tomorrow, more men could die. So many more."

Lif did not like anything about this situation. She chewed her lip, a habit she appeared to be forming, before questioning, "Do you really believe that the jötnar have set a trap for us and are lying in wait?"

"I can't be sure," rumbled the guardian, "but I wouldn't put it past them."

The morning was bright, the sun a solitary presence in the sky. The entire caravan had lined up just after dawn. More than half the men were on horses or manning the sleds, while the rest readied their new skis.

Lif had a horse of her own. The barrel-bodied thing was so wide that it was hard for her to spread her legs across its back. Whickering, it stamped its forehooves impatiently while she tried to keep it in place. Meanwhile, her siblings and Harekson were disputing Roden's assessment.

"Are you positive we cannot approach by another route?" Ottar asked again, as if hoping a fifth time would change the answer.

"I can only direct you on the straightest course. As I have said more than once, it is not as if I were reading a map. All I am able to do is sense the direction in which to travel. Nothing more. Nothing less."

"We will be heading right into them," snarled Harekson. There was no question that he was displeased.

Roden looked apologetic. "I don't know what else to tell you other than what I have already said."

"Then we march, following your course," sighed Ottar.

Harekson grabbed the blond man's arm. Ottar slowly shook his head and stepped away as Thorinheim's heir released his hold.

Ottar gave his command. "We march. Keep a keen eye and a sharp ear. We all know what we might face today." His voice dropped, and he quietly uttered, "May mighty Thor prevent *that* from happening."

Roden squeezed his stallion's ribcage with his legs, steering him through the copse and onto the plain on the other side. As soon as they had left the protection of their temporary refuge, one thing became uncomfortably clear. The lands beyond were deathly silent.

CHAPTER EIGHT

Every hoofbeat sounded thunderous, every exhale loud as a gale. The entire party understood that they had abandoned their mysterious realm of safety and entered into sinister lands. No one spoke. All instinctively remained silent. Yet the snow continued to crunch under pressure, and the sleds scraped against the ground.

Even the horses were unusually quiet. The whites of their eyes flashed, and their ears flicked about in that hyperawareness that animals display when traversing territory where predators roam.

Líf felt her mare shy under her as if ready to bolt back to the safety of the tree line. Yet the young woman somehow managed to keep the horse's head facing in the right direction.

When they neared the slope where she had last seen the jötnar waiting, she remembered the threat made by the three-eyed brute—that that the giants would slaughter her people if they ever returned. Even Hervor hesitated at that marker, her gray eyes never leaving the crest of the small hill.

Ottar coaxed his mount up the slope first. Maybe his second chance at life had given him extraordinary courage, for he did not appear fearful that a group of giants might lie in wait on the other side.

Roden accompanied her brother. His hooded eyes appeared narrower than usual. He kept his wits about him, one hand resting upon the hilt of his sword. His dark hair was flattened by his fur-trimmed cloth hat, whose pointed tip flopped over to one side. Líf wondered how dangerous it was for him not to wear a helmet like other men did. Yet he was Rus, and as far as she was concerned, they were a different sort of people.

Then again, how could she criticize the man when his companion was even worse? Úlfor was a mercenary, but he continued to wear Úlfhéðinn garb: a tunic over an undershirt, wrapped in his wolf-hide cloak. There was not one ring of chain mail on him. He was bareheaded, his long, unkempt hair falling over his shoulders and halfway down his back.

If they had been in the civilized world, Líf might have offered to trim his locks like the other crewmen's. Good grooming was a mark of her people: men wore their hair shoulder length and took care of their beards. The seafarers made an effort to maintain their hygiene, even during raiding parties and when circumstances precluded their weekly baths.

These inconsequential thoughts kept some of Líf's terror at bay. The group reached the peak and studied the terrain that lay ahead. There were no signs of the jötnar, whose large footprints had disappeared over the past few weeks. The land was bare and so white one had to squint to see.

Continuing to guide them, Roden led them away from the locale of the prior attacks, skirting ice-trimmed boulders and ascending rocky slopes. Sometime before midday, Líf realized they had passed their old camp without even noticing it. Their abandoned gear was lost under the powdery white stuff.

"At least we are moving at a respectable speed," consoled Thray. She always knew Líf's thoughts. "Now we can actually get somewhere."

The days slipped past as they had done in Glæsisvellir. Over time, the silence was broken by occasional whispered conversation and, eventually, by good-natured banter. Though caution was still of utmost importance, a fragile sense of calm pervaded the caravan.

In the evenings, while others set up camp and a defensive perimeter, Líf took lessons from Úlfor, who had brought the makeshift spear along just for that purpose. Líf soon learned that there was much more to spear fighting than propelling the elongated projectile at one's opponent. The weapon was too valuable for that. It was actually used more for jabbing and thrusting, though a blow to an enemy's head with the shaft worked as well. Only out of pure necessity was one supposed to throw the spear, for that last-stand maneuver could mean the end of your efforts.

At night, under the protection of darkness, the men spoke freely. Too freely, Líf thought. Often, she picked up wisps of conversation trailing in the still air that did not bode well for her siblings. Many of the men were disgruntled by the decision to continue the journey away from their homeland. Moreover, a slow erosion was taking place, a gradual loss of the hard-earned respect for the shieldmaiden's standing among the crew. Who was she to think a woman could have any say over a man? She might wear a mail shirt, but that did not give her male rights. And what sort of leader couldn't keep his sisters in check? Surely not one they should be following.

These and similar opinions drifted under the stars, leaving Líf no comfort except that found in her dreams. She had always been the most emotional of the three siblings; words and suggestive looks affected her in ways that would never bother Ottar or Hervor. She wished she could form the same thick skin as her taller, stronger kin. It seemed that her weakness was more than physical.

Fortunately, whenever the wooden spear was in hand, Líf was able to push aside her continual self-doubt. Though her arms grew tired of its weight, her legs became sore from springing and crouching, and her head throbbed from the explosive exercise, she felt powerful in the face of it all.

Just beyond the whittled point's swinging arc, Thray and the wolf sat and watched. Neither made a sound as they patiently waited for their people to finish their dance of war. Úlfor would swat her shins or her back with his own spear to make her straighten up or to correct her stance. He still said very little, but Líf understood his commands. Sweating despite the cold, she wore a grin whenever she had to pause for air.

"What is this?"

Líf looked up to see her sister standing nearby, the goshawk perched on one shoulder. The fierce bird looked more tangible than ever, though to the shieldmaiden it was nothing more than a patch of empty air.

"I'm learning the spear," Líf explained. She raised the simple weapon.

"I see what you are up to," snapped Hervor before turning to the Úlfhéðinn. "And you!"

Why was she so angry? Had Hervor not agreed that Líf should learn these skills? Flustered, Líf felt her jaw drop as her sister verbally attacked the warrior.

"You knew she was my student. How dare you presume to take over for me! And for what? A spear?"

"Hervor, he only—" Líf tried to interject as Hervor snatched away the wooden device and broke it across her knee.

The shieldmaiden seethed, "I have had enough of men assuming their place is higher than mine. Líf is not yours to teach. What a fool you are, Úlfor, daring to overstep your bounds."

The woman warrior strode up to him, her lips mere inches from his neck. Úlfor looked as if he would growl. His eyes glimmered in a bestial way. Would he attack? His hand still held the upright weapon at his side. "Do not dare to do so again," Hervor hissed.

Úlfhéðnar were supposed to gain their unnatural strength and ferocity from channeling the spirits of wolves. Líf wondered if the wolf warrior could smell the hot blood pulsing through her sister's veins.

Hervor stepped back and reached for Líf. "Come, now."

Úlfor spoke. "A spear and your axe are of equal worth."

The shieldmaiden rounded on him, the goshawk taking wing. Her weapon of choice was ready to punish the impudent fellow. Úlfor dodged the first strike, then jabbed his weapon at her. The battle began in earnest.

With an enraged cry, Hervor somersaulted away, then spun around, pulling out her seax with her other hand. The raptor's alarm call erupted overhead as the bird dove at the iridescent wolf. Both animals flickered with hot hues. Thray screeched and rushed toward Líf.

"Stop this!" Líf shouted as she threw a hard-packed snowball at the back of her sister's head.

The impact startled Hervor. She missed her strike and received a swift cut to her right arm. This only agitated the shieldmaiden even more. Now Úlfor retreated as Hervor expertly attacked.

"Stop," gasped Líf once more, not daring to try to split up the pair. They would kill each other. Their red rage was poisoning even their fylgjur, which were also in the middle of a full-on fight. Feeling her voice betray her, she barely coughed out, "You must stop."

Líf sprinted back to camp in search of anyone who might help. The first person she saw was Brasir, who immediately realized something was dreadfully wrong. As he approached her, she veered away at the sound of her brother's voice.

"Ottar! Ottar!" she cried. When he turned, she immediately pointed behind her. No other words were needed. With young Sigird at his side, Ottar raced to the place where two lives were on the line.

They were not the only ones. Líf's mad dash had alerted the entire camp to the fight, and a ring of onlookers pressed in as close as they dared. Some shouted; others cheered.

"Let me through!" Ottar demanded, and the men spread apart enough for him to slide past. Líf was at his heels, but Sigird was muscled out.

Three figures were in the center. Brasir, empty handed, had just jumped back from an unintentional swing. In all her wild beauty, Hervor resembled a Valkyrie come to claim the souls of the dead. With her axe facing the mercenary, she pointed her dagger at the black-skinned man. "Do not stop this!"

Ottar took in the scene. A sudden panic appeared to wash over him, then was gone in a blink of an eye.

"Brasir," he said, and by his tone the other man knew it was useless to argue. Brasir stepped back into the ring of onlookers as the two combatants began once again.

"They'll kill each other," said Líf, pointing out the obvious. But maybe it was not so clear. Why else would Ottar not stop this foolishness?

Her brother answered her unasked question. "This fight is for honor. We cannot interfere."

Inhaling sharply, Líf watched in horror at the deadly strikes each combatant attempted to land on the other. She had never seen her sister in hand-to-hand combat. This was nothing like observing her spar with crewmembers or batter around young upstarts in their home village. This was something else entirely. This was a fight for the highest stakes.

Hervor was breathtaking. Her movements were practiced perfection, her skill undeniable. There was no question of her high standing as a warrior among the elite. Even the mercenaries murmured at her impressive prowess. Yet her opponent was far more skilled.

Had Úlfor been any other kind of warrior, he would have been felled by the woman's deft strokes. Yet he was no *mere* warrior; he was Úlfhéðnar. Even without the assistance of the maddening drug that stripped away all fear, doubt, and pain, this man was something greater than human. A hitherto unseen savagery emerged, an unstoppable power erupting from a deep and rarely tapped source.

Clearly, he held the upper hand. With barely any effort, he took control of the fight, forcing Hervor to retreat as he circled her like a wolf assessing its prey. Now Líf understood. Here and now, her sister would lose, her hugr become an offering to the gods, her body left to feed the worms. Hervor would neither see what happened to the group or know whether their mission succeeded.

Hervor's honor had been challenged, and the only thing she could do was prove those in doubt wrong or die in the attempt. And who better to help solidify her status than the one man no others dared cross? The one better than all the rest?

There was no way for her to win. Could her pride have instilled in her the notion that she might succeed? Or was there some bit of honest truth buried deep within the shieldmaiden, warning her that this action would be her last? But was there a better way for a woman of war to die than to fall in battle at the hands of one who possessed superior skill? The honor that was taken from her would be returned in the tales of her death and the courage she had shown in meeting it.

This was what men were willing to risk in order to achieve renown. This was what they cared about: to gain fame during life, and immortality through song and spoken word in the generations to follow.

Yet now, face to face with such a sacrifice, Líf felt only disgust—for her sister, who valued her life so little; for the men, who had pushed Hervor to this point; and finally, for the belief that time in the realm of the living was so insignificant. A tear rolled down Líf's cheek, and she quickly wiped it away.

Úlfor knew he had the upper hand. You could see it in his eyes and in the way he moved. He was taller and stronger, the force of his strokes far more damaging. Yet his face never brightened in delight. He spat out no taunts or jeers like some of the watchers did. He kept his sight only upon his opponent and the flash of her two blades.

As Hervor leaped away from a swift thrust, she rolled on the ground. Her breathing was heavy, and her brow was filmed with sweat. She was near Líf's feet—so close, in fact, that the sisters could have touched.

In the moment between two breaths, an ironclad resolve washed over the female warrior. She hurled her axe at Úlfor, forcing him to dodge. The weapon spun past, catching the fringe of his wolf-hide cloak and scattering the onlookers.

At the same time, she stabbed her seax into the ground and rose to face the oncoming tip of the spear. She bent slightly backward. As the lethal point passed overhead, she grabbed its shaft with both hands.

Úlfor jerked the spear back. Hervor stumbled but held true. Both individuals clutched the deadly weapon with the grip of gods. The Úlfhéðinn growled low while the shieldmaiden snarled.

In another lightning-quick movement, Úlfor jerked the spear toward himself, and in the next moment his large, muscular arm was around Hervor's throat, crushing her windpipe against his chest. The woman flailed and reached up to the man's face to jab her thumbs into his eyes while Úlfor's other hand kept batting hers away.

As her face purpled, she flung out the toe of one boot, desperately trying to reach her discarded dagger, but the blade lay just out of reach. She gasped and sputtered but could not escape his grip.

All Líf wanted to do was dive on the knife and toss it to her dying sister. Who cared if Úlfor had done no wrong? Hervor was in trouble, and she could save herself if she had the blade. Yet that same sense of honor that filled Líf with such hatred also kept her from following through.

The entire camp watched in silence as the shieldmaiden kicked out several more times and then was still. Úlfor tossed her to the earth, where she rolled onto her back, gasping. Her lungs had to be crying out for air. Her neck had already begun to bruise.

The wolf warrior looked at Ottar but then seemed to think better of it. Standing over the incapacitated woman, he said, "Are we done here, or must I finish you off?"

Líf wanted to implore her sister to be sensible, but her tongue lay leaden in her mouth.

Hervor opened her eyes and, for a moment, beheld her sister's. In a voice not her own, the shieldmaiden gave in. "We are done."

Picking up his spear, Úlfor addressed his opponent in a voice loud enough for all to hear. "You are better than any woman—" Hervor winced and closed her eyes as he continued, "or man that I have ever fought." Noticing the gaping onlookers, the wolf warrior rumbled, "It is over. Go!"

The crew returned to the camp and their duties. The Úlfhéðinn headed away as well. Only the shieldmaiden remained, still sprawled on her back. For the first time, Líf pitied her oldest sibling. She had lost *and* she had lived. Was there a more a dishonorable way for her to exist? Hervor was no longer a woman feared but a woman scorned.

CHAPTER NINE

How swiftly Líf's world had changed once again! As she stepped away from her sister, she was struck by a difference among the men. Hervor had been held in high regard, wielding perhaps more power than even she had realized. But now that the shieldmaiden had been defeated, that fragile balance of power listed markedly in a new direction.

And what was Ottar without his sister? His personal crew had always held him in high esteem, but the hired hands did not understand how the older Lothbransons worked and had long questioned why a man would allow a woman's authority to be intertwined with his own. Without the shieldmaiden's fierce, punishing persona by his side, Ottar's standing had dropped lower than that of the jarl's son. Seeming to recognize this, Ottar gave orders with intensified precision and an ever-watchful mien.

By the same token, Líf sensed that Harekson's sway over the crew had instantly increased. She wondered how many of the men would support him if he chose to break his word with Ottar.

"We are at that man's mercy," she uttered in dismay.

The color in her cheeks paled even more as Thray growled, "Your sister was foolish."

"She must live with it," sighed Líf. She glanced at Hervor, who had pushed herself up to a seated position and now stared away from the camp, into the distance.

"Will she?" Thray's voice was as cold and sharp as Úlfor's spearhead. "Live with it?"

"She wouldn't kill herself," Líf hastily countered, but her heartbeat sped up at the thought. "That is not her fate."

"It was not like her to lose, either," noted Thray. Her little voice was unsympathetic.

"How can you be so cruel?" snapped Líf.

"I? It is your sister who thinks only of herself." Thray's fur bristled even more. "She is your elder. You have no spouse, so she is supposed to watch over you, as is Ottar. And what has she done?"

"Stop it, Thray," Líf warned.

"What *has* she done, Líf?" Thray was undeterred. "Risked the security of our family and set us on a path to ruin!"

"How dare you?" Líf shrugged her shoulders so violently that Thray almost tumbled to the ground.

Snapping her large teeth together as if preparing to bite, the squirrel chattered, "You wait and see. No good will come of this." The tiny fylgja leaped off and bounded away.

Líf's mood darkened. Aimlessly she wound her way through the previously claimed sleeping plots. Before long, her eyes rested upon Skeggi. He was the one man who adored Hervor. Surely, nothing could damage her reputation in his mind.

"What are you doing?" Líf asked.

The large, ruddy-haired man was furiously carving something into one of their fire logs. Skeggi blinked and looked at his haphazard work as if seeing it for the first time. He tossed the wood into the fire, sending sparks shooting up into the air with all the fury Fenrir bore. "Nothin'."

Not sure whether she should sit down or walk away, Líf admitted, "I'm worried." Why she had chosen to confess her fears to this man and not to her brother, she could not fathom.

As Skeggi looked at her, his eyes filled with sorrow and sympathy. "Remember, nothing remains. The only certainty we are guaranteed is Ragnarök and the end of time."

This was far from helpful and not what Líf needed to hear.

Skeggi continued, "Your sister was beaten by one better."

"But why should that ruin *us*?" Líf had meant to say *her*. She looked down at the ground in shame.

"When we were young," Skeggi began, "Ottar and I made a blood oath so that we would be brothers forever. I have always viewed you as my own family. Because of that, though I am no Lothbranson, I will never leave your side. I know this is not what you care to hear—"

Líf dropped to her knees and gave Skeggi a large hug. Until that moment, she had viewed him as nothing more than the drunken, teasing fool who had overshadowed much of her childhood. But hearing his words gave her a sense of security, meager though it was.

Whispering into his ear, she said, "Thank you." Before she pulled away, she added, "Brother."

If a blush could be seen under all his thick, shaggy facial hair, Skeggi surely would have sported one. Together they looked at Hervor. The light was dimming and the temperature dropping, yet the shieldmaiden remained motionless, in solitude, for a while longer.

Over the following days, the changing relationships were visibly reflected in the actual layout of the camp. Those closest to Ottar and Hervor laid their bedding alongside them. Others with weaker ties began to cluster near Harekson. No man was without a weapon within arm's reach. They even slept with their blades tucked among their blankets.

Even if Hervor had tried to offer advice or make a demand, the weight of her say in any matter of worth had been stripped away. But since her defeat, she had remained silent and distant, as if she were reliving the experience repeatedly in her mind.

To see her sister this way broke Líf's heart. Perhaps Hervor would have been treated better if she had been kinder to the crew. But had she not fought again and again for that hard-won respect? Where was their loyalty? Where was their esteem? None of them could have fought the shieldmaiden and succeeded. None but the Úlfhéðinn. Yet did that matter? No.

Had Hervor been born a man, her standing might have been merely bruised. The reputation of any common warrior who attempted to combat an Úlfhéðinn might have been enhanced. Yet she was a woman, so she was now one of the least respected people in camp, along with young Sigird and Líf.

Life was never fair for one born without a cock. Yet, in truth, was life ever fair? From birth, everyone was taught that existence was a struggle against all sorts of odds: neighboring kingdoms, the abysmal environment, even their place amid the other worlds of Yggdrasil. At every stage of life, one fought for food, for status, for honor, for immortality.

A person emerged from the womb kicking and punching and repeated those actions throughout life until dead and buried. Those few who showed great skill were selected to repeat those actions in the afterlife until Ragnarök. That was their truth, their certainty, and their prison, for being of human flesh.

"Don't be so bitter," Thray said. Though she had not apologized for her earlier words, she did seem to be trying to extend a greater kindness.

"I shouldn't have urged Ottar to ask Úlfor to come," Líf murmured as she worked at mending a crewman's shoes. The rocky terrain took a toll on the leather. "It would have been better if Úlfor had remained at Jarlbörg."

"Would it?" The fylgja's emotions were in check, for her fur shone with shimmering, iridescent hues. "Had he not been present, you would have been killed in Midgard."

Líf remained silent, though she could not help but wonder if that might not have been better for the party as a whole. For what was her life worth when weighed against her sister's?

"Líf?" Thray's tone indicated she understood the woman's dark thoughts. Suddenly the squirrel squeaked out, "He comes!"

Úlfor approached. He held a second spear, this one no wooden toy but a real weapon with an iron-barbed tip. Líf realized what he wanted.

"How dare you?" she gasped, appalled. "After what you did to my sister, you have the nerve to approach me?"

The wolf warrior stopped. "This is more important than what has occurred," he countered.

"No!" snapped Líf as she jabbed the sewing needle in the air between them. "Leave me alone, do you hear? Stay away from me."

The man inclined his head respectfully and moved away. Thray remained silent. For a time, the squirrel just stood there, unblinking. Then, as if nothing had occurred, she began to groom her fluffy tail.

"Lover's spat?" questioned Arto. He and several of his companions sat nearby, gnawing on frozen horseflesh. He was becoming increasingly confident around the Lothbransons. This was unfitting for one of his standing, yet one more reminder of how precarious her family's position had become.

Not wanting to encourage more snide behavior, Líf bent over her work and began to add another layer of leather to the sole of a boot.

"Are you mute as well as mad?" the man persisted. His goat fylgja pawed at the ground. "It's rude not to reply to a question."

"It's no business of yours," Líf retorted abruptly.

"Privacy only works in private. Out here," Arto said, gesturing broadly, "we have no secrets. *Everything* is shared."

At the man's words, Líf's cheeks flushed and her stomach knotted. She hurriedly gathered up her sewing equipment and as many boots as she could carry. As she walked away, Arto called out, "Come, now, it was only conversation we was havin'."

Líf took refuge on the opposite side of the camp, away from the men clustered around the few fires. She stared at the looming mountains in the distance, for that was their destination as far as anyone could tell. The long, narrow spires of stone shot up into the cloud-choked sky, their tops disappearing in the ever-gray haze.

It was always stormy over the range, the sky dark and ominous. Líf imagined that the place was the origin of the blizzards that had afflicted them since their arrival in Jötunheim. Maybe they were not the ribs of Ymir but the phalluses of some monstrous entity that impregnated the womb of the clouds, which birthed the harsh gales and icy precipitants.

When she shared her wandering thoughts with Thray, the squirrel cocked her head to one side. "You have the most vivid daydreams, Líf. I wish my mind could envision that which is not known."

"Do you not dream, Thray?" Líf had always assumed fylgjur could dream, but she had never before thought to ask.

The little creature paused but, instead of answering, turned her face in a new direction. "Look, there is Brasir, all alone. When was the last time you both talked? If I cannot remember, it has been a while."

Líf glanced at the dark-skinned fellow as he tended some of the picketed horses. He was brushing their thick fur with more care than most men took with their own mounts. When he discovered a sore where travel packs had rubbed against a horse's hide, he applied salve from a little jar. It was not as if these animals were quality livestock, yet he treated them as if they were the king's own herd.

"Well? Will you not speak with him?" Thray asked, her colors warming as she spoke.

"Why should I?" Líf countered. "We have nothing, absolutely nothing, to say to each other."

"That's not true," purred the squirrel.

"If he had anything of worth to tell me, he would have. Brasir is not shy, though he *is* a bit too reserved."

"He has much on his mind," noted the fylgja.

"Exactly," Líf said as she returned to her sewing. "Why should I get in the way of that?"

"I doubt he would view it the same way." Thray held back speech for a full breath before adding, "It was just a suggestion."

"Thank you," said Líf just as she pricked her finger with the needle. Sucking the bead of blood so not to the stain the boot leather, she mumbled, "But I can handle my own affairs."

"Well," mused Thray coyly, "I do like the way the muscles of his back flex as he works."

That caught Líf off guard. "How do you know? He wears so many layers that you cannot possibly tell. And didn't you just say that you were incapable of imagining things?"

Thray allowed her tail to slide slowly around the base of Líf's neck. "I said that I cannot envision that which is not *known*."

Líf felt herself blush. This time, she knew that her cheeks must have been as red as Thray's fur.

They had entered one of the many valleys that were all but swallowed between the mountains bordering them. The snowdrifts on the valley floor reached the horses' chests. Several men were sent ahead to shovel a path up the steep slopes, where they would be able to move more freely.

Large ridges and serpentine gorges wound up and down the sides of the great stone spires. Despite the sharp inclines, there was no loose rock to cause the mounts to slip or skiers to stumble. Still, their progress was slow and exhausting. But there was little fear that even an army of jötnar would discover them, hidden as they were amid the shaded nooks and crannies.

At the base of the third mountain, Roden halted the caravan. His face wore a look of perplexity. Sliding off his horse, he began to explore the area, climbing up the ridges and down to the valley itself. When he returned, his face appeared blanched, not from fear but as one near death.

"What is it, Roden?" Ottar hastily questioned. "Are we not on the correct course?"

The Rus hesitated. "We are," he began. His voice dropped to a whisper. "In a sense."

Harekson, who also rode up front, grunted, "I do not like riddles."

With an apologetic look, Roden began, "We are where we must be to reach Svartálfheim."

Harekson surveyed the endless mountain range surrounding them. All was stone and snow. Líf also glanced about, half expecting to see a hidden door embedded in the side of a cliff.

The Rus followed their line of sight before continuing, "But we cannot go any further lest we miss our mark."

"Is it behind us?" Ottar asked hopefully.

"No," Roden shook his head, sending the end of his pointed hat swinging. He cast his forefinger to the sky. "We must climb."

Chapter Ten

"You want us to climb the mountain?" Harekson asked in disbelief. Though he was the one who'd said it, all in earshot surely had the same thought. Líf knew she did. "It's far too steep for the horses. Only Thor's goats could clamber up those sheer cliffs."

"Nevertheless, if you want to access the world beyond," sighed Roden, "you must go up."

Immediately and without question, Ottar appraised their situation. "The horses can probably make it a little farther. After that, we will have to set them free and leave some of our less essential supplies. We can take only what we can carry. Everyone should keep a set of skis, for we do not know what we will face at the top. How many picks do we have? How many cords of rope?"

Harekson scowled. "This is folly. No sane man would climb that peak."

Tired and exasperated, Ottar was quick to respond. "Then leave. I release you from our agreement. You can return home at any time, but I will see this through. *You* ensured that back in Haugr."

The expression on Harekson's face changed from irritation to something akin to sympathy. "Your sons are well cared for. My grandfather has always treated his wards as well as his own blood kin." Glaring at Brasir, whose features were almost lost under the fur trim of his hood, he continued, "I will not return empty-handed. As my grandfather wishes you to find the truth of the slave's words, I will not interfere. But it will give me great pleasure to expose this for what it is, a mere delusion of the mind." He looked up toward the invisible peak of the mountain. "I have not climbed like this since we were youths."

"Nor have I," admitted Ottar. "We must find the best climbers to lead us on the safest course. May the gods look kindly on our quest."

"I can climb," Brasir volunteered. "My journey has taken me to lands far and wide. I have acquired many skills, including this one."

"I will climb as well." Hervor had barely said a word to anyone since her defeat, and the sound of her voice ringing out was almost as startling as her proposition.

"I cannot—" Ottar began, but she cut him off.

"You know I was always better at this than you." Then in a far humbler manner, she added, "Let me do this, brother."

Ottar nodded his consent. After careful consideration, five people were chosen to find a route and lead groups of climbers up the mountain. They would affix lengths of rope to any anchor point they could find, to assist others less skilled than themselves.

The caravan trudged up the slope as far as the horses could go before they began whickering and slipping. Following Ottar's instructions, the men unloaded supplies and hid the excess before releasing all but two of the steeds, which they slaughtered to replenish their declining food stocks. Sheltering under a slight outcropping, they made camp for the night, for no one knew how long it would take to reach the top. It would be better to start at daybreak.

The rumble of thunder was heard, although no lightning was spotted. From her vantage point, Líf scanned the valley of snow. Nothing moved as far as she could see, other than a few of their horses struggling in the drifts. They would all probably freeze over the next few days. Poor beasts. They could not know that their purpose, which was now fulfilled, had been the only thing ensuring their safety. They were merely pawns that had served at the pleasure of more intelligent masters.

Was this how the gods viewed humans—as simple-minded beings unable to comprehend the vastness of the deities' plans? And what of the Norns? Did those women look upon the Æsir and Vanir as no more than toys for their entertainment?

Such thoughts left Líf cold and depressed. And she was cold indeed, for the higher they climbed, the more frigid the air became. Each inhale felt like daggers stabbing her lungs. Before they started out, Brasir had shown them how to wrap a bit of cloth over the lower portion of the face. Líf could not tell if it helped, but she did not dare take it off.

In the morning, their climb started slowly and with extreme caution. Líf, who had never attempted anything like this before, trembled as soon as her feet left the security of solid ground. She was not asked to carry much on her person, although a small parcel of provisions was strapped to her waist. Ottar and Skeggi carried what she could not, bearing their swollen bundles without complaint.

She followed her sister's lead rope, preferring to clutch it rather than the hard surface of the mountain. Next to her, Roden used Brasir's rope. The Rus focused only on his hands and the holds just above eye level. His face was almost as white as the snow that had begun to fall during the night.

Ottar was below Líf, while Úlfor followed Roden. And so five lines of crew members hoisted themselves into the sky, leaving the domain of men and entering the world of birds and winged things.

Hervor's goshawk dove down and swooped past the crew, inspecting their progress and possibly judging their skill. Skeggi's portly seagull showed not the slightest inclination to expend more energy than necessary, but rather fluttered overhead to find a perch just high enough that she could wait until her human passed by.

Thray remained tucked behind Líf's apron, nestled amid layers of cloth. They did not speak to one another, for it took all of Líf's concentration to maintain her heavy breathing as the muscles of her thin arms began to tremble from exertion.

But what of the other fylgjur? Not all of them could take wing or were small enough to ride upon their humans. What would happen if they remained in Jötunheim while their people vanished into the unknown?

Trepidation caused Líf to look down. Paralleling the men were glimmering animals. Hoofed or clawed, it did not matter; the fylgjur climbed the steep cliff in ways their natural counterparts could not. Even Brasir's massive bear followed steadily, keeping her eyes upon her man's feet. It was as if some inexplicable force secured them to the mountainside. As long as the men were safe, so were their guardians.

The drawback to this discovery was that she realized how far they had ascended. All of a sudden, Líf felt lightheaded. She missed her next grip and began to tilt backward.

This was it. This would be her death: plummeting to the stony earth. No amount of snow would soften her fall. Her body would be smashed amid the rocks, blood oozing from mouth and ears.

As a child, she had seen it happen to someone else. A man known for his surefootedness had ended his life gurgling and spitting up red, all his bones shattered. Had she not leaped aside at the right moment, she would have shared his fate. It now appeared that she would.

With a cry, she flailed about with her free arm, fingers groping desperately for a handhold. At the same time, a strong pressure at her back forced her against the face of the mountain, stopping her perilous tilt. Ottar had saved her from a lethal fall.

After mustering her nerve, she started upward once more. This time, Roden did not keep pace alongside. The Rus gripped the rocks with white knuckles. Úlfor shifted away from the security rope to try to talk sense into the other mercenary's ear.

Líf could not wait to see what the issue was. Her own arms and legs were tiring, and her back had begun to ache. With no safe place to pause and rest, and with a line of men underneath her, all she could do was climb ever higher and pray that she had the strength to make it to safety.

In the early afternoon, salvation came in the form of a stretch of ledge large enough to hold them all. One by one, the climbers heaved themselves over the top. The men at the end of each line hauled up the ropes after their climb to ensure a good amount for the next leg of their journey.

Líf spied Úlfor pulling up the last length of his rope with great effort. Only when the pale hands of Roden appeared over the lip of the ledge did she realize that the Rus was being hoisted to the top. His eyes were wider than she had ever seen them, and he sprawled listlessly onto the stony platform.

"Roden's afraid of heights," she said in surprise.

Thray, who did not even attempt to poke her nose out, emitted a muffled reply. "The only sane one among this lot."

For several hours, everyone rested and ate, for they could not be certain of getting another chance to do so. A relentless stiffness crept into joints, an aching soreness into muscles. Ottar conferred with Harekson about continuing or pausing here for the night. Soon the more cautious decision was made: they would sleep here, for it was impossible to tell how much higher the stone spire rose. Far above, the ominous underbelly of the clouds flashed with the eerie, sallow glow of lightning.

It was hard to discern whether morning had actually arrived when Líf was awakened and told to gather her gear. Gloom from the overcast sky enveloped the camp. She felt as though she had not slept at all, and as she rose to her feet, her entire body complained. She felt as if she had climbed for miles, yet she could not be certain, for it took far longer to ascend these cliffs than to walk the same distance on level ground.

Blisters had appeared on her hands despite her gloves, and some had burst the day before. Young Sigird bandaged his hands, probably hoping to minimize the friction on his fingers.

All around, men lined up, and Líf took her position behind Hervor. Once again, the shieldmaiden began to climb the wall of stone. When it was her own turn, Líf hesitated, not out of fear but from sheer physical reluctance to force her body to further strain itself.

Roden's position had been shifted to that of last man on his line. The end of the rope was tied firmly about his waist so he could be assisted if he froze up again. Úlfor was positioned above his companion.

"You can do this, Líf," Ottar encouraged her. He must have thought her as terrified as Roden, yet that was not the problem. As long as she focused on her sister's heels, she remained less concerned about the altitude. No, it was not the height that terrified her; it was her waning strength. What if she could no longer grip the stone? What if her fingers loosened on the rope? If she fell, she would certainly take her brother and possibly others with her.

"You heard him, Líf," squeaked Thray. "Keep going. Come on. Maybe we can kiss the clouds!"

Líf did as she was bidden. As she eased off the ledge, she kept telling herself to reach one more handhold. She kept silent though her body cried out. But even if she had complained, the rumbles of thunder would have swallowed her sounds.

There was almost no wind. This was a surprise as well as a blessing, for Líf knew that even the slightest breeze might overwhelm her fragile balance. Moisture continued to build in the atmosphere; she could feel a thickness in the air, a heaviness weighting her limbs. Her muscles once again began to shake, and she felt a twinge in her tensed-up calf.

Buried in Líf's clothing, Thray encouraged her. "A little more, Líf. Just a little more."

Even beneath her gloves, she felt layers of skin slough off; her palms were moist and sticky. Hoisting her body higher, she saw the reddened prints of her hands as her blood saturated the cloth coverings.

Thray sensed her pain, her struggle. The small fylgja wriggled out into the frigid air and leaped onto the mountain itself. "Líf, Líf, you must keep going! Yes. Yes, like that. Look, Líf! You are about to reach the clouds."

The young woman tilted her face upward just as Hervor's feet vanished into the ceiling of gray mist. In a few more moments, she, too, had breached the clouds. Immediately, she felt a strange sensation. Though it was almost impossible to make out anything other than the rocky face of the mountain in front of her, she felt something brush her cheeks. Glimpsing crystal particles, she recognized them as either snow or sleet.

"Keep going, Líf! Higher!" urged Thray. The fylgja's shape was lost in the murk, although a faint glow just above told Líf that the squirrel was a bit higher than her head.

The cloud-filled sky was briefly illuminated. The fine hairs on Líf's arms and the back of her neck rose, and several shocks occurred where her clothing rubbed. Then came a rumble so deafening that she wanted to cover her ears but did not dare relax her grip on the rock.

That's when she heard the scream. The horrific sound grew fainter, though the man did not stop shouting. Somewhere below, a body would land—a crumpled shell that had once borne a fearless hugr.

Líf kept moving. Her body was damp, as if morning dew coated her. The temperature slowly rose, although it was still far from warm. The stone became slippery, and the dangerous film of moisture forced the entire party to slow down.

A second flash of lightning lit the sky; Líf could almost make out its jagged, golden branches. What if Roden was wrong? What if this was not the path into Svartálfheim but to Bilskirnir? Was Thor trying to prevent them from reaching his great mead hall?

Thray appeared out of the haze. Just as the little animal was about to speak, a third burst of lightning occurred. For the first time, Líf saw how the sparks affected the fylgja's fur. Energy was absorbed into her small body, causing her form to radiate even more brightly. No lanterns could match the brilliant luminescence of Thray in those following moments.

Even lacking the assault of rain, Líf's body felt drenched. Chilled droplets rolled down her face and into her eyes. Her handholds became less and less secure. How much longer could she continue?

"Líf, listen to me." Thray's voice teased the woman's awareness away from pure sensation. "You're almost there."

Every part of her body urged Líf to let go. Only Thray's encouragement drove her upward into the thickening darkness. She had to feel her way now. One hand slid up the rope; the other reached for grips in the rock. Her fingers dug into any crevice they could find, driving into the uneven markers, pushing through soft—

Retracting her hand, she squinted through the abysmal gloom at the small mound of soil in her palm. There had not been one speck of dirt during all their time on the mountain. Where had this come from, and why was there so much?

Líf pulled herself up inch by inch, and the stone gradually disappeared beneath a layer of soil and moss. Loose and dark, rich with moisture, the deepening layer of dirt appeared to be the ideal soil for farmland. The icy peak of the mountain had become lush, loamy earth. How could this be?

This strange turn of events was all the motivation Líf needed. She was soon climbing with a speed she had not dared to expect after so many hours of struggle and pain. Excitement boosted her spirits. Once again, she reached for the rope above her—but this time, her arm swung aimlessly in vacant air. Unprepared, she gasped and fumbled.

Suddenly the strong grip of her sister clasped her arm and hoisted her up into Svartálfheim.

THERE IS ALWAYS MORE TO COME...

Lif's adventure will continue in Volume Five of The Guardian's Speaker series. Fleeing from the land of the giants, her family ventures into darker realms full of creatures just as sinister as the environment.

The second omnibus of The Guardian's Speaker series will release in 2023!

NOTE FROM THE AUTHOR

As an author, writing the story is just the beginning. Next come revising, editing, formatting, proofreading, and marketing. Surprisingly, marketing requires a huge amount of time. If you enjoy an author's work and want her or him to publish more in a shorter time span, you can help! Spread the word on social media and by word of mouth. Post reviews on Amazon, Goodreads and other websites. Believe me, I would much rather write a new book than spend time promoting the one I have just finished. So go ahead—pin, tweet, post, review, and like. Thank you!

LEARN MORE AT
WWW.KATHARINEWIBELLBOOKS.COM

OR FIND ME ON:

Facebook	@KatharineEWibell	Pinterest	@KatharineWibell
Twitter	@KatharineWibell	YouTube	@KatharineWibell
Instagram	@KatharineEWibell	TikTok	@KatharineEWibell

HAVE FUN! Explore my Pinterest page and see how I envision the nine worlds amid Yggdrasil, Lif, Ottar, Hervor, Brasir, Wavecutter and so much more. Spoiler Alert! You'll get a sneak peek at upcoming characters not only in The Guardian's Speaker series but also in my other books! Have a suggestion? Contact me on my website or on Facebook! Follow my website Blog and dive even deeper from mythology to playlists!

MONTHLY NEWSLETTER SIGN UP!

Receive sneak peaks, giveaways, select deals, and my free Story Starter Collection!

ABOUT THE AUTHOR

Katharine Wibell's lifelong interest in mythology includes epic poetry like the Odyssey, Ramayana, Beowulf, and the Nibelungenlied. In addition, she is interested in all things animal whether training dogs, apprenticing at a children's zoo, or caring for injured animals as a licensed wildlife rehabilitator. After receiving degrees from Mercer University in both art and psychology with an emphasis in animal behavior, Wibell moved to New Orleans with her dog, Alli, to kick start her career as an artist and a writer. Her first literary works blend her knowledge of the animal world with the world of high fantasy. Read my Bio at KatharineWibellBooks.com

SPECIAL THANKS

Volume One

To April Wells-Hayes, my editor; to Karen Wibell, who served as reader and preserved my sanity; and OliviaProDesign for the cover.

I give homage to the Nordic skalds of old whose oral retellings kept their stories alive until they could be written down.

I thank all the modern translators of the Nordic and Icelandic sagas as well as Völuspá.org which provided the novella's epigraph. *Völuspá - The Prophecy of the Seeress.* (45.3-6) *Völuspá.org.* Web. Accessed 9 March 2021.

And I quietly respect my father's lineage from which so many fabulous and terrifying myths emerged.

Volume Two

To April Wells-Hayes, my editor; to Karen Wibell, who served as reader and preserved my sanity; and OliviaProDesign for the cover.

I give homage to the Nordic skalds of old whose oral retellings kept their stories alive until they could be written down.

I thank all the modern translators of the Nordic and Icelandic sagas as well as Völuspá.org which provided the novella's epigraph. *Völuspá - The Prophecy of the Seeress.* (1.1-4) *Völuspá.org.* Web. Accessed 9 March 2021.

And I quietly respect my father's lineage from which so many fabulous and terrifying myths emerged.

Volume Three

To April Wells-Hayes, my editor; to Karen Wibell, who served as reader and preserved my sanity; and OliviaProDesign for the cover.

I give homage to the Nordic skalds of old whose oral retellings kept their stories alive until they could be written down.

I thank all the modern translators of the Nordic and Icelandic sagas as well as Völuspá.org which provided the novella's epigraph. *Völuspá - The Prophecy of the Seeress.* (20.1-6) *Völuspá.org.* Web. Accessed 18 May 2021.

And I quietly respect my father's lineage from which so many fabulous and terrifying myths emerged.

Volume Four

To April Wells-Hayes, my editor; to Karen Wibell, who served as reader and preserved my sanity; and OliviaProDesign for the cover.

I give homage to the Nordic skalds of old whose oral retellings kept their stories alive until they could be written down.

I thank all the modern translators of the Nordic and Icelandic sagas as well as Völuspá.org which provided the novella's epigraph. *Völuspá - The Prophecy of the Seeress*. (2.1-4) *Völuspá.org*. Web. Accessed 18 May 2021.

And I quietly respect my father's lineage from which so many fabulous and terrifying myths emerged.

APPENDICES

APPENDIX I

Yggdrasil and the Nine Worlds

Yggdrasil is an immense ash tree that serves as the center of the cosmos in Nordic myth. All nine of the worlds are connected, from up in its mighty branches down to its roots. The gods, Norns, Jötnar, humans, and monsters live in and around this tree. For these reasons, Yggdrasil is often referred to as the *world tree*.

Asgard exists up in the branches of Yggdrasil and is the home of the race of gods known as the Æsir. Some prime examples of these deities are Odin, Thor, and Frigg. Asgard is the most fertile land in existence and has an abundance of jewels and gold. Valhalla, Odin's mead hall, is located in this world.

Bifröst is not a world but a rainbow bridge that connects Asgard to Midgard and is used by the gods whenever they want to visit the world of men.

Vanaheim is the world containing the other race of gods, known as the Vanir. These deities are associated with wisdom, fertility, and foresight. From this lineage come the god Frey and his sister Freya. Lush and peppered with waterfalls, it is also located in the canopy of Yggdrasil.

Álfheim is the third world that hangs in Yggdrasil's boughs. In this breathtaking realm of hardwoods and grasslands exists the race known as Ljósálfar (light elves). It is sometimes termed Ljósálfheim. The Ljósálfar are ruled by the goddess Freya, who, like them, is extraordinarily beautiful.

Midgard, which is analogous to Earth, is located in the center of Yggdrasil. This is the world of mankind, which is surrounded by water wherein resides the gigantic serpent, Jörmungandr.

Jötunheim is the world of the Jötnar, the giants for which it is named. Described as a desolate wilderness full of jagged mountains and the occasional copse of trees, this realm is as harsh as those who live there. It borders Midgard and is separated by a wall so massive that even the Jötnar are too small to scale it. This particular race of Jötnar is different from their fiery relatives, and they are sometimes referred to as *frost giants,* for they often reside in their mountain ranges. Hidden somewhere in this vast realm is Mímisbrunnr, the well that waters one of Yggdrasil's roots.

Svartálfheim is located below Álfheim and contains its own subterranean component called **Niðavellir**. These are the lands of the other two races of elves, the Døkkálfar (dark elves) and the Svartálfar (black elves). Though not overtly evil, these species are very unsavory. Here, too, are the subterranean dvergar, dwarves who are the most skilled smiths of all the races. Shadowy evergreen forests make maneuvering on Svartálfheim's terrain difficult.

Niflheim is one of the worlds located in Yggdrasil's roots. It is almost entirely composed of ice and mist. Brutally cold and all but barren, this realm is where the great dragon, Níðhöggr, feeds on the roots of the world tree in an attempt to kill the cosmos.

Muspelheim is the world of fire, counterbalancing Niflheim. Ruled over by Surtr, a fire jötunn, this land lies in wait to scorch the rest of existence if given the chance.

Helheim is the final world and the one located at the very base of Yggdrasil. It is the realm of the dead and is named after its ruler, the corpse-deity Hel. This afterlife is an eternity removed from torment and bliss alike. Those who die and are sent here continue to deal forever with the same sort of struggles they did in life.

Vígríðr is not a world but a plane, much like a field that exists all by itself. This is where the final battle of Ragnarök will take place, where it is predicted that all existence shall end

APPENDIX II

Glossary

Álfheimr	World of the light elves, the Ljósálfar
Althing	The largest council of elders and rulers. Held once every nine years, a representative of each jarl's household and the most important godis from all four quarters of the kingdom met with the king to establish new laws and deal with major grievances. Always held before the independent quadrants held their annual Things, at which a similar process occurred on a far smaller scale, the Althing was the only occasion on which the people held more power than royalty.
Æsir	The race of gods of whom Thor and Odin belong
Asgardians	The race of gods that live in the world of Asgard
Argr's fjord	A fjord in the lands to the north
aurochs	A species of currently extinct giant oxen that existed in the times of the Nordic peoples
berserker	A bear warrior; member of an elite force similar to Úlfhéðinn
Bilskirnir	Thor's mead hall
Blood Eagle	The worst punishment a person could be given
blót	Sacrificial religious ceremony
bragðr	A dicing game meant for gambling
bóndi	A freeman; member of the middle class
búðir	A tented or wooden structure created specifically for the Althing, in which a representative would live and convene with others when not in session
býta	A dicing game meant for gambling
Døkkálfar	One of three races of elves; also known as the dark elves
drakkar	A large, dragon-style longship, painted in bright colors with carvings on the keel and dragon heads on both ends

drengr	A man who has boundless courage, a high-minded nature, and is the manliest person around (see *drengskapr*). To be masculine in features and character as well as fearlessness in the face of certain death was esteemed above all else.
drengskapr	The supreme ideal; see *drengr*
ergi	The opposite of a drengr; a coward or a cheat. It can be used both as a quality of a person as well as refer to the person. If a man were seen doing women's work or suspected of showing affinity for his own sex, he was forever branded an *ergi*.
faering	A small, clinker-built boat seating two or four
Fenrir	The giant wolf who fathers all wolves and wolflike monsters
fjord	A long, narrow, deep inlet of the sea between high cliffs
Fólkvangr	The mead hall of Freya, where half of the worthy warrior dead go after death; shieldmaidens may have been included
Fornjót's bite	Frostbite
Freya	Goddess of love and protector of women
full outlawry	Among the most fearsome of punishments, exceeded only by the ritual of the Blood Eagle.
	A person sentenced to full outlawry was cast out of the kingdom forever unless they wished to be slain, with relatives or friends prohibited from avenging the death. To die in full outlawry was not only considered demeaning but would deny a person the right to enter Valhalla.
fulltrúar	Icons of patron gods for worship (sing. *fulltrúi*)
fylgjur	Female guardian spirits with animal forms (sing. *fylgja*); one of the four parts of the self
	Fylgjur have keener senses than humans. Their fur and eyes are iridescent, shimmering colors or have metallic sheens that reflect their moods. Most people cannot make physical contact with them, for they are invisible in all ways. They do not need to eat or drink; however, as they are connected with their person, they know what hunger feels like as well as drunkenness.

full outlawry	Among the most fearsome of punishments, exceeded only by the ritual of the Blood Eagle.
	A person sentenced to full outlawry was cast out of the kingdom forever unless they wished to be slain, with relatives or friends prohibited from avenging the death. To die in full outlawry was not only considered demeaning but would deny a person the right to enter Valhalla.
gandr	The staff of a völva
Geirröd	The jötunn who was one of the few opponents that ever came close to killing the god Thor, the protector of mankind.
Glæsisvellir	The glittering plains located within Jotunheim. A land of youth and eternal health. At its seat of power is Údáinsakr, the warrior's paradise.
godi	An elected official whose title lasts until death and is usually, but not always, passed on through bloodlines. There were specific numbers of godis for each region.
Grímnismál	A famed Nordic poem
Guðmundr	A mythic king whose last name was Úlfhéðinn. He was the first wolf warrior.
hamingjur	(Sing. *hamingja*) Invisible female spirits that represent a person's luck passed through family lines.
	Invisible to the naked eye, hamingjur can be good or bad. One of the four parts of the self, they may be thought of as a second self, a figure that is always behind the person, illuminating the human in an aura of light. They have faces or any specific features.
hamr	The physical body; one of the four parts of the self
Haugr	The sacred lands where the Allthing takes place.
Hel	The world of the common dead and the evil also known as Helheim. Ruled by the deity Hel, after whom the world is named.
hlaut	Blood blessed for ceremonial purposes.
hnefatafl	A chess-like board game with an attacking army and a defending army.
Höfund	Son of mythic King Guðmundr Úlfhéðinn.

hugr	Mind or soul; one of four parts of the self.
jarl	An earl or ruler of a village or small region.
Jarlbörg	The capital of the kingdom from where the Lothbransons come
Járnsaxa	The unusually beautiful jötunn, who became one of Thor's lovers. The only jötnar that the god of thunder ever looked upon kindly
Jól	Yuletide; a ceremonial season extending from the time of the winter solstice until Jólablót (January 12). celebration of the rebirth of the sun, for at that time of year, it is dark almost all day long. Jolfaðr comes. Straw goats for Thor are crafted for decoration.
Jólablót	A three-day period during which, like Winter Nights, the entire population was expected to migrate into Thorinheim to conduct their ritual offerings in the hopes that next season would bring a bountiful harvest. Jolfaðr's gifts are given out.
Jolfaðr	Odin's disguise when he would ride in on Sleipnir, his eight-legged horse, and bestow gifts upon the good children
Jörmungandr	The world serpent. A massive sea serpent wrapped around Midgard
jötnar	(Sing. *jötunn*) A race of giants or trolls who live in Jötunheim
Jötunheim	The world of the jötnar (giants)
karve	A type of small longship used for war, cargo and transportation of people; approximately 17 feet long
knarr	A large cargo ship (54 feet) capable of carrying up to 122 tons
Ljósálfar	The light elves; the race of the light
Lögberg	The Law Rock, a rock formation at the Althing into which the seats for the king and the Lögsögumaður were carved
Lögsögumaður	Speaker of the Althing, elected only for that specific year
longship	A long, narrow, specialized warship

Midgard	The world of mankind ("Earth")
Mímisbrunnr	The well of knowledge; located in Jotunheim
Mjolnir	Thor's war hammer; an amulet for protection of the common people
Muspelheim	The world of fire
nid	A formal insult delivered either verbally by a rune stick
Níðhöggr	The dragon at the base of Yggdrasil, the world tree
night sack	A sort of sleeping bag or bedding material
Norns	Three female entities who decide the fate of all beings, including the gods
Odin	King of the gods; protector of the upper class; god of wisdom, trickery, and war
Ragnarök	The prophesied end of times
Rán	Jötunn (giantess) deity of the ocean. All the drowned are to live until the end of times in her mead hall on the ocean floor.
Ratatoskr	The squirrel that lives in the Yggdrasil tree
rune staves	Rune-covered wooden planking or rods; used for seid and nids
Rus	A number of the Nordic ancestors ventured east and mixed their blood with the natives becoming what was now known as Rus.
seax	A small utility dagger worn by most Vikings at all times
seid	Magic
shieldmaiden	A female warrior
sigil	An inscribed or painted symbol believed to have magic power
skald	A poet
skeid	A large Viking warship which was neither as elegant nor ornately decorated as the drakkar
Skål	A toast, rather like "Cheers!"
Sormr	The Serpent's Strait; a river between Midgard and Jotunheim

Spákona	The place of unbridled sight, located on the cusp of civilization where the völva lives.
Sumarmál	A celebration of the beginning of summer, warmer months, and raiding season; new growth and fertility
Svartálfheim	The world of the black elves
Thing	An assembly of regional rulers (jarls) and governing officials (godi) where rules are created and laws formalized; serves as a court of law in many cases. Women are not allowed unless summoned.
Thor	God of thunder and lightning; protector of the common people; war god
Thorinheim	The largest trading village both on the island and in Midgard itself
Údáinsakr	The warriors' paradise, where no man could die of wounds or age. Located inside Jotunheim
Úlfhéðnar	(Sing. *Úlfhéðinn*) Wolf warriors. They do not use chain mail or helmets; however, they do wear wolf cloaks and typically use spears and swords. They are known to use drugs to increase strength and ferocity.
umbo	The central, knobbed grip on a shield dome (Latin)
Valhalla	Odin's mead hall, where half the best dead male warriors will be taken to feast and train until Ragnarök
valkyrie	A winged female spirit that claimed the souls of the worthy dead to take to Valhalla
Vanir	One race of gods that include Frey and Freya
vegvísir	The Wayfinder. Whoever bears that sigil will never lose their way, whether in storm or clear weather, even when the way is unknown.
völva	(Pl. *völvur*) A seeress; often carried a staff and wore a blue cloak
weregild	Compensation paid to the family of an injured party by the person who has committed the offense, especially if a death was involved
Winter Nights	A days-long celebration during which everyone in Thorinheim would come together to bring in the new year through feasting and small offerings to the gods.

As the veil between the lands of the living and the dead was considered thinnest at this time—around October 31—caution was used regarding what one said about the deceased, and there was much remembrance of those who had been lost. This was also the time when the people could petition the divine for future prosperity.

Yggdrasil	The world tree that contains the universe—all nine worlds
Ymir	The first jötunn and the one whose corpse formed Midgard

APPENDIX III

The Guardian's Speaker Volumes One through Four Phonetic Pronunciation

Æsir — AA-seer
Álfheimr — ALF-haym-er
Aurochs — AW-raaks
Bilskirnir — bil-skirnir
Blót — BLOTE
Bragðr — BRAG-there
Brasir — BRASS-ear
Bóndi — BONE-dee
Búðir — BOO-thir
Býta — BER-ta
Døkkálfar — DOLE-cal-far
Drengr — DREN-ger
Drengskapr — DREN-skah-per
Einar — AI-naa
Ergi — er-GHEE
Fjord — FYOHRD
Fólkvangr — FOLK-van-ger
Fornjót — FORN-yote
Fulltrúar — (fulltrúi singular) FULL-true-are/FULL-true-ee
Fylgja – Fylgjur (pl) –filg-JYA/filg-JYUR
Gandr — GAND-er
Garðar's Ile — GAR-thar's ILE
Gerðr's fjord — GER-thar FYORD
Glæsisvellir — GLAY-sis-veyl-leer
Godi — GO-dee
Gratti — GRAT-tee
Grímnismál — GREEM-nis-mall
Gunhild — GOON-hild
Guthorm — GOO-thorm
Hamingja — Hamingjur—HAHM-ing-jya /HAHM-ing-jyur
Hamr — HAM-er
Hnefatafl — NEH-fuh-taa-fl
Hlaut — HLAH-oot
Hugr — HOO-ger

Jarl — YARL
Járnsaxa — YARN-skg-ah
Jól — YULE
Jólablót — YULE-ah-BLOTE
Jolfaðr — YULE-fah-ther
Jörmungandr — YORE-mung-GAND-er
Jötnar — (Sing. *Jötunn*) YOT-nar
Jötunheim — YOT-un-heim
Líf — LEEF
Ljósálfar — LYO-sal-far
Lögberg — LOHG-berg
Lögsögumaður — LOHG-so-GUM-ah-THUR
Lothbrandóttir — LOTH-bran-DOE-ter
Mímisbrunnr — MEE-mess-BRUN-ner
Mjölnir — MYOL-nir
Muspelheim — MUS-pull-heim
Níðhöggr — NITH-hog-er
Ragnarök — RAHG-nuh-rok
Rán — RAHN
Ratatoskr — RAW-tah-TOE-sker
Seax — SAX
Seid — SAYD
Sigil — SI-gl
Sigird — SEE-grihd
Skeid — SKAYD
Skål — SKAUL
Spákona — SPAH-con-a
Sumarmál — SUE-mar-mall
Svartálfheim — SVAR-tal-heim
Thorinheim — THOR-en-haym
Úlfhéðnar — OOLF-hedth-nar
Valhalla — VAL-hal-uh
Valkyrie — Val-kr-ee
Vanir — vuh-NEER
Veðrfölnir — VEETH-fole-nir
Vegvísir — VEG-vee-ser
Völva — (Völvur pl.) –VOOL-va/VOOL-vur
Yggdrasil — EEIG-dra-seal
Ymir – EE-meer

Made in the USA
Columbia, SC
13 July 2022